THIEF OF SHADOWS

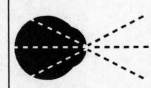

This Large Print Book carries the
Seal of Approval of N.A.V.H.

THIEF OF SHADOWS

ELIZABETH HOYT

THORNDIKE PRESS

A part of Gale, Cengage Learning

GALE
CENGAGE Learning®

Detroit • New York • San Francisco • New Haven, Conn • Waterville, Maine • London

GALE
CENGAGE Learning®

LIBRARY OF CONGRESS CATALOGING-IN-PUBLICATION DATA

Hoyt, Elizabeth.
  Thief of shadows / by Elizabeth Hoyt. — Large print ed.
    p. cm. — (Maiden Lane series) (Thorndike Press large print core)
  ISBN-13: 978-1-4104-5097-5 (hardcover)
  ISBN-10: 1-4104-5097-X (hardcover)
  1. Large type books. 2. Great Britain—History—18th century—Fiction.
I. Title.
PS3608.O9577T45 2012
813'.6—dc23   2012021313

Published in 2012 by arrangement with Grand Central Publishing, a division of Hachette Book Group, Inc.

This is for my favorite brother-in-law, Charles, an intriguingly talented interdisciplinary artist with interests in dance, theater, and visual arts who, nevertheless, does not mind slumming in the occasional romance novel video. ☺

ACKNOWLEDGMENTS

As always I need to thank the team of professionals who helped to polish a terribly rough draft into a final product somewhat more readable: my savvy agent, Susannah Taylor, my patient editor, Amy Pierpont, and my meticulous copy editor, Carrie Andrews. In addition, Amy's assistant, Lauren Plude, is always scandalously good-natured, Diane Luger from the GCP art department has once again outdone herself with the cover, and Nick Small and Brianne Beers from publicity have worked tirelessly to make sure you've actually heard of this book.

Thank you all.

CHAPTER ONE

Oh, gather 'round, my dears, and keep
the candles burning bright, for tonight I'll
tell you the tale of the Harlequin Ghost of
St. Giles . . .
— from *The Legend of the
Harlequin Ghost of St. Giles*

London, England
May 1738

The body in the road was the absolute cap
to the day.

Isabel Beckinhall — Baroness Beckinhall
— sighed silently to herself. Her carriage
had come to a standstill in the worst part of
London — the dirty streets of St. Giles. And
why was she in St. Giles as dark descended?
Because she'd volunteered to represent the
Ladies' Syndicate for the Benefit of the
Home for Unfortunate Infants and Foundling Children at the final inspection of the
new home, more fool she.

Never volunteer. Not even when pleasantly filled with warm scones and hot tea. Warm scones were obviously the work of the devil or perhaps of Lady Hero Reading, one of the two founding patronesses of the home. Lady Hero had refilled her teacup and looked at Isabel with guileless gray eyes, asking prettily if Isabel would mind meeting with Mr. Winter Makepeace, the home's dour manager, to look over the new building. And Isabel had blithely agreed like some scone-filled, mindless cow.

And the damned man hadn't even shown!

"Moo," Isabel muttered to herself just as the carriage door opened to admit her lady's maid, Pinkney.

"Ma'am?" Pinkney asked, her blue eyes wide and startled. Of course, Pinkney's blue eyes were nearly always wide and startled. She was one of the most sought-after lady's maids in London and a paragon of the latest fashion, despite being barely past one and twenty and somewhat naïve.

"Nothing," Isabel said, waving aside her bovine utterance. "Did you find out why it's taking so long to move the dead man?"

"Oh, yes, my lady," Pinkney said. "It's because he's not dead." Her pretty dark blond brows drew together. "Well, not yet anyway. Harold the footman is having a time

10

pulling him aside, and you wouldn't credit it, ma'am, but he's a comic actor."

It was Isabel's turn to blink. *"Harold?"*

"Oh, no, my lady!" Pinkney giggled until she caught Isabel's steady gaze. "Er" — the maid cleared her throat — "the not-yet-dead man is. A comic actor, that is. He's dressed as a harlequin, mask and all . . ."

Isabel was no longer listening. She'd opened the door and climbed from the carriage. Outside, the gray day was growing grimmer with the advent of nightfall. Fires flared to the west, and she could hear the rumbling of rioters from that direction. They were very near. Isabel shivered and hurried to where Harold and the other footman were bent over a figure on the ground. Pinkney had probably mistaken the costume or the man or the mask or —

But no.

Isabel drew in a sharp breath. She'd never seen the notorious Ghost of St. Giles in person, but she had no doubt at all that this must be him. The prone man wore black and red motley. His floppy brimmed black hat had fallen from his head, and she could see that his brown hair was tied back simply. A short sword was sheathed at his side and a long sword lay by one broad hand. A black half-mask with a ridiculously long nose

11

covered the upper half of his face, leaving his square chin and wide mouth revealed. His lips were parted over straight white teeth, the upper lip a little bigger than the bottom.

Isabel snapped her attention up to her footman. "Is he alive?"

"He's still breathin' at least, m'lady." Harold shook his head. "Don't know for how long, though."

A shout came from nearby and the sound of smashing glass.

"Put him in the carriage," Isabel said. She bent to pick up his hat.

Will, the second footman, frowned. "But, m'lady —"

"*Now.* And don't forget his sword."

Already she could see a mass of people rounding the corner down the street. The footmen glanced at each other then as one lifted the Ghost. Harold grunted under the weight, but he made no complaint.

A crowd gathered at the end of the street and someone gave a shout.

The rioters had spotted the carriage.

Isabel picked up her skirts and trotted after her footmen. Harold gave a great heave and dumped the Ghost and his sword into the carriage. Isabel scrambled rather inelegantly inside. Pinkney was staring wide-eyed at the Ghost sprawled on the floor of the carriage, but for the moment Isabel ignored him. She tossed the hat on top of him, lifted her seat, and withdrew two pistols from the hidden compartment underneath.

Pinkney squeaked in alarm.

Isabel turned and handed the pistols to the footmen at the carriage door. "Don't let anyone climb the carriage."

Harold's jaw tightened. "Yes, m'lady."

He took the pistols, gave one to Will, and mounted the running board behind the carriage.

Isabel closed the carriage door and knocked on the roof. "Fast as you can, John!"

The carriage started forward with a lurch just as something hit the side.

"My lady!" Pinkney cried.

"Hush," Isabel said.

There was a lap robe on the maid's seat, and Isabel tossed it over the Ghost. She sat back on her own seat, clutching the window as the carriage rocked around a corner. Something else knocked against the carriage. A grimacing face appeared suddenly at the window, its tongue smearing lewdly against the glass.

Pinkney screamed.

Isabel stared at the man, her heart racing but her gaze steady as she met his eyes. They were bloodshot and filled with maddened rage. The carriage jolted and the man fell away.

One of the pistols fired.

"My lady," Pinkney whispered, her face white, "the dead man —"

"Not-quite-dead man," Isabel muttered, eyeing the robe. Hopefully anyone glancing inside would see a robe thrown carelessly on the floor, *not* the hidden Ghost of St. Giles. She braced herself as the carriage swung wildly around a corner.

"Not-quite-dead man," Pinkney obediently repeated. "Who is he?"

"The Ghost of St. Giles."

Pinkney's robin's-egg-blue eyes widened. "Who?"

Isabel stared at her lady's maid in exasperation. "The Ghost of St. Giles? The most notorious footpad in London? Goes about in a harlequin's costume, either ravishing and murdering or rescuing and defending, depending on whose stories you believe?"

If Pinkney's eyes got any bigger, they might fall out of her head altogether.

"No?" Isabel waved a hand toward the window and the shouting and screaming outside and said sweetly, "The man that

14

mob wants dead?"

Horrified, Pinkney stared at the robe. "But . . . why, my lady?"

The second pistol fired with a deafening *BOOM!* Pinkney jumped and looked wildly out the window.

Dear God, they were out of ammunition. Isabel prayed the footmen were safe — and that they could hold off the rioters without their guns. She was an aristocrat, but just last year a viscount had been dragged from his carriage, beaten, and robbed in St. Giles.

Isabel took a deep breath and felt under the robe until she found the hilt of the Ghost's sword. She drew it out as Pinkney eyed her askance and put the heavy thing across her lap. If nothing else, she could hit someone over the head with it. "They want him dead because this morning he cut Charming Mickey O'Connor down from the gallows."

Pinkney actually brightened at this. "Oh, Charming Mickey the pirate! *Him* I've heard of. They say he's handsome as sin and dresses better than the king himself."

Of course her lady's maid had heard of a well-dressed pirate.

"Quite." Isabel flinched as something hit the window, cracking the glass. "They probably chased him all the way from Tyburn gallows, poor man."

"Oh." Pinkney bit her lip. "Pardon me, my lady, but *why* have we picked him up?"

"Well, it does seem a pity to let anyone be torn apart by a mob," Isabel drawled, not letting the girl see the fear that made her heart beat hard. "Especially a young, handsome man."

Pinkney looked timidly at Isabel. "But, my lady, if the mob wants him and he's in our carriage . . . ah . . ."

Isabel drew on all her strength to smile firmly. Her hand tightened on the hilt of the sword across her lap. "That's why we're not going to let them know we have the Ghost, are we?"

Pinkney blinked several times as if working through this logic; then she smiled. The child really was quite pretty. "Oh, yes, my lady."

The lady's maid sat back as if quite confident that they were all out of danger now that everything had been explained.

Isabel twitched aside the curtains to peer through the cracked glass. She wasn't nearly as sanguine. Many of the streets in St. Giles were narrow and twisting — the reason that her carriage had been traveling so slowly earlier. A mob could move much faster afoot than they. But as she looked behind

16

them, Isabel saw that the mob was beginning to fall away. John Coachman had found a straight stretch of road and was urging the horses into a trot.

Isabel let the curtain fall with a heartfelt sigh of relief. *Thank God.*

The carriage drew abruptly to a stop.

Pinkney shrieked.

"Steady on." Isabel gave her maid a severe look. The last thing she needed was Pinkney having the vapors if they were about to be attacked.

Isabel peeked out the window and then hurriedly shoved the sword back under the carriage blanket.

And only just in time. The carriage door opened to reveal a stern-looking dragoon officer in scarlet uniform.

Isabel smiled sweetly. "Captain Trevillion. How good to see you — *after* we've outrun the mob."

The captain's craggy cheekbones darkened, but he still cast a sharp eye about the carriage. For a moment his gaze seemed to linger on the blanket.

Isabel kept her eyes on his face, her smile firmly in place. Casually she lifted her feet and rested them atop the robe.

The dragoon's gaze snapped back to her. "Ma'am. I'm glad to see you and your party safe and sound. St. Giles isn't a place to be loitering today."

"Yes, well, we didn't know that when we started out this morning." Isabel raised her eyebrows in polite inquiry. "*Have* you caught that pirate yet?"

The captain's thin lips tightened. "It's only a matter of time. We'll get him *and* the Ghost of St. Giles. The mob has them both on the run. Good day to you, my lady."

She nodded, not daring to breathe until the dragoon had slammed shut the carriage door and given the word to John Coachman to move on.

Pinkney sniffed scornfully. "*Soldiers.* Their wigs are always terribly out of fashion."

Isabel slumped back against the squabs and gave her lady's maid a quick grin.

Half an hour later, the carriage was pulling up before her neat town house.

"Bring him inside," she ordered Harold when he opened the doors.

He nodded wearily. "Yes, m'lady."

"And, Harold?" Isabel descended the carriage, still clutching the sword.

"M'lady?"

"Well done. To both you and Will." Isabel nodded to Will.

A shy grin split Harold's broad, homely face. "Thank you, m'lady."

Isabel permitted herself a small smile before she swept into her town house. Edmund, her dear, late husband, had bought Fairmont House for her shortly before he'd died and had gifted it to her on her twenty-eighth birthday. He'd known that the title and estates would go to a distant cousin and had wanted her properly settled with her own property, free of the entail.

Isabel had immediately redecorated on moving in four years ago. Now the entry hall was lined in warm golden oak panels. A parquet wood floor was underfoot, and here and there were items that amused her: a dainty pink-marble-topped table with gilded legs, a laughing boy faun holding a hare in black marble, and a small oval mirror edged in mother-of-pearl. All items she loved more for their form than their worth.

"Thank you, Butterman," Isabel said as she tucked the sword under her arm and pulled off her gloves and hat, handing them to the butler. "I need a bedroom readied immediately."

Butterman, like all her servants, was impeccably trained. He didn't even blink an eye at the abrupt order — or the sword she carelessly held. "Yes, my lady. Will the blue room do?"

"Quite."

Butterman snapped his fingers and a maid went hurrying up the stairs.

Isabel turned and watched as Harold and Will came in, carrying the Ghost between them. The Ghost's floppy hat lay on his chest.

Butterman raised his eyebrow a fraction of an inch at the sight of the unconscious man, but merely said, "The blue room, Harold, if you please."

"Yes, sir," Harold panted.

"If you don't mind, my lady," Butterman murmured, "I believe Mrs. Butterman may be of assistance."

"Yes, thank you, Butterman. Please send Mrs. Butterman up as quickly as possible." Isabel followed the footmen up the stairs.

The maids were still turning back the sheets on the bed in the blue room when the footmen arrived with their burden, but the fire on the grate was lit.

Harold hesitated, probably because the Ghost was quite dirty and bloody, but Isabel gestured to the bed. The Ghost groaned as the footmen laid him on the spotless counterpane.

Isabel propped his sword in a corner of the room and hurried to his side. They were out of danger, but her pulse hadn't slowed. She realized she was a bit excited by this odd turn of events. She'd rescued the Ghost of St. Giles. What had started as an ordinary, almost dull day had become a curious adventure.

The Ghost's eyes were closed. He still wore his mask, though it was askew on his face. Carefully she lifted the thing over his head and was surprised to find underneath a thin black silk scarf covering the upper part of his face, from the bridge of his strong nose to his forehead. Two eyeholes had been cut into the material to make a second, thinner mask. She examined the harlequin's mask in her hand. It was leather and stained black. High arching eyebrows and the curving grotesque nose gave the mask a satyr-like leer. She set it on a table by the bed and looked back at the Ghost. He lay limp and heavy on the bed. Blood stained his motley leggings above his black jackboots. She bit her lip. Some of the blood looked quite fresh.

"Butterman said 'twas a man injured," Mrs. Butterman said as she bustled into the room. She went to the bed and stared at the Ghost a moment, hands on hips, before nodding decisively. "Well, nothing for it. We'll need to undress him, my lady, and find out where the blood's coming from."

"Oh, of course," Isabel said. She reached

for the buttons of the Ghost's fall as Mrs. Butterman began on the doublet.

Behind her, Isabel heard a gasp. "Oh, my lady!"

"What is it, Pinkney?" Isabel asked as she worked at a stubborn button. Blood had dried on the material, making it stiff.

" 'Tisn't proper for you to be doing such work." Pinkney sounded as scandalized as if Isabel had proposed walking naked in Westminster Cathedral. "He's a *man*."

"I assure you I have seen a nude man before," Isabel said mildly as she peeled back the man's leggings. Underneath, his smallclothes were soaked in blood. Good God. Could a man lose so much blood and survive? She frowned in worry as she began working at the ties to his smallclothes.

"He has bruising on his shoulder and ribs and a few scrapes, but nothing to cause this much blood," Mrs. Butterman reported as she spread the doublet wide and raised the Ghost's shirt to his armpits.

Isabel glanced up for a moment and froze. His chest was delineated with lean muscles, his nipples brown against his pale skin, with black, curling hair spreading between. His belly was hard and ridged, his navel entirely obscured by that same black, curling hair. Isabel blinked. She had seen a man — men, actually — naked, true, but Edmund had been in his sixth decade when he'd died and had certainly never looked like this. And the few, discreet lovers that she'd taken since Edmund's death had been aristocrats — men of leisure. They'd hardly had more muscles than she. Her eye caught on the line of hair trailing down from his navel. It disappeared into his smallclothes.

Where her hands were.

Isabel swallowed and untied the garment, a little surprised by the tremble of her fingers, and drew them down his legs. His genitals were revealed, his cock thick and long, even at rest, his bollocks heavy.

"Well," Mrs. Butterman said, "he certainly seems healthy enough *there*."

"Oh my, yes," Pinkney breathed.

Isabel looked around irritably. She'd not realized the maid had come close enough to see the Ghost. Isabel drew a corner of the counterpane over the Ghost's loins, feeling protective of the unconscious man.

"Help me take off his boots so we can bare his legs completely," Isabel told Mrs. Butterman. "If we can't find the wound there, we'll have to turn him over."

But as they stripped his breeches farther down his legs, a long gash was revealed on the man's muscled right thigh. Fresh blood oozed and trickled over his leg as the sodden material was pulled away.

"There 'tis," Mrs. Butterman said. "We can send for the doctor, my lady, but I've a fair hand with the needle and thread."

Isabel nodded. She glanced again at the wound, relieved it was not nearly as bad as she'd feared. "Fetch what you'll need, please, Mrs. Butterman, and take Pinkney with you to help. I have a feeling he won't be much pleased by a doctor."

Mrs. Butterman hurried out with Pinkney following behind.

Isabel waited, alone in the room save for the Ghost of St. Giles. Why had she rescued him? It'd been an action taken almost without thought — to leave a defenseless man to be ravaged by a mob was an idea that instinctively repulsed her. But now that he was in her house, she found herself more curious about the man himself. What sort of man risked his life in the disguise of a harlequin? Was he a footpad or a sword for hire? Or was he merely a madman? Isabel looked at him. He was unconscious, but he was still a commanding presence, his big body sprawled upon the dainty bed. He was a man in the prime of his life, strong and athletic, nearly bare to her gaze.

All except his face.

Her hand moved, stretching toward the black silk mask still covering the upper part of his face. Was he handsome? Ugly? Merely ordinary-looking?

Her hand began to descend toward the mask.

His flashed up and caught her wrist.

His eyes opened, assessing and quite clearly brown. "Don't."

This day was not going as planned.

Winter Makepeace stared up into Lady Isabel Beckinhall's clever blue eyes and wondered how, exactly, he was going to extricate himself from this situation without giving away his identity.

"Don't," he whispered again. Her wrist was warm and delicate, but he could feel the feminine strength beneath his fingers, and his own muscles were damnably weak at the moment.

"Very well," she murmured. "How long have you been awake?"

She made no move to pull her wrist from his grasp.

"I woke when you took off my leggings." *That* had certainly been an interesting way to regain consciousness.

"Then you're not as badly off as we thought," she drawled in her husky voice.

He grunted and turned his head to look about the room. A wave of nausea and dizziness nearly made him pass out again. "Where am I?"

He kept his voice to a low, barely audible rasp. Perhaps if he whispered, she wouldn't recognize him.

"My home." She cocked her head. "I won't touch your mask if you don't want me to."

He watched her, calculating. He was naked, in a strange house, and wounded. The odds were not in his favor.

She raised one elegant eyebrow. "If you'd let go of my wrist?"

He opened his hand. "Your pardon."

She rubbed her wrist, her eyes lowered demurely. "I saved your life earlier, and you're quite at my mercy now" — her eyes flicked over his nude body — "yet I don't think you truly ask my pardon."

She raised her gaze to his, intelligent, humorous, and utterly seductive.

The danger was palpable.

Winter's lips twitched. "Perhaps I'm just a rude fellow."

"Rude, undoubtedly." She flicked a finger over the small bit of material covering his pelvis, and his base flesh stirred in mindless response. "But ungrateful as well?" She shook her head sadly.

He raised his eyebrows. "I trust you do not blame me, madam, for my present state of undress. I do vow, I woke thus and know not who to blame but *you.*"

Her eyes widened just a fraction and she bit her lip as if to quell a tremor of laughter. "I assure you my, uh, curiosity was prompted merely by a desire to find out where you were wounded, sir."

"Then I am honored by your *curiosity.*" Winter felt as if he had tumbled down a hill and landed upside down. He never bantered thus with women, and Lady Beckinhall had made it quite clear on their previous meetings — when he was merely Mr. Makepeace, the manager of the Home for Unfortunate Infants and Foundling Children — that she did not hold him in high regard.

Perhaps it was the mask and the intimacy of the quiet room.

Or perhaps it was the knock on the head he'd received earlier. "Did you discover that which you sought?"

Her lips, wide and delicate, curved into a secret smile. "Oh, yes, I found all that I could wish for."

He inhaled, his pulse too fast, his head too light, and his cock too unruly, but the door to the room opened at that moment.

Instantly, Winter closed his eyes. He instinctively knew it was best that the others not know he was awake and aware. He couldn't logically explain this impulse, but since this type of instinct had saved his life countless times in the past, he no longer bothered to question the urge.

Carefully he peered from beneath his eyelashes.

His field of vision was limited, but at least two females entered the room.

"How is he?" one of the women — a servant, judging by her accent — asked.

"He hasn't moved," Lady Beckinhall replied.

She didn't mention that she'd been talking to him only seconds before, he noticed. But then he'd always known Lady Beckinhall was quick-witted.

"Shouldn't we take off his mask?" a different, younger, female voice asked eagerly.

"Do you think that wise?" Lady Beckinhall inquired. "He might decide he must kill us if we learn his identity."

Winter almost cocked an eyebrow at this outrageous suggestion. The younger servant girl gave a muted scream. Obviously she hadn't noticed how very solemn Lady Beckinhall's voice was — the lady was hiding her amusement.

The first servant sighed. "I'll sew his leg up quick and then we'll get him comfortable."

Which was when Winter realized that the next several minutes of his life were to be quite unpleasant.

His entire body ached, so he hadn't really noticed until that moment that his right thigh throbbed in particular. Apparently that was the wound Lady Beckinhall had been searching for.

He closed his eyes fully then and waited, breathing in and out slowly, letting his arms and legs lie as if weighted on the bed.

It's the shock that makes pain hard to bear, his mentor had said long ago. *Expect it, welcome it, and pain becomes simply another sensation, easy enough to brush aside.*

He thought of the home and the logistics of moving eight and twenty children into a new building. Fingers touched his wound, pinching the edges together with a sharp bite of agony as fresh, warm blood trickled over his leg. Winter was aware of the pain, but he set it aside, letting it flow through him and out again as he considered each child at the home and how he or she would react to the move.

The new dormitories were spacious rooms, lit by large windows carefully barred.

The sharp dig of the needle as it pierced his flesh. Most of the children would be happy with their new home. Joseph Tinbox, for instance, though already eleven years of age, would delight in running up and down the long hallways. *The draw and raw tug as the thread pulled through his skin.* But for a child such as Henry Putman, who had been recently left at the home and remembered the abandonment, the move might be troubling. *Another stab of the needle.* He would have to be especially aware of Henry Putman and others like him. *Fire burning over his leg as liquid was splashed on the wound.* Only Winter's many hours of training kept him from jerking from the searing pain. He breathed in. Breathed out. Let his mind drift as the stabbing began again . . .

Some time later, Winter realized that the poking of the needle had stopped. He surfaced from his internal musings to the feel of a cool hand on his forehead. He knew without opening his eyes that it was Lady Beckinhall who touched him.

"He doesn't feel feverish," Lady Beckinhall murmured.

Her voice was low for a woman and somewhat throaty. Winter seemed to feel her breath washing over his still-nude body and ruffling his nerve endings, but that was

30

fancy. Perhaps the knock on the head was worse than he'd thought.

"I brought some water to bathe him," the older maidservant said.

"Thank you, Mrs. Butterman, but you've done enough for tonight," Lady Beckinhall said. "I'll see to it myself."

"But, my lady," the second, younger servant protested.

"Truly, you both have been the greatest help," Lady Beckinhall said. "Please. Leave the water here and remove the rest of the things."

There was a rustling, the sound of something metallic dropping into a tin basin, and then the door opened and shut again.

"Are you still awake?" Lady Beckinhall asked.

Winter opened his eyes to find her looking at him, a wet cloth in her hands.

His body tensed at the thought of her hands on him. "There's no need for that."

She pursed her lips and glanced at his leg. "The wound is still bloody. I think it best. That is" — her eyes flashed up at him in challenge — "unless you fear the pain?"

"I have no fear of pain or anything else you might inflict on me, my lady." His whisper came out as a rasp. "Do your worst."

■ ■ ■ ■

Isabel inhaled at the flash of defiance she saw in the Ghost's brown eyes.

"You don't fear me or what I may do to you," she murmured as she approached the bed. He'd lain so still while Mrs. Butterman had sewn up his wound that she'd feared he'd fainted again, but now some color had returned to his cheeks, reassuring her. "You don't fear the wrath of the soldiers or a murderous mob. Tell me, Sir Ghost, what *do* you fear?"

He held her gaze as he whispered, "God, I suppose. Doesn't every man fear his creator?"

"Not all men." How strange to discuss philosophy with a naked, masked man. She carefully wiped at the dried blood upon his thigh. The warm muscle beneath her hand tensed at her touch. "Some care not at all for God or religion."

"True." His dark eyes watched her every movement. "But most men fear their own mortality — the death that will eventually take them from this earth — and the God that will judge them in the afterlife."

"And you?" she murmured as she squeezed out the cloth and wet it again. "Do you fear death?"

"No." His statement was cool.

She raised her eyebrows, bending over the wound to examine it. It was jagged, but Mrs. Butterman had stitched it very well. If it healed, there would be a long scar, but it wouldn't be too wide or unsightly. It would've been a great pity to mar such a beautiful male limb. "I don't believe you."

A corner of his mouth curled suddenly as if his own amusement surprised him. "Why not? Why should I lie?"

She shrugged. "Out of bravado? You do go about in a mask and harlequin's motley."

"Exactly right," he whispered. "I hunt the streets of St. Giles with my swords. Would I do such a thing if I feared death?"

"Perhaps. Some who fear death make a game of mocking it." She stroked up his thigh, coming perilously near the sheet laid over his genitals.

He made no move, but she knew his entire attention was on her. "Only fools mock death."

"Truly?" She inched her cloth under the wadded sheet. A tent was forming there. She straightened and plopped her cloth into the basin of water, rinsing it. "But mockery can be such an amusing game."

She moved to lay the cloth low on his belly.

He grabbed her wrist. "I think the game you play is not to mock, but to tease." There was a ragged edge to his whisper.

Isabel eyed the growing ridge beneath the bundled sheet. "Perhaps you're right." Her gaze flicked to his, her eyebrows raised. "Is it a game you like?"

"Would it matter?" His mouth twisted cynically.

Her eyebrows rose. "Of course. Why tease an unwilling man?"

"For the pure sport?"

She blinked at the twinge of hurt. "You wound me."

He tensed his forearm and, without any visible sign of strain, pulled her closer, until she was forced to bend over his form, her bodice nearly touching his bare chest. This close she could see a ring of amber about his dark irises — and his pupils large with pain.

"If I wound you, madam, I am sorry," he rasped. "But acquit me of stupidity. I am not a rag doll to be played with."

She cocked her head, wishing he'd remove his mask so that she could truly see him, this man who had captured her interest as no other had in a very, very long time. He parried her flirtation with disconcertingly plainspoken answers. She simply wasn't used to such frankness. All the gentlemen of her acquaintance knew to speak in elegant riddles that in the end meant nothing at all. Was he a common man, then, beneath his mask? But he didn't address her as an inferior.

No, his speech was quite familiar. As if he were her equal or more.

She inhaled and let her eyes drift down his form. "No, you certainly are no limp rag doll, sir. I beg your pardon."

His eyes widened as if in surprise and he abruptly let her go. " 'Tis I should beg pardon of you. You saved my life — don't think I don't know it well. Thank you."

She felt heat moving up her neck. Dear God, she hadn't blushed since she was a girl. She'd bantered with dukes, flirted with princes. Why, then, should this man's simple words make her feel suddenly self-conscious?

" 'Tis of no matter," she said, much less graciously than her usual manner. She tossed the soiled cloth into the basin. "You've lost a lot of blood. You may rest here until we can move you in the morning."

"You're very kind."

She shook her head. "We've already established that I'm not a kind woman."

He smiled slightly as his eyes closed. "I
think we've established just the opposite,
actually. You're kindness itself, Lady Beckinhall."

For a moment she watched him, waiting
to see if he'd add something more, but
instead his breathing grew sonorous.

The Ghost of St. Giles had fallen asleep.

The gray-pink light of dawn was peeking
through the window when Isabel next
opened her eyes. For a moment she merely
blinked, wondering fuzzily why her back
ached and why she wasn't in her own bed.
Then her gaze flew to the bed beside her.

Empty.

She stood stiffly and looked down at the
coverlet. It was neatly made, but blood
smeared the center. He had been there last
night at least. She placed her palm on the
counterpane, but the cloth was cool. He'd
left some time ago.

Isabel crossed to the door and called for a
maid. She'd make inquiries, but she already
knew in the pit of her stomach that he was
gone and, besides the bloodstains, he'd left
no trace.

She returned to stare moodily at the

empty bed while she waited for the maid, and in that moment she remembered something that had nagged at her too-tired brain the night before: Lady Beckinhall. He'd called her by her name, though no one had uttered it in his presence.

She caught her breath. The Ghost of St. Giles knew her.

CHAPTER TWO

Now you may not credit it, but once the
Ghost of St. Giles was merely a mortal
harlequin actor. He played with a traveling
troupe that wandered from town to town.
The Harlequin wore tattered red and
black motley and when he swung his
wooden sword at the villain of the play, it
clacked: *Clip! Clap!* and made the
children shout with glee . . .
— from *The Legend of the
Harlequin Ghost of St. Giles*

Winter Makepeace, mild-mannered schoolmaster and manager of the Home for Unfortunate Infants and Foundling Children,
crouched on the sloping roof shingles as the
sun came up over London. His back was to
the roof edge and the drop below. He
gripped the eve with both hands before
kicking out and letting his body fall over the
edge. For a moment he hung, three stories

up, his entire weight suspended only by his fingertips, and then he swung through the attic window below. He landed with a wince, not only because of the pain his injured thigh caused him, but also because of the soft thump he made as he hit the floor.

Usually he entered his room through the window without any sound at all.

He winced again when he sat on the bed and examined his motley hose. They were muddy and a large rip ran from his hip to nearly his knee on the right leg. His head pounded in a drumbeat rhythm as he peeled the filthy fabric from his bandaged wound. He bundled the torn hose with his jackboots, swords, mask, and the rest of his costume and shoved the whole mess under the bed. Providence only knew if he'd be able to repair the damage — his sewing skills were adequate but by no means accomplished. Winter sighed. He very much feared that he needed a new costume — one that he could ill afford.

Turning, he limped, nude, to the pitcher of water on his washstand and poured a bit into the basin. He splashed the cold water on his face and for the first time in his life regretted that he didn't own a looking glass. Were there bruises on his face? Telltale scratches? He could feel the scrape of his morning beard as he ran his palms over his jaw.

He grunted and for a moment leaned straight-armed on the shabby little wash-stand, letting the water drip from his face. He ached. He couldn't remember when he'd last eaten, and his head was spinning in a slow, nauseating rhythm. He had to dress, had to appear normal for the coming day. Had to teach small, recalcitrant boys at the day school, had to prepare the home's children for the move to the new building, and had to find out if his youngest sister, Silence, was safe.

So much to do.

So many people who depended on him.

So very tired.

Winter collapsed onto his narrow bed. Just a moment's rest first. As he closed his eyes, he seemed to feel the touch of a soft yet strong feminine hand.

Seductive, husky laughter whispered in his mind . . .

Bang! Bang! Bang!

Winter jolted upright, hissing as the sudden movement sent a stab of pain through his right thigh. Sunlight was streaming through his window now, illuminating every crack in the wall, every dusty beam in his attic bedroom. He squinted. It must be late morning, judging by the angle of the sun. He'd overslept.

The insistent knocking on his door began again, this time accompanied by a feminine voice. "Winter! Are you there, Brother?"

"A moment." He snatched his nightshirt from under his pillow and hastily threw it over his head. His breeches were nowhere in sight and he couldn't remember where he'd left them yesterday.

"Winter!"

Sighing, he draped the bedsheets around his shoulders like a banyan and stood to open his bedroom door.

Sherry-brown eyes narrowed in fear and concern met his. "Wherever have you *been?*"

Temperance Huntington, Baroness Caire, his elder sister, swept into Winter's room. Behind her was a girl of thirteen with black hair and rosy cheeks. Mary Whitsun was the eldest girl at the home and as such held the most responsibilities.

Temperance nodded at the girl. "You'd best go tell the others that we've found him."

"Yes, ma'am." Mary hesitated only long enough to say to Winter, "I'm so glad you're safe, sir." Then she was gone.

41

Temperance glanced about the room as if expecting to find an entire brothel hiding in the corner, then frowned up at him. "Dear Lord, Winter, we've spent half the night and all this morning searching for you! When you didn't come back yesterday and the riot spilled over into St. Giles, I quite feared the worst. And then we received word that you'd never made it to the new home."

Temperance plopped onto the bed. Winter eased back as well, careful to keep the covers over his lower limbs. He opened his mouth —

But Temperance evidently wasn't done. "And then Silence sent word that she has *married* Mickey O'Connor and has gone into some sort of hiding with him. We had to send the baby, Mary Darling, to her with two of O'Connor's more frightening-looking men." She added grudgingly, "Although, they did seem very fond of Mary Darling and she of they."

She inhaled for breath and Winter leaped into the breech. "Then our sister is safe?"

Temperance threw up her hands. "Presumably so. The soldiers were all over London yesterday — and still are today, for that matter — looking for Mickey O'Connor. Can you imagine? They say he was actually *dangling from the rope* when the

Ghost of St. Giles cut him down. Of course, that's probably an exaggeration. You know how these rumors spread."

Winter kept his features impassive. Actually, it was no exaggeration at all — he'd barely made it in time to save O'Connor's neck from the hangman's noose. But obviously he couldn't tell Temperance that.

"And Mr. O'Connor's wretched *palace* burned last night," Temperance said in a lower voice. "They say a body was found in the smoldering ashes this morning, and everyone presumes it to be O'Connor's, but Silence's note arrived *after* the fire, so he must be still alive, mustn't he? Oh, Winter! Will Silence be safe with him, do you think?"

That was one question he could answer without hesitation.

"Yes." Winter looked into Temperance's eyes so that she could see the assurance in his. Mickey O'Connor might be a very dangerous river pirate and the most notorious man in London at the moment — and Winter might dislike the man quite intensely — but he did know one thing: "He loves Silence and Silence loves him. I watched the man's face as he gave Silence up to us when he knew he could no longer protect her. O'Connor cares for her deeply. Whatever else happens, he'll keep her safe with his life."

"Dear Lord, I hope so."

For a moment Temperance closed her eyes, losing her rigid posture as she slumped against his pillow. She was but nine and twenty — a mere three years older than he — but Winter was startled to realize that a few fine lines had imprinted themselves about her eyes. Had they always been there and he'd never noticed? Or were they new, brought on by the excitement of the last few weeks?

As he watched her, Temperance opened her eyes, as alert as ever. "You still haven't answered my question. Where have you been since yesterday afternoon?"

"I got caught in the riot." Winter winced and settled himself companionably on the narrow bed, shoulder to shoulder with his sister. "I'm afraid I was already late to my meeting with Lady Beckinhall. I was hurrying to get there when the crowd overwhelmed me. It was rather like getting caught in a herd of cows driven to market, I suppose, except they were noisier, fouler, and much more mean than any bovine mass."

"Oh, Winter," she said, laying a hand on his arm. "What happened?"

He shrugged. "I was too slow. I fell and was kicked about some and my leg was hurt." He gestured to his right leg. "It's not broken," he added hastily at her exclamation, "but it did slow me down. I ended up ducking into a tavern to wait out the worst of the riot. I suppose I got home quite late last night."

Temperance frowned. "No one saw you come in."

"As I said, it was quite late."

Strange how facile he had become at lying — even to those closest to him. It was a flaw within himself that he would have to examine later, for it did not speak well of his character.

He looked at the window. "And now it is already near noon, I think, and I need to be up and about my duties."

"Nonsense!" Temperance's brows drew together. "You're injured, Brother. One day abed will not bring the house down about your ears."

"Perhaps you're right . . . ," he began, and then was startled when his sister leaned over to peer into his face. "What is wrong?"

"You're not arguing with me," she murmured. "You must really be hurt."

He opened his mouth to deny her statement, but unfortunately she jostled his leg at that moment, turning his protest into a gasp of pain.

"Winter!" Temperance stared at the bedsheet-covered leg as if she could see through the material. "How bad is your leg, exactly?"

"It's just a bump." He swallowed. "Nothing to be concerned over."

She narrowed her eyes, looking patently dubious of his claim.

"But I may take your advice and stay abed today," he added hastily to appease her. Truthfully, he wasn't sure he *could* stand for any length of time.

"Good," she replied, gingerly rising from the bed. "I'm sending one of the maids up with some soup. And I should get a doctor to see you as well."

"No need," he said a bit too sharply. A doctor would immediately realize that his wound came from a knife. Besides, Lady Beckinhall's maidservant had already sewed it up. "No, really," he said in a quieter voice. "I just want to sleep for a bit."

"Humph." Temperance didn't look at all convinced by his protest. "If I weren't leaving this afternoon, I'd stay and make sure a doctor saw to you."

"Where are you going?" he asked, hoping to change the topic of conversation.

"A house party in the country that Caire insists we attend." Temperance's face clouded. "There'll be all sorts of aristocrats there, I suppose, and all of them looking down their horsey noses at me."

He smiled — he couldn't help it at her description — but his words were tender when he replied. "I doubt anyone will be sneering. Caire would cut off their noses, horsey or not, if they dared."

A corner of her mouth tipped up at that. "He would, wouldn't he?"

And Winter was glad, not for the first time, that his elder sister had found a man who adored her completely — even if he *was* an aristocrat.

For a moment he felt a pang. Both Temperance and Silence — the two people he was closest to in the world — were married now. They had husbands and, presumably, would soon have families of their own. They'd always be his sisters, but now they would always be apart from him as well.

It was a lonely thought.

But he didn't let it show on his face. "You'll do fine," he told Temperance gently. "You have intelligence and moral dignity. Qualities I suspect very few of those aristocrats possess."

She sighed as she opened his door. "You

may be right, but I'm not entirely certain that intelligence and moral dignity are at all esteemed in aristocratic circles."

"Ma'am?" Mary Whitsun peered around the doorjamb. "My lord Caire says as how he's waiting for you in the carriage."

"Thank you, Mary." Temperance touched a finger to the girl's cheek, her countenance clouded. "I'm sorry to leave again so soon. We haven't had much time together lately, have we?"

For a moment Mary's stoic little face wavered. Until her marriage, Temperance had lived at the home and had grown especially close to Mary Whitsun.

"No, ma'am," the girl said. "But you'll be coming back soon, won't you?"

Temperance bit her lip. "Not for another month or more, I'm afraid. I have an extended house party to attend."

Mary nodded resignedly. "I 'spect there's lots of things you must do now that you're a lady and not like us anymore."

Temperance winced at the girl's words, and Winter felt a chill. Mary was right: The aristocratic world was apart from the ordinary world he and Mary lived in. Mingling the two never worked well — something he'd do well to remember when next he saw Lady Beckinhall.

■ ■ ■ ■

The current fashion in furnishings was opulent, Isabel reflected several days later, but even by modern standards the Earl of Brightmore's London town house was so beyond lavish it bordered on the ridiculous. Rose-colored marble columns lined the walls of Brightmore's main sitting room, topped with gilded Corinthian finials. And the finials weren't the only things that were gilded. Walls, ornaments, furniture, even the earl's daughter, Lady Penelope Chadwicke, shone with gold. Isabel personally thought that gold thread — which featured prominently in the embroidery on Lady Penelope's skirt and bodice — was rather absurd for an afternoon tea, but then she supposed it did make sense.

What else was the daughter of Midas to wear but gold?

"Mr. Makepeace may be intelligent," Lady Penelope was saying, her voice just slow enough to imbue her words with doubt about the manager's mental facilities, "but he is not suitable to run an institution for children and infants by himself. I think we can all be agreed on that point at least."

Isabel popped a bite of scone into her

mouth and mentally cocked an eyebrow. The Ladies' Syndicate for the Benefit of the Home for Unfortunate Infants and Foundling Children was holding an emergency meeting with those members currently in town: herself; Lady Phoebe Batten; Lady Margaret Reading; Lady Penelope; and Lady Penelope's companion, Miss Artemis Greaves, who, Isabel supposed, must be accounted an honorary member of the Ladies' Syndicate simply because she always attended with Lady Penelope. Missing were Temperance Huntington, the new Lady Caire; her mother-in-law, Lady Amelia Caire; and Lady Hero, all out of town.

Judging from the expressions of the other members of the Ladies' Syndicate, Lady Penelope's point about Mr. Makepeace *wasn't* universally agreed upon. But since Lady Penelope was, in addition to being a well-known beauty — eyes of pansy-purple, hair of raven-black, et cetera, et cetera — *also* a legendary heiress, not many ladies were brave enough to chance her ire.

Or perhaps Isabel had misjudged the courage of the assembled ladies.

"Ahem." Lady Margaret cleared her throat delicately but quite firmly. A lady with dark, curling brown hair and a pleasant face, she was one of the youngest members — older only than Lady Phoebe, who was still technically in the schoolroom — but she seemed a strong personality nonetheless. "It's a pity that Mr. Makepeace no longer has the help of his sisters in overseeing the home, but he *has* been the manager for many years now. I think he'll do quite well enough on his own."

"Pish!" Lady Penelope didn't snort, but she did come perilously close. Her pansy-purple eyes widened so much in incredulity that they nearly bugged from her head. *Not* a becoming expression. "It's not just the lack of feminine authority at the home that concerns me. You can't seriously think that Mr. Makepeace can represent the home at all the social functions he'll need to attend now that we ladies are patronesses?"

Lady Margaret looked troubled. "Well —"

"The home has new social standing because of the Ladies' Syndicate. He'll be invited to all manner of genteel gatherings — gatherings in which *his* comportment will reflect on *us* as his patronesses. There will be teas, balls, possibly even *musicales!*"

Lady Penelope waved a dramatic hand, nearly clipping the nose of Miss Greaves, sitting next to her. Miss Greaves, a rather plain young woman who hardly spoke, started. Isabel privately suspected she'd been dozing while holding Lady Penelope's silly little white dog in her lap.

"No," Lady Penelope continued, "the man is impossibly gauche. Just three days ago he did not appear for a scheduled appointment with Lady Beckinhall at the new home and didn't even send an excuse. Can you imagine?"

Isabel swallowed, amused at the other woman's theatrics. "To be strictly fair, there *was* a riot in St. Giles at the time." And she'd been busy saving a mysterious, masked man whose athletic form haunted her dreams at night. Isabel hastily took a sip of tea.

"To not send word to a lady is the *height* of impoliteness, riot or no riot!"

Isabel shrugged and took another scone. Privately she considered a riot quite sufficient excuse — Mr. Makepeace *had* sent an apology 'round the next day — but she hadn't the interest to argue with Lady Penelope. Mr. Makepeace might be a perfectly fine manager, but she had to agree that he would be a disaster in society.

"And with the new home's grand opening, we have need of a much more refined manager," Lady Penelope said. "Someone who can converse with a lady without offering insult. Someone who can rub shoulders with dukes and earls. Someone *not* the son of a beer brewer." Her lip curled on the last two words as if beer brewer were a step below whoremonger.

The Ghost of St. Giles would probably be quite at home conversing with dukes and earls — whatever his social standing under that mask might be. Isabel pushed aside the thought to focus on the conversation. "Temperance Huntington is Mr. Makepeace's sister and thus also the child of a brewer."

"Yes." Lady Penelope shuddered. "But at least *she* has married well."

Lady Margaret pursed her lips. "Well, even if Mr. Makepeace cannot overcome his accident of birth, I do not see how we can take the home away from him. It was founded by his *father* — that same beer brewer."

"He's now the manager of a large, well-funded home. A home that will, no doubt, in the future expand in both size and prestige. A home with all our names attached to it. In less than a fortnight he will be obliged to attend the Duchess of Arlington's grand ball. Can you imagine what will happen the first time the Duchess of Arlington asks Mr. Makepeace about the children in his home?" Lady Penelope arched a pointed eyebrow. "He's likely to spit at her."

"Well, not *spit*," Isabel protested. *Cut her dead, maybe . . .*

Sadly, Lady Penelope had a point. Because they had all given money to the home, Mr. Makepeace, as the home's manager, would now be an important figure in London society. He needed to be able to sail polite society's sometimes dangerous waters with ease. To be the face of the home, to perhaps solicit more monies, influence, and prestige for it as the home grew. All of which Mr. Makepeace was completely unprepared for at the moment.

"I can teach him," Lady Phoebe blurted out.

All heads swung toward the chit. She was a plump child of seventeen or eighteen with light brown hair and a sweet face. She should be in the midst of preparations for her first season — except Isabel suspected there wouldn't be any season for the poor girl. She wore round spectacles, but her eyes squinted vaguely behind them. Lady Phoebe was nearly blind.

Still, she lifted her chin. "I can help Mr. Makepeace. I know I can."

"I'm sure you could, dear," Isabel said. "But it would be quite inappropriate for a bachelor gentleman such as Mr. Makepeace to be taught by a maiden."

Lady Margaret had opened her mouth, but she closed it abruptly at Isabel's last words. Lady Margaret wasn't married either.

"The idea is a good one, though," Lady Margaret rallied. "Mr. Makepeace is an intelligent man. If someone pointed out the advantages to him of learning society's ways, I'm sure he would set himself to acquiring some sophistication."

She glanced at Lady Penelope. That lady simply arched her eyebrows and sat back in her chair with a moue of distaste. Miss Greaves was staring fixedly at the little dog in her lap. As Lady Penelope's companion, it would be suicide for her to voice dissent to the other lady's opinion.

Lady Margaret's gaze swung toward Isabel. Her lips curved into a mischievous smile. "What we need is a lady who is no longer a maiden. A lady with a full understanding of polite society and its intricacies. A lady with enough self-possession to polish Mr. Makepeace into the diamond we all know he is."

Oh, dear.

Three days later, Winter Makepeace carefully descended the wide marble staircase of the Home for Unfortunate Infants and Foundling Children's new residence. The staircase was a far cry from the rickety bare wood steps in their old home, but the slippery marble was also perilous to a man using a cane to support his still-healing right leg.

"Coo! Bet this banister would make a grand slide," Joseph Tinbox said somewhat unwarily. He seemed to realize his mistake as soon as the words had left his lips. The boy turned an innocently earnest freckled face up toward Winter. " 'Course, *I'd* never do such a thing."

"No, that would be quite unwise." Winter made a mental note to include a warning against banister riding in his next address to the children of the home.

"There you are, sir." Nell Jones, the home's right-hand woman, appeared at the bottom of the stairs, looking flustered. "You have a caller in the sitting room, and I don't know that we have any muffins left. There're a few sweet biscuits from the day afore yesterday, but I'm afraid they may be stale and Alice can't find the sugar for tea."

"Biscuits will be just fine, Nell," Winter said soothingly. "And I don't take sugar in my tea in any case."

"Yes, but Lady Beckinhall may," Nell

pointed out as she blew a lock of blond hair out of her eyes.

Winter stilled on the landing, aware that his heartbeat had quickened. "Lady Beckinhall?"

"She's in there with her lady's maid," Nell whispered as if the lady could hear her from down the hall and through the walls. "And she's wearing jeweled buckles on her slippers — the maid, not the lady!"

Nell sounded awestruck.

Winter repressed a sigh even as his muscles tightened in anticipation. His body might be eager to see the lady again, but the reflex was involuntary. He did not need the complication of Lady Beckinhall and her overly inquisitive nature today.

"Send in the tea and whatever biscuits you have," he told Nell.

"But the sugar —"

"I'll handle it," he said firmly, catching Nell's frantic gaze. "Don't worry so. She's only one woman."

"One woman with a fancy lady's maid," Nell muttered, turning toward the back of the house and the kitchen.

"And, Nell," Winter called, remembering the matter that he'd originally come down for, "have the new girls arrived yet?"

"No, sir."

"What?" He'd received word just this morning of two orphaned sisters, only five years of age, begging for scraps on Hog Lane not far from the home. Immediately he'd sent the home's sole manservant, Tommy, to bring them in. "Why not?"

Nell shrugged. "Tommy said they weren't there when he got to Hog Lane."

Winter frowned, troubled by the news. Only last week he'd gone to pick up a little girl of seven or so who had been left at St. Giles-in-the-Fields Church. Yet when he'd arrived, the girl had inexplicably disappeared. The whoremongers of St. Giles were often on the lookout for girls, but these children had vanished within minutes of his receiving word that they were on the street. That was awfully swift even for the greediest of whoremongers. Why would —

Someone pulled on his coat, and Winter looked down into Joseph Tinbox's brown eyes, grown wide with pleading. "Please, sir, can I go with you to see the lady and her maid? I ain't never seen jeweled buckles afore."

"Come." They'd reached the lower floor by now, and Winter tucked his cane discreetly in a corner, then placed his palm on the boy's shoulder. Hopefully this arrangement would be less conspicuous — the last thing he needed was Lady Beckinhall realizing that he was limping on the same leg that the Ghost had been wounded on. He smiled at Joseph. "You shall be my crutch."

Joseph grinned up at him, his face suddenly quite angelic, and Winter felt a quite inappropriate warmth in his chest at the sight. As the manager of the home, he should have no favorites. He should view all eight and twenty children equally and impartially, a benevolent governor above and apart from them all. His father had been such a manager, able to be both kind and distant. But Winter had a near-daily struggle to follow his father's example.

He squeezed the boy's shoulder. "Best behavior, mind, Joseph Tinbox."

"Yes, sir." Joseph composed his face into what he no doubt thought a solemn expression, but to Winter's mind it merely made him doubly mischievous-looking.

Winter squared his shoulders and let his weight settle equally on both legs, ignoring the pain that shot through his right thigh. He opened the sitting room door.

The sight of her was like a swift, cool wind through his frame, quickening his body, alerting all his senses, making him completely aware he was a male and she a female.

Lady Beckinhall turned as he entered. She was attired in a deep crimson gown, delicate layers of lace falling from the sleeves at her elbows. The lace was repeated in a thin line about her low, rounded bodice as if to frame her creamy bosom. More lace edged the frivolous scrap of beaded linen that served as a cap on her glossy mahogany hair.

"Mr. Makepeace."

"My lady." He crossed to her carefully, his palm still on Joseph's shoulder.

She held out her hand, no doubt so that he could bend over it and kiss her fingers, but he would do no such thing.

Instead he took her hand, feeling the small shock of her slim fingers in his palm, and shook it before quickly letting go. "To what do we owe the honor of your visit?"

"Why, Mr. Makepeace, perhaps you've already forgotten your promise to show me about the new home?" She widened her eyes mockingly. "To make up for our appointment last week?"

He suppressed a sigh. Lady Beckinhall's maid stood behind her, and Nell was quite correct: The girl was overdressed, her lace as dear if not dearer than her mistress's. Joseph had his head tilted sideways and was leaning slightly away from Winter's grip, presumably in an effort to catch a glimpse

60

of the fabled jeweled buckles.

"I must apologize again for missing our meeting last week," Winter said.

Lady Beckinhall inclined her head, making the teardrop pearls she wore swing from her earlobes. "I hear you were caught up in the mob."

He started to reply, but before he could, Joseph cut in eagerly. "Mr. Makepeace was near crushed, he was. He's spent almost the whole last week abed. Got up only when we moved to this here new home."

Lady Beckinhall's dark eyebrows arched in interest. "Indeed? I had no idea you were so gravely injured, Mr. Makepeace."

He met her gaze, keeping his own complacent, though his pulse had quickened. She wasn't a fool, this woman. "Joseph exaggerates."

"But —" Joseph began, his voice injured.

Winter patted him on the shoulder, then transferred his hand to the back of a settee. "Run to the kitchens and see if Nell has the tea ready, please, Joseph Tinbox."

The boy's face fell, but Winter looked at him firmly. Any show of weakness and Joseph would wriggle out of the request.

With a dramatic slump of his shoulders, the boy turned to the door.

Winter looked at Lady Beckinhall. "I'm

afraid we aren't settled yet in our new home, but should you come back next week, I would be pleased to show you around."

The lady nodded, finally — thankfully! — settling onto a winged chair. Winter sank into the settee, keeping his face bland even as his right thigh protested the movement. The lady's maid retired to a seat across the room and gazed rather vacantly out the window.

"Thank you, Mr. Makepeace," Lady Beckinhall replied in her throaty voice. "I'm looking forward to your tour, but that was not the only matter I came to see you about today."

He arched his eyebrows in silent inquiry, trying not to show impatience. He hadn't the time to play guessing games. Not only did he have work to do, but also every minute he spent in her company there was the danger that she might make the connection between him and the Ghost. The sooner she was out of his home, the better.

She smiled, quick and devastating. "The Duchess of Arlington's ball is next week."

"Yes?"

"And we — the Ladies' Syndicate — hope that you'll be attending to represent the home."

He nodded his head curtly. "I've already

informed Lady Hero that I would attend at her request, though frankly I do not see the need to do so. Nor" — he glanced at the door as it opened to admit Nell and two of the girls bearing the tea — "do I see what your interest in the matter is."

"Oh, my interest is quite personal," Lady Beckinhall drawled.

He looked back at her quickly. A tiny smile was playing about her lips, sensual, sly, and not a little roguish.

His eyes narrowed in sudden wariness.

Lady Beckinhall's blue eyes danced. "I've been elected to be your social tutor."

CHAPTER THREE

Twice a year the Harlequin's troupe came
to play in St. Giles. It happened one day
that a fine lady was riding by and her
carriage was stopped by the crowd
gathered to see the comic actors. The
fine lady drew aside the curtain on her
carriage and looked out. And as she
did so, her eye caught the gaze of
the Harlequin . . .
— from *The Legend of the
Harlequin Ghost of St. Giles*

Isabel watched as Winter Makepeace slowly
blinked at her news. It was his only reaction,
but it was a telling one from a man who
made stone statues seem animated.

"I beg your pardon?" he asked politely in
his low, slow voice.

She supposed he could be called a handsome man, but only if one overlooked his
severe demeanor. His face was pleasant

64

enough, his chin strong, his nose straight, his mouth firm, but she'd not often seen Winter Makepeace smile and never laugh. His dark brown hair was clubbed back simply without curl or powder, and he dressed in plain black or brown. He had the air of a man far older, for Mr. Makepeace couldn't be past thirty years of age.

He was sitting on the settee, seemingly relaxed, but she hadn't missed his slight limp as he'd entered the room — nor the fleeting expression of irritation on his face when the boy had mentioned his infirmity. For a moment she remembered the Ghost and how he'd looked, lying on the bed in her blue room: naked, muscled, and dangerously sexual.

Winter Makepeace, in contrast, no doubt had the soft body of a man of letters. His chest would be bony, his arms thin and spindly. Why, then, was she even dwelling on the thought of Mr. Makepeace nude?

Isabel leaned toward the tea things. Miss Jones and the other maids had finished setting out the trays, but they still hovered, looking wide-eyed between her and Mr. Makepeace. "Shall I pour?"

She saw a muscle knot in his jaw. His glance flicked to the maids and his expression softened a trifle. "Thank you, Nell.

65

That will be all."

Nell cast him a speaking glance as she left, but Mr. Makepeace's attention was already back on Isabel. He waited until the door closed behind the maids. "Please explain."

"Oh, dear," Isabel sighed as she poured the first cup of tea. "There doesn't seem to be any sugar. Shall I ring for the maids again?"

She smiled sweetly at him.

Apparently Mr. Makepeace was immune to her smiles. "We haven't any sugar. You'll just have to do without. Now, what —"

"That's such a pity — I do so adore sugar in my tea."

Isabel made a disappointed moue and was rewarded with the firming of Mr. Makepeace's lips. It was too bad of her, really, but for some reason it amused her no end to poke at this man. To subtly taunt and prod. He was so stiff, so utterly self-contained. Perhaps he simply had no emotions to restrain, but she didn't think so. No, Isabel knew deep in her heart that there was a volcano somewhere under that granite shell. And if it ever blew, she wanted to be there to witness the explosion.

"Lady Beckinhall," Mr. Makepeace gritted very softly. "I regret the lack of sugar for your tea, but I would be most apprecia-

66

tive if you explained yourself. Right. Now."

"Oh, very well." Isabel handed the cup of tea to him and spoke as she poured herself another. "The Ladies' Syndicate has decided that you would . . . ah . . . *benefit* from some lessons in social etiquette. It's nothing much really" — she waved a negligent hand as she sat back on the settee with her own teacup — "just a few —"

"No."

"— sessions." Isabel blinked and raised her eyebrows. Mr. Makepeace had a slight frown about his lips, which in any other man would translate into a full-fledged rage. "I beg your pardon?"

"I said *no*." He set his tea down untouched. "I don't have the time or inclination to waste on lessons in social etiquette. I'm very sorry, but —"

"You don't sound sorry," Isabel pointed out. "In fact, you rather prove my case, Mr. Makepeace. You delight in repressing your emotions, yet you can't be bothered to hide your disdain for a lady."

For a moment he simply watched her, his dark eyes lidded, and she wondered what he was thinking.

Then he inclined his head. "I am very sorry if I seem to disdain you, my lady. On my honor, I do not — quite the contrary.

67

But I do not see the need for your so-called social etiquette lessons. My time is limited as it is. Surely you would agree that it would be better spent managing the home than learning to flatter aristocrats?"

"And if your home — and your livelihood — depend upon flattering those aristocrats?"

His straight brows drew together. "In what way do you mean?"

Isabel sipped her tea, bitter though it was without her usual sugar, and marshaled her thoughts. He was a stubborn man, and if she couldn't make him understand the gravity of his situation, she very much feared that Mr. Makepeace would simply refuse her help. And then he'd lose his position at the home. Winter Makepeace might do a wonderful job of hiding all his emotions, but Isabel knew the home was very important to him. Besides, it didn't seem right that he should suffer the loss of his family's and his life's work simply because he was surly, dour, and a rather humorless man.

So Isabel lowered her teacup and gave Mr. Makepeace her best smile — the one that had made more than one young buck trip over his own feet in a ballroom.

Judging by Mr. Makepeace's expression,

she might've presented him with a codfish of uncertain provenance.

Mentally sighing, Isabel said, "You understand the importance of attending events in polite society now that the home has the patronage of ladies such as Lady Hero, the Ladies Caire, and Lady Penelope?"

His nod was so slight it might've been a twitch.

She'd take it anyway. "Then you must understand the need to make your appearances in society properly. Everything you do, every movement you make, and everything you say will reflect not only on yourself, but also on the home — and its patronesses."

He stirred impatiently. "You fear I will embarrass you."

"I fear," she said as she deliberated over her choice of sugar biscuits, "that you will lose the home."

For a moment he was silent, and had he been any other man, she would've said he was stunned.

"What do you mean?" he asked very carefully.

"I mean that you risk losing either your position as the home's manager or your patronesses — or if worse came to worst, both." She shrugged and took a bite of the sugar biscuit, which turned out to be terribly stale. "No society lady wishes to be associated with an uncouth gentleman. If you cannot learn some polite manners, you will either be replaced as the home's manager or you will lose your patronesses."

She took a sip of her bitter tea to wash down the dryness of the biscuit, watching his face over the rim of the teacup. He gazed straight ahead, his face immobile, as if he debated something within himself.

Then he looked at her squarely and she had to repress a gasp. It felt as if he touched her physically with the intensity of his stare and the effect was . . . heady. Oh, yes, there were certainly emotional depths to this man. Did he let those emotions free when he was intimate with a woman? And why was she thinking this of Mr. Makepeace? He was the least sensual man she knew.

She was so confused by her thoughts that it took her a moment to realize he had spoken.

"No." Mr. Makepeace rose, his hand perhaps unconsciously rubbing his right leg. "I'm afraid I have neither the time nor the inclination to learn etiquette from you, my lady."

And with those blunt words, he left her.

■ ■ ■ ■

Why did lady Beckinhall imperil his usual reserve?

Winter Makepeace limped down an alley as the last rays of the dying sun retreated over the mismatched roofs of St. Giles. Even after a half hour spent in the lady's company earlier this afternoon, he could still make no sense of his dangerous attraction to her. She'd been very brave, true, to rescue him from the mob. She liked to act the frivolous flirt, but her actions had been kinder than he'd seen from most people, poor or aristocratic. She'd brought him into her home, tended to his wounds, and nursed him with her own hands. The lady had shown a wholly unexpected side to herself, and if she were the daughter of a cobbler or butcher, he might've been very tempted to find out more about that part of her she kept so well hidden.

Winter shook his head. But Lady Beckinhall was no butcher's daughter. He knew — *knew* — she wasn't for him. And yet, as he'd been mentally lecturing himself that he must stay as far away from Lady Beckinhall as possible, he'd found himself almost agreeing to her ridiculous plan to "tutor"

71

him. It had been harder than it should've been to walk away from the lady. And that simply wasn't logical.

Lady Beckinhall was as far above him as Hesperus, the evening star. She'd been born to wealth and privilege while he was the son of a beer brewer. He was by no means rich and at times in the past had teetered on the edge of penury. She lived in the best part of London — an area with wide, straight streets and gleaming white marble, while he lived . . .

Here.

Winter leaped a stinking puddle and ducked around a crumbling brick wall. The gate in the wall had been vandalized and swung open, creaking in the wind. He entered the dark cemetery beyond, careful to watch for the low, tablet-like headstones set into the ground. This was the Jews' burial place, and he knew that during the day he would see the inscriptions on the headstones in a mixture of Hebrew, English, and Portuguese — for most of the Jews in London had fled that country and its terrible laws against those who were not Christians.

A small, black form darted away as he neared the other side of the cemetery — either a cat or a very large rat. The wall here was low, and Winter scrambled over it and into a narrow passageway, biting back an exclamation at a twinge from his leg. This let out into another alley next to a chandler's shop. Overhead, the chandler's wooden sign swung, squeaking, in the wind. It was in the crude shape of a candlestick, but whatever paint had once outlined the flame and stick had long since flaked away. A single lantern hung outside the little shop, the flame flickering uncertainly.

It was the last glimpse of civilization the alley could boast — farther on, no lantern lit the black shadows. Only the most courageous — or foolhardy — of St. Giles's residents would brave the dark alley after nightfall.

But then he wasn't an ordinary resident, was he?

His boots clattered on the remaining cobblestones in the alley as the grim shadows enveloped him. Most would bring a lantern out at night, but Winter had always been more comfortable making his way by moonlight.

A cat screeched with amorous intent nearby and was answered by an equally loud rival. Was he as mindless as the tomcats? Driven by the scent of a willing female and his own innate animal drive?

He shook his head as he entered a covered lane — more a tunnel, really. The walls dripped with slimy moisture and his footfalls echoed off the low arch. Up ahead, something — or someone — moved in the gloom.

Without breaking stride, Winter unsheathed the sword hidden in his greatcoat. As a commoner, he wasn't technically allowed to carry either it or his short sword, but he'd long ago made peace with his necessary circumventions of the law.

Sometimes it was a matter of life or death, after all.

The lurker ahead made a sudden movement as if to rush him. Still advancing, Winter casually swung his sword up in front of his body. *By boldness of attack you'll seize the advantage,* the old words of his mentor whispered across his mind.

The robber thought better of his action. There was a scuttling sound and then the way ahead was clear.

He should've felt relief at the lessening of danger — that the potential for conflict and the possible need to harm his fellow man had disappeared. Instead, Winter fought down a wave of irritation mixed with disappointment. He had the primitive urge to fight, to feel the pull and bunch of muscle, the thrill of peril, the satisfaction of victory over another.

Winter stopped dead, breathing quietly in the black night, listening to the drip of fetid water on the tunnel walls.

I am not an animal.

That was, in part, what the mask was for: to let loose some of his baser urges. Carefully. With great control. But he wasn't wearing the mask tonight. Winter sheathed his sword.

The covered lane let out into a tiny courtyard that was hemmed in on all sides by tall buildings with overhanging balconies that seemed on the point of tumbling down to crush any so unlucky as to be standing beneath. Winter quickly crossed the courtyard and knocked twice on a low cellar door. He paused and then rapped once more.

Inside he could hear the scrape as a bolt was drawn back and then the door opened, revealing a face creased by time like the pages of a prayer book.

"Mistress Medina," Winter murmured.

Instead of greeting him, the little woman impatiently beckoned him inside.

Winter bowed his head to clear the low lintel and stepped into the cozy room. A fire crackled on the hearth, gently steaming the clean laundry hung overhead on a wooden frame made accessible by a crude rope and pulley. Directly in front of the fire was a low stool and small table, set all about with lit tallow candles. And on the table were the tools of Mistress Medina's trade: scissors, chalk, pins, needles, and thread.

"I've just finished it," she said as she closed the door behind him and locked it. She limped over to the bed and held up the tunic that had been lying there.

Black and red diamonds paced across the fabric. *People see only the surface,* his mentor used to say. *Give them a showy costume, a mask, and a bit of cape and they'll swear to phantoms in the night and never notice the man beneath.*

Winter crossed to the old woman and fingered the sleeve. "You've done excellent work as always, Mistress Medina."

She scowled at his praise. "Best take care of it, then, 'adn't you? I don't know if I can ever make another. My eyes are going." She jerked her chin at the smoking tallow candles. "Even with all them candles, I can't see to place my stitches 'alf the time."

"I'm sorry to hear it," Winter said, and meant it. He could see now that her eyes were red-rimmed and watering. "Have you another means of making your way?"

She shrugged. "Might try to 'ire on as a

cook. I made a fair pie in my day."

"You did," Winter said gently. "I can remember enjoying one of your apple pies."

"Aye, and I remember making you the first one of these," she said softly, caressing the new hose that went with the tunic. "You were but a shiverin' lad. I never would've thought you could even 'old the swords were it not for Sir Stanley swearin' you were the quickest learner 'e'd ever seen."

There was a faint, nostalgic smile at the corner of her mouth. Winter wondered — not for the first time — if the little seamstress had been more to his mentor, Sir Stanley Gilpin, than merely a servant.

Her gaze suddenly sharpened. "You've filled out some since then, 'aven't you? And become 'arder."

Winter lifted his eyebrows. "That was nine years ago," he said mildly. "Is a boy of seventeen ever the same as a man of six and twenty?"

She snorted and began bundling his new costume. "That I don't know, but I wonder sometimes if Sir Stanley knew exactly what 'e was about when 'e gave you them swords and mask."

"Do you disapprove of my actions?"

She waved an impatient hand. "Don't try to trap me with your arguments. All I know is that 'tisn't natural for a man to spend all 'is time roamin' the streets of St. Giles, making other people's troubles 'is own business."

"Would you have me ignore people in trouble?" he asked in simple interest.

She turned abruptly and pinned him with her gaze. Her eyes might be ruined from years of sewing in too-dim light, but her regard was still acute. "I saw the knife cut in that old pair of leggings you brought to me — *and* the dried blood about the edges. There must be a terrible wound 'iding beneath your breeches."

He shook his head, amused. "I'm young and strong. I heal fast."

"*This* time." She pushed the bundled costume into his chest. "What'll you do when the wound is deeper? Longer? You ain't immortal no matter what Sir Stanley might've told you, Winter Makepeace."

"Thank you, Mistress Medina." He took the clothes and retrieved a small purse from his pocket — most of the money he'd saved since the home had had the fortune to gain patronesses. "Call around at the home tomorrow morning. We're in need of a cook, I think, now that we've new quarters. In the meantime, I'll keep your admonitions in mind."

"Humph." She took the purse and unlocked the door for him, scowling. But as he passed by her, he heard her say gruffly, "Take care, Mr. Makepeace. St. Giles needs you."

"Good night."

He pulled his greatcoat more securely about himself as he headed into the chilly dark. If he were wearing his harlequin motley, he could go in search of other people's troubles right now and lose himself in the night and danger. Winter shrugged irritably at the thought. His shoulders itched to swing a sword or throw a blow. He'd lain abed for almost a week, letting his leg heal, and now he was almost ready to charge the filthy walls of the little courtyard.

Tomorrow night, he promised himself. Tomorrow would be soon enough to find someone to help. To find someone to fight.

The thought pulled him up short. He'd always regarded himself as a man of peace — despite his nocturnal wanderings. He went out as the Ghost of St. Giles to right wrongs. To help those unable to help themselves.

Didn't he?

He shook his head at himself. Of course he did. St. Giles was a weeping wound of humanity. Those too poor to live elsewhere came here. The prostitutes, the thieves, the ones enslaved to gin. All the dregs of London. And with them came their problems: rape and thievery, starvation and want, abandonment and despair. He'd long ago learned that there weren't enough hours in the daytime to help the destitute of St. Giles, so he'd taken to the night. Some wrongs needed more than good intentions and prayer to correct.

Some could only be helped with the point of a sword.

Winter walked around a corner and into a slightly wider street, startling a skeletally thin, small mongrel that looked like a terrier of some kind. The dog yipped once and cowered back into the pile of rags it lay on. Winter passed the animal, but something made him pause. Perhaps he sensed movement or the scent of something else besides the dog.

Or perhaps it was Providence.

In any case, he turned and took another look. A pale thing lay against the dog's dark fur, like an exotic starfish lost from the sea: a child's hand. Winter bent and lifted away a rag, ignoring the uncertain rumbling coming from the dog's thin chest. A frightened face cringed away from him, the eyes wide and staring, the mouth stretched in a rictus of terror.

He crouched to make himself less intimidating. "I'll not hurt you, child. Are you all alone?"

But the little creature seemed too petrified to speak.

"Come. I know a warm, safe place." Winter carefully lifted the child, bundled rags and all, ignoring the creature's feeble attempts to push him away. Lord only knew what had made the child so terrified, but he could not leave it here to freeze to death.

The dog tumbled from the rags, falling to the street with a yelp.

The child whispered something and held out a pleading hand to the mongrel.

Winter lifted his chin to the dog. "Best you come along, too, then."

And without looking back to the mongrel, he turned to continue toward the home. The dog would follow or not, but in either case the animal was not his main concern.

The child was.

He could feel the little body shaking against his chest, whether from fear or cold, he couldn't tell.

Half an hour later, the new Home for Unfortunate Infants and Foundling Children loomed ahead. The building was utilitarian brick, but it still stood out from its surroundings, a shining beacon of hope. Winter stumbled at the thought. What would he do if Lady Beckinhall was correct and he was driven from the home? He had no idea — the home and helping the children within it were all he'd ever wanted to do in his life. Without it — without *them* — he was less than nothing.

He shook away the thought and continued walking. The child needed to get inside. There was a rather grand front entrance with a set of wide stairs, but Winter chose the more accessible servant's entrance at the back.

"Lord love you, sir!" Alice, one of the maids, exclaimed as Winter came in. The servant's entrance opened into the kitchen, and Alice appeared to be enjoying a before-bed cup of tea at the kitchen table. "I didn't know you were out this late, Mr. Make-peace."

"Pour a cup of tea with lots of milk and sugar, please, Alice," Winter ordered as he brought the child to the hearth.

"Shoo, you!"

Winter turned at Alice's angry words and saw she was attempting to wave the mongrel back out the door.

The child whimpered in distress.

"That's all right, Alice," he said. "Let the

dog stay."

" 'Tis a smelly, filthy beast," Alice muttered, sounding scandalized.

"Yes, I can see that," Winter said drily. The mutt had crept to the fireplace, apparently torn between staying close to the child and fleeing before strangers, and the odor of rotten fish drifted from its matted fur.

"Here you are, then." Alice handed Winter the milky tea, then hovered as he held the cup steady for the child's trembling hands so it could drink. "Poor, wee mite."

"Indeed," Winter murmured. He smoothed the child's lank hair away from its dirty little face. The child looked to be four or five, or maybe older, for many children in St. Giles were too small for their age.

The dog sighed and slumped into a corner of the hearth.

The child's eyelids were heavy with fatigue. Winter tried not to disturb the creature as he gently drew aside the rags. A little chest was revealed, almost blue with cold, the ribs in pitiful relief.

"Bring a blanket to warm by the fire, Alice," Winter murmured.

"He needs a bath," the maid whispered when she returned with the blanket.

"Aye," Winter said. "But he's been through

enough for tonight, I think. We can give him a thorough washing tomorrow morning."

Assuming the child lived through the night, that is.

Winter drew off the last piece of clothing and then paused, brows raised. "I think you'd best finish this, Alice."

"Sir?"

He wrapped the sleeping child in the warm blanket and turned to the maid. "She's a girl."

Lady Margaret Reading — better known simply as Megs to her intimates — stepped into Lady Langton's ballroom that night and deliberately did *not* look eagerly around. For one thing, she knew most of those who would be attending the ball: the very cream of London society, including her brother Thomas and his wife. Distinguished members of parliament would mingle with society hostesses and, no doubt, one or two slightly risqué ladies or gentlemen. They were people she'd associated with ever since she'd come out nearly five years ago — the usual roster of invitees to an event such as this.

But that wasn't the only reason she didn't bother looking around. No, it was much more discreet to not gawk after *him* like a besotted milkmaid. She wasn't ready yet to let everyone — her brother included — know about their connection. Right now it was a delicious secret she held close to her breast. When they announced their attachment, it would immediately become public property. She wanted him all to herself for just a little longer.

And the third reason she didn't scan the crowd? Well that was the simplest of all: The first sight of him was just so wonderful. She felt a thrill every time. A quiver in her tummy, a rush of light-headedness, a wobbliness in the knees. Megs giggled. She was making Mr. Roger Fraser-Burnsby sound like a head cold.

"I see that you're in fine fettle tonight, Margaret," a rich masculine voice murmured behind her.

She turned to find her eldest brother, Thomas, smiling down at her.

Funny, that. Until recently — until his marriage to the rather notorious Lavinia Tate last December, in fact — Thomas had never bothered smiling at her. Not really anyway. He always had a social smile, of course. As a leading member of parliament and the Marquess of Mandeville, Thomas was always acutely aware of his public aspect. But since the advent of Lavinia into the Reading family, Thomas had been different. He'd been *happy,* Meg realized now. If love could excite a man as stuffy as her eldest brother, think what it could do to the average person!

"Oh! Is Lavinia here already as well?" Megs asked, grinning.

Thomas blinked as if surprised by her enthusiasm and replied cautiously, "I did escort Lady Mandeville here tonight."

Hmm. Obviously love could only help so far in such a stodgy case.

"Good. I'd hoped to have a chat with her." Megs made her expression more sedate.

"You'll have to seek her out, then. Lavinia is up in the boughs over this escaped pirate business, and the moment we were past the door, she sought out her bosom bows to gossip with. She was telling me all the details about his burned body on the ride here. Quite gruesome, really, and not at all what a lady should be interested in." Thomas frowned ponderously.

Megs, not for the first time, felt a twinge of sympathy for her new sister-in-law. It might not be correct, strictly speaking, for a lady to be interested in burned-to-a-crisp pirates, but it was very hard not to be. "Most everyone in London is talking about it, I think, both the pirate and the Ghost of . . ." Megs trailed off as she suddenly lost interest in the conversation.

She'd caught sight of Roger at last and her knees were wobbling right on schedule. He stood with a group of other gentlemen and his head was thrown back in laughter, his strong, tanned throat working. Roger wasn't exactly handsome in the traditional sense. His face was too broad, his nose too flat. But his eyes were a warm brown and his grin was quite infectious. And when he turned that smile on her . . . well, the rest of the world seemed to fall away.

". . . a soiree or ball or some such. I expect you'll attend," Thomas murmured next to her.

Megs started slightly. She had no idea what "some such" he was talking about, but she could find out later readily enough. "Of course. I'll be quite pleased."

"Good. Good," Thomas said vaguely. "And Mother will be in town by then as well. Too bad Griffin and Hero have run off to the country. Odd time to do it, in the middle of the season."

"Mmm." Roger was talking to three other gentlemen who Megs knew were close friends of his: Lord d'Arque, Mr. Charles Seymour, and the Earl of Kershaw. Unfortunately, she didn't know the other gentlemen at all well and was thus rather shy around them. In fact, Lord d'Arque was a notorious rake. If she could only catch Roger's eye, perhaps she could signal a meeting in the garden.

Plum-colored silk overembroidered in gold and silver thread blocked her line of sight.

"Oh, Lady Margaret, I'm so relieved to see you here!" Lady Penelope spoke to Megs, but it was at Thomas that she batted her eyelashes. Beside her, Miss Greaves smiled shyly at Megs. "I must speak to you about Mr. Makepeace."

"Makepeace?" Thomas frowned. "Who is this chap, Megs?"

Megs opened her mouth, but Lady Penelope was already talking. "He is the manager of the Home for Unfortunate Infants and Foundling Children, my lord. Or I should say the *current* manager, for I must speak frankly and say that I am deeply doubtful of Mr. Makepeace's qualifications. I think if we could only find a more *polite* manager, the home would be vastly improved."

Thomas looked both confused and bored by this explanation, but Megs couldn't let it go by unchallenged. Mr. Makepeace might be nearly as stodgy as Thomas, but he'd devoted his entire life to the home. It seemed a shame to let a bully like Lady Penelope take it away from him.

Megs smiled sweetly. "We've appointed Lady Beckinhall as Mr. Makepeace's tutor in matters social. Shouldn't we give her a chance to educate Mr. Makepeace?"

Lady Penelope sniffed. "Lady Beckinhall has all my admiration, of course, but I have little hope that even she can effect such a drastic change in Mr. Makepeace. Rather, I believe that an entirely new manager must be found. To that end, I have just today started interviewing men I think might be suitable for the position."

Megs stiffened at this information. "But we already have a manager —"

"Not, as we've already agreed, an *appropriate* one." Lady Penelope smiled prettily, though quite a few of her teeth were showing. "The gentlemen I've agreed to interview all have lovely, polished manners and are recommended by some of my most intimate friends."

"But do they have experience running an orphanage?" Thomas arched an eyebrow in amusement.

"Pish!" Lady Penelope waved an airy hand. "The man I hire can learn, I am sure. And if need be, I can always hire *two* gentlemen."

Miss Greaves cast her eyes heavenward for a second and Megs wished she could do the same without being seen by Lady Penelope. At least Lady Penelope seemed aware of the huge amount of work Mr. Makepeace did all by himself.

"I don't think we can make any drastic changes while both Ladies Caire and Lady Hero are away from the city," Megs said firmly. "After all, *they* are the original founders of the Ladies' Syndicate."

Lady Penelope's bottom lip stuck out in a pretty pout, and Megs felt a welcome wash of relief. Lady Penelope must know she could not act in Lady Hero's and the Ladies Caire's absences without damaging her cause irrevocably. Megs made a note to write all three ladies so they might be aware of the danger to Mr. Makepeace.

At that moment, Roger looked over, catching Megs's eye, and all thought of the home fled her mind. He winked and tilted his head imperceptibly in the direction of the garden terrace.

"Oh, I see a dear friend," Megs murmured. "If you'll excuse me?"

Megs only vaguely heard Thomas's and Lady Penelope's polite words. Roger was already moving obliquely toward the French doors. She must be careful, but soon — so soon! — she would be in her lover's arms.

CHAPTER FOUR

*Now wise men have tried to explain love
— and they have failed. All I can say is
that the Harlequin and the fine lady fell in
love that day. True and lasting love that
cares not for man's rank or place in the
world: a thing both grand and awful . . .*
— from *The Legend of the
Harlequin Ghost of St. Giles*

"They say the king himself has put a price
upon his head," Pinkney said chattily the
next morning.

Isabel glanced up at her vanity mirror and
watched as the lady's maid placed a pin
precisely in her hair. Her mouth was dry as
she asked, "The Ghost?"

"Yes, my lady."

A price on his head. With Charming
Mickey dead, the authorities had obviously
concentrated their ire on the Ghost of St.
Giles. Perhaps he'd lie low, avoid the streets

now that they had suddenly become much more dangerous. Isabel bit her lip. Except in the short time that she'd talked to him, the Ghost hadn't seemed the type to avoid danger. Oh, why was she worrying over the man anyway? It'd only been chance that had set him in her path and her own perhaps overlarge sense of right and wrong that had picked him up and saved him from the mob in the first place. She'd probably never see the man again in her life.

Isabel scowled at herself in the mirror.

"I do hope they don't catch him," Pinkney said, not even noticing her mistress's expression. A slight frown knit itself between the maid's brows as she worked a curl into position. "He's so handsome and dashing. And with the death of Charming Mickey . . . well, we shan't have *any* handsome rogues left in London soon."

Pinkney's expression had turned tragic.

"That certainly would be a pity," Isabel said drily.

"Oh, I forgot!" Pinkney exclaimed. She stuck her hand into the slit in her dress and rummaged in the pocket underneath, drawing out a letter. "This came for you this morning."

"Thank you," Isabel said, taking the letter.

"It was delivered by a boy, not the post," Pinkney said. "Perhaps it's a love letter."

Isabel raised her brows in amusement as she broke the seal. Unfolding the letter, she read:

Lady Penelope is interviewing gentlemen to replace Mr. Makepeace.

Isabel frowned, turning over the letter. It wasn't signed, and besides her name, there wasn't anything else written on it. Still, she had a good idea who the note was from.

"Not a love letter?" Pinkney asked curiously.

"Um . . . no," Isabel murmured.

The dratted man had walked out on her the last time she'd talked to him. He probably wouldn't even see her if she tried to warn him — or talk some sense into him. Yet, if she didn't make an effort to once again change his mind, he was sure to lose the home. Isabel rose and threw the note into the fire, watching as the flames devoured the paper. She had an invitation to go riding this afternoon and had thought about shopping before that and perhaps calling on some acquaintances.

She wrinkled her nose. None of her plans were that important. They never were. "Have John Coachman ready the carriage, please."

"Yes, ma'am," Pinkney said, bustling to the door.

Isabel squared her shoulders and paced before the fireplace as she waited. She must be firm this time and not take his refusal. If need be, she'd corner the wretched man in his bedroom. The shock alone at her scandalous behavior might turn the tide —

Her foot hit an object on the floor that went tumbling away. Isabel bent to pick it up. It was a painted wooden top, no bigger than her palm. For a moment she stared blankly at the toy before carefully placing it on her vanity table and leaving her bedroom.

Downstairs, Pinkney was tying on a bonnet. "Shall we be shopping, my lady?"

"No, we're to the home again," Isabel replied, ignoring the slump of her lady's maid's shoulders. "Please tell Carruthers that there's a toy on my vanity table. I'd like her to take it away."

"Yes, my lady." Pinkney scurried to do her bidding.

In another few minutes, the carriage was ready and they were away. Isabel smoothed the skirts of her emerald gown. It was much too fine for visiting the home and he'd no doubt make note of that fact. She lifted her chin. Well, she didn't care a fig for what Mr.

Makepeace might think of her or her attire. The man had the dreary aspect of someone three times his age. *That* she would correct along with his manners.

They met with no delays and her carriage rolled to a stop a little over half an hour later outside the new home's entrance. Harold opened the carriage door and set the step for her.

"Thank you," Isabel murmured as she got out of the carriage. Pinkney, who'd dozed in the carriage, stifled a yawn and followed. "Tell John Coachman to take it 'round the corner, please. I'll send a boy when I'm ready to leave."

Isabel lifted her skirts and climbed the home's front steps with Pinkney beside her.

"Shall I knock?" the lady's maid asked.

"Please."

Pinkney lifted the heavy iron knocker and let it fall. The lady's maid fussed with her ornately embroidered turquoise skirts as they waited, and Isabel wondered — not for the first time — if her maid wasn't upstaging her.

The door opened to reveal a freckled face.

Isabel couldn't remember the boy's name, but fortunately that didn't matter at the home — all the boys had been christened "Joseph" and all the girls "Mary."

"Good afternoon, Joseph," she said with determined brightness. "Is Mr. Makepeace in?"

"He's with the girl," the boy said obscurely, his manner very solemn. He turned before Isabel could ask another question and led her back into the house.

The former Home for Unfortunate Infants and Foundling Children had been a tall, narrow building, nearly falling apart from age and poor structural materials. It had burned over a year ago, at which point the Ladies' Syndicate for the Benefit of the Home for Unfortunate Infants and Foundling Children had been formed to construct this new building. The hallway that Isabel now traversed was wide and well lit, the plaster walls painted a soothing cream. To the right was a sitting room where visitors to the home might be received, and where in fact she'd seen Mr. Makepeace only the day before. But the boy led them past the sitting room. Directly ahead, the hall led back to a dining room and then the huge kitchens, and to the left was a wide marble staircase that gave access to the upper floors. The bones were all here, but Isabel couldn't help thinking that they needed a bit more decoration upon them before the

97

new home lost its current austere appearance.

The boy mounted the stairs without a word, and Isabel followed with Pinkney panting behind. They could hear the chatter of children and the slower murmur of adult voices as they passed the classrooms on the first floor above the ground floor. On the second floor were the dormitories, empty now during the day. Past the dormitories, at the end of the corridor, Joseph opened an unmarked door.

Inside was a small but cheerful room with a bright blue and white tiled fireplace and two tall windows to give light. Four cots were distributed along the wall, only one of which was occupied. A tiny child lay under the snowy sheets and counterpane, her dark brown hair spread upon the pillow. Curled beside her was a funny little dog with wiry white fur spotted in brown.

Winter Makepeace looked up from where he sat in a chair beside the bed. Fatigue lined his severe face, but his eyes widened in sudden alertness at the sight of her.

"Lady Beckinhall," he said, his voice grating with weariness as he stood, "to what do I owe this second visit?"

"Pure stubbornness?" Isabel murmured whimsically. "Oh, do sit back down." Obviously the man had spent the night caring for a sick child. She approached the bed and peered at the little face as the dog gave a tentative growl. "What's wrong with her?"

Mr. Makepeace looked at the child, his face calm, but she could see a flicker of worry in the tightening of his lips. For the first time she noticed that his upper lip was wider than his bottom lip. A memory tickled at the back of her mind, faint and elusive. Where had she seen —

"I don't know," he answered her, scattering her train of thought. "I found her last night in an alley, the dog beside her. We've had the doctor in to see her, but he can give no more information than that she suffers from malnutrition and exhaustion."

Isabel's brows knit. "What's her name?"

Mr. Makepeace shook his head. "She won't speak."

"She told me her dog's name is Dodo," Joseph offered. He'd taken the seat on the opposite side of the bed and his hand had crept to pat the little girl's thin arm.

Mr. Makepeace inclined his head. "I beg your pardon. I should've said that the child will not speak to *me* — or any other adult. Joseph Tinbox says, however, that she has communicated with him briefly when they were alone."

Joseph Tinbox nodded emphatically. "And her name is Peach."

The adults all looked at him. Pinkney giggled. Isabel shot her a glance and the lady's maid half choked as she stifled her laughter.

There was a pause, and then Isabel cleared her throat delicately. "Peach seems a rather . . . odd name."

Joseph Tinbox looked stubborn. "It's what she's called an' we shouldn't go changin' it."

"Naturally we shall call her whatever she wishes," Mr. Makepeace said mildly. "But I think we'll wait to see what that is when she wakes."

Joseph Tinbox opened his mouth — no doubt to argue — but the little girl woke at that moment. She glanced around, her eyes widening in panic, and then she squeezed her eyelids shut again. She'd moved to grip Joseph Tinbox's hand and was holding it desperately.

Mr. Makepeace frowned as he watched the child. "I think I shall take Lady Beckinhall down to the sitting room, Joseph Tinbox. Perhaps you can see if . . . Peach . . . would like to try some of the broth that was sent up earlier."

He patted the boy's shoulder, then stood

and ushered Isabel and Pinkney to the door, closing it behind them.

"I apologize for our disorder, Lady Beckinhall," he said as he went to the stairs. "I'm afraid that finding the child has disrupted our normal proceedings here at the home."

"I do understand," Isabel murmured as she followed him down the stairs. "Why do you think she won't speak to anyone but Joseph Tinbox?"

"Undoubtedly she trusts him," he said as they made the ground floor. He looked at her over his shoulder, his expression wry. "And undoubtedly she does *not* trust me."

"Oh, but . . ." Isabel instinctively began to protest. Whatever his faults, it was patently obvious that Mr. Makepeace cared for all the children in his home. She couldn't imagine him hurting any of them.

Mr. Makepeace shook his head as he opened the door to the sitting room. "I do not take her suspicion personally, my lady. For a child to have learned distrust at such a young age, she must've been badly mistreated by the adults she has known. It would be natural, therefore, for her to place her trust in Joseph Tinbox instead."

"Oh." Isabel absently sank onto a settee. She hated the thought of the frail little girl upstairs enduring physical punishments, perhaps whippings. She shuddered. She remembered then his hand on the boy's shoulder. "He's a favorite of yours, isn't he, Joseph Tinbox?"

Mr. Makepeace stiffened. "I don't have favorites."

She raised an eyebrow. She'd seen the fond look he'd given the boy. "Oh, but —"

Mr. Makepeace dropped into an armchair, propping his head in his fist.

Isabel's eyes narrowed, and she addressed her lady's maid who had followed them downstairs. "Pinkney, please go to the kitchens and ask for some luncheon. Some meat, cheese, and bread. Any fruit there might be. And a strong pot of tea."

"There's no need," Mr. Makepeace began.

"When did you last eat?"

His brows drew together in irritation. "Last night."

Isabel pursed her lips. "Then there is every need."

Once again his look was wry. "I bow to your expertise in the matter."

"Humph." His teasing words warmed her, even as she felt alarm looking at the stubble on his chin. Had he slept at all last night? He must be truly weary to relax enough to banter with her. Another thought struck. "We really must find a cook for the home, now that the children are settled in the new building. Nell Jones and the other maidservants have enough to do without preparing the meals as well."

He stifled a yawn behind a fist. "The girls are taught to cook."

"Yes, but they can't see to every meal. Besides, I've eaten the girls' efforts, and while their biscuits are, er . . . very *interesting,* it might be a good idea to have someone who can cook things that are rather more standard, don't you think?"

She looked at Mr. Makepeace expectantly, but his only reply was a soft snore. The wretched man had fallen asleep, his head still propped in his hand. For a moment Isabel simply watched his sleeping face. The lines around his mouth had softened in relaxation, his eyelashes were black and rather thick, and he might've looked boyish were it not for the beard shadowing his jaw. His stubble gave him a rakish air.

Isabel's lips curved at the last thought. Any man less rake-like than Mr. Makepeace she'd yet to meet. Why, he spent so much of his time caring for his home and the inhabitants that he'd fallen asleep in front of her in the middle of the day. It made her wonder what, if anything, he did when he had a moment to himself. Did he read?

Perhaps he kept a diary or enjoyed touring churches? She considered, but couldn't come up with any more activities for the man. He was rather an enigma, wasn't he? His life was given to self-sacrifice, but he still kept a large part of himself secret. If only —

The door to the sitting room opened and Isabel looked up, expecting Pinkney.

Instead, a small elderly woman stood in the doorway. "Oh! Beggin' your pardon, ma'am."

"Mistress Medina," Winter Makepeace's voice was raspy with sleep. He hadn't moved, but he'd evidently woken up as soon as the door had opened. "We have need of your services."

The little woman cocked her head. "Sir?"

He indicated Isabel. "Lady Beckinhall was just chiding me for lack of a good cook."

Isabel's eyebrows snapped together. "I did *not* chide —"

He ignored her protest, turning toward Mistress Medina. "Can you start at once?"

"Certainly, sir."

"Good, then —"

A gaggle of little girls bearing trays trooped into the sitting room, herded by Pinkney, looking less than her usual neat self.

"Here's the tea, my lady," Pinkney said.

"Excellent." Isabel smiled and waved a hand to a side table. "You can place the tea there and we'll dine as I discuss matters with Mr. Makepeace."

Winter Makepeace cleared his throat ominously. "What matters are those?"

Isabel smiled firmly. "How I'm going to help you keep your position."

Naturally all the little girls goggled at Lady Beckinhall's words.

Winter had not slept more than a few minutes since finding "Peach" the night before, but Lady Beckinhall's presence was strangely invigorating.

Even if it was irritating as well.

He turned to the girls. "Mary Whitsun, please show Mistress Medina to the kitchen. She's to be our new cook, so you must obey her and give her any help she might need. The rest of you girls are due in the school-room for lessons, I believe."

There was a general slumping of shoulders, but the girls filed out. Mary Whitsun nodded briskly and smiled at Mistress Medina before leading the new cook from the room.

He turned back to Lady Beckinhall, looking dangerously attractive in a dark green dress that gave her hair mahogany high-lights. "Now, what are you about?"

"Luncheon first." She rose and found a plate and began heaping it with meat, cheese, and bread. It looked like a lot of food for a lady. "I find arguing — and we do seem to argue quite a lot — is best done on a full stomach."

He stared at her, perplexed. What was she up to now?

Lady Beckinhall turned, saw him scowling at her, and beamed. "Have something to eat. That'll make you feel better."

And she handed the full plate to him.

Well, he couldn't continue to frown at her when she was being so nice. Winter took the plate, feeling warmth creep into his chest. It wasn't often that someone else provided for him. Usually it was the other way about.

He cleared his throat before saying gruffly, "Thank you."

She nodded, unperturbed, and selected a small wedge of cheese and a slice of bread before reseating herself on the settee. "Have you thought about putting something in that corner?" She waved her wedge of cheese at the right side of the fireplace. "A statue, perhaps? I have the most wonderful little white marble statuette. It's of a stork and a frog."

He blinked, bemused. "A stork."

She nodded. "And a frog. Roman, I think. Or perhaps Greek. Maybe it represents one of Aesop's fables — he *was* Greek, wasn't he?"

"I believe so." Winter set his plate aside, bracing himself. "Charming as this visit is, I think we need to get to the point now, my lady."

She smiled ruefully. "The arguing so soon?"

That smile sent a bolt straight through his middle, but he soldiered on, keeping his face expressionless. "If we must."

"Oh, I think we must," she said softly. "I've heard that Lady Penelope intends to hire a new manager for the home."

He'd been expecting something like this, but the blow was hard nonetheless. This wasn't just the children's home — it was his as well. Last night's rescue of Peach had made him realize that. He could no more walk away from the home than he could cut off his right hand.

But he didn't let those ragged emotions show on his face. They were carefully hidden. Carefully contained. "And how will you help me keep the home?"

She shrugged elegantly, though he noticed

107

that she couldn't quite conceal the tension in her face. Perhaps he wasn't the only one concealing emotions. "I'll tutor you in social manners, prove that you can be as graceful as any popinjay Lady Penelope finds. It's the only way to defeat her plans."

He raised his eyebrows in amusement at her choice of words. "And you've appointed yourself my savior? Why?"

"Why not?" She smiled carelessly. "I've found I've acquired a taste for saving gentlemen lately. Did you know that I helped the Ghost of St. Giles escape from a maddened mob the other day?"

His heart stopped. "No, I did not."

"Quite brave of me, don't you think?" Her lips curved mockingly at her own words.

"Yes," he said with perfect seriousness. "I do."

She glanced up and he snared her eyes. Her soft mouth wobbled. What was she thinking, this beautiful, exotic creature? She didn't belong here in his plain sitting room, didn't belong in St. Giles or in his life. And yet he had a near-impossible-to-resist urge to drag her into his lap and kiss her.

He took a deep breath, beating down the animal. "Well, then. I suppose I'd best put myself under your tutelage."

"Good." She rose abruptly and without

her usual grace. "Then we shall start tomorrow morning."

The next morning, Winter stood looking up at the facade of Lady Beckinhall's town house. It was exactly what he'd expected: new, ostentatious, and in the most fashionable part of London.

The inside was another matter altogether.

Winter paused on the threshold of the grand doors, giving his right leg a rest and trying to understand the difference, ignoring for a moment the supercilious butler who had admitted him. The house was grand, yes, rich and elegantly appointed, but there was something else here as well.

The butler cleared his throat. "If you'd care to wait for Lady Beckinhall in the small sitting room, sir?"

Winter tore his gaze from the sunbeam dancing across the marbled entryway floor and nodded absently at the man.

He was ushered into the "small" sitting room, which, naturally, wasn't small at all — it was nearly the size of the new home's dining room. But the room had been appointed in such a way that its large size didn't seem cold or uncomfortably formal. The walls were a buttery yellow with a gray-blue wainscoting. Groups of chairs and settees were scattered here and there, making smaller, more intimate seating spaces. Overhead, cherubs frolicked on the painted ceiling, peeking from behind billowy white clouds. Winter snorted under his breath at the sight. He strolled toward a fireplace at the far end of the room, not bothering to hide his limp now that he was alone. A pink and white gilded clock ticked on the mantel, its face nearly hidden by curlicues and cupids. The sitting room was at the back of the house and the sounds from the street were muffled, making the room pleasantly quiet.

Winter touched the clock. It was a silly thing, and yet . . . oddly adorable and utterly fitting in Lady Beckinhall's sitting room. He frowned, puzzled. How could a clock be adorable?

Something scuttled behind one of the pink settees.

Winter raised his brows. Surely Lady Beckinhall wasn't troubled by rats? But perhaps she had a lap dog like so many fashionable ladies. He stretched to peer over the back of the settee.

Large brown eyes stared back from a small boy's face. The child couldn't be more than five, but he was dressed in a fine scarlet coat and breeches with lace at his throat. Not a servant's child, then.

He hadn't known she was a mother. The thought made something in his heart contract.

Winter inclined his head. "Good day."

The boy slowly rose from his place of hiding and scuffed one foot in the thick, plush carpet. "Who're you?"

Winter bowed. "Mr. Makepeace. How do you do?"

Some instinct — or more likely hours of tutelage — made the child bow in return.

Winter felt his lips twitch in amusement. "And you are?"

"Christopher!" The answer came not from the boy, but from a frazzled-looking female servant at the door. "Oh, I'm sorry, sir, if he was bothering you."

Winter shook his head. "No bother at all."

Lady Beckinhall appeared behind the maidservant, her face expressionless. "Christopher, you've worried Carruthers terribly. Please make your apologies to her."

Christopher ducked his head. "Sorry, 'Ruthers."

Carruthers smiled fondly. "That's all right, Master Christopher, but I think it's past time for your bath now if we're to see the park this afternoon."

The child dolefully left the room, no

doubt doomed to a soapy fate.

Winter looked at Lady Beckinhall as the door closed. "I did not know you had a son, my lady."

For a split second he was shocked to see pain on her face. Then she smiled brilliantly as if to mask whatever true emotions she might be feeling. "I don't. I don't have any children."

He lifted an eyebrow. "Then why —"

But she had already turned to seat herself on the settee, talking all the while. "I thought we'd start simply this morning. The Duchess of Arlington's ball is one week away, and unless you know how to dance . . . ?"

She obviously didn't want to talk about the child. Interesting. He shook his head at her inquiring look.

"No, of course not," she sighed. "Then we'll have to begin dancing lessons very soon. You'll need to at least know the steps — I have no hope that you'll actually master them, but if we can get you to the point where you don't step on a lady's toes, I'll be more than pleased."

"You're too kind," he murmured.

Her eyes narrowed as if she'd taken exception to his dry-as-dust tone. "I think a new suit is in order as well. Perhaps something in cream or light blue silk?"

His pride balked. "No."

Her lush lips firmed. "You can't appear in polite society in the dingy clothes you're wearing now. That coat looks to be at least a decade old."

"Only four years," he said mildly. "And I cannot accept such a lavish — such a *personal* — gift from you, my lady."

She tilted her head, studying him, and he was reminded of a crow looking one way and then another to figure out how to crack a nut. "Think of it as a gift from the Ladies' Syndicate. We appreciate the work you do for the home, and a new suit of clothes so you can move about in society is hardly a wasted extravagance."

He wanted to decline, but her gentle argument made sense. He sighed silently. "Very well, but I must insist upon somber colors. Black or brown."

She clearly had to bite back the urge to try and persuade him to wear something outrageous — bright pink or lavender, perhaps — but in the end she must've seen the wisdom of a compromise.

"Very well." She nodded briskly. "I've sent for tea so we can at least practice that today. And naturally I thought we'd make conversation."

"Naturally."

"And while sarcasm *does* have its place in polite company, it's best used in moderation," she said sweetly. "Very *strict* moderation."

There was a short silence as she held his gaze. Her blue eyes were surprisingly determined. Surprisingly strong.

Winter inclined his head. "What would you have us converse about?"

She smiled again, and he felt it deep in the pit of his belly, the pull this woman had on him. Pray it did not show upon his face.

"A gentleman often compliments a lady," she said.

She wanted *compliments* from him? He searched her countenance for signs of a jest, but she seemed in earnest.

Winter sighed silently. "Your home is very . . . comfortable."

He realized now *that* was the feeling her house exuded: a sense of comfortableness. Homey. That was what it was.

He glanced at her, rather pleased with himself.

Lady Beckinhall looked as if she were trying to restrain a smile. "I'm not sure that is exactly a compliment."

"Why not?"

"You're supposed to compliment a house's

decor," she said patiently. "The taste of its mistress."

"But I care not for decor or this taste you speak of." He found himself invested in his argument. "Surely the quality of a home should be measured by the comfort one receives there? In which case, calling your home very comfortable is the highest of compliments."

She tilted her head as if considering his words. "I suppose you are quite correct. One should be comfortable in a home. I thank you then for your kind compliment."

Odd, her accession to his argument lit a small flame of warmth in his breast. Naturally, he made no indication of this. Instead, he inclined his head in acknowledgment.

"But," she continued, "society places no value on comfort in a home, so as kind as your words are to me, they will not do in a ballroom or musicale, as I think you already know."

The door opened behind him and a phalanx of maids entered bearing tea trays.

He waited until the maidservants had placed their burdens down and been dismissed.

Then he looked at her, this woman too intelligent for the frivolous society she wallowed in. "You would have me change my entire aspect, I see."

She sighed and leaned forward to pour the tea. "Not entirely. Besides" — she shot him another of her quick, devastating smiles as she set down the teapot — "I doubt you're such a frail personality as to be so easily changed. Come. Please sit down with me."

He was still standing, despite the ache in his right leg, as if ready to either flee or fight. This woman made what social graces he had vanish.

Winter took the settee across from Lady Beckinhall, a low table with the tea things forming a protective barrier between them. He resisted the urge to massage his injured leg, which had begun to throb unpleasantly.

She cast him a challenging glance but made no comment on his choice of seat, instead handing him one of the teacups. "You take no sugar or cream, I believe."

He nodded, taking the dish of tea. It was hot and strong and of a quality that he didn't often drink.

"Now, then," Lady Beckinhall said as she stirred sugar and cream into her own tea. "Although I appreciate your compliment of my home, most compliments you'll be obliged to offer in a ballroom will be of a more personal nature. Something about the lady's eyes or hair or dress, for instance, would be most suitable."

She sipped her tea, watching him over the rim with those damnably perceptive blue eyes.

And he couldn't seem to control his own gaze. He perused her form as he sought a *suitable* compliment. Ladies were supposed to sit correctly upright, even he knew that, but Lady Beckinhall seemed somehow to lounge bonelessly on the cushions, shoulders back, feet tucked beneath the settee. The position thrust her bosom into prominence, though he did not think it deliberate on her part. She wore a low-cut gown of deep gold, the cloth tenderly cradling her pale, soft breasts.

I would do violence for one glimpse of your naked breasts. Bleed for one taste of your nipple on my tongue.

No, that was probably not the type of compliment she was looking for.

He cleared his throat. "Your voice, my lady, would make a nightingale jealous."

She blinked as if surprised. "No one has ever complimented me on my voice before, Mr. Makepeace. Well done."

Were her cheeks a shade pinker than before?

Her lashes lowered. "A few more comments such as that one, Mr. Makepeace, and you might be flirting with me."

He felt his brows rise. "You wish me to flirt with you?"

She shrugged. "Most of the conversation between a lady and a gentleman at social events is, in essence, flirtation."

"Then you must flirt with dozens of gentlemen in a night."

"Do I detect a tone of reproach, Mr. Makepeace?" she asked softly.

"Not at all." He ordered his thoughts. "I merely observe that in this you are far more knowledgeable than I."

"More experienced, you mean?"

He merely watched her, for the answer was self-evident. She was more experienced — in flirtation and, no doubt, in other, more basic interactions between women and men. The thought sent an unpleasant rush of some foreign emotion through him.

It took a moment for him to recognize — in some astonishment — that what he felt was jealousy. He lived a life of careful constraint. Ladies — females of any kind — were strictly forbidden by the life choices he'd made. And yet . . .

And yet there was a part of him — a part he'd never noticed before — that had become impatient with his own rules.

"But you must have flirted before," she was saying, her voice low and velvety. Welcoming and seductive. Everything that was utterly feminine and alluring.

"No."

Her delicate brows winged upward. "I know your life is busy, but surely you've had a *tendre* for some young girl before? A friend of your sisters' perhaps? Or a neighbor?"

He shook his head slowly. "No one." Did she understand to what he confessed? The beast within yawned and stretched. "I lay myself completely in your hands, Lady Beckinhall. Please. Teach me."

CHAPTER FIVE

The fine lady and the Harlequin became lovers, but such things are very hard to conceal, for the fine lady had suitors both rich and jealous and soon they heard the gossip about the Harlequin. One night when the moon was full, they followed the Harlequin into St. Giles and there set upon him with their steel swords. The Harlequin had but his play sword of wood with which to defend himself. The fight did not last long and when it was done, the suitors left the Harlequin dying in the street . . .

— from *The Legend of the Harlequin Ghost of St. Giles*

Isabel swallowed at Mr. Makepeace's low words. His voice sent a shiver across her nerves, making her nipples tighten. Had she heard correctly? Had he just confessed to being a virgin? He was unmarried, true, and

120

by his own admission had never had a sweetheart, but still. Many men resorted to prostitutes — and he lived in an area where they abounded.

But one look at Mr. Makepeace's proud, stern face disabused her of that notion. Somehow she knew: he would never pay for such an intimate act.

Which meant he was a virgin . . . and he'd just asked for her tutelage. Surely he didn't mean —

"Your silence is uncharacteristic, my lady," he said, still in that deep, precise voice that feathered across her senses. "I hope I have not shocked you with my inexperience . . . in flirting."

Flirting. Of course. *That* was what they were discussing. But she hadn't imagined the gleam in his dark eyes — or the subtle pause before he'd said "flirting."

Isabel straightened. *She* was the experienced one here, after all. "I believe we must work on your introduction, then."

He merely raised one eyebrow.

She cleared her throat. When had she last been this out of sorts? And over a plain, rigid schoolmaster — a man *younger* than she! "Flirtation is best begun immediately, even before the introduction. Can you show me your bow?"

121

He stood slowly and, still holding her eyes, bowed shortly.

She frowned. "No. Something more elegant. Shall I demonstrate?"

"No need." His gaze was ironic.

This time he backed up a step and pretended to doff an imaginary hat, bowing from the waist, his arms outstretched gracefully.

Isabel's eyes widened. "If you've known all along how to give a proper bow, why haven't you?"

He straightened slowly and shrugged broad shoulders. "A simple nod of the head gives enough deference without such silly flourishes."

She rolled her eyes. "Well, from now on flourish, please, when in polite company."

"As you wish," he said gravely.

"Now." She had to stop to inhale, for oddly she found herself out of breath. "Now, I would like you to practice kissing the hand of a lady."

She extended her hand, hoping he wouldn't notice the faint tremor of her fingers.

He paced toward her, took her hand, and bent over it. For a moment, his bowed head obscured their hands, but she felt the brush — warm and intimate — of his lips on her knuckles.

She gasped. "You're supposed to kiss the air *above* the lady's knuckles."

He raised his head, still bowed over her hand, the position bringing his face much closer to hers. She could see tiny shards of gold in his brown eyes. "Isn't this a lesson in flirtation?"

"Yes, but —"

He straightened to his full height. "Then it seems to me that a real kiss is more to the point than a pretend one."

Only now did she see the shadow of a smile lurking at the back of his eyes.

Her own eyes narrowed as she attempted to withdraw her hand from his. His grip remained firm.

"Mr. Makepeace."

He opened his hand, but only slightly, so that as she withdrew her hand, his fingers seemed to stroke across her palm.

"Perhaps you have no need of instruction after all," she muttered.

"Oh, but I do, I assure you." He resumed his seat across from her. "How many lovers have you had?"

She frowned at him, genuinely shocked. "You can't ask that."

"You already did of me," he reminded her, unperturbed.

"I certainly didn't use the word *lovers*," she retorted.

"But the meaning was the same, was it not?"

"Perhaps." *Of course the meaning had been the same.* She pursed her lips.

"I apologize. I wasn't aware your sensibilities were so delicate."

The wretched man was laughing at her! Oh, his expression was serious enough, but she could tell by the way he watched her that he meant to provoke.

Isabel settled back against the settee cushions and tilted her head. "Three."

His chin jerked — very faintly, but she'd seen it. She'd surprised him.

Hiding a smile, she waved a hand airily. "Four, if one counts my husband, but I don't think husbands *should* be counted as lovers, do you?"

His eyelids half lowered. "I would not know. Did you take lovers when you were married?"

"No." She made a considering moue. "Rather bourgeois of me, I know, but there it is. I never strayed from my marriage vows."

"Did he?"

She looked away. "I don't like these questions."

"I'm sorry. I did not mean to hurt you." His voice was deep and sincere.

"You haven't." Desperately she fought to regain her social face. She tilted her chin defiantly, gazing at him frankly.

The corner of his lips curved just a bit. "Then you took your lovers after your husband's death?"

How had she let him lead her into this dangerous conversational territory? Yet now that she was here, she wouldn't back down. "Yes. I waited a decent amount of time after dear Edmund was buried, naturally."

"Naturally."

She would've sworn he would be disapproving of a lady taking lovers, but she couldn't detect disapproval in his tone. He folded his hands in his lap, his manner as relaxed as if they discussed the price of fresh oysters.

"Do you have a lover now?"

What would it be like to teach such a man the arts of the bedroom?

The whispered thought startled her. He wasn't of her milieu, wasn't the type of man she would usually consider taking as a lover. She liked sophisticates. Men who were quick with an amusing witticism. Men who knew how to entertain, perhaps surprise in the bedroom, but who were discreet — even distant — out of it. Men who didn't take an *affaire d'amour* with any seriousness.

Her heartbeat quickened. "No." How far was he willing to take this? She leaned forward, her manner seductive. "Are you interested in the position?"

If she'd hoped to make him back down, she was sadly disappointed. His lips quirked, drawing her eyes to that fuller upper lip. Her brows knit in thought.

"I'm interested in many things," he said, his deep voice precise and unhurried, "but I cannot believe you offer me the position in earnest, my lady. After all, I have already confessed my lack of credentials."

Any other man would've looked abashed to remind her of his inexperience. Mr. Makepeace, in contrast, seemed perfectly complacent, even self-assured. Somehow she knew he would take a love affair very seriously indeed. Once that pinpoint focus was engaged, he would throw himself body and soul into the liaison. Into the *woman* he decided to take as a lover.

A shiver ran through her at the thought. To be the object of such ferocious regard was an alluring prospect, but it also gave her pause.

Caution, her intellect whispered. *Don't engage this man without proper consideration.*

126

He won't be as easily cast aside as the sophisticates of London society.

Isabel slowly sat back again, regarding her pupil. "Then we'll need to work on your social skills, won't we?" She smiled as she dumped her cooled tea and poured herself another dish. "Shall we practice dinner conversation?"

He nodded, and if she saw disappointment in his eyes, she ignored it. She might like to flirt and tease, but she wasn't without common sense after all.

"I am at your command," he drawled.

Winter watched as Lady Beckinhall took his teacup, dumped the contents, and poured him a fresh cup. Somehow he'd scared her away from their risqué conversation, and now she was set on talking about the weather or some other boring topic.

The strange thing was that he felt a twinge of disappointment. He'd liked sparring with her. Liked even more the small glimpse under the social mask she wore. She'd been truly hurt by her husband, and while he didn't want to remind her of sad memories, he did want to see again the naked face she'd shown. The true Lady Beckinhall.

She looked at him now, the role of hostess firmly in place. "Have you seen the new opera at the Royal Playhouse?"

"No." He took a sip of tea, watching her. "I've never attended an opera."

Her eyes narrowed slightly in, if he weren't mistaken, irritation. "A play, then?"

He silently shook his head.

"A musicale? The fair?"

He merely looked at her and waited.

She hadn't much patience, his Lady Beckinhall. "I declare you're the most boring man I've ever met, Mr. Makepeace. You must do something besides constantly toil at the home."

He felt the corner of his mouth curve.

"Sometimes I read."

"Don't tell me." She held out a commanding small palm. "You secretly devour the frivolous novels of Daniel Defoe."

"I admit to liking *Robinson Crusoe*," he said. "And I found his pamphlets on gin and gin distilling interesting if utterly wrongheaded."

She blinked as if interested in spite of herself. "Why?"

"Defoe argued that gin distilling is integral to the well-being of our English farmers because they sell their grain to the distillers. That argument may be correct, but it doesn't take into account what gin does to the poor of London."

She was already shaking her head. "But Defoe wrote later that gin was spoiling the offspring of those same London mothers who drank the — Why are you smiling at me?"

"Reading political pamphlets, my lady?" He tutted as if shocked. "Do the rest of the Ladies' Syndicate know about this?"

She blushed as if she'd been caught doing something naughty, yet she lifted her chin stubbornly. "You'd be surprised how many ladies read political pamphlets."

"No," he said slowly, "I don't think I would. I've never doubted that the fairer sex was as interested as men in politics and the social wrongs of London. I am, however, a bit surprised that *you* are."

She shrugged. "Why shouldn't I be?"

He leaned forward. "Because you make every effort to pretend disinterest in anything serious. Why?"

For a moment he thought she would actually give him a straight answer. Then she looked away, her hand waving indifferently. "I'm supposed to be teaching you dinner conversation. Politics is never a good topic for mixed company —"

"My lady," he began in warning.

"No." She shook her head, determinedly not meeting his eyes. "You shan't draw me in again. Novels are a *much* more proper topic of conversation."

She wasn't going to change her mind, he could see, so he humored her. "Even *Moll Flanders*?"

"Especially *Moll Flanders*," she said. "A novel about a woman of ill repute is sure to be a lively topic of conversation."

"And yet," he said softly, "despite Moll's dramatically tragic downfall, I cannot like her as much as Mr. Crusoe."

She visibly wavered, and he thought she'd stick to her usual society mask. But then she leaned forward, as eager as any girl. "Oh! When he found the footprint in the sand!"

He grinned. "Exciting, wasn't it?"

"I stayed up all night to read it to the end," she said, slumping back with a satisfied sigh. "I've read it again twice since." She suddenly fixed him with a gimlet eye. "And if you ever tell one of the ladies that I much prefer *Robinson Crusoe* over *Moll Flanders*, I'll cut out your liver."

He bowed solemnly. "Your secret is safe with me, my lady."

The corners of her lush mouth quirked. "Who would've thought," she murmured, "that the so-serious Mr. Makepeace would like adventure novels?"

He cocked his head. "Or that the frivolous Lady Beckinhall would prefer adventure novels to scandalous biographies?"

For a moment — only a moment — she dropped the facade and smiled at him almost shyly.

He smiled back, his heart beating in triple time.

Then she looked away, biting her lip. "Oh, where has the time gone? I think that's enough for today, don't you? I'll come to the home tomorrow and we can continue your studies there."

He didn't bother arguing. He'd obviously pushed her as far as she could go today. Instead, feeling protective, he stood and bowed, and with a few murmured words left her.

But as the butler showed him the door, Winter wondered: Who was uncovering who in their little game?

Isabel sat at her vanity that night brushing her hair, having already dismissed Pinkney for the evening. She was playing a dangerous game, she knew, with Mr. Makepeace. He wasn't of her station, wasn't even the same age as she. Yet she was strangely addicted to his intent regard. It was heady, being the focus of such a serious man. No man had ever looked at her the way Winter Makepeace did — not her lovers, and certainly not her husband.

She lowered her brush. Was that why she found herself wanting to provoke him into . . . what? Dropping his mask, perhaps?

Odd thought. For now that she considered it, his bluntness of speech rather reminded her of another man — the masked Ghost of St. Giles. He, too, had declined light flirtation for more direct conversation with her. How bizarre that Mr. Makepeace, a staid schoolmaster, should remind her of the roguish Ghost of St. Giles.

A movement in the mirror caught her eye. The drapes on the bed behind her twitched.

Isabel set her brush down on the vanity, turned, and looked at the bed. "Christopher?"

There was a pause and she began to wonder if she'd been mistaken, and then a small voice said, "Ma'am?"

She sighed. "Christopher, I think I've told you before that you mustn't hide in my rooms."

Silence.

Isabel stared at the bed, perplexed. What if he refused to come out? Should she have the boy pulled from the bed? Spanked by his nanny? Damn it, where was Carruthers?

132

The curtains rustled again as if small fingers had trailed across them. "I like it here."

She looked away, biting her lip, tears smarting in her eyes. He was only a small boy. Surely she could deal with a small boy?

She inhaled. "It's past your bedtime."

"Can't sleep."

She looked about the room as if searching for help. "I'll send for some warm milk."

"Don't like milk."

She stared at the curtain, exasperated. "What do you like?"

"Can . . ." She could hear the hesitation in his little voice and it made her heart squeeze. "Can you tell me a story, my lady?"

A story. Her mind was a blank. All she could think of was Cinderella, and she had the feeling that a little boy wouldn't be interested in the exploits of a girl and a handsome prince. She looked down, thinking, and saw the brush.

Isabel cleared her throat. "Have you heard of the Ghost of St. Giles?"

The curtain paused in its twitching. "A ghost? A real ghost?"

"Well . . ." She knit her brows in thought. "No, he's a living man, but he moves like a ghost and he hunts at night like a ghost."

"Who does he hunt?"

"Wicked men," she replied, sure of her ground now. She'd heard the stories of the Ghost ravaging maidens and kidnapping ladies, but having actually met the man, she was sure that the stories were false. "He punishes thieves and footpads and those who prey on the innocent."

"Pray like in church?"

"No. Prey like a cat catching a mouse."

"Oh."

She glanced at the bed and saw that Christopher had parted the curtain. One brown eye peeped out at her.

Isabel tried a smile. "Now, I really think you must go to bed, Christopher."

"But that wasn't a story," he pointed out.

Her chest tightened in near panic. "It's the best I can do for now."

"Are you my mother?" That single brown eye was wide and unblinking.

She had to look away first. "You know I'm not. I've told you so before." She got up and briskly opened the curtains to her bed, careful not to touch the boy. "Shall I ring for Carruthers or can you find the nursery yourself?"

"M'self." He jumped down from the bed and walked slowly to her door. "G'night, my lady."

Her voice was husky when she replied.

"Good night, Christopher."

Luckily, she held back the tears until he'd shut the door behind him.

"Lady Beckinhall's carriage is outside," Mary Whitsun said as she entered the home's sitting room the next afternoon.

Winter looked up from the letter he was reading just in time to see a little white and black terrier trot into the room as if he owned the place.

"Oh, come here, Dodo," Mary exclaimed. She bent and picked up the dog, who submitted without even a half-hearted growl.

Winter raised an eyebrow, impressed. Dodo had continued his warning growl whenever he came near. "Has Peach come down?"

"No, sir," Mary said regretfully. "She's still abed and not speaking, poor thing. But Dodo here has decided to explore the home. Just this morning Mistress Medina had to chase the dog away from some tarts she had cooling on a table in the kitchen."

"Ah." Winter eyed the terrier, who'd shut his eyes as if ready for a nap in Mary Whitsun's arms. "We'd best assign some of the little boys to look after him and see he goes into the alley to do his business. Can you

135

see to it, Mary?"

"Yes, sir."

The girl turned to the door, but Winter had remembered something. "Just a moment, Mary."

She looked at him. "Sir?"

He rummaged in the papers on his lap before finding a small, folded letter. This he held out to Mary. "My sister enclosed a note to you in her letter to me."

The girl's face lit up, and Winter realized with a start that Mary Whitsun was growing into a lovely young lady. They were going to have to watch the lads around her in another couple of years. "Oh, thank you, sir!"

She snatched the letter from him and was out the door before Winter could protest that he hadn't done anything worth being thanked for.

He'd just bundled the letter together when the door opened again. Lady Beckinhall swept in, already taking off her bonnet, followed by her lady's maid holding a basket. Behind them was a spare little man in a beautifully cut peach silk suit.

Winter rose and bowed. "Good afternoon, my lady."

"Good afternoon." She turned to her lady's maid. "Send for some tea, will you, please, Pinkney?" She glanced back at

136

Winter as she took the basket from Pinkney and set it on a table. "I've brought the most lovely little iced cakes. You must have three at least."

He raised an eyebrow and said mildly, "I just ate luncheon."

"But not enough, I'll wager," she said, eyeing his middle disapprovingly.

"Do you have plans to fatten me up, my lady?"

"Among other things," she said airily. She wore a deep blue and white striped dress today, which brought out the blue of her eyes.

Winter tore his gaze away from her form. "And who is this?" he asked, nodding at the little man in the peach suit.

"Your tailor." Lady Beckinhall smiled sweetly. "Kindly take off your breeches."

The lady's maid walked back in as she said this. Naturally the maid giggled before slapping a hand over her mouth and retiring to a chair in the corner.

Winter looked at Lady Beckinhall. "If I'm truly to be measured for a suit, perhaps you and your maid should leave before I disrobe."

She sniffed as she withdrew a blue-flowered plate from her basket and began laying dainty little iced cakes on it. "Pinkney and I are quite capable of turning our backs, I assure you."

His mouth tightened as he tried to tamp down the alarm in his chest. "I would prefer you leave."

"And *I* would prefer to stay in case Mr. Hurt needs to consult with me over the cut of the suit I wish him to make."

He narrowed his eyes at her. Besides the impropriety of undressing in the same room as two women, there was the possibility that the tailor would see his scars — most notably the one from last week — and ask inconvenient questions.

But she was busy ignoring him. Two girls had entered with the requested tea and now Lady Beckinhall directed them in setting it out.

"The Duchess of Arlington's ball is in just five days. You can make up a suit in that amount of time, can't you, Mr. Hurt?" she asked after the girls had been dismissed. She poured two cups of tea, handing one to Winter before adding both sugar and cream to hers.

The tailor bowed. "Yes, my lady. I'll set all my lads to the task of making Mr. Makepeace's suit."

"Splendid!" Lady Beckinhall took a sip of tea. "Oh, I say, this is much better than last time I visited."

"I'm so glad it meets with your approval," Winter said.

"Sarcasm, Mr. Makepeace. We've discussed this before," she chided, then without waiting for a reply, said, "I think your conversation is much improved, but we never did get to dancing yesterday. So after Mr. Hurt is finished . . ."

The tailor took his cue. "If you'll stand and remove your outer garments, Mr. Makepeace."

Winter sighed silently, setting aside his cup of tea. He noticed that both Lady Beckinhall and, behind her, her maid had stopped what they were doing and were staring at him. He arched an eyebrow.

"Oh! Oh, of course." Lady Beckinhall straightened and motioned for her maid to turn around. She glanced questioningly one last time at Winter, and when his expression didn't change, she turned as well, muttering something about "Puritan ideas of modesty."

Winter waited a moment to make sure she wouldn't turn back and then stripped off his coat and waistcoat. It was brought home with forceful memory that he'd been nude before this woman only a sennight ago.

Even if she didn't know it.

His breeches followed and then he was in shirtsleeves and smalls. He glanced at the tailor.

"The shirt as well, sir," Mr. Hurt said. "The fashion is for a tight-fitting waistcoat and coat."

"Yes, indeed," Lady Beckinhall called over her shoulder, "I want the suit to be in the first stare of fashion."

Winter grimaced but took off his shirt.

The tailor nodded. "That shall do for now, sir."

Winter stood with arms outstretched, feeling exceptionally silly as the tailor moved about him, wielding a measuring tape.

"Have you been practicing flattery?" Lady Beckinhall asked just as the tailor's thumb, holding the tape, pushed up the lower edge of Winter's smallclothes.

"As per your instructions," Winter replied, watching as Mr. Hurt caught sight of the end of the scar revealed by the rucked smalls.

The tailor hesitated, then continued his work.

Lady Beckinhall sighed very quietly.

Winter's attention snapped back to her. "I am in admiration of the way in which you can order tea so very . . . er . . . efficiently, my lady."

Mr. Hurt shot him a pitying look.

There was a slight pause.

"Thank you, Mr. Makepeace." Lady Beckinhall's voice was choked. "I must say, you give the most *imaginative* compliments."

"Your tutelage has inspired me, ma'am."

The tailor looked doubtful.

Winter cleared his throat. "And, of course, who would not be, ah . . . *exhilarated* by the loveliness of your countenance and form."

He arched an eyebrow at Mr. Hurt.

The tailor made a face as if to say, *Not bad.*

Which was probably as good as Winter was likely to get at this art.

But Lady Beckinhall wasn't done. Her head had tilted to the side at his words, making some type of jeweled ornament in her glossy dark hair sparkle in the light. "My form, Mr. Makepeace?"

Ah, this was dangerous territory. "Yes, your form, my lady. It is a strong and feminine form, but I think you already know that."

She chuckled, low and husky, sending shivers over his arms. "Yes, but a lady never tires of hearing compliments, sir. You must keep that fact in mind."

Her little maid nodded vigorously in agreement.

"Indeed?" Winter stared at Lady Beckinhall's back, wishing he could see her face. Her plump mouth would be curved slightly in amusement, her blue eyes dancing. His body reacted at the thought and he was heartily glad that Mr. Hurt had moved to his back.

"But you must be awash in a sea of compliments, my lady," Winter said. "Every gentleman you meet must voice his admiration, his wish to make love to you. And those are only the ones who may voice such thoughts. All about you are men who cannot speak their admiration, who must remain mute from lack of social standing or fear of offending you. Only their thoughts light the air about you, following you like a trail of perfume, heady but invisible."

He heard her startled inhale.

The maid sighed dreamily.

Mr. Hurt had stopped his quick, capable movements, but at Winter's glance, he blinked and resumed his work.

"Thank you, Mr. Makepeace," Lady Beckinhall said quietly. "That . . . that was quite wonderful."

He shrugged, though she couldn't see him. "I only speak the truth."

"Do you . . ." She hesitated, then said throatily, "Do you think me shallow for

142

enjoying such compliments?"

Her back was confident and straight, but her neck, bared by her upswept hair, was white and slim and held a hint of vulnerability. She was so forthright, so assured of herself that he'd not noticed the tender spot before.

"I think you sometimes like to hide behind a facade of gaiety, my lady." He cleared his throat. "I also think that when you enter a room, all eyes turn to you. You blaze like a torch, lighting the darkest corners, brightening even those who thought they were already well lit. You bring joy and mirth and leave behind a glow that gives hope to those you've left."

"And you, Mr. Makepeace? Are you one of those who thought themselves well lit?"

"I am as dark as a pit." Now he was glad her back was turned. "Even your torch will have difficulty lighting my depths."

A dark pit? Isabel couldn't help but turn around at Mr. Makepeace's words.

He stood, arms outstretched to either side, as Mr. Hurt measured the length of his sleeve. She caught her breath. The pose was a living *Vitruvian Man* sketch. And, like a masterpiece by da Vinci, his bare chest was a work of art. Muscles rolled over his outstretched arms, the veins at his biceps clearly delineated. The plains of his chest were smooth and broad. Only a sprinkle of curling hair was scattered between his dark nipples, while thicker tufts grew under his arms.

Isabel found her breath quickening at the sight. This was wrong, she knew. She shouldn't stare at the man. Shouldn't wonder how a schoolmaster had come to be so wonderfully muscled. It was as if he'd dropped a layer of concealment along with his clothes. His form was as masculinely lovely as that of the last nude man she'd seen — the Ghost of St. Giles. As her eyes dropped to his legs, he pivoted slightly, hiding his right thigh. For a moment her eyes narrowed.

The tailor gave a little gasp, bringing Isabel out of her reverie. Her gaze flew up to meet Mr. Makepeace's eyes. Despite his insistence that she turn her back when he disrobed, he showed no trace of embarrassment now at standing in front of her in only his smalls.

His eyes met hers, proud and challenging, but she could see at the back those depths he spoke of.

"Why are you a pit of darkness?" she asked.

He shrugged, his shoulders moving elegantly. "I live and work in the bleakest part of London, my lady. Here people beg, steal, and prostitute themselves, trying to obtain the most basic of human needs: food, water, shelter, and clothing. They have no time to lift their heads up from their toil, no time to live as human beings, graced with God's gifts of laughter and love."

He'd dropped his arms as he spoke, unconsciously stepping closer to her. Now he raised his hand and pointed to the ceiling, the muscles on his forearm rigid. "Peach still lies abed above. She was abandoned and used. A *child* who should've been cherished and loved as the very embodiment of all that is good in this world. *That* is what St. Giles is. *That* is what I live in. Wouldn't you find it strange, therefore, if I capered and skipped? Laughed and giggled?"

His bare chest heaved with his vehemence, nearly touching her bodice he was so close. She had to tilt her head back to keep his gaze, and she found that every inhale brought with it his heady scent.

Man, pure man.

She swallowed. "Others work here and are not a black pit. Your sisters have worked here. Do you think them any less discerning than you?"

She saw his nostrils flare as if he, too, had caught her scent. "I do not know. I only know that the darkness almost consumes me. It is an animal I battle every day. Darkness is my burden to bear."

Was this the real Winter Makepeace, hidden under the mask he wore normally? She wanted to touch him, wanted to stroke his cheek, feel the warmth of his skin and tell him that he must prevail, must fight the darkness invading him. Tell him that *she* would beat it back for him if she could. At the same time, she reveled in this part of him. Was the man beneath really all darkness?

Or was he part passion as well?

But Mr. Hurt cleared his throat at that moment. "I believe I am finished, my lady."

Mr. Makepeace immediately stepped away, his eyes shuttering, and picked up his shirt.

"Of course." Isabel's voice came out in a near squeak. She swallowed. "Thank you, Mr. Hurt, for your time."

"My pleasure, my lady." The tailor bowed and hurried from the room with his notes.

Mr. Makepeace was donning his breeches now, his back turned.

Pinkney watched him avidly from across the room.

Isabel sent her a stern look even as she searched for something to say to him. It was just so hard to have an intimate conversation with his back. "I hope that my . . . my torch, as you term it, can bring light into your darkness, Mr. Makepeace. I truly —"

He turned abruptly, catching up his waistcoat and coat. "I beg your pardon, Lady Beckinhall, but I have tasks to do today that really cannot wait. I hope you will excuse me."

Well, she certainly knew a dismissal when she heard one. Isabel smiled sunnily, trying to hide the sharp crystal of hurt his words had engendered in her breast. "Naturally, I wouldn't dream of interrupting your work. But we do need to start your dancing lessons. Shall we say tomorrow afternoon?"

"Yes, that will do," he said brusquely, and with an abbreviated bow, he strode from the room.

"He's going to need a lot more tutoring," Pinkney said, apparently to herself. She caught Isabel's look and straightened. "Oh, I'm sorry, my lady."

"No, that's all right," Isabel replied absently. Mr. Makepeace *did* need a great deal more tutoring — perhaps more than could be done before the Duchess of Arlington's ball.

Isabel sent Pinkney to find a boy to fetch the carriage and then paced the small sitting room, considering the problem of Mr. Makepeace. His curtness — which at times verged on outright rudeness — was more than simply learning social manners. After all, the man hadn't been born in some cave, left to be raised by wolves. No, he'd come from a respectable family. His sister, Temperance, had managed to obtain all of the social graces — so much so that she adapted easily to being the wife of a baron — even if she hadn't been entirely accepted by aristocratic society.

Pinkney came back to announce that the carriage had arrived. Isabel nodded absently and led the way out the home's door to the carriage. She murmured a word of thanks to Harold as he helped her in and then settled back against the squabs.

"Have you decided what you'll wear to the Arlington ball?" Pinkney asked hesitantly from across the carriage.

Isabel blinked and glanced at her lady's maid. Pinkney was looking a might droopy. "My newest cream with embroidery, I think. Or perhaps the gold stripe?"

Talk of fashion always perked up Pinkney.

"Oh, the embroidered cream," the maid said decidedly. "The emeralds will be lovely with it, and we've just got a half dozen of those lace stockings I ordered. Made in the French fashion."

"Mmm," Isabel murmured, her mind not really on the topic. "I suppose I can wear the cream embroidered slippers as well."

There was a disapproving silence from the other side of the carriage that made Isabel look up.

Pinkney's pretty eyebrows were drawn together in what was nearly a stern frown. "The creams are frayed about the heel."

"Really?" Isabel hadn't notice the fraying, so it must be small indeed. "But surely it's not enough —"

" 'Twould be better to get new ones — perhaps in cloth of gold." Pinkney looked eager. "We could call on the cobbler this afternoon."

"Very well." Isabel sighed, resigning herself to an afternoon of shopping.

Usually the activity was quite enjoyable, but at the moment her mind was on the conundrum of Mr. Makepeace, for she'd just come to an important realization about the wretched man.

If Mr. Makepeace's rudeness didn't come from his upbringing, then it must be innate to him — an essential part of his character. If this was so — and Isabel very much feared it was — then teaching him graceful manners was a much more difficult matter than she realized. For either Mr. Makepeace must learn to wear a constant mask of false propriety in society — one that he in no way believed in — or she must bring him into the light and teach him to view the world as a more cheerful place.

And *that* was a daunting task indeed.

CHAPTER SIX

As the Harlequin lay on the ground, his life's blood running into the channel in the middle of the street, a strange man approached. The man wore a cape that hid most of his form, but still one could see that he walked on a goat's cloven hooves. The man sat down beside the dying Harlequin and took a white clay pipe from his pocket. He lit the pipe and looked at the Harlequin. "Now, Harlequin," said he, "would you like to revenge yourself on your enemies . . . ?"

— from *The Legend of the Harlequin Ghost of St. Giles*

Winter Makepeace leaped the gap between building roofs and landed lightly. He slid backward a bit on the steeply pitched second roof, his boots scraping on the shingles, but he caught himself with the ease of long practice.

151

Tonight he was the Ghost of St. Giles.

He heard a faint gasp on the street below as he passed, but he didn't stop to look. He was taking a risk, for the sun had not yet set, and he preferred to do his Ghostly activities under cover of night, but he wasn't going to lose another child. Earlier this evening, the residents of the home had barely sat down to supper when word had come that a child was in need of their help. A harlot had succumbed to one of the many diseases that plagued her profession, leaving behind a child of only three.

Sadly, this was a common tale in St. Giles — and the reason for the home's existence. Winter could not count the times that he had sent a servant or gone himself to find an orphaned or abandoned child and bring him or her back to the home. What was different in this case was the fact that someone had beaten the home's emissary to the child the last two times they had been sent out.

Winter very much feared that someone — someone organized — was stealing orphaned children off the streets of St. Giles.

Winter ran along the peak of a house and jumped down to its lower neighbor. The buildings of St. Giles had not been properly planned. Tenements, shops, warehouses, and workshops had all been built, higgledy-piggledy, cheek by jowl, sometimes literally one on top of another. It made for a confusing warren of buildings to the outsider, but Winter could traverse St. Giles with his eyes closed.

And by rooftop at that.

Naturally, he'd sent Tommy out to fetch the child back to the home, but Winter hoped to reach the child before Tommy. He'd excused himself from the supper table, saying his leg was bothering him again, hurriedly donned the costume of the Ghost, and set out from his bedroom window under the eves.

Now he glanced down and saw that he was over Chapel Alley. The chandler shop owner who'd reported the orphan had said that the child's mother had lived in a room just off Phoenix Street, only a stone's throw away. Winter leaped to a balcony below, ran along the rail, and used the corner of the brick building for fingerholds as he climbed down to the alley.

By the alley wall, a girl of about ten had watched his descent with wide eyes, clutching a basket to her bosom. A few wilted posies at the bottom of the basket were obviously leftover from her day of hawking flowers.

"Where does Nelly Broom live?" Winter

asked the girl, giving the name of the dead whore.

The girl pointed to a crooked house at the end of the alley. "Second floor, back o' th' 'ouse, but she died this morn."

"I know." Winter nodded his thanks. "I've come for the child."

"Best pick up your feet, then," the flower girl said.

Winter paused to look back at her. "Why's that?"

She shrugged. "The lassie snatchers 'ave gone in already."

Winter turned and ran. *Lassie snatchers?* Was that the organized group of kidnappers working in St. Giles — and were they so well known that a little girl called them by name?

He shoved open the outer door to the house the girl had pointed to. Inside, a narrow staircase directly faced the outer door. Winter ran up it on the balls of his feet, careful not to alert his quarry.

The stairs let out into a tiny landing with a single door. Winter opened it, surprising a family at their evening meal. Three children crowded their mother's skirts, mealy bread crusts clutched in their hands. The father, a gaunt fellow with a full head of red hair, pointed a thumb over his shoulder to where

Winter could see another door. Winter nodded silently at the man and swept past. The door led into a smaller room that had obviously been divided off from the main room. Two bedraggled women cowered together in a corner. Across from them, the window stood open.

Winter didn't have to ask. He strode to the window and leaned out. The drop to the street was at least twenty feet, but a narrow ledge ran directly below the window. Winter swung his leg over and, gripping the top of the window, stood on the ledge. About a foot above him, he could see a man's legs disappearing over the eves. Winter grasped the crumbling edge of the eves and hauled himself up. On the roof stood a man and a youth, and in the youth's arms, a child, so frightened it wasn't even crying.

The man gave a yell at the sight of Winter coming over the eves. "Th' Ghost! 'Tis th' Ghost come to drag us to 'ell!"

"Leg it!" cried the youth, and they turned.

But Winter was on them already, the blood pumping in his veins, righteous rage nearly blinding him. He grasped the man's coat, pulling him backward. The man threw a frantic punch that Winter absorbed on his shoulder before laying the man flat with a blow to the jaw.

The youth hadn't stopped. He was near the roof edge, debating whether he could make a six-foot leap across to the next building. He backed a step in preparation, the child still in his arms.

And then Winter caught hold of him.

The youth whipped around, as lethal as a snake, and sank his teeth into Winter's wrist.

Winter grit his teeth and grabbed the boy by his hair, shaking him like a rat. The youth let go of his wrist at the same time as he let go of the child. The child tumbled down, narrowly missing the roof edge, and lay as if stunned, small eyes staring up at Winter unblinking.

With his free hand, Winter took hold of the child's foot and dragged him away from the roof edge. The child had been wrapped in a blanket, which caught on the roof tiles as he was dragged, leaving him entirely nude.

Winter bent and flung the edge of the blanket over the child. "Stay there," he whispered.

The little boy nodded mutely.

Then Winter turned to the youth he still held by the hair. He shook him again. "You might've dropped that babe over the edge."

The youth shrugged. "Plenty more where

'e came from, innit there? 'Sides, it's a *boy.*"

Winter's eyes narrowed. "The whoremonger you work for doesn't take male children?"

"Don't 'ave a lassie's nimble fingers, do they?" The youth bared his teeth like a feral dog. " 'Sides, I don't work for no stinkin' whoremonger. You'd best be afeared of the man who pays me — 'e's a toff, 'e is."

"What toff?"

The youth's eyes flicked over Winter's shoulder.

Winter ducked to the side, just avoiding the blow meant for his head. The older man skipped back. But the youth was free now, racing after the older man as they fled away over the rooftops.

Winter instinctively started in their direction but drew himself up abruptly when he remembered the little boy. He turned back to the child.

The boy lay where Winter had left him, still unmoving. His eyes widened as Winter approached and picked him up, bundled in the ragged blanket. He felt too light. No doubt he was undernourished as so many children were in St. Giles. If the child had had clothes before his mother's death, the other inhabitants in the house where he lived had obviously stolen them.

A black weight seemed to settle on Winter's shoulders. He might've saved this little boy, but no doubt the "lassie snatchers" were running somewhere else in St. Giles, still plying their evil trade tonight even as he stood here.

"What's your name?" Winter whispered to the boy, pushing golden curls back from the little forehead.

The child reached out a chubby hand and fingered the curved nose of Winter's mask in wonder. As he did so, a scrap of paper fell from his little fist.

Winter bent and picked up the paper. The child was nude, so he must've somehow grabbed the paper off the lad who'd snatched him. Winter couldn't tell what, if anything, the paper had written on it, but he could feel a part of a waxen seal. He placed it carefully in his pocket and then wrapped both arms about the little boy.

"Best we get you to the home, Joseph Chance."

"Now, then," Isabel said early the next afternoon. "The most important thing to remember when dancing with a lady is not to step upon her toes."

Winter Makepeace, dressed as usual in his black coat and waistcoat, looked rather like a faintly bemused scarecrow. He nodded somberly. "I shall endeavor to preserve your toes, my lady."

"Good." Isabel inhaled and faced forward. They were in her ballroom — a delightful space with green and black marble floors and her prized harpsichord, painted red with gilt trim. "Mr. Butterman has some talent with the harpsichord and has agreed to provide our dancing music."

The butler bowed gravely from his seat at the harpsichord.

"How kind," Mr. Makepeace murmured.

Isabel darted a sharp glance at him but was slightly surprised to see no sarcasm in his expression. Indeed he nodded his thanks to her butler, who, looking a tad surprised himself, nodded back. Perhaps he saved his sarcasm solely for her.

Depressing thought.

"Shall we begin?" she asked briskly, holding out her hand to him.

He took her hand in his warm fingers and looked down at her gravely. "As you wish."

"On three. One and two and *three*." She moved forward in the steps she had previously demonstrated for Mr. Makepeace and was astonished to realize that not only had he understood them on the first introduction, but also that he moved gracefully.

She darted a glance sideways at him and found him looking back, a faintly amused expression on his face as if he knew her thoughts. "When did you learn to dance, my lady?"

They faced each other for a beat and then separated and paced gently backward away from each other.

"Oh, as a young girl," she said breathlessly, even though the dance was slow. "I had a dance master when I was twelve and shared his lessons with my girl cousin who, sadly, I did not get on with."

They turned and paced in a parallel line together.

"You had no brothers or sisters?" he asked.

"None that I knew," she replied. "I had an older brother who died in infancy before I was born. Now take my hand."

He did so, his large hand enveloping hers in warmth as she circled him.

"Yours sounds like a lonely childhood," he murmured, low enough that Butterman couldn't hear.

"Does it?" She faced him again. "But it wasn't. I had many friends and that same girl cousin I argued with when young is now an intimate. There were parties and teas and picnics in the country. I had a very happy girlhood."

She curtsied as he bowed. "When I was old enough, I came out — to great acclaim, if I do say so myself."

His dark eyes lit. "I can believe it. You must've had scores of young aristocrats at your feet."

"Perhaps."

He shook his head. "Did you think about what you were looking for in a husband? What type of man you wanted to spend the rest of your life with?"

What was he getting at? "I suppose I thought mostly of elegance and form, like most young girls," she said cautiously.

His eyes narrowed. "And yet you married Beckinhall?"

She laughed; she couldn't help it. "You make poor Edmund sound like a dire fate. He wasn't, you know. I was quite fond of him, and he of me."

His face was expressionless. "He was also much older than you."

"No, to the left here." She shrugged as he circled her in the direction indicated. "What of it? Many marriages are made with differing ages." She glanced at him slyly with a sudden urge to provoke — he was so grave today! "I do assure you that I was quite . . . *satisfied* . . . in my marriage."

They linked hands, about to skip sideways,

but he tugged over hard on her fingers, making her fall against him.

"Oof!" She looked up at him, startled.

The harpsichord clanged in discord before Mr. Butterman caught himself.

"Oh, dear," Mr. Makepeace drawled. "I do beg your pardon."

Isabel narrowed her eyes. Each breath she took pushed her breasts into his chest. "Do be careful, Mr. Makepeace. Complicated maneuvers such as the one you just tried are better left to those more experienced."

"Ah, but, Lady Beckinhall," he said as the corners of his mouth twitched, "I hope under your tutelage to be experienced quite soon."

"Yes, well . . ." She stepped back, trying to regain her breath. "Shall we try again?"

He bowed. "As you wish."

"I do wish." She nodded at Butterman.

Once again they faced forward, repeating the steps, though she wasn't sure why since he seemed to have already learned them in a damnably short time. When she glanced at him, he was studying her thoughtfully.

"A penny for your thoughts," she murmured.

"I was just thinking," he said as he paced toward her, "how very stupid your husband must've been to stray from you."

She braced herself, but still his words hurt. "I never said that."

He merely looked at her.

She inhaled. "I assure you I thought nothing of it. Marriages among my rank are often more friendly than passionate."

"And yet you are a passionate woman," he whispered as he took her hand and raised it. They circled each other as he spoke. "Has anyone cherished you just for yourself?"

She looked up and laughed at him. "This question from the man who takes care of everyone yet whom no one takes care of?"

He frowned slightly. "I don't —"

"No, no," she said softly, placing her hands on his hard hips and turning him. "Like this. And you do know exactly what I mean."

They stopped dancing, oblivious to the music still playing.

"Do I?" he asked.

"We might come from terribly divergent backgrounds, Mr. Makepeace," she murmured. "But I do assure you I can recognize one as lonely as I."

He stilled. "You keep surprising me, my lady."

"What do you do at night," she whispered impulsively, "after all the children have gone to bed? Do you lie in your own lonely bed — or do you walk the streets of St. Giles?"

His face closed as surely as if a door had shut. "You also keep drawing me in," he murmured as he stepped away from her, "when I know you are a danger to my mission in St. Giles."

She knit her brow. *Mission?* That sounded very religious. Surely he couldn't —

"I think our lesson must be over with for today," he continued.

He bowed and was out the door before she could react.

"Shall I retire, my lady?" Butterman asked diffidently from the piano.

"Yes. Yes, that will be all, Butterman. Thank you," Isabel replied absently, then reconsidered. "Wait."

"My lady?"

She looked at her butler, a man who'd been in her service since her marriage. She'd never really thought about it, but she trusted him implicitly. That made up her mind. "I'd like you to do something a little out of the ordinary for me, Butterman."

He bowed. "I'm always at your service, my lady."

"And I thank you for it," she said warmly. "I'd like you to find out everything you can about the Ghost of St. Giles."

Butterman didn't even blink. "Of course, my lady."

She continued staring at the door where Mr. Makepeace had left long after the butler had gone about his business.

She'd hit a soft spot somehow in their sparring, and his reaction hadn't been what she'd expected. She'd have to think long and hard on what to do next.

Supper at the Home for Unfortunate Infants and Foundling Children was always a somewhat chaotic affair.

"Amen." Winter raised his head as a ragged chorus of childish voices gave end to the evening grace.

It was good to be back at the home after the afternoon's sparring with Lady Beckinhall. The lady was getting too close — both to the Ghost of St. Giles and to his own inner beast. Last night he'd found himself dreaming about her in quite an explicit manner. He'd woken with his base flesh hard and eager, and it had taken an hour of preparing lessons and writing letters for his cock to subside. Even now, the memory of those luminous dream breasts held in sweet offering was enough to —

"Can you pass the salt?" Joseph Tinbox said, interrupting his inappropriate reverie.

"Yes, of course," Winter replied, doing just that.

He eyed his plate with some anticipation. Tonight they appeared to be dining upon a wonderfully thick beef stew with crusty bread and a creamy cheese as accompaniments. Mistress Medina had exceeded his expectations as cook for the home.

"Cor! I loves beef stew," Joseph Tinbox exclaimed from his seat across from Winter, giving voice to his own thought.

"I love beef stew, Joseph Tinbox," Winter gently corrected.

"Me too," Henry Putman piped up from beside Winter, oblivious. "Do you like beef stew, Joseph Chance?"

"Aye!" The new little boy nodded vigorously as he raised a big spoonful of stew to his mouth.

"If I had my druthers," Henry Putman declared, "we'd have beef stew *every* night."

"Couldn't have fish pie, then," objected Joseph Smith from Winter's other side.

"Don't hardly ever have fish pie anyways," Joseph Tinbox pointed out. " 'Sides, no one likes fish pie but you, Joseph Smith."

Sensing that culinary tastes might be a potential source of conflict, Winter cleared his throat. "How far have you progressed in your study of the Bible, Joseph Tinbox?"

"Revelations," Joseph Tinbox said. "Right corker it is, too, sir. All about dragons and blood running in streams, and —"

"Yes, quite," Winter said hastily. "And you, Henry Putman, what Psalm is your class memorizing this week?"

"Psalm 139," Henry said dolefully. "It's *long*."

"But very lovely, don't you think?" Winter said. " 'If I say, Surely the darkness shall cover me: even the night shall be light about me/Yea the darkness hideth not from thee, but the night shineth as the day: the darkness and the light are both alike to thee.' "

Henry scrunched up his nose doubtfully. "If you say so, sir. I just can't make out what it all means."

"It means that the Lord can see in the dark," Joseph Tinbox said with eleven-year-old authority.

"And also that whether in the daytime or the nighttime, there's no hiding from God," Winter said.

For a moment there were alarmed faces about the table.

Winter sighed gently. "What else has happened at the home while I was away today?"

"Dodo got in a fight with Soot," Joseph Smith said.

"Aye!" Henry Putman waved his spoon,

nearly getting stew in Joseph Chance's hair. "Dodo came into the kitchen and went too close to Soot — he was sleeping by the fireplace. And Soot leaped up and scratched Dodo's nose. But Dodo fought back and barked until Soot ran outside."

Winter raised his eyebrows. "Indeed? That was quite brave of Dodo. I didn't know he was such a fighter."

"She," Joseph Tinbox said. "Dodo is a lady dog."

"Is she?" Winter pulled apart his bread.

"Aye," Joseph Tinbox said, "and she likes cheese ever so much."

"Hmm." Winter cast a stern eye on the boy. "Dogs often like cheese, but it doesn't always like them. Besides, we don't want to waste good cheese on a dog, do we?"

"Noooo." Joseph drew out the negative as if uncertain that he agreed.

Winter decided to let it pass. "And how is Peach herself doing?"

"She's sitting up." Joseph Tinbox brightened. "An' she can hug Dodo."

"Ah. Has she said anything else?"

A line of worry drew itself between Joseph's eyebrows. "No, not yet. Prolly she just has to get stronger, don't you think, sir?"

Winter nodded absently as the boys

turned the conversation to the best kind of sweet. Privately, he had reservations, though. The child didn't seem to be intellectually deficient, and from the reports he'd been given by Nell and Mary Whitsun, Peach was improving physically. Yet she refused to speak to anyone but Joseph.

So at the end of the meal, Winter made sure the boys were safely on their way to their evening prayers and then he slipped into the kitchens.

Mistress Medina was supervising the scrubbing of the cooking pots, but she looked up at Winter's entrance.

"Come to see 'ow I'm doin', are you, Mr. Makepeace?"

"Not at all," Winter said. "I've actually come to beg a favor, Mistress Medina."

"An' what's that?"

"Have you any more of that excellent cheese you served at supper?"

" 'Appens I do." Mistress Medina bustled over to a cabinet and unlocked the upper door with a key hanging from her waist. "Didn't get enough to eat at supper, then?"

"Actually, I ate quite well," Winter murmured. "This is for . . . er . . . Peach."

"Ah." The cook nodded wisely as she cut a wedge of cheese and wrapped it in a cloth before giving it to Winter. "That mite needs a bit of extra, from what I 'ear."

"Indeed she does," Winter said gravely.

Mistress Medina gestured to a tray. "I made up a supper tray for 'er, but none of the maids 'ave 'ad a minute to bring it to 'er room, poor lass. Mind if I take it up with you?"

"Not at all," Winter replied. Perhaps the presence of a motherly woman would help Peach with her speech. "That's quite kind of you."

"Ain't nothing special," Mistress Medina said gruffly. She seized the tray and together they mounted the stairs to the sickroom.

When he entered the room, Winter thought both girl and dog asleep in the narrow cot. Then Dodo raised her head and gave her customary halfhearted growl. When he looked at Peach's face, he saw the girl's eyes were wide open.

Mistress Medina grunted as she placed the tray on a table. "Scrappy is that one. Got into a fight with the tomcat in the kitchen this afternoon."

"So I heard," Winter said drily as he drew up a chair next to the bed. "Good evening, Peach."

The child gave no sign that she'd heard, yet her large dark eyes were fixed on his face.

Winter nodded as if Peach had given a

full rejoinder. "I don't know if you remember me, but I was the one who found you in that alley."

No response save the tightening of thin arms about the dog's neck.

"Ah. I almost forgot."

Winter took the wedge of cheese out of his pocket. Dodo craned her head forward, sniffing eagerly even before he had fully unwrapped the cheese. Joseph Tinbox had been quite correct: the dog did like cheese.

"Mistress Medina, our cook, has made you some supper. I can attest that it's quite tasty." He glanced back at Mistress Medina, who had taken up a silent position by the door.

Mistress Medina caught his eye and nodded soberly at him.

Winter looked back at the girl. "I brought a present for your dog, Dodo, as well. Would you like to give it to her?"

For a moment he was afraid his ruse wouldn't work. Then Peach stretched out a hand.

Winter broke off a bit of cheese and placed it in her tiny palm.

"You must have been very scared and cold that night," he said, watching as she gave the dog the cheese. He broke off another piece and held it out.

171

After a hesitation, that, too, was fed to the dog.

"I've been wondering where you might've come from." Winter went on giving her bits of cheese. "It was quite cold that night, so I don't think you'd been there very long. Did you live close? Or had you walked there, you and Dodo?"

Silence, broken only by the munching of the very happy dog.

The last of the cheese was gone, and Winter had the feeling that the girl wouldn't eat her supper while he was still in the room.

He rose. "When you are able, I would very much like to hear your voice, Peach."

He was turning away, so he nearly missed the whisper from the bed.

Winter looked back. "I'm sorry?"

"Peela," the child whispered. "Me name's Peela."

Winter blinked. "Peela?"

"Pilar," Mistress Medina said suddenly. Winter saw she had a strange look on her face. She took a step toward the bed. "It's Pilar, isn't it?"

The child nodded once, jerkily, then shrunk into her covers.

The cook glanced at Winter and then left the room. He followed, closing the door softly behind him.

"How did you know her name?" Winter asked curiously. "Pilar is a Spanish name, isn't it?"

Mistress Medina had her hand over her mouth and for a moment he thought he saw tears sparkling in her eyes.

Then she took her hand away and he saw her mouth was twisted with anger.

"Pilar's also a Portuguese name." She pronounced *Portuguese* with an accent that wasn't English. "I know because she's like me. She's a daughter of Abraham."

"I cannot wear this," Winter Makepeace stated with maddening calm five days later.

Isabel prevented herself from rolling her eyes only by the greatest of willpower. "It is black and brown. *Quite* sedate."

Mr. Makepeace looked at her dubiously, probably because while the breeches and coat of his new suit were indeed black and the waistcoat brown, the waistcoat could be called sedate only by the most outrageous stretch of imagination.

The coat and breeches were superbly cut of shimmering midnight silk, so black it had a bluish cast. Embossed silver buttons trimmed the pockets, sleeves, skirts, and front. And the waistcoat. Well, the waistcoat was a masterpiece. Isabel sighed as she looked at Mr. Makepeace's fine torso. It really was a crime to call the waistcoat's color "brown." The waistcoat was the loveliest shade of tobacco, elegantly embroidered along the edges and pocket flaps in apple green, silver, light blue, and pink.

"That," Isabel said as she lounged on one of the settees in her sitting room, "is the most refined waistcoat I think I've ever seen. A duke wouldn't be ashamed to wear it."

She couldn't hide her satisfaction — both with the excellent cut of his suit and the fact that he'd finally returned to her home. Since the dancing lesson, Mr. Makepeace had sent his excuses, avoiding another lesson, or even a meeting, until tonight. She'd begun to think that she'd scared him off entirely.

Now he was standing before her mantelpiece mirror making perturbed little pokes at his neck cloth. He shot her an ironic glance. "I'm not a duke."

"No, but you'll be mingling with dukes." Isabel stood and caught Mr. Makepeace's hand. "Stop that. You'll undo all the good that my rented valet did dressing you."

Mr. Makepeace turned his hand suddenly so that now he gripped her fingers. He cocked his head at her, watching her with those mysterious brown eyes, and then slowly — so very slowly — lowered his head and kissed her fingertips.

She inhaled and met his eyes. Damn him! Why should the touch of this man's lips on her *fingers* of all things make her belly heat? And why was he playing with her thus?

"As you wish," he murmured as he straightened.

"I do wish," she said rather incomprehensibly. She snatched her hand away and smoothed her skirts. "The carriage is waiting, if you're finished having maidenly nerves."

"Quite finished." His mouth quirked as he held out his arm to her.

"Good," she humphed, just to say something, and laid her fingertips on his forearm as he led her to the door.

The night was pleasantly cool against her shoulders as he helped her into the carriage. Tonight she wore her embroidered cream, the skirts heavy and sweeping, and it occurred to Isabel as she settled in the carriage that Mr. Makepeace's colors complemented her own quite nicely.

She looked across at him as he sat. There was a rustling sound as he moved and she noticed that the pocket of his coat was tented.

"Have you something in your pocket?" she

175

asked. "I can't believe Mr. Hurt even made them to work."

"I asked him to." Mr. Makepeace shot her a look as he drew a crumpled piece of paper out of the pocket. "It seemed a waste of material to make false pockets."

"But you'll ruin the line if you go putting things in your pocket." Isabel leaned forward to peer at the splotch on the paper. "What is that anyway?"

He shrugged. "Something I found in a little boy's hand."

"That's d'Arque's emblem," she said as she finally realized she was looking at a red wax seal. "Who was the little boy who had it?"

"You recognize this?" His broad thumb smoothed over the blob of hardened wax.

"I think so." She took it from him, holding it up to the swaying carriage light. "Yes, you can see the owl. It's quite distinct in the d'Arque coat of arms."

The paper looked like it had been torn from a letter, the seal still attached to one edge. On it, scrawled in a hand that looked barely literate, were two words:

chapl allee

She looked on the other side. Here there

176

was more writing, but in an elegant, cultured hand:

12 Octob

The last two letters of *October* had been torn off. She turned the paper back over and looked up at him. "I doubt this is d'Arque's handwriting on this side, though the date might be and the seal is definitely his. How strange. How do you suppose a small boy in St. Giles found such a thing?"

He took the scrap of paper from her hand, turning it over thoughtfully. "That's a good question. Tell me about this d'Arque."

She looked away from him and shrugged carelessly. "You'll meet him soon enough — I'm sure he'll be here tonight. He's the Viscount d'Arque. Inherited the title from his uncle, I believe, not that long ago — perhaps three years?"

"He's a young man?" He'd sat back against the cushions, so a shadow was cast across the upper half of his face. She couldn't read his eyes and could see only his lips.

"Young is relative, isn't it?" She cocked her head, staring at him. "I suppose he's not much older than I, if you call that young."

He smiled faintly. "I do."

She could feel the blush creep up her cheeks — damn the man! "Most wouldn't, I think. I'm two and thirty and have buried a husband. I'm far from a dewy maid, Mr. Makepeace."

"But you're also far from a doddering crone, my lady," he retorted. "Do you consider Lord d'Arque old?"

"Of course not." She sighed and looked away. "But then men age less rapidly than women. Many would consider him to be in his prime."

"Do you?"

She smiled — not kindly — and looked back at him. "Yes. Yes, I suppose I do."

His mouth tightened. "He's a handsome man."

Was he jealous? And why did the possibility send a wicked thrill through her?

"Yes." She couldn't help it — her voice emerged a throaty purr. "He's tall and well built and he moves with a kind of animal grace that makes ladies stare. And he's witty. He has the knack of saying the most mundane things — and only afterward do you realize the double entendre or the devastating put-down. It's quite a talent, really."

"Mmm." Those mobile, wide, sinfully delicious lips hardly moved. "And I only speak frankly — too frankly most often."

"Yes."

He leaned forward suddenly, the movement startling a squeak from her. He thrust his face into the full light and she could see an edge of anger — hot and wild — in his usually calm brown eyes.

Her heart began to beat in triple time.

"Would you like me more if I knew how to simper and twist my words?" he demanded.

His sudden aggression made her reply without thinking, straight from her heart. "No. I like you as you are."

She licked her lips at her admission and his gaze settled broodingly on her mouth. It felt like a brand, that look. A physical touch more intimate than any embrace. Her lips parted in wonder and his eyes rose slowly to meet hers, for once unshielded.

Dear God, what she saw in that look! How he had hidden these many years behind the guise of a simple schoolmaster, she didn't know. Anger, passion, lust, and surging hunger swirled in his stormy eyes. Emotions so stark, so strong, she didn't understand how he kept them under control. He looked as if he were about to attack her, ravish her, and conquer London and the world itself.

He could've been a warrior, a statesman, a king.

The carriage drew to a halt, and it was he who moved first.

He held out his hand to her. "Shall we descend so I can meet this Viscount d'Arque?"

As she laid her trembling fingers in his, she wondered, *Why does it feel like I've just accepted a challenge?*

CHAPTER SEVEN

With his last breath, the Harlequin whispered, "Yes." The mysterious man's eyes glowed red even as the Harlequin's lost all color, becoming the white of death, and he whispered, "Let it be." At once the Harlequin was whole again, his limbs straight and strong. In every respect he was the same as ever, save for two things: his eyes remained white and now he carried two swords . . . and neither one was made of wood . . .

— from *The Legend of the Harlequin Ghost of St. Giles*

Winter felt Isabel's slim fingers on his arm and knew a thrill of satisfaction. She might be attracted to this d'Arque — a *witty* man closer to her age and of her same social standing — but right now it was *his* arm she held.

He stepped from the carriage and remembered to turn and help her descend. She smiled her thanks as another carriage began pulling away. Winter glanced up in time to see the distinctive owl in a coat of arms on the carriage door. He squinted, staring at the coachman, who looked ominously familiar.

"There's no need to be nervous," Isabel whispered, evidently mistaking the reason for his pause.

He nodded down at her. "Naturally not with you on my arm, my lady."

Only then did Winter face the Duchess of Arlington's town house. It was one of the grandest houses in London, rumored to have been partially paid for by a former duchess's royal liaison. Even so, the present duchess had entirely redecorated the house, putting her husband's estates into deep debt.

Not that one could tell from the opulence of the ball.

Scores of liveried footmen showed the guests into a wide hall, brilliantly lit with huge chandeliers. A sweeping staircase led to the upper floor and a grand ballroom already crowded with sweating, perfumed bodies.

Winter leaned down to whisper in Isabel's ear, aware that she smelled of lavender and lime. "You're sure mingling with these aristocrats will do the home good?"

"Positive," she breathed, laughter in her husky voice. "Come, let me introduce you to some people."

They stepped into the ballroom, and Winter felt his senses quicken. D'Arque was here tonight. Soon he would meet the man who was his only connection to the lassie snatchers in St. Giles.

Isabel's fingers were on his arm, but it was she who guided him discreetly through the mass of people. The walls of the ballroom were a soft shade of blue-green, highlighted in cream and gold. It should have been a soothing room with those colors, but it was anything but. Around them people laughed and talked loudly. A quartet of musicians attempted to play dancing music, and the stench of burning candle wax and humanity was nearly overpowering.

Strange that the perfumed ballroom of the aristocracy could be nearly as foul as the manure-smeared streets of St. Giles.

"Who do you intend for me to meet tonight?" Winter murmured as they slowly made their way.

Isabel shrugged. "Oh, the very cream of society, I think." She leaned toward him and tapped his arm with her folded fan. "Those people who can do the most for the home, in fact."

His eyebrows arched. "Such as?"

She nodded toward two upright gentlemen who seemed to be the very epitome of pillars of London society. Their heads were bent together as they obviously discussed something important. "The Duke of Wakefield, for instance."

He glanced at the tall, dark man. "Lady Hero and Lady Phoebe's elder brother, I recollect."

"The very same." Isabel nodded. "He's quite powerful — and of course fabulously wealthy. Wakefield is a guiding force in parliament. It's rumored that Sir Robert Walpole doesn't make a move without consulting him. And his companion, the Marquess of Mandeville, is nearly as influential. He's Lady Margaret's elder brother, of course. I'd introduce you now, but it rather looks as if they are intent upon some serious discussion."

"Then we look for other quarry."

"Indeed." Isabel made a slight moue as she scanned the crowd.

Winter had to tear his gaze away from the sight of her pursed lips.

"Oh, poor man!" Isabel exclaimed gently.

"Who?"

But she was already leading him to a man who stood by himself at the side of the room. He wore a gray wig and his eyes were aloof behind half-moon spectacles. He seemed entirely removed from the crowd. The gentleman was facing partly away from them and didn't turn until they were nearly upon him.

"Mr. St. John," Lady Beckinhall greeted him.

St. John's brown eyes widened behind his spectacles, flicking between them and then shuttering so quickly that most would've missed the reaction. "Lady Beckinhall." He took her fingers, bowing over them.

She waved her other hand gracefully at Winter. "May I present Mr. Winter Makepeace, the manager of the Home for Unfortunate Infants and Foundling Children? Mr. Makepeace, Mr. Godric St. John."

Winter held out his hand to the other man. "Actually, we've already met."

Lady Beckinhall raised her eyebrows. "You have?"

"I'm a friend of Lord Caire," St. John said as he took Winter's hand. He didn't smile, but his manner was pleasant enough. "I was there when the old home burned last year. Good to see you again, Makepeace."

"And you, sir," Winter replied. "You were

185

quite a help that night as I remember. I was surprised not to see you at my sister's wedding."

A muscle flexed in the other man's jaw. "I regret not attending. It was soon after Clara —" St. John clamped his mouth shut and looked away.

"I was very sorry to hear of Mrs. St. John's death," Lady Beckinhall said quietly.

St. John nodded once, jerkily, and swallowed.

"But we must be moving on, as I have other gentlepersons to introduce Mr. Makepeace to," Lady Beckinhall continued smoothly.

Godric St. John seemed not to notice as they moved away.

Lady Beckinhall leaned her head close to Winter's jaw, making her delicate scent for a moment break through the stinking miasma of the room. "Mr. St. John lost his wife last year after a long illness. They were quite devoted to each other. I hadn't known he had reentered society."

"Ah," Winter murmured. He glanced over his shoulder. St. John was standing alone again, staring into space. "He's like the walking dead."

"Poor, poor man." Lady Beckinhall shivered. "Come. I see some gentlemen I'd like to introduce you to."

"Lead the way."

Lady Beckinhall smiled brilliantly as they came upon a small group. "Gentlemen, I wonder if you all have had the pleasure of meeting my companion, Mr. Winter Makepeace?"

At the general murmur in the negative Isabel introduced Winter to the three gentlemen.

"The Home for Unfortunate Infants and Foundling Children, eh?" Sir Beverly Williams said. "Quite the mouthful, ain't it? In St. Giles, you say?"

"Indeed, sir," Winter said.

"Best move it out of that cesspit, is my advice," Sir Beverly snorted. "Ought to be farther west in the newer parts of the city. Hanover Square or such."

"I doubt we could afford the rents in Hanover Square," Winter said gently. "Besides, our customers don't frequent the newer parts of London."

"Eh? Customers?" Sir Beverly looked confused.

"He means the orphans, Williams," said the Earl of Kershaw, a congenial man with a broad nose and twinkling eyes in a round face. "Isn't that right, Makepeace?"

Winters bowed to the earl. "Quite correct,

my lord. The orphans come from St. Giles; therefore the home is situated there."

"Makes sense," said the third man, Mr. Roger Fraser-Burnsby. "St. Giles is a dangerous spot, though. Isn't there a madman who runs about the place?"

"The Ghost of St. Giles." Kershaw shook his head with a wry smile. "Tell me you're not afraid of bogeymen, Fraser-Burnsby? It's a legend, no more."

Winter felt Isabel glance at him, but he was careful to keep his face pleasantly interested.

"I've met the Ghost," she said. "It was a fortnight ago. I found him insensible in the street and naturally stopped my carriage to help." Her blue eyes met his in challenge.

Winter nodded calmly. "The Ghost must be very grateful to you indeed."

"Good Lord, had you no care for your precious person, Lady Beckinhall?" Sir Beverly sounded quite scandalized.

"How brave of you." Fraser-Burnsby grinned boyishly. "But I'm very glad you escaped unscathed, my lady."

She shrugged elegantly. "He was hardly in a position to attack me."

"We must thank God, then," Kershaw rumbled. "For keeping you safe, for he sounds a lunatic if even half the accounts are true. Have you seen this Ghost, Mr. Makepeace?"

"Only at a distance," Winter replied casually. "He appears to be a shy fellow. Now, if you will excuse us, I've promised Lady Beckinhall a glass of punch."

The three gentlemen bowed as he led Isabel away.

"Why did you do that?" she hissed as soon as they were out of earshot.

He looked at her, brows raised. "Wasn't that the proper way to excuse ourselves?"

"Yes, of course, quite proper," she said grumpily. "But we could've stayed longer with them."

"I thought the point of this ball was to meet an array of people," he said with quiet amusement.

She wrinkled her nose as if ready to argue.

"Oh, Lady Beckinhall, how nice to see you tonight." Lady Margaret Reading slipped in front of them and exchanged with Isabel the odd pretend cheek kissing that lady friends seemed to favor.

Lady Margaret hesitantly extended her hand to him. Winter took it and kissed the air over her knuckles.

The girl beamed as he straightened, as if he were a spaniel who had performed a particularly clever trick. "Mr. Makepeace, you look quite wonderful."

"Thank you, my lady," he replied.

Isabel narrowed her eyes at him, probably because of the dryness of his tone.

He cleared his throat. "Your smile brightens this room, Lady Margaret."

"Oh, thank you." She glanced rather distractedly over his shoulder, and Winter had to repress the urge to look. This wasn't St. Giles — presumably he was safe from attack here.

Or at least the type of attack he was used to.

"Lady Beckinhall, I quite fear I'd grown limp with worry that you would not attend this night," a tall, handsome man drawled from Isabel's other side. "And yet here you are and I find my entire constitution lifted with the glory of seeing you."

Isabel laughed at this ridiculousness and took her hand from Winter's arm to offer it to the newcomer. "La, Lord d'Arque, where do you come up with such creative flattery? If I don't take care, my head may be turned."

"Only if you don't take care?" d'Arque asked lightly as he bent over her hand.

Winter repressed an urge to growl, for he was sure the other man wasn't just pretending to kiss her knuckles.

D'Arque straightened languidly, his eyes intent on Isabel. "I needs must practice my flattery it seems, my lady. But perhaps you could help me? Under your gentle tutelage, I have hope of rising to meet your sweet regard."

Winter cleared his throat. "She already has one man to tutor."

Isabel started as if she'd truly fallen under the spell of this jackanapes. "My lord, may I present Mr. Winter Makepeace, the manager of the Home for Unfortunate Infants and Foundling Children? Mr. Makepeace, this is Adam Rutledge, the Viscount d'Arque."

"Ah, Makepeace," Lord d'Arque said after they'd made their bows. "What's this about tutoring?"

"Lady Beckinhall has kindly offered her services to give me some polish," Winter said in a flat voice. "In order to better represent the home."

D'Arque's eyebrows rose lazily. "But what's the point, pray tell? After all, I shall be replacing you soon as the home's manager."

Winter stilled, the pounding of his pulse loud in his ears. "I beg your pardon?"

D'Arque tilted his head as if intrigued. "I was given to understand by Lady Penelope that you would be resigning as manager of the home. Don't tell me you've changed your mind? I had my heart quite set on the position."

"I do not have any intention of relinquishing my position at the home," Winter said through clenched jaws. "Now or ever."

Winter Makepeace looked absolutely furious.

For a man who normally kept his emotions under strict control, the sight was rather frightening. Isabel instinctively started to take a step back from him, but he slapped his hand over her fingers on his arm, keeping her close.

Lord d'Arque's heavy-lidded eyes flicked to where Winter had trapped her hand, and his cynical smile became fixed. "I'm told that you've outstayed your usefulness at the home, Makepeace."

Isabel opened her mouth to deny the charge, but Winter was already speaking, low and lethally. "I've no doubt that Lady Penelope is the source of your information. The lady knows her slippers and gloves, but she has no practical experience running an orphanage in the heart of St. Giles. I have been and will be the best person to manage the home."

"Is that so?" D'Arque's lips curved cruelly.

"You may still be happy at the home, but as I understand it, the home has grown beyond you. Forgive me, but I believe with the illustrious patronesses it now has, you may even be an embarrassment."

"Adam!" Isabel's shocked gasp was out before she could think. She felt Winter's forearm turn to steel beneath her fingers at the use of d'Arque's Christian name.

Lady Margaret glanced at her curiously while d'Arque's expression grew smug.

Isabel's eyebrows rose coolly at him. She and Adam Rutledge may've been playing a sophisticated game of seduction for the last year, he may've made it subtly known that he was interested in a liaison, and she may've hinted that she wasn't averse to the idea, but she'd never committed herself.

He had no right to look so damned complacent — and certainly no right to attack Winter in a show of male possessiveness.

Lady Margaret cleared her throat in the awkward silence. "I think Mr. Makepeace is an excellent manager and . . . and representative of the home."

D'Arque bowed at Lady Margaret. "Your defense of Makepeace reflects well on your gentle character, my lady."

Lady Margaret smiled tightly. "You make me sound like a tabby cat, my lord."

"A tabby cat with claws." Isabel grinned. "It really is too bad of you to tease Mr. Makepeace so, my lord. What do you care about managing an orphanage in any case?"

The viscount shrugged indolently. "Perhaps I've discovered a newfound urge to do good works?"

"Or perhaps you have an interest in something else in St. Giles?" Winter asked softly.

D'Arque's brows knit in puzzlement, and Isabel looked up at Winter sharply.

"Such as?" the viscount drawled. "Do you accuse me of a secret taste for gin?"

It was Winter's turn to shrug. "There are other things to consume in St. Giles besides gin. Girls, for instance."

D'Arque's brows slowly arched. "Surely you don't think I prefer boys?"

"I have no idea," Winter said coolly. "I don't know you, after all, my lord, and there are some who are so depraved as to enjoy debauching children."

"I do assure you that I like my females fully, ah, *matured.*" The viscount cast Isabel a significant glance.

She arched a brow and looked away.

D'Arque suddenly clapped his hands, the gesture so abrupt and violent that Lady Margaret, standing beside him, shied. He was a man who had a well-established polite

194

facade, but there was real anger now in his light gray eyes.

"Come," the viscount cried. "Let us put our social skills, mine and Mr. Makepeace's, to the test. I propose a contest of gentlemanly manners with an evening at the opera the first playing field. What say you, Makepeace?"

Isabel started to shake her head. The opera seemed a tame enough outing, but she didn't trust Viscount d'Arque in his present temper.

"Done." Winter's voice was even and low, but there was no doubt that he was picking up a gauntlet thrown down.

"Splendid!" D'Arque's eyes gleamed cruelly. "And to spice the stew, I shall invite several other gentlepersons of quality to help judge us."

"Very well." Winter inclined his head. "And now you must pardon Lady Beckinhall and me, for we are in search of the refreshments."

"Ah." D'Arque bowed ironically. "Please, don't let me keep you from your social rounds."

Winter turned and strode away through the crowd. People took one look at his face and stumbled out of his way, while Isabel skipped to keep up with his long legs.

"You needn't run from the room," she panted, trying to keep her voice low.

"You would prefer I stay and knock that ass down?" Winter snapped.

"You would never do such a thing — it's not in your nature."

His oblique glance was sharp. "Perhaps you know nothing of my nature."

She lifted her chin. "I think I do. I think you take pride in repressing all your emotions, carefully tucking them away behind the bland mask you wear in public. I think you fear to feel too deeply, perhaps fear to feel at all."

He cast her an incredulous look.

"It's true. I've been studying you this last week. Besides," she said more practically, "hitting d'Arque would merely make his point."

They had come to an alcove off the main ballroom, discreetly hidden by several large vases and statuary. He pulled her inside then halted and swung her around, and she saw his eyes were burning black. He took her upper arms, holding her in an angry grip.

"His point that I'm some kind of half-ape, barely fit for civilized society?" he demanded, his voice a low vibration of outrage. "Is that what you think? Are you mortified to be seen on my arm in front of your lover?"

"He's not my lover," she hissed.

"He wants to be."

"Yes, he does!" she flung out, tired of male rage, tired of this man flirting with her and then withdrawing.

"And is that what you want, too?" he growled, his mouth twisted harshly. "Do you want to lie with him?"

She lifted a taunting shoulder. "Perhaps."

His face was so close to hers that she could feel his breath upon her lips. His eyes dropped to her mouth and she knew: He was going to kiss her. She'd finally feel Winter Makepeace's mouth on hers, finally find out what lay beneath the mask. For a moment she forgot where they were, *who* they were. She wanted him. Wanted to tear the neck cloth from around his throat, open his shirt, and lay her mouth there, against the hot beat of his heart. She lifted her face, parted her lips, urged him on with her eyes.

Instead he raised his head, blinking as if he were coming out of a darkened room.

Winter Makepeace looked at her and she saw it, the moment his eyes shuttered, the second he regained his mask and drew away from her, both physically and emotionally.

He stepped back, lifting his hands. "I beg

your pardon, Lady Beckinhall. That was quite unforgivable of me."

She wanted to scream with frustration. Instead she inhaled, wishing she could free herself from passion as abruptly as he appeared to. "No, Mr. Makepeace, what is quite unforgivable is your apology."

He'd nearly broken his unspoken vow. He'd nearly kissed a woman — nearly kissed Isabel.

A girl had once kissed him when he'd been young — before he'd reached seventeen. Before he'd realized what his true purpose in St. Giles and this life was. He'd met her on a trip to Oxford and could no longer remember her name — perhaps he'd never known it. Their kiss had been awkward and fumbling, and he'd not seen her again.

Isabel was as the sun to a candle compared to that girl so long ago. He wanted to touch her more than he wanted his next breath. More than he'd wanted food when he'd been his hungriest. More than he'd wanted water when he'd been his thirstiest. She was a craving under his skin so great that even now he felt his body actually canting toward her. He wanted to take her, to consummate this hunger within himself. Bury his flesh inside hers and conquer her as primitively as any Viking savage.

And he *could not.*

The children of the home — the children like Pilar — depended on him. He'd made a mistake, let himself have too much free rein, pretended that he was something other than what he truly was. Winter stared into Isabel's beautiful, stormy blue eyes and was aware that a part of him was utterly seduced by this woman and this moment. She made him forget his duty. Made him forget all that depended upon him. She was temptation personified.

He turned away.

She caught his arm, her grip surprisingly strong — but then she'd been taking him by surprise with her feminine power ever since she'd found him dressed as the Ghost and insensible in St. Giles.

"Where are you going?" she demanded.

He looked away from her face. "We need to return to the ball."

"Why?"

He grimaced. "I'm supposed to be meeting dignitaries, remember?"

"I remember that you appear to be about to dismiss me as nothing."

He finally faced her again — it seemed he must find a way to fight this gut-deep pull, and now was as good a time as any.

Her plush lips were pressed together, her eyebrows knit, and her fine eyes looked . . . hurt. *Dear Lord.* Something inside of him began to bleed.

"What would you have me do?" he murmured, conscious that the ball — and all the people attending it — was only feet away. "I've apologized and you are insulted."

"You are avoiding the subject." She dropped her hand and he felt the warmth seep from his arm where she'd touched him. "You are avoiding *me.* You were about to kiss me a minute ago. I felt it and —"

"But I didn't." He wanted to tear at his hair, punch the wall, grab her again, and give in to temptation. Kiss her until that awful look left her face.

He did none of those things, of course.

"No, you didn't," she said slowly. "Obviously I am easily resisted."

"Easily." He scoffed at the word, folding his arms across his chest to keep his hands contained. How could she think this was *easy* for him? "I've no doubt that you are used to men kissing you and more when you look at them the way you just looked at me."

Her lips parted. "Are you calling me a *whore?*"

200

His head jerked back. "*No.* I don't —"

She stepped up to him, toe-to-toe, and jabbed a finger rather painfully into his ridiculously embroidered waistcoat. "I may not meet your monkish standards of conduct, but that in no way makes me a loose woman. Do you understand that, Winter Makepeace? I enjoy the company of men and I enjoy bedsport. If you are made uncomfortable by that fact, then perhaps it is *your* standards that you should look to."

Isabel turned in fine fettle, obviously about to sweep out of the little alcove and leave him flat.

Winter snaked out an arm. It was his turn to arrest her. "I don't think any of those things about you," he said, attempting to get her to face him.

"Then why *not* take the next step?" she asked, her face averted.

"I *can't.*"

She turned and he nearly closed his eyes, so blinded was he by her blazing look. "Why not? Are you physically incapable?"

His mouth twisted. "No. At least not to my knowledge."

Her eyes softened. "If this is the fear of inexperience, I assure you that I won't expect an expert lover — at least not at first."

Winter's lips twitched. "No, it isn't that. You don't understand —"

"Then explain."

He exhaled and tipped back his head to stare at the plump cupids cavorting on the Duchess of Arlington's ceiling. "I am dedicated to the home and St. Giles. I have pledged to help those who need my help — need it desperately — in that wretched area of London."

"You sound as if you've made a priestly vow," she said wonderingly.

He glanced away from her, marshaling his thoughts. He'd never put this into words, never told another living soul his mission.

Then he inhaled and faced her. "It is very similar, in intent if not philosophy, to a priestly vow. I'm not like your society rogues, Isabel. I regard physical lovemaking as something sacrosanct to love. And if I loved a woman enough to take her to my bed, then I would love her enough to marry her. I don't intend ever to marry, ergo, I do not intend to ever get close enough to a woman — physically or emotionally — to make love to her."

"But you're *not* a priest," she said. "Surely you can have both a wife and family and help those in St. Giles."

He glanced down at her, so beautiful, so

full of that life. "No, I don't believe so. A husband and father's first duty is to his wife and family. Everything else is secondary. How can the people of St. Giles ever come first if I am married?"

Her eyes widened in astonishment. "I don't believe this. You're attempting to become a saint."

His mouth tightened. "No, I've merely dedicated my life to helping others."

"But *why?*"

"I've told you why," he said, trying to still his impatience. This discussion was like cutting open his chest, putting a hand in, and stirring his organs about. He did not like it at all. "The children, the poor of St. Giles, the terrible lives they lead. Did you not hear me when I spoke?"

"I heard you well enough," she snapped. "I'm asking why *you.* Why must *you* be the one to make this sacrifice of your entire life?"

He shook his head helplessly. She was of the privileged class. She'd never known want, never counted coins to calculate whether they should go to pay for coal to warm the body or bread to feed it, for they would pay for only one, not both. She simply could not understand.

Winter dropped his hand from her arm

and stepped back, putting prudent distance between them. His voice was carefully modulated when he spoke.

Carefully gentle. "If not me, then who?"

Megs sighed and arched her back, luxuriating in the lovely feeling after lovemaking. This had been one of many revelations she'd discovered since dear Roger had initiated her into the secrets of the bedroom: how boneless, how utterly relaxed her body felt afterward.

Not that they'd ever had the opportunity to meet in a bedroom.

At the moment, she lounged on a settee in a very dark receiving room at the back of the Duchess of Arlington's house. She could hear the sounds of the ball, muffled by the walls and intervening rooms, but it was still a lovely, cozy refuge for just the two of them.

"Time to get up, my love," Roger whispered in her ear.

"So soon?" Megs pouted.

"Yes, at once," he mock-scolded her. Roger sat up and put himself to rights. "You don't want the matrons in the ballroom to notice your absence, do you? Or worse — your brother the marquess."

Megs shuddered at the thought. Both her brothers in their own ways had made rather scandalous marriages, but that didn't mean they would look at all favorably at even a hint of impropriety from her.

She sat up reluctantly and began straightening herself.

"Besides," Roger continued casually, "I do want to remain on good terms with my future brother-in-law."

Megs caught her breath and looked up, joy rushing into her breast.

Roger burst into warm laughter at the expression on her face. "Did you think I wouldn't want you for my wife, sweet Meggie? Haven't you realized yet that I'm head over heels in love with you?"

When she just stared at him, frozen, his face fell. "That is, if you are amenable to my suit? I fear I may've overstepped my —"

She flung herself on him before he could finish.

"Oof!" Roger fell backward onto the settee under her onslaught.

"Yes, yes, yes!" Megs muttered in between covering his sweet, dear, *wonderful* face with rather messy kisses. "Oh, Roger, how can you ever think otherwise than that I love you with all my heart?"

He caught her face and held her still for a much longer, more expert kiss on the lips.

"Oh, sweeting," he whispered as he broke

away. "You've made me the happiest man in the world."

She lay her head beside him, simply enjoying the moment.

Then he lurched beneath her and slapped her rather familiarly on the bottom. "Up, up, up."

Megs groaned, but complied. She hurriedly checked herself in a small mirror and then turned to Roger. "Shall we have a short engagement?"

"Yes, please." He grinned down at her, the dimple she'd grown quite fond of flashing in his right cheek. "But a small favor? Can we keep our engagement secret until I can order my estate and make a proper suit to your brother? I'm not as rich as I'm sure he would like, but I've a business offer that—"

"Hush." She placed her fingertips over his lips. "I'm marrying you because I love you, not because of your money."

He frowned. "You could marry a title. Marry a much richer man."

"I could but I won't." She smiled up at him, blissfully happy. "And I'll be sure and make that point to Thomas when the time comes."

He laid his forehead against hers. "I do love you."

"I know." She stood on tiptoe to brush a kiss against his lips. "I'll not tell anyone of our engagement as long as you promise not to wait too long to talk to Thomas."

"A fortnight, no more." His roguish brown eyes grew grave. "Truly, it's an excellent investment, Meggie. If all comes to fruition, even your brother will be impressed."

She shook her head fondly, whispering, "You don't need money to impress me, Roger Fraser-Burnsby."

She stood a second, looking into his eyes, wanting to say so much more and unable to find the words.

Instead, in the end, she touched his cheek, turned, and slipped from the room.

Isabel backed into the doorway of the ladies' retiring room and stared down the hallway thoughtfully. If she wasn't mistaken, Lady Margaret had just exited a room farther down the hall, where the passage became dimly lit. Now why — Isabel's eyes widened, then narrowed. Mr. Roger Fraser-Burnsby had just come out of the room Megs had left.

Well.

She was enough of a woman of the world to know that clandestine tête-à-têtes sometimes took place at balls. But Lady Margaret was an unmarried heiress. True, Mr. Fraser-Burnsby seemed like a nice enough young man, but Megs risked her reputation and thus the rest of her life by meeting him in private.

Isabel checked that her skirts were straight and then started back to the ball. She'd have to find a way to gently hint to Megs that she wasn't quite as discreet as she thought she was. But in the meantime, Isabel had to return to the ball and Winter Makepeace. She'd already taken too long in the retiring room and had the sneaking suspicion that she might've been hiding from him. Isabel sighed. She'd never been a coward before. She'd just have to face the man and make light conversation until this wretched evening was over.

And then she must find a way to put Winter Makepeace from her mind — and perhaps her heart.

CHAPTER EIGHT

That night the Harlequin took revenge upon those who had wronged him. His attackers had not even left St. Giles when he found them, and though they screamed at his unholy white eyes and tried to defend themselves, they were ill matched against the Ghost of St. Giles! He fought with inhumane strength and skill and he killed them all without word or look of mercy. But he didn't stop there. The Harlequin went hunting the next night as well. Soon, all who had ever done a misdeed knew to stay well away from St. Giles at night, for the Ghost was thirsty for blood . . .

— from *The Legend of the Harlequin Ghost of St. Giles*

"Oh, my lady, those stockings are the very height of elegance," Pinkney exclaimed the next night as Isabel rolled her new lace stockings over her calf. "And such a reasonable price. Shall I order another dozen?"

Isabel pointed her toes to better view the embroidered clocking overlaying the lace on the outside of her ankle. It really was rather fine. No doubt Winter Makepeace would think clocked lace stockings a shocking waste of money.

She nodded defiantly to Pinkney. "Buy two dozen."

The lady's maid grinned, ever enthusiastic when it came to the procurement of expensive clothing, and held open Isabel's petticoat for her to step into. "I will indeed, my lady."

"Good," Isabel said absently as she studied herself in the mirror. Her chemise had heavy lace on the elbow-length sleeves and neck, and the gossamer material revealed the deep red of her nipples. Would such a sight tempt the priestly Winter?

Did she even want to tempt him?

"My lady." Pinkney held out her silk stays and Isabel nodded, raising her arms so that the maid could slip the stays on over her head.

Pinkney came around to Isabel's front and began to tighten the laces while Suzie the little undermaid knelt to hold the stays firm.

He'd said that he didn't want a liaison

with her, or any woman, in as plain language as she'd ever heard. He'd devoted himself — mind, soul, and cock, it seemed — to St. Giles and its people. Why humiliate herself chasing a man — a mere schoolmaster at that! — when other gentlemen were willing? Lord d'Arque, for instance. He was handsome and witty and would no doubt be a very experienced and skilled bed partner.

The maids stood and began gathering her skirts. Tonight Isabel wore a violet brocade with a darker purple medallion pattern woven into the material. She stepped carefully into the pool of fabric and stood as the maids drew the skirt up and began fastening it about her waist.

The problem was that she wasn't particularly interested in a romantic affair with d'Arque — or anyone else save Winter. Strange how only a week or so ago she would've laughed at the mere notion — she and the home's manager. But in the past week, her perception of him had changed. He spoke to her as an equal, as if her rank and his position simply didn't matter. But it was more than that. Many men considered women either ethereal beings to be placed on a pedestal or childlike and unable to hold logical thought. Winter talked to her as if she were as intelligent as he. As if she would be interested in some of the same things that engaged him. As if he might want to know what she thought about. He talked to her as if she mattered.

And considering it now, she realized no one had ever been curious about her, Isabel the woman. She had been wife and daughter, lover and witty society lady. But no one had ever looked beneath those masks to find out what the woman who wore them really thought.

Was it so terrible to want to be closer to a man who saw her as a person?

Pinkney helped her slip into the tight bodice of her dress. She slid the V-shaped embroidered stomacher in front of the bodice and then carefully pinned the edges of the dress to the stomacher. The maid picked and tugged gently at the lace of the chemise so just the edge showed at the square bodice and then tied the sleeves of the dress at Isabel's elbows to show the fall of lace beneath.

"There." Pinkney stood back reverently. "You do look splendid tonight, my lady."

Isabel arched her brow, turning first one way and then another to examine herself in the mirror over her vanity. "Splendid enough to seduce a priest, do you think?"

"My lady?" Pinkney wrinkled her brow in

confusion.

"Never mind." Isabel touched the jeweled red silk rose in her coiffure and nodded to herself. "Has Mr. Makepeace arrived yet?"

"No, my lady."

"Curse the man," Isabel muttered just as she caught sight of a small foot sticking out from under one of her armchairs. "Go ahead and make sure the carriage is ready. I'll be down in a few more minutes."

Isabel waited until both maids left and then approached the armchair. "Christopher."

The foot withdrew under the chair. "My lady?"

She sighed. "What are you doing down there?"

Silence.

"Christopher?"

"Don't want to have a bath," came the tiny, mutinous mutter.

She bit her lip to keep from smiling even though he couldn't see her. "If you never bathe, you'll become caked with dirt and we'll have to scrape it off with a shovel."

A giggle drifted out from under the armchair. "Can you tell me about the Ghost again, my lady?"

She cocked an eyebrow at the armchair. Was this blackmail in one so young? "Very well, I'll tell you a story about the Ghost of St. Giles, but then you must go back to Carruthers."

A heavy sigh. "All right."

Isabel cast her gaze about her bedroom for inspiration. Butterman had reported on his findings about the Ghost just this afternoon. Most of it was silly rumors and fairy tales, obviously meant to frighten little children. The Ghost was scarred in some and ate the livers of maidens. He could be in two places at once and his eyes burned with an orange flame. In others he could fly and knocked at the windows of misbehaving boys. But some of the stories sounded like they might have a grain of truth in them.

"My lady?" The small foot was inching back out from under the armchair and Christopher's voice sounded impatient.

Isabel cleared her throat. "Once upon a time . . ." Didn't all stories begin thus? "There lived a poor widow who sold currant buns. Every morning she would get up well before the rooster crowed and bake her buns. Then she would pile them onto a great, wide basket and, placing the basket on her head, walk the streets of London crying, 'Currant buns! Currant buns! Ye'll ne'er taste better! Buy my currant buns!'

"All day she walked and cried, and by suppertime her basket was empty and her feet sore, but the poor widow would have a few pennies in her pockets from her labors. Then she would buy a bit of meat, a bit of bread, and a bit of milk and walk home to feed her children."

Isabel paused to see if she'd lost her listener, but almost at once Christopher said, "But what about the Ghost?"

"I'm coming to that," she said. "One day as the widow walked home, a gang of men set upon her and beat her and took all her pennies. 'Oh, stop, stop!' the widow called. And, 'Who will help me?' But all were afraid of the robbers and none would come to help. The widow was left crying in the street and had to sell her shawl to pay for her children's dinner. The next day she baked and sold her currant buns, but again as she walked home, she was set upon by the same gang of robbers. Again they beat the poor widow and took her pennies and they merely laughed when she called, 'Who will help me?' "

"Oh," Christopher whispered from under the armchair. "If'n I had a pistol, I would shoot those men for her!"

"That would be very brave of you." Isabel had to clear her throat — a lump had formed at the thought of the little boy wanting to help a stranger. "This time the poor widow had to sell her shoes to pay for her children's dinner. The third day the widow was in despair, but she could do naught but bake her currant buns and walk the streets of London in her bare feet to sell them. When she headed for home that night, her feet were bloody and she was very weary. When the robbers again set upon her, she could only whisper, 'Who will help me?' " Isabel paused. "But this time someone heard her. The Ghost of St. Giles swept down upon those mean robbers like a terrible windstorm."

"Huzzah!" Christopher's head peeked out from under the armchair and he hugged himself with excitement as Isabel continued.

"The Ghost has two swords, you know, one long and one short, and he used both as he attacked those robbers. He made them yell with pain and fear, and by the time he was finished with them, he'd shredded the clothes from their bodies. The robbers were forced to run naked and barefoot through St. Giles to escape the Ghost. The people of St. Giles made sure they were very sorry for the sorrow they'd caused the poor widow and they never bothered her again."

"Oh!" Christopher said as he hugged himself. "Oh!"

His eyes were wide and his cheeks red, and Isabel hoped she hadn't overexcited him.

"That's the best story ever," Christopher said.

Isabel smiled, feeling a bit embarrassed, for she'd gotten carried away in the story herself. Strange to think that she'd actually met the dashing, mythical Ghost. Stranger still, she had a mad suspicion of who he might be under that grotesque mask.

She blinked and focused on the boy. "There's more. Would you like to hear it?"

Christopher nodded.

The epilogue wasn't as full of action, but it was Isabel's favorite part. "The next morning when the widow got up to make her currant buns, guess what she found next to her oven? A bag of money — more than she'd lost from the robbers — and a pair of new shoes."

"How did the Ghost get in her house? Was it locked?"

"Yes, it was," Isabel said. "No one knows how he got in."

Christopher's eyes widened as he contemplated that bit of information.

"Now," Isabel said. "I have to go to an opera and you must go to your bath, remember?"

Christopher wrinkled his nose, but he got out from under the armchair readily enough. He paused by her door. "Will you come say good night to me later?"

She swallowed. Telling him the story — and his obvious enjoyment — had given her confidence in her dealings with Christopher. Now she felt on shaky ground again. "You know I can't."

He nodded, not looking at her, and left.

She stared after him, perplexed. What did he want from her? And whatever it was, could she give it? She hadn't time for this. She had an opera to go to. Isabel strode to her bedroom door and out into the hallway, nearly running down the stairs. One would think she ran from a demon instead of a small boy, she thought bitterly.

Downstairs, Butterman was standing by the front door. He bowed. "John Coachman says that Mr. Makepeace has sent word that he has been unavoidably detained and will meet you at the opera."

"Oh, very well," she muttered irritably. What was Winter thinking? Did he mean to forfeit Lord d'Arque's contest of manners before it had even begun? "I shall leave at once, then. Oh, and, Butterman?"

"My lady?"

She inhaled, steadying her breathing.

"Please tell Carruthers that Christopher was in my rooms again."

Butterman's expression changed not at all. "Of course, my lady."

"Tell her not to be too harsh on the boy, please?"

He nodded and snapped his fingers at a footman, who hurried back to the servants' stairs while Butterman held the door for her.

Isabel frowned as she descended her front steps. Perhaps it was time she asked Louise, Christopher's mother, to find different accommodations for the child. The problem was the silly woman had never had a head for money — what she had of it — and couldn't afford to house Christopher. Not to mention the company she kept . . .

"Good evening, my lady." Harold bowed as he held out his hand to help her into the carriage.

"Thank you, Harold." She settled herself back against the soft squabs, watching idly as the carriage rocked through the darkened streets of London.

Carriages lined the street outside the Covent Garden opera house, and her own ground to a halt as they waited their turn in a long line. Isabel craned her neck, searching for any sign of Winter. She saw d'Arque's carriage with its distinctive coat of arms, and a minute later the viscount himself, ushering two ladies into the opera. Her heart sank as she realized it was Lady Penelope and her companion, Miss Greaves, that he escorted. Wonderful. He'd chosen Winter's worst critic as judge of this silly contest of manners.

And Winter Makepeace himself was nowhere to be seen.

In a storage room of the opera house, Winter stripped his clothes off with swift, efficient movements.

He'd been delayed at the home by a last-minute emergency when one of the youngest toddlers had gone missing. Mary Morning, barely two, had eventually been found safe and sound and hiding in one of the kitchen cupboards. He'd left the toddler in Nell's capable hands, but the search for Mary Morning had made Winter's arrival at the opera house later than he'd planned.

Winter pulled on his harlequin tunic and calculated that he'd have barely twenty minutes to finish changing into the Ghost of St. Giles costume, run through the back of the opera house, find d'Arque's coachman, and question the man on why he seemed to have a nighttime job as a lassie snatcher in St. Giles. For Winter had recognized d'Arque's coachman at the Duchess of Arlington's ball: he'd been the older of the two lassie snatchers who'd tried to kidnap Joseph Chance.

He took his mask out of the soft sack he'd brought with him to the opera house. He'd wanted no questions on the way to the opera, so he'd walked there with his costume and swords hidden in the sack; later, when the evening was over, he'd walk back to the home again. Now he tied the mask onto his face and reveled in the familiar feeling of freedom it gave him. It was as if he were a big cat, uncoiling his limbs, mentally stretching before the hunt.

Contain the animal.

Something within him growled. He must release the beast when he was the Ghost, but he had to control it at the same time. Just a little freedom. Just a bit of fresh air. What would he do if he ever met Isabel Beckinhall in this guise again? Would he take what he dared not in the light of day?

Winter pushed the disquieting thought from his mind and stowed his soft bag with his clothes behind the door. Cautiously, he peered into the corridor. Twenty minutes and when he'd have his answers from d'Arque's coachman, he'd return and change back into his suit. Draw the protective shell of Winter Makepeace about himself and became again the rigid, upright schoolmaster and orphanage manager.

A man who only dared think about kissing Isabel Beckinhall in his dreams.

Isabel's carriage finally drew opposite the opera house's front doors, and Harold's plain, honest face appeared at the carriage door. "My lady."

"Thank you," she murmured as she stepped down.

The carriage pulled away, and Isabel mounted the steps to the opera house alone. She'd simply have to arrive at d'Arque's box sans her pupil — even if it would count badly against Winter. Lady Penelope would certainly take note of his tardiness.

The crowd became thicker as she entered the opera. Brightly gowned ladies chattered with gentlemen no less elegantly dressed. Overhead, the vestibule ceiling arched high, recessed box molding painted in blue, cream, and crimson.

"Pardon me," Isabel murmured as an elderly lady in a fussy lace cap bumped against her. The woman pivoted and Isabel felt the distinctive pull of her skirt. She looked down and saw a bit of lace hanging off her hem.

"Drat," she muttered under her breath.

She remembered that a retiring room lay in a corridor just off the main lobby. Carefully, Isabel lifted her skirts and headed that way. If she hurried, she should have time to pin up the lace and get to d'Arque's box before the opera started.

The corridor was ill lit, but the retiring room was the first door on the right. Isabel began to push it open when she saw a form dart at the far end of the corridor.

Black and scarlet motley flashed.

Surely not. Isabel told herself that she must've mistaken the pattern even as she began making her way down the dim corridor. The Ghost had never been seen outside St. Giles. Well, except for the day she'd found him. That day he'd ventured out as far as Tyburn to keep a pirate from swinging from the gallows. Further, Winter Makepeace was supposed to be attending the opera *right now.* If he were indeed the Ghost . . .

Isabel's heart was beating in a quick, fluttering rhythm as she neared the place where she'd seen the flash of scarlet. She glanced around. Only a few candles in sconces on the wall lit this part of the hall. Judging from the bare wood floor and unadorned walls, this must be a service passage of some kind. Isabel tiptoed down its length, passing a half-opened door to a storage room. At the end, the hall made a right-hand turn. She peered around the corner. A narrow staircase leading up.

Empty.

She sighed and straightened in disappointment.

"Looking for something, Lady Beckinhall?" The whisper was husky and low, but quite distinctly masculine. She whirled.

He leaned against the hallway wall, as indolently graceful as a lounging leopard. She hadn't seen him standing last time — then he'd been wounded and ill. Now he was tall and virilely athletic, the formfitting harlequin's costume outlining muscles on legs, chest, and arms, while the long-nosed mask gave him a faintly satanic aspect.

He tilted his head, his mouth — that familiar, sensuous mouth — curving in sardonic amusement. "Or do you search for *someone*, my lady?"

"Maybe I do." She raised her chin even as she felt the blush heat her cheeks. "What are *you* doing here?"

"Mischief, mayhem, merrymaking?" He shrugged. "Does it matter?"

She took a cautious step closer to him.

The voice was the same, and the body was the right height and build, but he had a freedom, a daring recklessness that Winter Makepeace had *never* shown her. But then Winter Makepeace had never shown any sign of violence, either, and if the stories were to be believed, the man in front of her was not only used to violence, but also skilled at it.

Isabel was utterly fascinated. "It matters if you have no fear for your life. You must know that many wish your arrest and even death."

"And if they do?" Unbelievably, he sounded *amused.*

Another step. "I might be . . . disheartened . . . should anything happen to you."

"Would you?"

She slowly reached out and ran a finger down the length of the deformed nose of his mask. "Who are you?"

His beautiful mouth twisted. "Whoever you wish me to be."

She laughed then, a little breathlessly. "Don't make promises you can't keep, sir."

"I never do." His words whispered across her senses.

She met his eyes, brown behind the eyeholes in his mask, and reached around the back of his head. Her fingers found the tie holding his mask and gently pulled.

He lifted his hand and for a moment she was disappointed, thinking he meant to stop her.

Then he took the cured leather mask away from his face.

As he had the last time, he wore a thin black silk half-mask under the leather one.

He cocked his head. "Is this what you want?"

"No," she whispered, standing on tiptoe, her hands flat against his hard chest. She'd find out for certain one way or another. "*This* is."

She opened her lips against his. He claimed her like a barbarian marauder. The kiss was rough, unpracticed, and without finesse, and yet Isabel felt a trembling thrill go through her. She was used to civilized embraces, carefully thought out, impeccably implemented. Mannered and cool. The Ghost of St. Giles, in contrast, was a storm breaking over her, all passion and emotion.

All real man.

She felt his arms come about her, pulling her tight against his chest as he bent her helplessly, lost, falling, her heart half beating out of her breast. And she knew — *she knew* — that she kissed not only the Ghost of St. Giles, but Winter Makepeace as well.

She drew back, gasping, her eyes searching for the familiar features beneath the mask.

And then a hand clamped down on her shoulder and she was torn from his arms.

"How dare you!" d'Arque shouted as he flung Isabel at the wall.

She blinked, shocked, and looked at the Ghost.

He was tying the leather mask onto his face.

"Answer me, you coward," d'Arque demanded. He drew his sword.

"No!" Isabel screamed, but it was too late.

D'Arque lunged toward the Ghost of St. Giles, his bare sword flashing.

Winter drew his sword only just in time to counter d'Arque's attack. He growled under his breath at the cavalier manner in which the other man had handled Isabel and thrust d'Arque's sword away contemptuously. Winter backed toward the stairs around the corner of the narrow passage. It wasn't that he was afraid to duel the viscount, but if he pushed the other man, he would retreat . . . into Isabel, who was behind d'Arque. He simply couldn't risk her becoming entangled in their swords.

But the viscount wasn't so easily dissuaded. Evidently thinking he had the Ghost of St. Giles on the run, he pursued Winter.

Winter gritted his teeth and dealt a flurry of thrusts that should've had d'Arque on the defensive. The viscount grinned and slapped away Winter's blade. For a moment Winter stared at the man, nonplussed.

Then he turned and swiftly ran up the stairs, his breath coming in quick pants.

D'Arque followed — the ass — forcing Winter to turn at the top only just in time to avoid a stab in the back.

"Running, Ghost?" d'Arque sneered. He didn't even seem winded by the run up the stairs. "I hadn't heard you were such a coward, but then it is easier to fight in the dark and against those untutored in the arts of the sword."

Oh, but it would be wonderful to reply! Winter didn't dare — he'd risked enough talking to Isabel. Instead he lunged, silently, his front foot stomping forward with his thrust.

D'Arque caught his blade, his biceps bulging in his tight-fitting pale blue velvet coat. The viscount's eyes widened as he teetered on the top of the stairs.

One hard thrust. That was all it would take to send the other man down those stairs and to oblivion. Winter's breath was tearing at his throat, his pulse beating like a war drum.

He wasn't an animal.

Winter stepped away, back toward a door behind him, reaching to open it —

D'Arque recovered and leaped toward him.

Winter raised his sword, meeting d'Arque's savage thrust, the blades shrieking against each other. He half fell through the doorway and was dimly aware of a woman's scream.

They were in a hallway behind the opera boxes. Around them, people arriving for the opera filled the corridor.

Winter pushed his sword down and away, disengaging their blades, and then kicked d'Arque in the thigh with the flat of his boot. He felt the scrape of the viscount's blade against his leather jackboot as the other man flailed to keep his balance.

"Damn me!" a florid elderly gentleman exclaimed as Winter backed into him.

D'Arque was flushed, a sheen of sweat showing now at his brow, but he grinned, teeth white against swarthy skin. "Surrender yourself to me, thief."

Winter bared his teeth and shook his head once.

Then he darted into one of the boxes.

It was occupied, of course. Two gentlemen scattered, leaving a young lady alone, gaping at him.

"Pardon," Winter whispered to her as he passed by.

He leaned out over the edge of the box. They were only on the first tier, but it was a twenty-foot drop to the pit below. The wide railing ran in a horseshoe all around the theater, ending on either side at the stage. If he could just —

Behind him, the young woman gasped.

Winter whirled. The viscount was already on him, sword flashing. Winter parried, but there wasn't much room to move. Suddenly d'Arque's sword was at his throat, held off only by Winter's own sword. Winter stumbled back a pace, the small of his back hitting the balcony behind him. The blades ground together, shrieking as if for blood, as d'Arque leaned his entire weight against him. Slowly, agonizingly, Winter bent backward over the balcony. He could feel the heat of the other man's breath, smell his too-sweet perfume mixed with the sharp acid of sweat. His head and upper body hung over nothing but air.

Behind him was a two-story fall.

The viscount panted with his effort as he

snarled, "Give up. You're cornered."

"No!" cried a familiar, feminine voice from below in the pit. "Adam, no! You must let him go."

Slowly, Winter grinned, his eyebrows raised behind his mask.

The viscount didn't like that. His pale eyes narrowed and Winter rather thought that Isabel might've sealed his death warrant.

Or she would have if Winter hadn't spent many, many long nights practicing his sword craft. He took advantage of the viscount's momentary distraction to shove with all his strength against the other man.

D'Arque fell back and Winter leaped onto the balcony rail.

He heard a scream from the pit below, but he dared not look down. D'Arque leaped onto the rail as well. The other man's sword flashed out, headed for Winter's face. Winter batted d'Arque's sword aside and thrust low toward the man's pelvis.

No man liked to be hit there. D'Arque's reaction was too jerky and for a second his balance wavered, his free arm windmilling in the air over the pit.

Gasps from below.

Winter softly tutted.

"Damn you," d'Arque growled, lunging anew.

Winter didn't like the man, but then again, he didn't want to kill the viscount either. He had no clear evidence against d'Arque. The man might still be innocent. Winter skipped backward on the railing, parrying d'Arque's attack as he retreated toward the stage. He almost laughed aloud. His heart was racing, his limbs were strong and quick, and he felt *free.*

Only fools take victory for granted. The ghostly voice of Sir Stanley echoed in his mind.

They fought along the rail, nearing the stage, the occupants scattering as they passed each box.

D'Arque slashed at Winter's face. Winter leaned to the side and pinked the viscount on the upper left arm. The point of his sword slid through the viscount's pale blue silk coat, ripping a long diagonal hole as Winter jerked it free.

Red began to stain the pale blue.

D'Arque lunged in awkward rage, and Winter easily avoided the attack. But the viscount had put too much weight on his outer foot. He tilted over the pit and began to fall as shrieks rose from below.

Winter didn't stop to think. He simply grabbed the man's free arm, pulling him back from death.

D'Arque's sword fell to the pit, stabbing into a plush chair, where it stood upright, wobbling from side to side.

Winter looked back up and into d'Arque's wide eyes.

The other man swallowed. "Thank you."

Winter nodded and let go of the viscount's arm. He turned and ran the few feet along the railing to the stage. Behind him, there were shouts and someone tried to grab his cloak as he ran past. He reached the stage and found the rope to the curtain, tied to a cleat at the side. Two slashes from his sword and the rope was free. Winter held it, feeling the sharp burn in his biceps as he swung out over the stage. Below, the musicians rose in a wave from their seats.

He dropped onto the stage, landing lightly on the balls of his feet, his sword still in hand. But he needn't have bothered. The stagehands nearest him backed away. Winter turned and ducked into the wings, running away from the stage and the commotion the duel had caused. He shoved past another stagehand, and then he was sprinting along a darkened corridor, hopefully toward the rear of the theater and a back door into an alley.

This had been madness. He should never have alerted Isabel to his presence. It had

233

been a much too risky move. But when he'd seen her and realized that she'd seen him — was in fact trying to find him — well, he hadn't been able to control the urge to confront her. To trade quips with her. To kiss her uninhibitedly.

The Ghost could do at night what Winter Makepeace never dared during the day.

The corridor abruptly dead-ended on a door that looked ancient and rarely used. There was a lock, but it was rusted and Winter easily pried it off.

Cautiously, he eased open the door. This was even better than an alley. He was on a side street and all the carriages that had taken the nobility to their opera were lined up, waiting. Now because of the swordfight he had only minutes to discover the information he'd come for.

Winter sheathed his long sword and took out his short sword.

He slipped through the door and crept along the carriage line, keeping to the shadows. A group of coachmen and footmen were standing in a group ahead, smoking pipes, but he didn't see d'Arque's coachman.

Farther along, he spotted the owl on the side of a carriage — and on the seat, the dozing coachman.

Winter leaped onto the seat and grabbed the man's collar before he'd even woken.

"What're you about?" the coachman sputtered before he caught sight of Winter's blade. His eyes widened as he saw the harlequin's mask.

Even in the dim light from the carriage lanterns, Winter could see this was indeed the same man who had nearly kidnapped Joseph Chance.

He shook him like a rat and whispered, "Who do you work for?"

"M-my lord d'Arque," the coachman sputtered.

"Why is he having girls kidnapped from St. Giles?"

The coachman's eyes slid away. "Don't know what you mean."

Winter pointed the tip of his short sword at the man's eye. "Think."

"It's n-not d'Arque," the man stuttered.

Winter narrowed his eyes. "*Not* d'Arque? What do you mean?"

The man shook his head, clearly frightened.

Winter placed the tip of his sword on the man's cheek. "Talk."

"Oi!"

They'd attracted the attention of the pipe smokers. With a sudden twisting movement, the coachman slithered out of his grasp. Winter lunged — and missed — as the man fell off the other side of the carriage, picked himself up, and ran into the night.

Hastily Winter jumped from the other side of the carriage and rushed into the shadows. When he was at a safe distance, Winter paused and leaned against a wall, catching his breath. His arms ached from the duel and swinging over the stage, he hadn't learned a thing from the coachman, and the night wasn't over yet.

He still had an opera to attend.

CHAPTER NINE

Now, the Harlequin's True Love soon heard tales of his fate. How he'd been attacked and left for dead. How he'd somehow survived and now roamed the streets of St. Giles at night killing the wicked. She knew that the man she loved was never that violent and so she determined to find the Harlequin and talk to him to see if she might bring him to his senses . . .

— from *The Legend of the Harlequin Ghost of St. Giles*

Ten minutes later, Lady Penelope said, "Here at last is Mr. Makepeace," and Isabel finally drew breath.

She kept herself facing forward as he greeted the other occupants of Lord d'Arque's lavish opera box. Lord d'Arque had invited a crowd to oversee his defeat of Winter in their silly contest of manners, it seemed. Besides herself, Lady Penelope, and Miss Greaves, there was also his friends, the Earl of Kershaw and Mr. Charles Seymour, along with Mrs. Seymour, a rather plain-faced woman older than her husband.

"I think it obvious that Mr. Makepeace has lost the duel of gentlemanly manners," Lady Penelope said. "Shall we declare my lord d'Arque the winner?"

"I am flattered, my lady," came d'Arque's habitual drawl, "but because of the unexpected appearance of the Ghost, I think it best to call this round a draw and reconvene on a different night. Perhaps we can use my grandmother's ball tomorrow night?"

"But —" Lady Penelope began.

She was interrupted by Miss Greaves's soft voice. "Oh, well done, Lord d'Arque. Fairness toward one's opponents is surely the greatest mark of a gentleman. Don't you agree, Mr. Makepeace?"

Isabel nearly laughed. Miss Greaves had thoroughly spiked Lady Penelope's guns. She just hoped the lady's companion wouldn't pay for her presumption later.

"I do, Miss Greaves," Winter replied, and the matter was settled.

Isabel stared sightlessly at the stage where two men were wrestling the stage curtain. It wouldn't do to let Winter Makepeace know how sick with worry — and rage — she'd been. If he wanted to run about in a mask and cape, think himself invincible and her a fool, well then let him!

A moment later she heard the slight rustle of clothing as he sat beside her. "Good evening, my lady."

She nodded without turning his way.

After the turmoil of the duel, the excited inquiries and exclamations over Lord d'Arque's minor wound, the viscount had settled his party into his opera box situated directly over the stage. The viscount had arranged for sweetmeats and wine to be served to them in the box, and Isabel thought rather cynically that Winter would've lost the contest of gentlemanly manners even if the duel hadn't already made Lord d'Arque the hero of the night.

Below, the stagehands — who had succeeded in tying up the curtain — were taking elaborate bows from the stage to cheers from the pit.

"It seems that you have decided not to talk to me." Winter Makepeace sighed. "I do apologize for my delay in arriving. I was detained at the home. One of the children —"

She pursed her lips impatiently. She'd had quite enough of his lies. "I'm sure you've heard by now that you missed an appearance by the notorious Ghost of St. Giles."

At last she turned to look at him. His mouth was set — an expression that she'd learned meant he was impatient — but otherwise he seemed exactly as usual.

On her other side, Lady Penelope fanned herself vigorously. "I nearly fainted when I saw that Lord d'Arque was risking his *life* battling that fiend! If you had fallen from the balcony . . ." She shuddered dramatically. "Truly your bravery saved us all this night, my lord."

Viscount d'Arque had long since regained his habitual aplomb. The wound at his shoulder was wrapped rather dashingly in a scarlet handkerchief. Several ladies had nearly come to blows vying for the privilege of offering their fichus, handkerchiefs, or even petticoats in sacrifice for his bandage.

Lord d'Arque looked a trace sardonic as he bowed to Lady Penelope. "Had I given my life in such service, I would deem it a more-than-worthy sacrifice."

"It is only too bad that no *other* gentleman was brave enough to challenge the Ghost," Lady Penelope said with a significant glance at Winter.

"Some of us are a bit aged to be hopping about on a balcony with swords," Lord Kershaw said drily. His words were meant sardonically, for he couldn't be more than forty years. "Although I'm sure Seymour could've given the Ghost a good fight — he's rather renown at the fencing club. Beat both Rushmore and Gibbons last time you were there, didn't you, Seymour?"

Beside him, Mr. Seymour looked modest.

But Lady Penelope ignored them both. "I *meant* a younger man — such as Mr. Makepeace, perhaps."

"But Mr. Makepeace was not here — and besides, he does not wear a sword," Miss Greaves protested softly. "Even had he been here when the Ghost was running amok, surely one wouldn't expect a gentleman to fight without a weapon."

"True, but then I don't believe Mr. Makepeace has the right to wear a sword, has he?" Lady Penelope asked archly. "Only an aristocrat may do so."

"Quite correct, my lady," Winter murmured, unconcerned.

"Would you wear a sword if you could do so?" inquired Miss Greaves.

Winter bowed in her direction. "I believe that civilized men can find ways to settle arguments other than with the use of violence, ma'am, so no, I would not."

Miss Greaves smiled.

Isabel snorted under her breath, causing Winter to shoot her a sharp glance.

"What a noble sentiment," Lord d'Arque drawled. "But I fear that when I saw the Ghost accosting Lady Beckinhall, I had more concern for *her* welfare than a philosophical argument."

Lord Kershaw shot Isabel a pointed look. "I was not aware you were accosted by the Ghost, my lady."

Isabel lifted her chin and met his gaze directly. "I'm sorry I had not informed you, my lord."

"Your consideration becomes you, Lord d'Arque," Lady Penelope continued, oblivious. "I'm sure Lady Beckinhall must've been near mad with fear." Her brows knit in puzzlement. "How *did* you find yourself alone with the Ghost of St. Giles, my lady?"

Trust Lady Penelope to point out the most awkward part of the whole evening.

The earl arched an eyebrow and smiled. "You said once that you'd rescued the Ghost. Are you better acquainted than we know?"

Isabel cleared her throat. "I saw the Ghost sneak into a backstage passage and followed him."

"On your own?" Lady Penelope's lovely dark eyebrows nearly disappeared into her hairline. "How very brave of you, my lady, to confront him all by yourself. Did you mean to arrest him on your own or did you have another reason to follow him into a dark passage?"

"I fear curiosity overpowered my good judgment, my lady." Isabel smiled through gritted teeth.

"Alas, curiosity has killed many a soft-hearted pussycat," Winter murmured.

Lord d'Arque's eyes narrowed as he looked between Winter and herself. "Curiosity is certainly not worth your precious life, Lady Beckinhall. I trust you will rein in your more risky urges in the future."

"You're advocating prudence, my lord?" Isabel cocked her head skeptically.

"In the case of mad murderers, yes." The viscount looked quite grim. "I don't wish to cross verbal swords with you, my lady, but when I discovered you with the Ghost, you seemed . . . imperiled."

Isabel drew in a sharp breath. Up until now, Lord d'Arque had been quite gentlemanly tonight. He'd not breathed word of the embrace he'd found her in with the Ghost, only hinting vaguely that the Ghost had threatened her. She'd been grateful for his circumspection — if knowledge got out about a kiss, her reputation would become notorious.

Now she caught a hint of an implicit threat from the viscount. Nevertheless, she couldn't allow him to slander the Ghost. "I do not believe I was in any danger."

"No?" the viscount murmured.

"No," she replied flatly.

"How can you say that when the Ghost is a well-known murderer?" Lady Penelope cried.

"I believe the rumors of his murders are just that: rumors," Isabel said. "The Ghost has never offered me harm."

"How many times have you met him?" Mrs. Seymour asked.

Isabel felt heat climb her neck. "Once before. Now twice."

"Many in St. Giles have run into the Ghost here or there," Winter said vaguely. "From what I've seen of him, he seems almost gentlemanly."

Isabel glanced at him skeptically.

His mouth twitched. "And whoever he is, the Ghost never threatened me. Quite the contrary, in fact. He helped to capture a dangerous murderer last year."

"Then perhaps Lord d'Arque shouldn't have fought him," Miss Greaves said, sounding distressed. "Perhaps the Ghost is innocent of any crime at all and should not be pursued."

"Ridiculous." Lady Penelope snorted. "Your heart is too soft, my dear Artemis. Those who have done awful crimes do not deserve our sympathy. They belong either in bedlam or prison or hung from the gallows."

Miss Greaves went suddenly white.

"In any case, I am not of the same opinion." Lady Penelope shuddered dramatically. "Lord d'Arque's courage and wonderful skill with the blade saved us from a tragedy, I think."

The viscount bowed to Lady Penelope. "I thank you, my lady. 'Twas my pleasure indeed."

"There's one thing I don't understand," Lord Kershaw said.

Isabel raised her eyebrows. "My lord?"

"Why was the Ghost here tonight at all?" the earl asked. "I was given to understand that he frequents St. Giles — hence his name."

Isabel cleared her throat. "He did venture as far as Tyburn only a fortnight ago."

"He's a criminal. No doubt he planned to attack and rob all of us," Lady Penelope stated assuredly.

"Or he could've come to save someone," Miss Greaves said.

Lady Penelope rolled her eyes.

"Perhaps he was hunting," Winter said.

"Exactly as I said," Lady Penelope snapped.

"Your pardon, my lady," Winter said, "but I meant that perhaps he sought someone who had done him wrong — or had done wrong to those he protects in St. Giles."

"What a very odd idea," Lord d'Arque said.

Winter looked at him, his face expressionless. "Is it?"

Did the wretched man *want* to be discovered?

"I believe the opera is about to begin," Isabel interrupted. The orchestra had ceased their vague tuning noises and started into Mr. Handel's latest wonderful composition.

"Yes." Miss Greaves leaned forward eagerly. "There is La Veneziana. She's said to be the greatest soprano of our age."

"Is she?" Lady Penelope employed a pair of jeweled opera glasses. "But she's such a scrawny little thing."

Isabel peered at the soprano on the stage. She wore a spangled red and white dress, and even with her lack of height, she commanded the stage.

And that was before she opened her mouth.

As the high, sweet voice soared through

the opera house, Winter leaned close to Isabel. "Her voice is magnificent," he whispered. "One might even forget her scrawniness."

She turned and looked at him and saw that his grave dark eyes were sparkling with mischief. Her senses suddenly spun. Only half an hour before, those same eyes had stared at her through the holes of a mask with passion and yearning and a blunt hunger that had taken her breath away. She felt the exact moment, the sudden loss of footing, the sensation of falling, and knew sheer terror.

Dear God, this man could utterly destroy her.

It was past midnight by the time Winter made his way wearily back to the home. The opera house was less than a mile away from St. Giles, and it seemed a terrible waste of money to hire a hack for such a short ride. Not to mention that he had a soft, long sack containing his Ghost costume and swords slung over his shoulder — something he'd rather not have to explain to anyone.

A carriage rumbled by and Winter hastily skipped back as the wheels hit a puddle in the road and sent up a wave of foul water and mud. Splatters hit his legs and he looked down ruefully at the dark splotches on his formerly white stockings. Wonderful. Now he reeked of the sewers and would have to wash out his stockings before he went to bed.

Winter sighed. What matter if his new stockings were stained? The only reason he'd not lost the bet with d'Arque before it had even begun was because d'Arque had declared the night a draw. Lady Beckinhall had been chilly the rest of the evening, shooting him suspicious glances and making snide asides to him — when she would speak to him at all. Did she know he was the Ghost? She must at least suspect after that kiss . . . or did she? Surely such an outspoken woman would've taken him to task already if she knew he was the Ghost. And if she *didn't* suspect he was the Ghost, maybe she wasn't interested in Winter Makepeace at all. Maybe she just liked kissing masked men. Winter kicked a broken cobblestone so savagely it ricocheted with a *clang* off the bricks of a building.

Winter stopped to calm his breath. He never should've kissed her. Had he not been in the Ghost's disguise, he would've been able to resist her — or at least he hoped he would've been able to resist her. The truth was, the moment she'd touched her mouth to his, he'd been lost. Isabel tasted of heat and mint, honey and longing. When she'd stroked her tongue across his mouth, he'd come fully, achingly erect. With that one touch, she'd opened a Pandora's box of passion within him.

Prudence demanded that he stay as far away from the lady as humanly possible. He should take tonight as a warning and retire. Yet he knew he would not. Isabel offered the only hope that he might continue at the home. More, she offered a means to investigate d'Arque, for without Isabel and her "tutelage," he would not normally frequent the rarified circles that d'Arque swam in.

Winter snorted. He'd be lying to himself if he thought that was the real reason he would see her again. As important as the home and discovering d'Arque's involvement with the lassie snatchers were, he knew in his heart that he simply couldn't stay away from Isabel. She drew him. Whether it was animal instinct rising to the surface — the male part of him that he'd thought he'd long ago suppressed — or something more spiritual, it hardly mattered. He could no more leave the lady alone than he could stop breathing.

For a moment Winter leaned against the crumbling corner of a brick house. He was dangerously involved with Isabel. And he was chasing his tail with d'Arque. What had d'Arque's coachman meant when he said that it *wasn't* the viscount? Was some other "toff" behind the lassie snatchers? And if so, then why had Joseph Chance been clutching a scrap of paper with d'Arque's seal on it?

Winter straightened, shaking his head. He was probably making the whole thing too complicated. No doubt the coachman had been lying simply to save his master's — and his own — neck. D'Arque must be involved, otherwise why —

The sudden clatter of hooves on cobblestones made Winter draw back into the shadows, but there wasn't much room to hide.

Captain Trevillion came around the corner, followed by a half dozen of his dragoons.

Trevillion must've seen Winter, for he drew his gelding to an immediate halt. "Mr. Makepeace, St. Giles isn't a safe place to loiter late at night, as I'm sure you know."

"I do know." Since the dragoon captain had already spotted him, Winter emerged into the moonlight. "Out hunting old women gin hawkers, Captain?"

Trevillion's lips tightened and Winter

wondered how much ribbing the captain might've taken over his less-than-successful campaign to clean the gin makers and sellers out of St. Giles.

"I've bigger prey tonight," Trevillion said in a clipped voice. "The Ghost has been spotted near St. Giles-in-the-Fields."

"Indeed?" Winter arched a brow. "Then he is quite active tonight. I come from the opera, where he also made an appearance earlier in the evening."

"The opera?" One of Trevillion's eyebrows rose sardonically. "You move in rarified circles for a man who lives in St. Giles, Makepeace."

"And if I do?" Winter replied coolly.

A corner of the captain's stern mouth actually cocked up at that. "Then it is none of my business, I suppose." Trevillion jerked his chin at the bag over Winter's shoulder. "And do you always carry such a heavy load to the opera?"

"No, of course not," Winter said, his manner easy. "I stopped by a friend's house on my way home. He has donated some books to the home."

Winter kept his gaze steady even as he held his breath. If the dragoon captain asked to look in his bag, he would have no explanation for the Ghost's costume.

Trevillion grunted and glanced away. "See that you take care on your walk home, Makepeace. I've enough to deal with without you getting yourself murdered."

"Your worry for my person is touching," Winter said.

Trevillion nodded curtly and wheeled his horse about.

Winter watched until the soldiers were swallowed by the night. Only then did he sigh and let his shoulders slump.

The rest of the journey home was without incident. Twenty minutes later, Winter let himself into the home's kitchen. Soot, the black tomcat, stretched by the fireplace, his sharp claws scratching softly against the red brick hearth, before straightening and padding over to bump his big head against Winter's shins in greeting.

Winter bent to scratch the old tom behind the ears. "On the watch, are you, Soot?"

Soot yawned and returned to his warm hearth. A lamp had been left burning for Winter and he lifted it, turning toward the back stairs that would lead to his rooms under the eaves. Only as the light hit the corner by the stairs did he realize that he wasn't alone.

Joseph Tinbox sat slumped in a chair, his eyes closed, his breathing soft and regular.

Winter's heart twisted at the sight. Had the boy waited up for him?

He laid a gentle hand on the boy's shoulder. "Joseph."

Joseph blinked, his eyes sleepy and confused. Winter was reminded suddenly of the two-year-old toddler he'd found on the old home's front steps nearly ten years before. He'd been towheaded, his little face streaked with tears and with an empty tin box tied to his wrist. The little boy had sighed deeply when Winter had picked him up, and he'd laid his head against his shoulder with all the trust in the world.

Joseph Tinbox blinked again and sudden awareness came into his face. "Oh, sir, I was waitin' up for you."

"I can see that," Winter said, "but it's past your bedtime now."

"But, sir, it's important."

Winter was well used to what boys considered "important" — squabbles with other boys, lost spinning tops, and the discovery of kittens in the alley.

"I'm sure it is," he said soothingly, "but —"

"Peach talked!" Joseph interrupted urgently. "She told me where she came from."

Winter, who'd been on the point of chastising Joseph Tinbox for interrupting, paused. "What did she say?"

"I think she should tell you for herself," Joseph said with the solemnity of a lord in parliament.

"She'll be asleep."

"No, sir," Joseph said. "She's frightened. She said she'd wait for your return."

Winter arched his eyebrows. "Very well."

Joseph Tinbox turned and led the way up the back stairs.

Winter followed with the lamp and his bag, still over his shoulder.

The house was quiet this late at night, the lamp's light flickering against the plain plaster walls of the staircase. Winter wondered what secret would keep a child from talking for over a week. He eyed Joseph's narrow back. He had the feeling the boy had had to use all his considerable powers of persuasion to get Peach to talk to him tonight.

Joseph stepped out onto the dormitory floor. It was quiet here, too, but now and again faint sounds could be heard: a murmured word, a sigh, and the rustling of bedclothes. Joseph glanced over his shoulder at Winter as if to make sure he still followed, and then tiptoed down the hall to the sickroom.

When Joseph cracked the door, Winter

saw that the boy was quite right: Peach was wide-awake. The lass lay in the exact middle of the sickroom cot, the covers pulled to her chin, one arm around Dodo the dog. A single candle was lit by her bedside.

Winter looked at the candle and then Joseph.

The boy reddened. "I knows you say that a candle left burning might start a fire, but —"

"I don't like the dark," Peach said quite clearly.

Winter looked at the girl. She stared back at him, frightened but defiant, her brown eyes so dark they were nearly black.

He nodded and dropped his bag to the floor before taking the chair by the bed. "Many dislike the night. It's nothing to be ashamed of, Pilar."

"I likes Peach, if you please, sir."

Winter nodded and watched as Joseph Tinbox went to the other side of the bed and took Peach's hand. "Peach, then. Joseph tells me that you have something to say to me."

Peach nodded once, her pointed little chin digging into the white covers. " 'Twas the lassie snatchers what got me."

Winter felt his pulse quicken, but he remained calm and casual, as if what the girl had said weren't of great import. "Oh?"

Peach gulped and clenched a hand in Dodo's wiry fur. The dog twitched, but otherwise showed no sign that the girl was pulling at her fur. "I . . . I was on a corner by th' church."

"St. Giles-in-the-Fields?" Winter murmured.

The girl scrunched up her forehead. "I guess. I was beggin' there."

Winter nodded. He didn't want to interrupt the flow of Peach's story, but there was something he needed to know. "Were your parents there, too, Peach?"

Peach hunched a shoulder and turned her face away. "They're dead. Mama died of fever an' Papa of the cough, an' little Raquel, too. They all died."

Winter felt his heart contract. He'd heard this story so many times before — families devastated by disease and poverty, leaving orphaned children forced to somehow make their way in an indifferent world. It didn't make this hearing any easier.

"I'm sorry," he said quietly.

Peach shrugged and chanced a peek at him. "Papa asked Mistress Calvo to take me in before 'e died. I stayed there a bit. But Mistress Calvo said she already 'ad too many mouths to feed an' that I must leave."

"Coldhearted witch," Joseph muttered angrily.

Winter gave him a chastising look.

The boy ducked his head, but he still scowled.

"Please continue, Peach," Winter said gently.

"Well, I tried to find work, really I did, but there weren't any," Peach said. "An' beggin' wasn't much better. Kept 'avin' to move so's the bigger ones wouldn't beat me."

There were gangs who ran stables of beggars and others who preyed upon beggars by demanding a percentage of their daily take. A child alone like Peach wouldn't have stood a chance against the gangs.

"Tell him what happened then, Peach," Joseph Tinbox whispered.

The little girl stared up at the boy as if drawing courage from him, then took a deep breath and looked at Winter. "Th' second night I were at th' church, they got me. The lassie snatchers. Woke me up and carried me away. I thought" — the little girl gulped — "I thought they might kill me, but they didn't."

"What did they do, Peach?" Winter asked.

"They took me to a cellar. An' it were full of girls, it were, all sewin'. At first I thought it weren't too bad. I don't mind work, really I don't. Mama said I was a good 'elper. An' Dodo was there, though no one 'ad named her and they kept trying to chase 'er away."

The little girl hid her face in Dodo's neck as the terrier licked her ear. She whispered so low that Winter had to lean forward to catch her next words. "But they didn't feed us 'ardly anything at all. Jus' gruel and water and there was bugs in the gruel." Peach began to sob.

Joseph Tinbox bit his lip, looking worried and anxious. He hesitantly reached out a hand to the girl, but then stopped, his fingers hovering over her thin shoulder. He glanced at Winter.

Winter nodded at the boy.

Joseph awkwardly patted Peach's back.

Peach shuddered and lifted her head. "An' that weren't the worst. They beat us, too, if'n we didn't work fast enough. There was a girl called Tilly. They beat her so long she fainted, an' the next morning she weren't there no more."

Peach looked at Winter, her eyes huge and haunted. She didn't say the words, but somewhere in her childish mind she knew that her friend Tilly must be dead.

"You were very brave," Winter said to the little girl. "How did you escape?"

"One night," Peach whispered, "the lassie snatchers came with a new girl. They argued with Mistress Cook — she was the one who made us all work. But they left the door unlocked behind them. I saw it was open a crack. So me an' Dodo, we ran — ran as fast as we could, until they weren't shouting behind us no more."

Peach panted as if she were reliving the terror of running through the night, chased by people without mercy.

"Brave, brave girl," Winter murmured, and Joseph nodded fiercely. "Do you know where the cellar was, Peach?"

The girl shook her head. "No, sir. But I know it's under a chandler's shop."

"Ah," Winter said, trying to beat down his disappointment. There were dozens of tiny chandler's shops in St. Giles. Still, it was better than nothing. "What a smart girl you are, Peach, to make note of such a thing."

Peach blushed shyly.

"Now, I think it's to bed for the both of you," Winter said as he stood. He watched as Joseph gave Peach one last reassuring pat before following Winter to the door. Winter opened the door, but then paused at a thought. "Peach?"

"Sir?"

"What were you and the other girls making in the cellar?"

"Stockings." Peach said the word as if it tasted foul. "Clocked lace stockings."

Winter yawned widely the next afternoon as Isabel's butler let him into her town house.

The butler raised a disapproving eyebrow a fraction of an inch. "Lady Beckinhall is waiting for you in the small sitting room, sir."

Winter nodded wearily and fell into step behind the butler. He'd been on the streets of St. Giles at first daylight, searching for a chandler shop with a workshop in the cellar beneath, but so far he hadn't been able to find the place. Nor had anyone heard of a Mistress Cook. Peach may've been mistaken about the chandler's shop — she'd been ter-rified, after all, when she'd fled Mistress Cook and the lassie snatchers — or Mistress Cook may've moved her illegal workshop.

Of course, there was a third — more disturbing — possibility. Several of his usual sources of information had been quite nervous and cagey. Perhaps the denizens of St. Giles were too afraid of the lassie snatch-ers and Mistress Cook to give away their location.

The butler opened a yellow painted door, and Winter braced himself as he entered the small sitting room. Isabel was standing by one of a series of tall windows on the far side of the room, her face in delicate profile, the sunlight glinting off her dark glossy hair.

His chest squeezed hard, the first glimpse of her almost a physical blow. Usually repeated exposure to an irritant dulled the shock after a time. Yet with Isabel, each sight quaked him anew, seized both limbs and mind. He very much feared that repeated exposure to her merely made him crave her more intensely.

"Mr. Makepeace," she said as she turned toward him. She was silhouetted now against the bright frame of the window, her face in shadow. "I had wondered if you would come at all today."

Ah. She had not forgiven him for his tardiness the night before.

"Indeed, ma'am?" he said, cautiously advancing. "But I see that you already have tea laid." He indicated the service spread on a low table. "I did say I would arrive at four of the clock and it is, by the clock on your mantel, exactly that."

She stepped away from the window, and he saw by the look on her face that she was hardly pacified by his words. "A new — dare I say *unique* — circumstance for you, Mr. Makepeace."

"Isn't it time you call me Winter?" he murmured, trying another tack — he certainly wouldn't win any arguments on his punctuality.

"Is it?"

"It is." He smiled hard. "Isabel."

She frowned. "I don't —"

Just then, a tiny sob came from the direction of an ornately carved sideboard.

Both he and Isabel looked at the piece of furniture, and oddly her expression turned from anger to uncertainty. She started forward, but then stopped.

She made no further move, so Winter strode to the sideboard, crouched with one knee on the floor, and opened the door to the cupboard underneath.

A tear-stained face peered out.

"Christopher," Winter said, remembering the boy's name from the first time he'd come here. He glanced over his shoulder, but Isabel seemed frozen. He looked back at the boy. "Is it comfortable in that cupboard?"

The boy drew a velvet sleeve across his nose. "No, sir."

"Would you care to come out?"

The boy nodded mutely. Winter gently reached in and lifted the child in his arms. This close he could see that Christopher was a handsome boy of only four or five. Winter stood, still holding the boy, and turned to Isabel. Many women were naturally inclined to take a child from a man — the maternal instinct being considered stronger than the paternal, perhaps — but Isabel made no such move. Indeed, she'd folded her arms as if to keep herself from reaching for the boy.

Winter raised his eyebrows at her and she shook her head as if coming to her senses. "I'll ring for Carruthers."

"Want to stay," Christopher whimpered.

Isabel swallowed. "I . . . I think it best that you return to your nanny."

When had Lady Beckinhall ever been unsure of herself, let alone stuttered? There was something here that he was missing.

Winter cleared his throat and murmured to the boy, "I was thinking of trying one of those scones on the tea tray. Would you like one, too?"

Christopher nodded.

Winter sat on a settee by the low table, the boy on his knee, and gave one of the pastries to Christopher before selecting one for himself.

He bit into the flakey scone, eyeing Isabel's stiff back. She'd gone to stand by the window again, completely ignoring him and the boy. Strange.

"Good, isn't it?" he said to the boy.

Christopher nodded and whispered rather wetly, "Cook's scones are the best."

"Ah." For a moment they munched in companionable silence.

"Where is Carruthers?" Isabel muttered from across the room.

Christopher, who had been about to take another bite of the scone, lowered the pastry and gripped it between sticky fingers in his lap. "She doesn't like me much, most of the time."

Winter wished he could deny the boy's words, but he'd never believed in lying to children, and Isabel was across the room, obviously trying to pretend the boy wasn't in it. He leaned forward and poured some of the milk from the pitcher into a teacup and added a couple of drops of hot tea. He held the teacup up for the boy.

Christopher dropped the scone — onto the floor, regrettably — and took the teacup with both hands, eagerly drinking. When he lowered the cup, milky tea stained his upper lip. "She told me a corker of a story last night, though."

The boy looked wistfully at Isabel's back.

The nursemaid, a rather plain woman of middling years, ran into the room. "Oh, my lady, I am so sorry." She came over to scoop up Christopher from Winter's arms before turning back to Isabel. "It won't happen again, my lady, I promise."

Isabel still had her back to the room. "Please see that it doesn't."

Poor Carruthers blanched before curtsying and hurrying out the door with Christopher.

Winter thoughtfully poured himself a cup of tea.

"You think I'm mean," Isabel said.

Winter looked at her. Her back was straight, but he could tell by the bow of her shoulders that she'd folded her arms about herself as if to shield her center.

"I think," he said slowly, "that I would like to know who Christopher is and what he means to you."

There was a long moment of silence in which he wondered if she was going to answer him; then her voice came, steady and without emotion. "Christopher is my late husband's son."

Winter's brows knit, but before he could ask the question, she turned and paced to the middle of the room.

Her beautiful mouth was compressed into a straight line as if to contain some overwhelming emotion. "His mother was Edmund's mistress."

"I . . . see," Winter said, though he didn't. "And he lives here with you? Was this your husband's wish?"

She shrugged. "I never knew about Christopher and Louise — his mother — until after Edmund's death. He appears to have made no provision for them."

He simply looked at her, waiting, wishing the distance between them weren't so wide.

Isabel clasped her hands at her waist. "Louise came to me a month after I'd buried Edmund. She said that Edmund had set her up in a little town house, but with his death, the lease on the house was no longer paid. She had no money. I've since learned that she doesn't understand even the most fundamental basics of managing her funds. She asked me for some money and I . . ." She trailed off, shrugging again.

She looked so forlorn standing alone in the center of the room, her hands clasped as if for an unpleasant but necessary recital. "Isabel, come have some tea."

To his great relief, she came toward him, sitting on the settee opposite him, watching numbly as he poured her a dish of tea and added plenty of milk and sugar.

"You shouldn't pour for me," she said absently as she accepted the dish.

He gave her an ironic glance. "No one pours for me at the home, I do assure you."

"Oh." She took a sip of her tea. "Yes, of course."

He watched her uneasily. There was something here that he was missing. Something she hadn't yet told him. "Did you know your husband kept a mistress?"

She shook her head as she lowered the dish of tea to her lap, holding it there between both her palms. "No, not really, but I wasn't at all surprised. Edmund had been widowed for many years before we wed and he had his needs."

He took a sip of his own tea, grown cold now. "You told me before that you were faithful to your husband. It must have been a betrayal to find he was not to you."

Her look was cynical. "You forget that such things — a man keeping a mistress — are considered almost de rigueur in my circles. I was surprised to learn of Louise, but not shocked. Ours was not a love match, after all. Edmund always showed me the greatest courtesy. He provided for me even after his death. What more can a woman ask from a man?"

"Faithfulness. Passion. Love," Winter said too quickly. Too sharply.

She looked at him, her cynical expression

dissolving into curiosity. "Truly? Is that what you think marriage is made of?"

"Yes."

Her eyes shuttered. "Then it's a pity you've decided never to marry, Mr. Makepeace."

It was his turn to look away. "Why didn't you simply give Louise money?"

She circled the rim of her tea dish with one finger. "I did, but . . . she moves from place to place and my house is big." She bit her lip. "Christopher was little more than a baby at the time, and Louise seemed an absentminded mother."

"So you invited her to leave him with you?" he asked. "Your husband's child?"

She nodded. "Yes."

"That was very kind of you."

She wrinkled her nose. "It was no hardship, especially when Christopher was small. I hired Carruthers, made sure he was provided for . . ." Her voice trailed away uncertainly.

"But?" he prompted.

She darted an irritated look at him. "But as Christopher has grown, he has become oddly fascinated with me. He sneaks into my rooms, hides in the drapes and under the bed, looks through my dresser and jewelry box."

Winter blinked. "Does he take things?"

"No. Never." She shook her head firmly. "But still . . . why would he do it?"

"It's not such a mystery as all that," Winter replied. "You're the head of the household, beautiful, and charming. It's natural that he would be fascinated by you."

She smiled for the first time since he'd seen her that day. "Why, Mr. Makepeace, I do believe that's the loveliest compliment you've given me."

He refused to be distracted. "The boy bothers you. Why?"

He almost regretted his question, for her smile faded and she looked away from him. "Perhaps I'm not very fond of children."

Then why become a patroness of an orphanage? he thought, but fortunately did not say.

"Well." Isabel drank the rest of her tea, set the dish down, and then stood. "Lady Whimple — Lord d'Arque's grandmother — is having a soiree tonight at d'Arque's town house. I suggest we practice your dancing."

Winter sighed. Dancing had become his least favorite activity.

"That is," Isabel said sharply, "if you intend to attend tonight?"

Winter rose, looking down into Isabel's

bright blue eyes. The invitation to d'Arque's town house would provide a perfect opportunity to search the man's study and bedroom. "Oh, I wouldn't miss it for the world."

CHAPTER TEN

For two nights, the Harlequin's True Love
braved the dangerous alleys of St. Giles,
searching, searching for her love — only
to return home at dawn disappointed. But
on the third night, the True Love found
him, standing over the body of a thief
he'd just slain. "Harlequin, oh, Harlequin!"
the True Love cried. "Do you not
remember me?" But he only turned aside
and walked away as if he could neither
hear nor see her . . .
— from *The Legend of the
Harlequin Ghost of St. Giles*

Despite Winter's assurances that he would
attend Lady Whimple's ball, Isabel entered
Lord d'Arque's ballroom that night with no
real expectation of seeing him. Once again
he'd chosen to arrive separately, this time
with the excuse that his schoolmaster duties
kept him late.

She was growing tired of such stories — tired of thinly disguised lies from a man who was otherwise strictly moral. Was he ever going to confess to being the Ghost? Or did he think she was so stupid that she couldn't recognize him under the mask and motley? The longer he pretended that nothing was out of the ordinary, the more her ire rose.

Isabel took a deep, steadying breath and glanced about. The ballroom was extravagantly decorated, naturally, and painted an elegant crimson. Lord d'Arque appeared to have spent a fortune on hothouse carnations — his grandmother's favorite. White, red, and pink mounds were everywhere in the room, perfuming the air with the heady scent of cloves.

Viscount d'Arque stood next to his grandmother to receive their guests, and as Isabel drew abreast of them, she curtsied to the elderly lady. Lady Whimple lived with her grandson now. She was rumored to have been a beauty in her youth, but age had placed a hand on her face and pulled down, bringing with it the skin around her mouth, eyes, and neck. Her eyelids drooped on either side of the peak of her eyebrows, making her look as if she perpetually grieved, but the light gray eyes beneath sparkled with intelligence.

"Lady Beckinhall," the elderly lady drawled, "my grandson has informed me that you have championed the cause of the manager of some home for children."

Isabel smiled politely. "Indeed, ma'am."

Lady Whimple sniffed. "In my day, society matrons were more interested in romantic intrigue and gossip, but I suppose you gels of today are more saintly for your charitable work." Her tone made plain that saintliness was not an attribute to be prized.

"I hope I can bear up under the strain," Isabel murmured.

"Hmm," Lady Whimple replied skeptically. "D'Arque has also told me that he himself is interested in managing this home for urchins, but he does like to bam me, so I've taken no notice."

"Grand-mère." The viscount bent to buss his grandmother on the cheek — a move that seemed to irritate her. "I know the idea of my doing anything not immediately beneficial to myself is very strange indeed, but we must learn to move with the times." He slid a mocking glance at Isabel. "And if I should become bored with the home I can always hire others to oversee it."

Isabel narrowed her eyes at him. D'Arque was merely baiting her now with his show of fickle ennui. The only good thing about his mercurial moods was that he might grow bored of this "contest" and give up the whole thing before it was too late.

"Ha. Just as long as I'm not expected to join in this madness," Lady Whimple muttered.

"I concur, my lady," a masculine voice said beside them.

Isabel turned to see that Mr. and Mrs. Seymour had come up behind her in the receiving line.

Lord d'Arque smiled. "Have you thrown your lot against me as well, Seymour?"

"Not against you, d'Arque." Mr. Seymour chuckled while his wife looked bored. "But you must admit that Lady Whimple has it right when she says that 'tis odd to think of you as the manager of an orphanage."

"Odd or not, 'tis my ambition," d'Arque said stubbornly. "If only because several lovely ladies are patrons of the home. 'Sides, London has begun to bore me. Overseeing urchins might be terribly amusing."

His grandmother snorted.

"If you say so," Mr. Seymour replied, shaking his head ruefully. "And it'll do me no good, I wager, to try and dissuade you. So I'll turn to Lady Beckinhall instead and ask if she's recovered from her encounter with her friend the Ghost of St. Giles."

Isabel frowned, about to make some objection to his words, but the viscount spoke first.

"And here is my rival," d'Arque continued. "Points for arriving on time, I think."

Winter was there suddenly, close beside her, his presence overwhelming her senses. He wore the new suit with the tobacco waistcoat, and she was struck anew at how handsome he looked in it.

"My lord." Winter Makepeace bowed shortly to the viscount. He took Isabel's arm. "If you'll excuse me, your receiving line grows long."

Isabel barely had time to nod to the others before Makepeace dragged her away. "That was not well done."

"Wasn't it?" His air of aloofness was wrapped firmly around him tonight. "But isn't it rude for the host to make his guests wait so long in line?"

"Perhaps." Isabel faced forward as they began to move through the room. "But it was almost as rude to walk in and simply snatch me away without a greeting."

"I did greet the viscount."

She stopped and faced him. Why was he being so argumentative this evening? "But not me, nor Lady Whimple, nor Mr. and Mrs. Seymour."

His mouth tightened. "I believe they are about to begin a dance."

Her brows rose incredulously. "Is that an invitation?"

He looked at her and then away as if *he* had a right to be angry with *her.* "If you want it to be."

"I do," she said simply, because she did want to dance with him, in spite of her anger. In their lessons, he'd been surprisingly graceful, but more, despite his mood, despite his avowal to not become involved with her, she wanted to be with him.

Wanted *him.*

So when he held out his hand, she took it and let him lead her to the dance floor. It was a country dance, the steps brisk and intricate, but she was aware all the time of his large body, weaving around hers. The subtle slide of his shoes against the floor, the way he bent and leaned with an economy of movement that was elegance itself. She'd never seen a more graceful male dancer, and yet he drew no notice to himself; he was not at all showy.

When at last they halted, face-to-face, holding hands, he wasn't even out of breath, though her chest rose and fell faster than usual.

He looked down at her, his brown eyes

brooding and a little sad.

She cleared her throat. "Is there something you wish to say to me?"

He cocked his head, his gaze growing wary. "I cannot think of anything. If you want me to apologize for my abrupt dismissal of d'Arque, I shall not."

Her lips firmed. So he still meant to keep her in the dark about the Ghost!

"No?" She breathed deeply. "Then it's just as well that I referred to something else."

"And what is that?" He wasn't even looking in her direction.

She smiled tightly. "I referred to last night. You never did explain why you were so late to the opera that you missed an appearance of the Ghost entirely."

"I did try to tell you that there was an emergency at the home —"

"That seems to happen quite often," she snapped.

He finally looked at her, his eyes dark and expressionless. "Yes, it does. It is a home for children after all, and children are quite unpredictable."

"They aren't the only ones."

He stared at her a moment, then looked away. "You seem perturbed. Perhaps if I fetched a cup of punch, you would find yourself refreshed."

And he walked away before she could say she loathed punch.

He *walked away from her,* leaving her flat in the middle of the dance floor. Such a thing had never happened to her before. Good Lord, did he think he was the King of England? Did he think *she* was a common strumpet?

She smiled fixedly at a matron who was staring at her openly, and then turned and made her way off the dance floor. A few acquaintances called greetings and she wasn't even sure what she replied. Long moments later, she found herself back at the dance floor and couldn't remember how many times she'd circumvented the room. She had some choice words to say to Winter when he got back. Where was he anyway? It shouldn't take this long to get a cup of punch. Not unless he was avoiding her altogether or had snuck out of the ballroom like a coward . . .

Or snuck out to do some Ghostly activity.

The realization hit her. Her head jerked up as she scanned the ballroom. He was nowhere in sight. Surely he wouldn't . . . not *here.* But as she moved from room to room, she soon discovered that Winter Makepeace was not in any of the public areas.

Which, of course, left the family quarters.

Isabel was by the side of the ballroom. It took only a half-dozen steps to slip into a hallway. She'd been in Viscount d'Arque's house once before, and she remembered that a library lay at the end of this hallway. Swiftly she went to the door and peeked inside. One candelabra lit the room, but she could see it was empty. Another few minutes was all it took to discover that Winter wasn't anywhere on this floor.

Isabel took a deep breath and crept up the stairs to the next level. She was risking her reputation here. When she was merely searching the same floor as the ballroom, she could always say she'd become turned around if discovered. Harder to plead confusion when she was on another floor.

She cautiously opened a door and found a lady's bedroom, probably Lady Whimple's. Fortunately there was no lady's maid inside, but Winter wasn't here either. The corridor made a turn and she found herself in front of another bedroom door. Isabel took a deep breath and eased inside.

The room was decorated in masculine deep reds and browns — obviously Lord d'Arque's private rooms. A huge bed with hangings took up most of the center of the room with matching curtains hiding the windows behind. Various heavily carved pieces of furniture lay against the walls. Isabel crept inside and, feeling silly, looked under the bed. Nothing. She was just beginning to feel disappointed when she realized that someone was humming in the next room over. Good Lord, it must be Lord d'Arque's valet — and by the sound he was headed into the bedroom. Isabel stood, about to flee —

When a strong arm shot through the window curtains and dragged her into the alcove behind.

She gasped — a tiny sound — but he clamped a hand over her mouth. Her eyes weren't yet accustomed to the dark, but she knew who it was instantly. He bent, the nose of his long mask sliding against her hair as he whispered, "Hush."

She froze, her heart beating like a trapped rabbit's. He held her tight against his body as they both listened to the still-humming valet move about the room. His hand was hot even through the leather of his glove, and she could feel his hard chest against her back. Now her heart was beating quickly for an entirely different reason.

An entirely inappropriate reason.

There was the slide of what sounded like a drawer being opened from outside the curtains. His breath was even and deep. They might've stood in a tearoom so unaffected was he.

Outrage hit her hard and low. How dare he be so calm, so collected? How dare he make her nipples tighten, her belly warm? How dare he do everything he'd done to her — and never acknowledge a thing?

Her hands had been clutched around his arm, but now she let them drop. The valet started a new tune, something familiar, though she couldn't quite recognize it. She felt behind her, her fingers touching a smooth material laid tightly over his thighs. He shifted as if to retreat from her, but there was simply no space in the alcove. The floor-length window was behind them, the curtain in front.

He could not escape her. She stroked her hands behind her as far as she could reach in this awkward position. She could feel his thighs and the beginning curve of his hip, but no more. She balled her hands in frustration and then made the decision.

Swiftly she turned in his arms. He could've prevented her, naturally, but any kind of struggle would've alerted the humming valet.

She looked up and saw his eyes glinting behind the strange mask. Was he angry?

Curious? Aroused?

It hardly mattered. She was tired of waiting for him to acknowledge who he was. Tired of donning a false mask of gaiety when she was so much more — *felt* so much more — beneath. No one had ever noticed her mask. No one but him. If he couldn't or wouldn't make the first move, then damn it, she would.

She dropped to her knees.

He inhaled sharply. She felt the movement even if she didn't hear the intake of breath. Reaching up, she found the buttons of his fall and began working at them.

His hands clamped around her wrists, holding her hands still against his groin.

She looked up as the distinctive sound of a door opening and closing came to them.

Silence.

His head was tilted as he stared down at her, the muscles of his thighs hard and tight against her forearms.

She waited, but he made no move.

Slowly she leaned forward and whispered a kiss against the thin leather of his gloves. Opened her mouth. And bit his knuckle.

He jerked in reaction. Small, a movement barely noticeable, but she felt it nevertheless and grinned.

"Don't," he whispered, so low it might've

been a sigh.

Beneath her captured hands, he was fully erect.

Her words were soft but distinct. "Let me."

Slowly, as if fighting himself, he opened his hands.

She didn't wait to see if he'd change his mind. Bending forward, she tugged at his fall, dragging it open, feeling within, finding what she sought.

He was as she remembered: thick and heavy and oh so beautiful. She drew his cock out from his smalls and breeches and ran her fingers over the hot, taut skin.

He'd stilled as if ready to either flee or do battle, so her next movement was quick and sure: she opened her mouth and engulfed the head of his cock.

Above her, he whispered a word, short and harsh.

She closed her eyes, reveling in the scent of him, musky and sensual. He tasted of salt and man, and she suckled him eagerly, feeling the life beneath her tongue. She moved her right hand, stroking him softly but firmly, for she wanted to make this last. Wanted this to be something he never forgot as long as he lived.

His big hands moved hesitantly, touching

her hair, her cheeks, whispering over her forehead in the gentlest of caresses.

Tears pricked her eyes and she gasped, letting him fall from her mouth but still holding him in her hands. She looked up, the tears streaming down her cheeks, and felt him stroke one away with the fingertip of his glove. He made her feel . . . feel too much. Made her want things she could never ever have.

His perfect lips parted. "Isabel."

"No," she murmured, and returned to her task.

The silly tears wouldn't stop, and she tasted them as she licked along his length. He was so hard, so hot! She lapped against the head, flattening her tongue on the very tip, hearing him groan softly.

And then she took him once more into her mouth and sucked.

He rocked back on his feet as if pushed hard, and the reaction made her lips curve about him in satisfaction. She closed her eyes once again and let her surroundings, the sorrow inside her, and even the man himself drift away from her. She focused only on the penis within her mouth. So hard, so needy, so entirely at her mercy. She stroked dreamily along his shaft, finding each throbbing vein, delving in his breeches to palm his tight balls. And all the while sucking and sucking and sucking.

Until his fingers grasped her hair almost painfully and she knew he was at his point. She looked up then, desirous of seeing him in his throes, watching as his head rolled restlessly on his bunched shoulders, as his mouth opened, his bared teeth glinting in the moonlight.

The first spurt was strong and almost tasteless on her tongue, but the second brought salt and man and a groan from his lips as if he suffered untold agonies, and she flexed within in sympathy.

She sucked and sucked, gripping his hips to keep him within her mouth, for she'd worked for this prize and thus she'd earned every drop. When at last he began to soften, she relented and instead licked him gently. She was wet between her thighs, her body primed and ready to receive him, but he wouldn't be able to —

His sharp movement caught her by surprise. One moment she was on her knees before him; in the next he'd hauled her upright. The grip on her arms was painful and she gave a little yelp, her eyes widening as she saw —

Then his mouth was on hers, his tongue taking possession of her, his strength all around her. She sagged against him, ready for anything he would do . . .

And then he was gone.

Isabel blinked, touching her bruised lips with her fingertips. Dear God, what had she done? The rest of the world came rushing back — who she was and, more importantly, who *he* was. For the moonlight had shone upon his face before he'd kissed her and she'd clearly seen them sparkling in his eyes:

Tears.

Winter Makepeace stumbled to a halt in a dark corner and leaned against the wall, pushing his mask up and rubbing his hands over his face. It was wet with his tears. He'd cried like a babe. Dear Lord, what Isabel had done was earth-shattering. To be so close to another human being, for her to actually kneel before him and . . . It was as if another new sense had suddenly opened up. He'd *felt* her, felt the world around him, and at the same time knew that they were the very center, just the two of them. In that moment, the animal he'd tried to bind and cage for years had broken entirely loose and *roared.*

He gasped, straightening, and replaced his mask. Did she know who he was? Had she been doing *that* to Winter Makepeace or to the Ghost? If it was the Ghost, he'd feel like dying, but if it was Winter Makepeace, then she'd just changed everything. Beautiful, stubborn, terrible woman! What was she playing at?

He shook his head angrily. He could've stopped her. He was bigger than she, stronger than she. But he simply hadn't *wanted* to stop her. At that moment with her hands upon his fall, his cock straining for release, he might've died had she walked away and not touched him. It'd been all he could do to keep his hands off her as long as he had. And when she'd finally held him — her sweet, beautiful mouth on the rude head of his cock . . .

Merely thinking about it made him hard again.

Winter cursed and cautiously stepped away from the shadows. He should rejoin the ball, should put in an appearance, but he had other matters to consider now. Footsteps sounded on the stairs. Swiftly, he ducked inside a room. It was small and dark — a dressing room, perhaps — but there was a window, dimly lit by the moon. He picked up the bag containing his clothes, which he'd hidden here after changing into his Ghost costume. It'd been safer to search d'Arque's house as the Ghost, in case he'd been discovered. His plan had been to don his suit again and go back to the ball, but no more.

Winter crossed to the window and threw up the sash, looking out. He was over the back garden, the moonlight casting shadows on geometrically trimmed hedges, and he was still three stories up. Fortunately, though, there was a decorative ledge under each windowsill. Only three inches wide — if that — but it should be sufficient.

Five minutes later, Winter dropped to the ground. He bent to take out the scrap of paper he'd hidden in his boot and tilted it so the moonlight illuminated the scrawled words: *10 Calfshead Lane.*

A St. Giles address. He'd found the paper tucked in a drawer in d'Arque's desk. His lip curled. Was d'Arque so sure of himself that he'd written down the address where the children were held? It seemed unlikely, but Winter wasn't going to ignore the lead.

A woman's laughter drifted on the night wind. Winter stilled, looking toward the house. Light spilled out into the garden as a door opened and a couple came out. The lady was leaning toward her suitor, obviously quite enthusiastic about whatever might happen in a dark garden.

Winter picked up his bag and turned

away, running lightly on the mown grass, heading for the gate that would let out into the mews.

Had their tryst been merely a game for Isabel? A frivolous distraction during a frivolous ball?

Or had she known who he really was?

Isabel hurried back to the ballroom, hoping that her absence had not been missed, but she need not have worried.

Something else had the room buzzing.

People were crowding around a man by the entrance of the ballroom, shocked murmurs and cries coming from that area. Isabel was too far away to hear what the commotion was about. She started forward only to find Lord d'Arque in front of her.

She grasped his sleeve. "What is it? What's happened?"

He glanced distractedly down at her. "I don't know. I couldn't hear what he said. Come, let us find out."

The viscount led the way through the crowd and Isabel fell in behind him. As they neared the doorway, Isabel saw that the man was in dark green livery — d'Arque's colors were white and blue — and he was agitated. She was shocked to see tears streaming down his face.

"My lord!" the man cried as he caught sight of the viscount. "Oh, my lord, it's terrible."

People were exclaiming and talking, but quite distinctly, Isabel still heard someone say, "No." She looked to her left and saw Lady Margaret.

The girl's face had gone ashen.

Isabel started for her.

"What is it?" Lord d'Arque said, his aristocratic voice seeming to calm the man. "Tell me."

Isabel had reached Lady Margaret by now, and she touched the other woman's arm. Lady Margaret gave no sign that she saw her. Her large brown eyes were fixed imploringly on the servant.

"My master . . ." The footman gulped as fresh tears spilled from his eyes. "Dear God, my lord, Mr. Fraser-Burnsby has been murdered!"

A woman screamed. Lord d'Arque went white, his face as if graven from stone, and Isabel remembered that he was — *had been* — good friends with Mr. Fraser-Burnsby.

"I . . . I didn't know where else to go, my lord," the footman said before breaking down again.

Around them, the crowd's murmuring rose, but Isabel's attention was caught by

Lady Margaret. The girl swayed where she stood, her mouth open, but no words were emerging. She looked like a small child suddenly struck in the face.

Isabel caught her arm. "Don't."

Her words at least had the effect of making Lady Margaret turn toward her, though she stared sightlessly. "Roger . . ."

"No," Isabel whispered fiercely. "You mustn't. Not now."

Lady Margaret blinked dazedly. Suddenly she sank straight toward the floor without a sound. Isabel moved, but she wasn't nearly fast enough to catch the girl.

Fortunately, someone else was. Mr. Godric St. John swooped with lightning-fast speed, catching Lady Margaret before her head could hit the ground. He stared as if mesmerized down at the girl's white face.

Isabel touched his arm. "Come with me."

He arched an eyebrow, but without a word swung the girl's limp form into his arms. Isabel couldn't help noticing how easily he lifted her. Odd. She wouldn't have thought Mr. St. John, a man known for being a scholar of philosophy, was so strong.

But that mattered little at the moment. Isabel walked swiftly toward the side of the ballroom, away from the chattering crowd, away from all the potential gossips.

"Bring her in here," she instructed Mr. St. John. She'd found a little sitting room, just off the ladies' retiring room. Fortunately there was no one around — they'd all gone to see what the commotion in the ballroom was.

He placed Lady Margaret gently down on a settee, then looked at Isabel, speaking for the first time. "Is there anyone I can send for?"

"No." She knelt by the settee, touching Lady Margaret's cheek. The girl was moaning softly as she woke. She glanced at Mr. St. John. "Thank you for your help. It would be best if this isn't talked about."

His lips firmed. "You can rely on my discretion."

He glanced once more at Megs and then quietly left the room.

"Roger?" Megs whimpered.

"Shhh," Isabel murmured. "We can stay here a little while, until you've regained your composure, but we mustn't stay too long. Someone will notice your disappearance and put it together with Mr. Fraser-Burnsby's death and —"

"Oh, God," Lady Margaret gasped, and began to sob so hard her body shook.

Isabel closed her eyes for a moment, overwhelmed by the other woman's soul-deep grief. What right had she to intrude? What right to make the girl realize that she must not let anyone else know of her despair — and the love for Mr. Fraser-Burnsby that must've caused it.

But there was no one else.

So Isabel opened her eyes and sank down next to the sobbing Lady Margaret. "There, there," she said inadequately as she wrapped her arms around the girl. "You mustn't take on so. You'll become sick."

"I loved him," Lady Margaret whimpered. "We were to be married. He'd just . . . just . . ." She shook her head, as if unable to say the words.

Oh, why must there be death in the world? Despair and grief? Why must a sweet young girl have her hopes dashed, her dreams of a family and love crushed? It simply wasn't fair — wasn't *right.* When men plotted and schemed against each other every day, what kind of god punished an innocent girl?

Isabel's mouth twisted bitterly. Except Lady Margaret would never be innocent again. She'd drunk of the cup of sorrow and loss and it would mark her evermore.

Isabel inhaled. "Come. We can find your mother and —"

But Lady Margaret was shaking her head. "She isn't here. She's away at a house party in the country."

"Then your brother, the marquess."

"No!" Lady Margaret looked up dully. "He doesn't know about me and Roger. No one knows."

Isabel bit her lip. "We must be discreet, then. If the guests out there see you taking on so, they'll think the worst — *say* the worst."

Lady Margaret closed her eyes. "They'd be right. We are — *were* — in love."

Ah. Well, Isabel wasn't one to judge. In fact, she rather admired the other woman's simple statement: there was no shame in Lady Margaret's voice over her affair, only grief.

Which didn't change the fact that Lady Margaret would be ruined beyond repair if word got out that she and Roger Fraser-Burnsby had been lovers.

"All the more reason to pull yourself together," Isabel said gently.

"I don't care," Lady Margaret whispered.

"I know, dear, but in the future you will." Isabel's words were blunt to the point of cruelty, she knew, but they must be spoken. "Pull yourself together, my lady. We need to walk through that ballroom to your carriage. Now, who did you come with tonight?"

"My . . . my great aunt is staying with me

while Mama is away."

Isabel had a vague recollection of an older, gray-haired woman sometimes accompanying Lady Margaret. "Good. I'll get you settled in the carriage first and then send her to you."

It wasn't as simple as that, of course. It took another fifteen minutes and much cajoling on Isabel's part, but at last Lady Margaret was ready to step from the room. Her eyes were red-rimmed, her face puffy, and she'd obviously been crying, but at least she no longer was.

"You only need to get to your carriage," Isabel murmured as she accompanied the girl back to the ballroom. "A few steps and then you can relax."

Lady Margaret nodded mechanically.

"Good girl," Isabel said. They'd reached the ballroom. People were still crowded around the entrance, and no one seemed to pay them any attention, thank goodness. "We'll simply tell your aunt that you've a migraine. Can you trust your lady's maid?"

"What?" Lady Margaret looked dazed.

The girl probably hadn't thought how fast gossip spread among servants. "Never mind. Just get rid of your lady's maid as soon as she helps you to undress. Lock your door and rest."

"Lady Beckinhall, there you are!" The voice was masculine and to Isabel's side.

She turned, half blocking the speaker's view of Lady Margaret. Mr. Seymour stood with Lord d'Arque. Both men looked grave. The viscount was still a bit green about his mouth.

Mr. Seymour's color in contrast was hectic. "Monstrous, this business. The cold-blooded murder of a gentleman right here in London." He glanced curiously at Lady Margaret. "The news must've been overwhelming for those of delicate sensibilities."

Isabel sent the man a quelling glance. "Quite. And even for those who have normal sensibilities. Mr. Fraser-Burnsby was a very nicely mannered gentleman, and a favorite to many. He will be missed."

Lord d'Arque muttered something under his breath and abruptly strode away.

"They were close," Mr. Seymour said, nodding in d'Arque's direction. "Apparently were at school together. I had no idea. D'Arque keeps everything close to the vest, and Roger was friendly to everyone." He shook his head. "We'll find his murderer, never you fear, ladies. We've called in the dragoons and they're searching St. Giles even now. We'll have him in prison by dawn."

Isabel stared, perplexed. "Who?"

Mr. Seymour raised his eyebrows at her words.

"Who killed Roger Fraser-Burnsby?" Isabel asked impatiently.

"I beg your pardon, Lady Beckinhall, but I thought you'd heard," Mr. Seymour said gently. "Roger Fraser-Burnsby was murdered by the Ghost of St. Giles."

CHAPTER ELEVEN

The Harlequin's True Love wept bitter
tears, but she did not give up. The
next morning she went to consult a
wisewoman. "Ah!" said the wisewoman
when she'd heard the True Love's tale.
"The Harlequin has relinquished his soul
to the Master of the Night and can no
longer walk in the sunlight. He will spend
eternity thus, neither seeing nor truly
hearing those about him, bent only on
revenge. It is a thing not easily done, but
if you want to bring him back into the
light, you must first bind him with Love,
then wash his eyes with Sorrow, and
finally make him touch Hope . . ."

— from *The Legend of the
Harlequin Ghost of St. Giles*

The moon hung low in the night sky, a goddess guiding his way as Winter Makepeace
leaped from one rooftop to another half an

hour later. He landed on all fours, but was up at once, running lightly over the shingles. So close. He was so close now he could feel it in his veins. The children who needed his help were near and he would find and rescue them. He must try to forget the emotions that Lady Beckinhall provoked. Try to recapture and contain everything she'd let loose. He would be strictly Winter Makepeace with her, make sure she never met the Ghost again. If he could do that, then perhaps he had a chance of going on with his life exactly as he had been before. Because as wonderful as it was to be with her, he'd pledged himself to another path. *This.* This was what he was made for: bringing justice to those who had no voice.

Righting the wrongs that threatened to overwhelm St. Giles.

He jumped from the rooftop down to a wall and thence into Calfshead Lane. Number 10 was a crooked doorway with no light outside. Above his head, two doors down, a sign swung in the wind, but if it had something painted on it, it was too dark to see. Winter tried the door handle, and when that refused to give, he backed a pace and simply kicked in the door.

It swung back on rusty hinges, banging against the wall inside and rebounding.

Winter caught it with one hand and peered inside.

"Go 'way!" a shrill voice shouted from inside.

Winter peered into the gloom. A woman crouched just inside the door, a knife held in one wavering hand. "Dear God, 'tis the devil himself!"

"Where are the children?" Winter rasped.

The woman stared around dazedly. "Children? Ain't no children 'ere."

Winter advanced inside as she scurried back. "I know there are children here. Where are they?"

The woman's rheumy eyes opened wide. " 'Ave you come to take me to 'ell?"

Winter stared at her. A couple of shapes — dead or dead drunk — lay in the corner of the tiny room, but they were obviously adult. And the woman before him didn't seem capable of running a child work mill. "Is there anyone else here?"

She blinked, her mouth hanging half open. "Not since th' pawnshop owner left. That were months ago now."

Swiftly Winter went to the only door in the room and opened it. Beyond was a bare little space, the ceiling not even tall enough for a man to stand upright in it.

And it was entirely empty.

Disappointment tightened his chest. This was supposed to be the place where the children were kept. The address was the only clue he'd been able to find in d'Arque's bedroom. If it was false, then he was lost.

The *children* were lost.

From without came the clatter of hooves on cobblestones.

Winter ran from the room.

Outside, a phalanx of mounted men were bearing down. Trevillion's dragoons, holding torches high. In the flickering light, he just had time to catch sight of the sign two doors down as they galloped toward him.

On the sign was a candle.

"Halt!" the captain bellowed.

Well, he wasn't doing that. Winter leaped, grabbing hold of the corner of the building. He began scaling it, using only his fingertips and toes. The wall exploded by his face, sending shards of brick into his mask. Belatedly, the sound of the shot rang out.

"Come down or I'll shoot you where you are," Trevillion called.

Winter grasped the edge of the gutter and was up and over the roof just as another shot hit the tiles by his heels. He ran, flat out, unmindful of his footing, aware that the horses were following him below. He made for the crest of the roof, bounding

301

over it and down the other side of the house, tiles loosened by his feet clattering to the ground. The dragoons rounded the corner and galloped into the alley below. The leap across to the next house was too great; he couldn't make it without falling, and falling meant immediate capture.

"Give it up!" Trevillion shouted. "We have you cornered."

And indeed he could see that the dragoons were in the lane to his right as well. There were dozens this time. Why had Trevillion suddenly decided to bring out all his troops?

He had no choice now.

Winter backed two paces and began running along the roof edge, toward the house closest.

"You'll never make it, man!"

A shot rang out and he grunted as he leaped. Too far. Too far.

Winter hit the edge of the next building, the impact sending searing pain through his chest. His arms were outstretched, his fingertips scrabbling, and then he began to fall. He slid backward, the leather of his gloves tearing on the rough shingles.

And then he caught.

Only a moment he hung, whispering thanks to God, and then he pushed up with his toes against the house wall and was up and over the edge.

Running for his life.

The sound of gunfire boomed through the night.

Isabel gasped as if she'd been hit herself. She opened the carriage door and, hanging on to the strap inside, stuck her head out of the moving vehicle. "Drive toward the gunshots, John Coachman!"

Her coachman was usually an imperturbable man, but at her words he swung around, his expression alarmed. "Are you sure, my lady?"

"Yes, yes. Just do as I say."

Isabel shut the door again but stayed near the window, peering anxiously outside. As soon as she'd heard that the Ghost was being blamed for Mr. Fraser-Burnsby's murder, she'd known that Winter was in dire peril. He'd left before the news of the murder and thus did not know that this night of all nights he must not go out as the Ghost.

She cocked her head, listening anxiously. The shots had been very near. If it was Winter being shot at, then he must be close. Unless the shots had hit their target . . .

A shadow moved in the gloom.

Her heart jolted. Isabel flung open the

door even before she recognized the long-nosed mask. "Quickly! In here."

He leaped inside the carriage without waiting for it to slow. Isabel slammed shut the door and rapped on the roof. "Home, John!"

Then she sat back on the squabs and stared across at him. His gloves were torn, but otherwise his costume was in place. He was alive. Alive, alive, alive! Thank God and all the angels and any saint that happened to be hanging about. Dear God, she was so relieved!

He took off his floppy hat and threw it on the cushions and then began removing his gloves as if he weren't put out at all. As if she hadn't just died a thousand deaths looking for him. And — *and!* — were it up to him, she wouldn't have been looking at all because she wouldn't have known he was the Ghost. Rage — white, hot, and clean — began boiling in her breast.

"You idiot man," she hissed low. "Don't you know that every soldier in London is searching for you with orders to take you dead or alive?"

He simply sat, breathing hard, not saying a word as he tucked the gloves into his belt.

She wanted to shake him. "Winter!"

He stilled before tearing the leather mask

from his face and the silk mask underneath. His expression was forbidding, but she could see that his eyes were burning even in the dim carriage. "So you know."

"You weren't ever going to tell me, were you?" She laughed angrily, too many emotions swirling in her breast. "Of *course* I know. Do you think I can kiss a man and *not* know who he is?"

If anything, his face became more stern. "Then you knew earlier tonight when you . . ."

"Sucked your cock?" If she thought to shock him, she was disappointed.

He didn't even flinch. He simply watched her with eyes she could not read, no matter how she tried.

Her laughter this time verged on the hysterical. "Were you jealous of yourself, Mr. Makepeace, or did you think me such a wanton that I seek out gentlemen at balls specifically to —"

He never let her finish the awful words. He lunged across the carriage, grabbing her in strong arms, and hauled her back before she could even gasp. She lay across his lap like some thief's prize, entirely at his mercy.

Something inside of her quieted.

"Don't," he muttered, staring at her mouth. "I swore I wouldn't do this. Do you have any idea what you've done?"

He never let her answer; instead he caught her mouth with his.

Her mouth trembled and she sobbed, just once. For the scare he'd given her, for the grief Lady Margaret suffered, for all the hopes and dreams that would never be.

That was all behind her, though. Here, now, there was only this man.

So Isabel framed his face with her palms, accepting his kiss, opening her mouth for his tongue, reveling in his sudden aggression. He was big and hot beneath her, his kiss urgent with male need. It lit an answering fire within her. She wanted this man. Wanted him inside her. Wanted him *now*. She caught his bottom lip between her teeth and gently bit down and was rewarded by a feral growl from him. His wildness should put fear into her heart, make her more cautious. Instead it spurred her own feminine urges.

She slid her hands down his tunic, feeling the hard muscles of his chest beneath her fingers. He was like a young tiger, all muscle and passion, and she wanted to ride him — not to tame the beast, but to feel for a small moment all of his vitality.

She reached for his falls, and he groaned and canted his head to kiss her even more desperately. He was already erect beneath her fingers, alive and hot. She fumbled, her usually nimble fingers made clumsy with want, and for a moment she thought she might have to rip the cloth, so desperate was she for his bare flesh.

But the buttons finally gave way and she mewled into his mouth as she felt his hot skin against her palms. He was so hard it was like grasping iron draped in velvet: soft and yet unyielding. She caressed his flesh, squeezing gently.

When he began to urgently pull at her skirts, she lifted her bottom to help him drag them aside.

This was madness; this was delirium.

He found her bare hips under her skirts and flexed his hands against them, his kiss growing wilder. She felt his fingers stroking her buttocks, then circling her thighs.

They were in a carriage, for God's sake. She should end this now. But she didn't want to; it was as simple as that. So much was denied her — was it terrible to take what she could?

She threw one leg over his and straddled his lap, then reached under herself and found him again.

He tore his mouth from hers. "Wait."

"No." She looked him frankly in the eyes.

"I don't care if you spill at once. I need you inside me now."

His beautiful eyes widened and then narrowed. "You'll not always hold the reins, my lady."

She smiled sweetly. "Naturally not, but I do now."

And she placed him at her entrance. She was already so slick that he slid partially in at once.

He moaned and his eyes closed, his head tilting back against the carriage seat as if she were torturing him.

The sight made her wetter.

She slowly slid down on him, biting her lip, smiling with the pure pleasure of it, watching his face as she sat completely on him.

He swallowed, his throat working, the muscles of his neck standing out in strong relief. Gently, tenderly, she rose, careful to keep his cock inside her, the friction making her sigh with pleasure.

"Don't," he whispered. "I'll spill too soon."

"I know," she crooned, and licked his neck. "But you'll never forget this. Never forget me."

His eyes opened, his sensuous upper lip twisting in a snarl. "I'll never forget you no matter what."

And he grasped her hips firmly, shoving up into her. He was untried, inelegant, jerky, and rough — and she loved it.

She flung back her head and laughed breathlessly.

"Damn you," he growled, jamming himself in and out of her, his cock ruthless and hard. "Do it."

She looked down at him, a goddess supreme. "Fuck, you mean?"

His eyes narrowed to slits. "Make love. Make love to me. *Now.*"

His low words started her climax. She shivered, no longer laughing now, frantic to bring this to an end no matter what he cared to call it. She leaned against him, raising her bottom, slamming it down on him, making him gasp with the feel of their bodies working together.

She wanted . . . longed for . . . *something.*

She was a thing of pure desire. The carriage rocked through the streets and she rocked against him, amplifying the motion. Until stars glowed behind her closed eyelids. Until heat rose in a wave from her loins. Until she gasped, unable to draw breath, unable to think, able only to *feel.*

Him. In her.

And when he groaned, loud and long, she

opened her eyes to see him grit his teeth as he pulled her savagely against himself. His cock was buried deep and she swore she felt the pulsations, the searing heat of his seed, filling her to the brim. It went on and on, like nothing she'd ever felt before, as if he were marking her in some primitive way.

At last she gasped, finally able to draw breath, and fell against him like a flower wilting in the heat.

She licked her lips, sighing, and said, "They think you murdered Roger Fraser-Burnsby."

His arms tightened around her. "He's dead?"

"Yes." She braced her palms against his chest and pushed upright. His head was still tilted back on the seat and he watched her through half-open eyes. "Mr. Fraser-Burnsby's footman told everyone at the ball the news — after you left."

He didn't even blush at the implied censor. "I didn't murder Fraser-Burnsby."

She grimaced. "I know that. You were with me."

He lifted a brow. "Would you think the worst of me if I hadn't been?"

"No, of course not," she said impatiently. "You aren't capable of murder."

"You know me so well, then," he said

neutrally, though his tone was skeptical.

"I may not know everything about this" — she fingered the Ghost's motley tunic — "but I think I know *you* well enough to believe that you would never do murder no matter what guise you wore."

"Hmm," was his only comment.

"Will you tell me?"

He glanced out the window. They were nearing her town house. "Tell you what?"

She stroked down the tunic. "Why you do this?"

He looked back sharply at her. "Perhaps. But now I have to leave before your carriage gets to your house."

"What?" Isabel found herself deposited without ceremony on the seat opposite.

She watched, dumbfounded, as he put himself to rights with a few swift movements. "You can't leave! The dragoons are out looking for you."

He glanced up impatiently as he tied on the silk mask. "I have work yet to do tonight."

"Are you *insane?*"

His mouth quirked beneath the leather, long-nosed mask. "Perhaps, but I have to do this."

"No, you don't —" she began, but he'd already opened the carriage door and jumped outside.

Isabel looked around the empty carriage. His seed still seeped from inside her, uselessly, but then that was nothing new.

Megs sat in the window seat in her bedroom and stared out at the dark night.

Endless, endless night.

She'd wept when first she'd come home. She'd held it in until she could dismiss the maids and then she'd cried. Silently, relentlessly, until her eyelids had grown sore from the salt of her tears, until she lay, spent, openmouthed, lost. Now she was empty of tears and everything else.

Her mind turned in weary circles like an animal too long caged. Roger was dead. She'd seen him only days before and he'd been alive — gloriously alive, strong and intelligent and loving. But now he was dead.

Alive, then dead.

Perhaps they had made a mistake. Perhaps some other man — oh, wicked thought! — had been brutally murdered instead of Roger. Perhaps Roger had merely been wounded and the footman in his terror had rushed away to give the news too soon.

But no. They had retrieved his body. Her maids had told her so as they were undressing her. Gossip traveled so fast among the servants, and their voices had been almost eager as they had described how Roger had been laid, all bloody and lifeless, in Lord d'Arque's carriage and brought home. Lord d'Arque would not have mistaken someone else for Roger.

Megs had had to fight not to slap the maids — a thing she'd never done before. Instead, she'd ordered them away much too sharply. Lady Beckinhall would disapprove. Her tone had not been discreet, and her maids had looked at her curiously as they'd left.

Somehow Megs found it impossible to care.

Her left foot had gone to sleep. She shifted, the sudden prick of the pins and needles an unwelcome sign of life. As she shifted, something rustled. She felt underneath her and brought out a letter. Of course. It was from Hero, her brother Griffin's wife, and had been delivered as she'd been dressing for the ball tonight. She'd tossed it to the window seat to enjoy later.

Well, this was later.

Megs stood and lit a candle from the fireplace embers before returning to the window. Concentrating carefully, she lifted the seal and unfolded the piece of paper.

Dearest sister, Hero began. It was rather sweet. As soon as she'd married Griffin, Hero had taken to addressing Megs thus when writing. Megs almost smiled before she remembered. The letter was long and chatty, telling of a new wing on Griffin's country home, a difficulty with the cook, and the planting of apple trees in the garden. Hero saved the news that must've excited her most until the last:

. . . and, darling, I think you will be happy to hear my secret: I am increasing and over the moon with happiness. Your brother is delighted, but quite annoying sometimes with his concern over my welfare. I think he will be a proud papa come winter.

For a moment, Megs simply stared at the paper in her hand. Happy, she should be happy for her brother and for Hero.
She bowed her head and wept.

He'd just experienced the most wondrous thing.
Winter glided into the shadows of a doorway and paused to watch Isabel's carriage disappear around a far street corner. Had she felt the same? Was it as glorious for her

314

as it had been for him? Or was he like every other man she'd tupped before?

His upper lip lifted in a snarl at the thought before he even realized it. He refused to be just another lover to her — easily discarded, easily forgotten. He might be a mere schoolmaster and she a baroness, but together, just the two of them, he was a man and she a woman. Some things were fundamental.

He pushed aside the hot tide of jealousy. It would do him no good and he had other matters to attend to before he could confront Isabel again.

Winter turned and loped toward St. Giles. No doubt the dragoons would still be looking for him — the murder of an aristocrat was shocking business to those who held the power in London. They would put every soldier at their disposal into the hunt for him. Winter wondered who had really killed Fraser-Burnsby, but then he dismissed the matter from his mind. Probably it had been a robbery and the Ghost of St. Giles was a convenient culprit.

Twenty minutes later, he neared Calfshead Lane, moving cautiously. He glided past 10 Calfshead Lane without pause. The chandler's shop sign was beyond it. He'd caught the sign out of the corner of his eye

just as Trevillion's dragoons had borne
down on him. He must have missed it in his
previous searches of St. Giles. The sign was
small and worn — easily overlooked in the
myriad of signs that perched above the
streets and lanes of St. Giles like a flock of
dingy crows.

The door under the sign was narrow and
battered, but the lock on it was newer and
in better shape. Winter tried the handle and
was surprised when the door swung easily
inward. The room inside was pitch-black.
Winter waited for his eyes to adjust, but
there was no light at all. Closing the door
again, he retraced his steps back down the
lane to a shop where a small lantern hung.
He snagged the lantern and returned to the
tiny chandler's shop.

This time when he opened the door, his
borrowed lantern illuminated a wide but
shallow room. Narrow shelves and hooks
were placed haphazardly on the walls,
presumably for the chandler's wares. They
were all empty, though, and from the dust,
had been so for some time.

A sudden gust of wind rattled the door
and something scurried in the shadows.

Winter raised the lantern and saw a rat
trotting along the wall. The vermin didn't
even pause in its nightly round.

Behind the rat, though, was another door. Winter crossed to it and cautiously put his ear to the wood. He waited a beat, listening to his own breathing and the scrabbling of the rat, but heard nothing on the other side.

Backing a pace, he drew both swords, and set down the lantern on the floor where it would illuminate the room when the door was opened.

Then he kicked in the door.

He stood to the side, away from any attack from within, but none came. The room seemed empty.

Winter waited, listening. Nothing came to his ears but the wind. Cautiously, he sheathed his long sword, picked up the lantern, and advanced inside. There was a faint stink about the place that made the hair stand up on the back of his neck: urine, vomit, fear. The place was empty save for the skeletal remains of a rat and a few rags.

Something glittered in the cracks of the floor when he turned around, holding the lantern high. He bent and examined the dusty floorboard. A glittering thread was caught there. Carefully he prized it out with the point of his short sword and held it up to the lantern's light.

A silk thread.

He set down the lantern and drew off his

glove with his teeth. Then he picked the thread from the tip of his sword and tucked it into his tunic.

There was nothing here for him. They'd obviously deserted the place. Was the workshop permanently closed, or had they simply moved the children and their terrible work?

It didn't matter at the moment: either way, he'd failed this night. He hadn't saved the children.

Winter picked up the lantern and left. Outside, the wind had risen, blowing raindrops into his face. He listened, but there was no other sound save the creaking of the chandler shop sign overhead. The dragoons must be hunting in another part of St. Giles. He replaced the lantern and then bent into the wind, walking swiftly. Twice he darted into alleys or doorways to avoid another night pedestrian, and once he was forced to take to the rooftops to avoid the dragoons. He did all this almost mechanically, and it wasn't until he stood in a neat garden on the west side of London that he realized which way he'd taken.

He stood outside Isabel's town house, staring up at the windows in back, wondering which was her bedroom. Odd that his feet should instinctively take him here. She was not of his world. She wouldn't offer him tea and bread toasted over a fire like a housewife in St. Giles. Wouldn't understand the gaping hole of want that was St. Giles or the need that drove him to try to fill it. Or perhaps she would. Isabel had proven herself a more complex woman than he'd first thought.

But their differences were of no consequence anyway when what drew them together was as old as Adam and Eve. She'd brought out the beast, made him feel when he'd always lived in a cold, still world. No other woman had ever done that. No other woman ever would. She was the only woman for him now. Perhaps he ought to show her that.

As he stood there, the clouds opened up and the rain began in earnest. Winter lifted his face to the downpour, letting the rain wash away doubts and the failure of the night. Letting the rain wash him clean.

A light began to glow in a ground-floor window. It was well past midnight. Perhaps a maid was tidying up. Or a footman was taking an illicit drink of brandy. Or maybe Isabel couldn't sleep.

In any case, he'd soon find out.

CHAPTER TWELVE

The True Love thought long and hard
about the wisewoman's words. Then she
unbound her long, golden hair and,
plucking several strands, began to
braid them into a fine cord. And as she
did so, she thought of all the hours
she had known the Harlequin, all
the moments she'd longed for him,
and all the thousands of seconds
she'd loved him . . .
— from *The Legend of the
Harlequin Ghost of St. Giles*

This was stupid.

Isabel stared sightlessly at Edmund's carefully compiled library. Her late husband had enjoyed owning an outrageously expensive collection of books, though he'd hardly read any of them. Still, they were a source of solace for her on nights like this when sleep stubbornly stayed just out of her grasp.

She sighed and took a small book of erotic poetry off the shelf. It was rather banal — the poet had been entirely too pleased with his own wit — but perhaps that would make her drowsy. She'd already taken a hot bath and called for both warm milk and a glass of wine. Little else was left to try if she were to get any sleep this night.

Isabel settled into a deep leather chair before the unlit fireplace, tucking her slippered feet beneath the skirts of her wrap. The room was a bit chilly without the fire, but she wouldn't stay long enough to make it worthwhile to light it.

She opened the book, tilting it to catch the light of her candle, and began to read.

The poetry must've done its job, for she didn't know how much longer it was when next she looked up, and at first she wondered if she might be dreaming.

He stood there, only a few paces in front of her, still in full Ghost of St. Giles regalia.

Her heart leaped with foolish joy. Until now she'd wondered if it had only been a physical relief for him. Like eating a nice meal when one was particularly peckish. One was grateful and happy for the meal, but one never really thought about it afterward.

He'd come to her again unbidden, though.

At least she wasn't a steak and kidney pie to him.

"You're dripping on my hearthrug," she said.

He took off his mask, moving rather slowly. "You need new locks."

She raised her eyebrows and closed her book. "My locks aren't that old."

"Yes, but" — he drew off the silk mask as well and let it drop to the hearthrug — "they're more ornamental than useful."

She watched as he doffed his hat. "Does that explain how you got in?"

"Partially." He unbuckled his sword belt and carefully laid it on the tiles before the fireplace. "I would've gotten in anyway, no matter how good your locks, but I shouldn't have gotten in quite so easily."

He began unbuttoning his tunic.

"Perhaps I don't have anything worth locking away," she said a bit distractedly.

He shot her a sparkling glance from underneath lowered brows. "You have yourself."

Gratifying. Why did his plain words mean so much more than any number of flowery flatteries she'd received in the past?

Isabel bit her lip. "What are you doing here?"

He removed his tunic but didn't bother

322

looking up as he sat to take off his boots. "I want you to show me."

"Show you what?"

He did look up at that, one boot in his hands, and his eyes bored straight into her woman's soul. "Everything."

She swallowed, for she'd clenched internally at his single word. "What makes you think I'm interested in teaching you?"

He stilled and his sudden and complete lack of movement made her heart beat faster, as if he were a predator readying to pounce. "Do I presume?"

She licked dry lips. "No."

"Don't tease, Isabel." He bent to the other boot.

She watched for a minute as he stripped the boot from his foot and then unbuttoned his shirt. "Why do you do it?"

He shrugged and pulled the shirt over his head, revealing again that wonderfully muscled chest. "No one misses them."

"Who?"

"The poor, the children of St. Giles." He paused, his hands on the fall of his breeches, and glanced at her. She saw that there was an angry fire in his eyes. "They send soldiers in for the death of one aristocrat, yet dozens of children die every month and they care not."

She cocked her head to the side, realizing that she must speak cautiously. "Roger Fraser-Burnsby was a good man."

He nodded. "And had he beat his servants, seduced maidens, and neglected his elderly parents, his murderer would still be hunted just as ferociously."

"True." His anger was more fresh tonight. Something had happened after he'd left her carriage. "What would you have society do, exactly?"

"Care." He ripped open his breeches and stepped from them, standing only in his smallclothes. His erection strained at the thin material. "I want them to care just as much about a poor child as they do a gentleman. I want them to make sure every child is fed and clothed and housed. I want them to see that London cannot continue this way with people dying in the gutter."

"You talk revolution," she murmured.

"And if I do?" His hands clenched into fists. "Perhaps we need another revolution — one of necessity instead of religion this time. I'm tired of rescuing orphaned and abandoned children. I want to never nurse a child through the night and see him die before daybreak, never have to bury another baby, never have to search for abandoned children only to find . . ." He choked sud-

324

denly, looking away from her.

Ah, they were drawing closer to what made him so edgy. She wanted to wrap her arms around him but was afraid he would rebuff such compassion. "What happened tonight?"

His mouth twisted. "I've been hunting for a workshop run by child kidnappers who make the children labor with no money and little food. I thought I'd found the place tonight — finally, after days of searching — only to discover the shop empty. The children are missing again, either removed to another place or perhaps even killed to leave no evidence."

He looked at her, and she caught her breath at the anguish in his eyes. "Surely you alone cannot expect to bear this burden? Isn't that a sin of pride, Mr. Makepeace?"

Any other man would've scoffed. He closed his eyes instead. "Perhaps. Perhaps I have too much pride." His eyes flashed open. "But that does not excuse the fact that I was too late. I failed those children."

She bowed her head. How could she help him, this man who felt too intensely, who bore all the problems of St. Giles on his shoulders? What could she offer him except what she'd already given him — her body?

She carefully put her book down on the

table by her candle. Then she picked up the candlestick and crossed to the fireplace. The coals were already laid. She knelt and put fire to them.

"What are you doing?" he asked behind her.

She straightened and turned to face him. "I thought we might need some warmth for what you want."

Then she let her wrap drop to the floor. Underneath was her night rail, a frivolous thing of lace and silk. She drew it off over her head and kicked the slippers from her feet. That left her naked and standing before him like some aging Venus. She threw her shoulders back, smiling at him defiantly.

Except his gaze wasn't at all disappointed. In fact, he looked a little awestruck.

She wet her lips, noting that they trembled slightly, and walked toward him. "Now, what exactly do you want me to show you?"

"Everything," he repeated.

A daunting word, for with another man it might be hyperbole. With Winter Makepeace it was not.

"Then touch me," she said huskily.

His hand was broad and fit almost exactly over her left breast. He laid it there, hot and strong, then lifted to stroke around her areola delicately.

"Like this?" His words were rumbled, his gaze intent on what his hand touched.

"Yes, that's nice," she said.

His eyes flicked to hers. "Nice."

She smiled. "Pinch my nipple."

He squeezed gently — too gently.

"Harder."

He frowned. "I will not hurt you."

"You won't," she whispered.

The pinch this time went straight to her feminine valley. He cupped both hands over her breasts, fondling and pinching until her breath became heavy.

Then he stepped back.

"What are you doing?" she asked, a bit sharply, for simply standing there receiving his ministrations had been oddly arousing.

"Lie down," he said. "I want to see all of you."

She swallowed but carefully straightened her silk chemise on the hearthrug and lay down upon it. She watched as he stripped his smalls off and then knelt beside her, entirely nude.

The firelight made his skin glow, sent shadows and light dancing over the hard muscles of his arms and chest. His hair was tied back still, but as he paused to stare at her body, she reached up to pull away the simple black cord.

He looked at her, startled.

She smiled, threading her fingers through his straight brown hair. It was shoulder-length, and when it was about his face, he looked less civilized. "Fair is fair."

Was that a blush darkening his lean cheeks?

"I want to touch you," he said low. "Feel and . . . taste."

She nodded, the breath suddenly gone from her lungs.

He bent over her, bracing one arm by her face, like a wildcat claiming its prey. She watched as he lowered his head toward her breast and then had to close her eyes as his tongue touched her nipple. He was gentle, exploring. Was this how Adam had first touched Eve? With wonder, even reverence?

He closed his teeth suddenly on her nipple and she gasped.

He released her at once, looking at her through his hair. "I hurt you?"

"No." She bit her lip. "It's . . . it's fine."

He stared at her a moment longer as if analyzing her reaction, then bent toward her again. This time he lapped at her nipple with long, firm strokes before suddenly sucking the tip into his mouth.

She had to ball her fists so as not to make a sound. He might stop if she did and she'd really rather he didn't.

Abruptly he abandoned her breast, sitting back to stare at her once more. "I want to discover all of you."

"Then do so," she said, her voice a low purr.

He traced with gentle fingertips the curve of her breast, following it up to her armpit and over to her collarbone. Then he took her hand and pulled her arm over her head to stroke the underside of her upper arm.

She squirmed.

He darted a look at her. "It hurts?"

"No, of course not," she gasped. "You're tickling me!"

The corner of his mouth kicked up and his hand suddenly dove for the vulnerable skin just under her armpit.

"Oh!" She convulsed, giggling, and he flung himself on top of her to keep her from wriggling away.

"Lie still," he said sternly, his mouth only inches from hers.

"Then stop tickling me," she murmured. She watched his eyes, deep and mysterious, and felt the firm nudge of his erection on her belly.

His face grew grave again. He nodded and levered himself off her slowly, as if waiting to see if she'd flee.

She spread her arms wide on the hearthrug and smiled, though her lips trembled.

He watched her a moment and then backed, lowering his head to her belly.

She sucked in a breath.

"Tickles?" he murmured against her skin.

"No," she whispered.

"Mmm." His hum vibrated against her belly, making her toes flex.

He skimmed, openmouthed, around her belly button and then slowed as he explored her lower tummy with his tongue. When he got to her maiden hair, he paused.

"Your skin is so soft," he rumbled. "Teach me. I don't know what to do."

His breath warmed her maiden hair and his knuckles skimmed her cleft, making quite explicit what he wanted her to teach him.

She widened her legs and took a steadying breath. "There is a little nubbin, hidden at the top of my slit."

His fingers were there, parting, discovering. "Here?" He brushed gently against her.

She closed her eyes in reaction. "Yes. Just . . . touch me there."

He stilled and she could almost hear him thinking. Had his fingers been anywhere else, she might've smiled, but at the moment . . . well, it was simply beyond her. She waited, breathing in, breathing out and listening to the gentle crackle of the fire. Strange. Men had touched her there before, but they'd never asked *how.* If they'd been skilled, she'd rejoiced; if they hadn't, she'd directed them elsewhere. Male pride was such a delicate thing. Never had she thought to tell them how to touch her.

Tell them what she liked best.

Finally he moved, a tentative poke.

She bit her lip. "Could you . . . stroke?"

"Like this?"

She inhaled. "Softer."

"This?"

She laughed, but the sound was frustrated. He was too high, hadn't quite found the right place. Perhaps she should —

"Isabel," he suddenly breathed by her ear. "I have all night. Surely by dawn I can learn this. Please show me."

Well, that was quite frank. And oddly, he didn't sound as if his male pride was hurt. He merely sounded . . . curious.

If he could speak of this frankly, then so could she. After all, she was supposed to be the more sophisticated, the more worldly. Surely that meant she was more open to sexual exploration than he.

Didn't it?

Or perhaps there was an entire side to simple schoolmasters that she'd never seen.

She'd hesitated too long.

"Isabel."

"Just . . ." She reached down and encountered his hand, large and capable. For a moment her fingers entangled with his. "It's not very big, merely the size of a large pea, yet it's quite sensitive and must be stroked on the right spot."

She guided him. "There's a little hood — like your foreskin, I suppose. Touching it produces the strongest sensation, but I don't like to have it drawn back. If you'll merely . . ." She moved his middle finger in a gentle circle — the touch she liked the best. The touch a man had never done for her.

"This?" he asked quietly. She felt his breath on her thigh.

"Yes, yes, that's quite . . ." She gulped, for it really was a wonderful sensation, lying here, letting him pet her. But if he continued . . . "Perhaps we should move on now."

"Fair is fair," he said, and there was dark laughter in his voice. "I like watching you. I like smelling you."

Dear Lord!

She felt him spread her thighs wider, felt his chest settle between them, felt his arms wrap around her legs. His face must be directly over her femininity, watching as she . . .

His mouth settled on her parted labia and she gasped, unable to draw breath. His finger still worked her and —

"Am I hurting you?"

"No!" She grasped his hair and pulled him down, uncaring of modesty, sophistication, worldliness.

And he was a quick learner. He licked her, his tongue swirling against his finger, parting her folds, kissing her deeply, until she was blown over by the storm, hard and fast, panting, gasping, losing all sense of herself and time. She arched under him, vaguely aware that he'd grasped her hips to keep from being dislodged, racing with the wind.

When at last she opened her eyes, he was lounging beside her, waiting patiently, his hand placed possessively on her belly.

She stretched out a hand, tracing the lines around his mouth wonderingly. "Come to me."

She spread her legs invitingly and he mounted her. She took his hard penis in her hand and guided him to her wet entrance, watching from under drooping eyelids the tense expression on his face.

"Now," she whispered, "now."

He rose, moving on her, moving in her, but obviously holding back.

She arched her hips. "Let go."

"I don't want to hurt you," he said through gritted teeth.

"You won't," she whispered, smiling. "I want to feel you. Every inch of you." And she pinched his nipple between thumb and forefinger.

Something seemed to give way inside him. He reared and thrust into her, hard and fast. His eyes were locked with hers, determined, even as the orgasm took him, convulsing his features, tightening the tendons on his neck. He shoved into her one last time and held himself there, tight against her, as if to claim her forever.

Her smile wobbled. Forever wasn't for them.

For a brief moment in time, Winter's mind stopped. All of his concerns and worries, all of his *thoughts,* simply ceased to be. He lay on the hearthrug, his chest rising and falling rapidly, and only *felt* the relaxation of all his muscles. The wonderful warmth of the woman lying next to him.

Total peace.

Isabel ran her fingers across his chest, tickling a bit. "Winter?"

"Hmm?"

"How did you come to be the Ghost of St. Giles?"

He opened his eyes, thoughts and memories flooding back so quickly to fill his empty mind that it was nearly painful. "A man named Sir Stanley Gilpin taught me."

She propped herself up on one elbow, leaning over him. Her breasts swung gently at the movement, for a moment capturing his attention. "What do you mean?"

Her hair was still confined in an elaborate coiffure and he wished she would let it down. He'd never seen her hair down. "Sir Stanley was an old friend of my father's and the home's benefactor before he died two years ago. He was a widower. When I was young, he'd come to our house to debate religion and philosophy with Father. They were friends from childhood, but very different."

"In what way?"

He absently pulled a pin from her hair as he thought. "My father was quite serious."

She smiled. "Like you."

He nodded, finding and removing another pin. "Yes, like me. He worked hard all day and at night read the Bible and heard my brothers' and my lessons. What spare money he had he saved and eventually spent to found the orphanage. He believed one should devote one's life to helping others."

She folded her hands on his chest and laid her chin on them. "And Sir Stanley?"

"My father loved him as a friend but considered him frivolous. Sir Stanley liked reading novels and poetry, enjoyed the theater and opera, and even wrote some plays, although I have to say they weren't very good."

"He sounds a delight." Isabel grinned.

Winter blinked, his hands stilling in her hair. He'd never thought about it before. "I suppose he was. In any case, he was quite the opposite to Father, and I rather admired him as a boy."

He felt a familiar guilt. Father had been everything a good man should be — pious, hardworking, generous. In contrast, Sir Stanley had been flamboyant, full of extravagant ideas, not very practical — and oddly compelling to a young lad.

"It would be hard not to be attracted to such a man," Isabel said gently.

He glanced at her face. Did she know the guilt he'd felt? He shook his head, returning to the story. "Sir Stanley was a canny businessman in his youth. He made his fortune in stock in the East India Company. Later I believe he owned a theater. In any case, by the time I was seventeen, I was helping Father at the home —"

She suddenly pushed up on her arms. "You started so young?"

He'd succeeded in freeing one long lock of hair. He wound it about his finger as he watched her. "Yes. Why? Many have a trade by that age."

Her fine brows knit. "Of course, but" — she shook her head, thinking — "did you have any say-so in deciding to be the home's manager?"

"You mean did I ever think to desert the home and all the children therein —"

"Winter," she chided.

He gently tugged her lock of hair. "That's what it would've been."

She looked mutinous.

He found another pin and pulled it free. "If it makes you feel any better, I enjoy my work and always have."

"And if you didn't?"

"I'd do it anyway," he said gently. "Someone has to."

She sank to lie on his chest again. "But that's just it. Why must it always be *you?*"

"Why not?" A second lock of hair fell to her shoulders, and he pulled it forward to run it over his lips. Her hair smelled of violets. "Do you want to continue to argue the point or hear about how I became the Ghost of St. Giles?"

She wrinkled her nose adorably, and a single spark of pure, sweet happiness shot through his breast. "Ghost."

He nodded. "When I'd been working at the home for three or four months, an . . . incident occurred."

He concentrated a moment on untangling a pin from the hair at her nape, aware that he was stalling. She waited quietly, not moving or saying anything, and at last he met her eyes.

Winter swallowed. "I'd been sent to pick up a child who we were told had been orphaned by his father's death. When I arrived at the wretched rooms where he and his father had lived, he was being auctioned off by a whoremonger."

He heard the sharp intake of her breath. "Dear God."

Dear God indeed. He remembered the cramped room, the dozen or so adults crowded into it, and the terrified little boy. He'd been a redhead, his hair shining like a beacon in the midst of the wretchedness.

"What happened?" she asked, her low, throaty voice luring him back from awful memories.

"I attempted to stop the auction," he said

carefully, concentrating on the feel of her silky hair in his fingers. *Ham-handed fists. The searing pain of broken ribs. The boy's tear-stained face as he'd been led away.* "I was unable to rescue the child."

"Oh, Winter," she whispered. Suddenly she was kissing him, her soft hands cradling his face. "I'm sorry. I'm sorry. I'm sorry." Each word was a kiss against his face, neck, and lips.

He reached up and held her head still so he could kiss her properly: deep and frankly. The old pain mixed and merged with the present sweetness until at last it faded. A little.

He drew back reluctantly, stroking her cheek with his thumb. "Thank you."

She looked angry. "You never should've had to face such a thing when you were so young."

"What of the little boy?" he asked gently.

She looked even angrier. "He shouldn't have faced it either."

His smile was sad. Did she not know that such things happened every day in St. Giles? "In any case, Sir Stanley learned of the matter when next he came to call upon my father. He took me aside and asked if I would like to learn of a way to honorably defend myself. I said yes."

Sir Stanley had been about sixty at the time, and Winter remembered that his broad, red face, usually merry and smiling, had been quite grave.

He withdrew the last pin from her hair and ran his fingers through the thick locks, combing and spreading them. "Sir Stanley invited me to his house and for the next year taught me how to use the swords as well as various acrobatic maneuvers. He'd learned it all in the theater and he was a rigorous master."

"But didn't your father object?"

"He didn't know what I did there." Winter shrugged. "Father was busy with his brewery and the home. I think he was glad that Sir Stanley had taken an interest in me. Sir Stanley may've also slightly altered the truth about what I did at his home."

She arched one eyebrow. "*Altered the truth?* Winter Makepeace, did you *lie* to your saintly father?"

He felt his face heat. "It was wicked of me, I know."

She grinned and quickly kissed his nose. "I think I like you more when you're wicked."

"Do you?" He searched her eyes. "And yet I strive to control the wicked part of myself every day."

"Why?"

"Would you have me run the streets as a mad beast?"

"No." Her forehead wrinkled as she cocked her head, studying him. "But I think there is no danger of that happening. Doesn't everyone have a small bit of wickedness in them?"

He frowned. "Perhaps. But my wickedness is dark."

Her hair was gloriously free about her shoulders. "The dark pit you spoke of before?"

"Yes." He grimaced. "Maybe. You once asked why my sisters were not as affected as I by St. Giles. I think there is something within me that absorbs the evil in St. Giles. There are times when I see someone being hurt or when a child has been abused that I have the urge to . . . kill."

"But you don't."

He shook his head. "I don't. I battle that urge and I fight it down and I'm very careful to hurt only those who deserve it."

"Have you . . ." Her brows knit as she reached out and stroked a finger down his breastbone. "Have you ever had to kill anyone?"

"No." He inhaled beneath her touch. "I've come close, but I've always been able to refrain."

She wrapped her arm across his chest. "And I think you always will. You may fear the darkness in you, but I don't. You're a good man, Winter Makepeace. I think you absorb the evil in St. Giles, as you put it, because you feel so deeply."

The corner of his mouth quirked. "There are many who have accused me of not feeling at all."

She gave him a knowing look. "Because you've made sure to hide your feelings — your emotions. Not all of it is dark, you know. Some of it might be quite . . . nice."

Was she right? He stared at the ceiling of her library, thinking. She might be. Isabel was a very perceptive woman, he'd found. But if she was wrong, if he let go only to lose control altogether . . . no, the risk was too great.

"You don't have to decide now," she said. "Tell me about the harlequin's costume. Whatever made you don it?"

"It was Sir Stanley's invention," he replied, relieved by the change of subject. "He was the original Ghost of St. Giles, you see, in his youth."

"What?" She sat up again. "You mean there's been more than one?"

"Oh, yes." He smiled at her incredulity.

"In fact . . . Well, suffice it to say that the legend of the Ghost of St. Giles has been around for quite some time. Decades, at least. Perhaps even longer than that. Sir Stanley simply took the legend and made it real. His theatrical background gave him the idea for the costume. People see what they want to see, he always told me. If you present them with what *looks* like a spectral figure, supernatural and possessing powers beyond the earthly, they will believe that is what they see. It's a great advantage in a fight. Sometimes one's opponent is so frightened by the mask and costume that they simply run away."

"Mmm," she murmured as she traced a circle about his left nipple. He was aware that he was growing hard again and wondered if his randiness would dismay her. "And so by day you run the home and by night you run about St. Giles as the Ghost. Is that right?"

He frowned. Her tone was carefully neutral. "Not every night, naturally —"

"Oh, naturally," she said, her voice almost a growl. "I suppose you must sleep some nights. At least one or two nights a week."

He watched her, wondering what had aggrieved her.

She sighed and straddled his hips. He was

immediately distracted, aware that her moist, feminine parts were very near his cock. "And will you always do this?"

"What?" He brought his attention back to her face. She was scowling down at him. "Run about St. Giles?"

"What happens if you're wounded?" She leaned down, nearly nose to nose with him. Her breasts swung temptingly and he caught one in his palm, feeling the soft weight. "Winter! What happened after I brought you home wounded from St. Giles?"

He shrugged, stroking his thumb over her nipple. "I came back to the home and rested, like the other times."

"The other times?" Belatedly, he realized he'd made a mistake. His admission only seemed to drive her ire higher. "How many times have you been wounded?"

"Not often," he soothed. Oddly her anger did not dampen his ardor. Quite the reverse, in fact. But even as new to lovemaking as he was, he knew that he would have a greater chance of repeating their previous encounter if she were in a softer mood.

"How many?" she demanded, a nude fury.

"Three, perhaps four times," he replied, hedging the answer a bit. In reality, he couldn't count the number of times he'd been wounded as the Ghost.

"Winter!" She looked truly distressed. "You must find a way to quit this activity."

He arched his brows mildly. "Why?"

She slapped her hand down on his chest rather painfully. "Can't you see? Eventually you'll be maimed or even killed!"

"Hush." He caught her hand and brought it to his lips, caressing her palm. "I'm well trained and I've done this for years before I met you, Isabel."

"Don't brush my concern away like so much dust," she said, her other hand coming down equally painfully.

"Isabel." He caught that hand as well and thrust her hands out wide.

"Oof!" Overbalanced, she fell against him, her breasts pleasantly crushed to his chest. "Winter, you must —"

He was weary of this useless argument, so he pulled her closer and kissed her. For a split second she resisted. Then, with a sigh, she submitted to him, her mouth opening beneath his, giving him what he craved. He made a sound at the back of his throat, a deep groan that was almost a growl. She stripped him of civility — of reason and will. All he could do was feel and act. His beast came roaring to the forefront. His hips were already moving beneath hers, urging her closer. He was so hard he could feel the beat of his pulse in his cock, the ache of want, of sexual need.

He needed her.

As if she knew his extremity, she made a soothing sound. At some point he'd let go of her wrists. She petted him, like a child soothing a savage beast, and one part of him wanted to laugh at the thought.

Another only wanted to take what she offered.

Thankfully she lifted and grasped him then. He gritted his teeth at her touch and opened his eyes.

She was watching his face as she lowered herself to him. "Shhh. I have what you need."

Did she mock him? It hardly mattered. He'd accept her if she did or not — he was too far gone to deny either her or his own need.

She engulfed the head of his cock and it was such bliss he nearly came at once. He bit the inside of his cheek to prevent the ignominy. To prevent this ending too soon.

He watched her through slitted lids. She seemed lost in her own pleasure, her head thrown back, her lovely hair cascading down her back. Something savage and unthinking awoke at the sight. This was *his* cock she took within herself. *His* body that brought her such ecstasy. She might think this was merely a physical joining, but he knew far better.

He was claiming her as his. He'd warned her once before what this physical act meant to him. This was a union. This was forever. But he had enough wits about him to know she didn't yet see it as such. He must go slowly. Bide his time.

And in the meantime, if she wanted him only for the sex, then he would use it to bind her to him.

So he reached up with both hands and fondled her breasts in the way she liked, and when she gasped in answer, he knew a fierce joy. *This* woman. This woman was his.

He trailed one hand down her belly to the fine curls that decorated her nest. Searching, seeking that little nub that she'd shown him. Circling, softly petting.

She gasped again and opened blue eyes lit with erotic mischief. "Are you trying to steal the reins from me?"

Even with his penis buried deep within her, even moments from climax, he arched an eyebrow. "You have them only by my permission."

"Watch."

She placed her hands behind her on his legs, her back slightly arched, her pelvis tilted, and slowly rose. The position gave him a splendid view of his glistening cock emerging from her delicate folds. He stared, unable to tear his gaze away as she slowly reversed course and his ruddy flesh bore into her sweet hole.

"Good?"

He heard her laugh breathlessly and looked up. She was flushed, a sheen of perspiration making her face glow. She was a goddess.

A mocking goddess who meant to drive him insane.

He moved without thinking, grabbing her hips, arching, turning. She lay flat on her back and he rose over her, having kept his place even as he'd repositioned them.

He braced his hands on either side of her startled face and smiled — though it near killed him to do so. "Watch."

Her gaze went to where they were joined, and he felt himself flex within her. Slowly he withdrew, each inch a blissful agony, until only his head was still lodged within her. Then he reversed and slowly, deliberately, thrust back into her, all the way, until his hips met hers firmly.

He leaned down, his mouth less than an inch from hers. Sweet. Tempting. And whispered, "Good?"

"Oh, God, Winter," she moaned, her blue eyes dazed with arousal, "do that again."

"With pleasure," he ground out.

And he did. Again. And again. And again. Until she was moaning with each thrust and withdrawal. Until his chest was so tight he thought it might explode. Until she clawed at his buttocks and begged.

Until he could hold back no longer. Until he let the beast go and pounded into her, out of control, out of his mind with lust.

In the end, when he arched in a rictus of honeyed pleasure, she looked up at him with swimming blue eyes and gently touched his sweaty cheek with one finger, and he knew.

He'd poured his soul along with his seed into her.

CHAPTER THIRTEEN

Next, the True Love took a little glass vial and sat down and thought about what the Harlequin meant to her and how she mourned his loss from her life. As she contemplated these sad thoughts, tears dripped from her eyes and each one she carefully caught in the glass vial . . .

— from *The Legend of the Harlequin Ghost of St. Giles*

It was still dark when Isabel mounted the stairs back up to her bedroom, but it wouldn't be for long. She'd lain with Winter after they'd made love for the second time, dozing a bit, just enjoying being close. When at last he'd roused and dressed, she'd been loath to leave the library. Only the knowledge that the servants would find it strange that she'd spent the night there made her move. She trusted her servants — and paid them very well — but they were human, after all. No point in giving them more to gossip about than her actions with the Ghost of St. Giles already had.

It was too early for even the chambermaids to be up and stirring the fireplaces, but Isabel realized she wasn't alone when she got to her bedroom. A little form lay just outside the doorway.

Isabel paused and looked down at Christopher, perplexed. There was a carpet in the hallway, but even so, the floor could hardly be a comfortable bed. Yet the boy was curled on his side like a little mouse, his chest rising and falling gently in deep sleep. He looked so young in sleep, almost a baby. He had his mother's fair hair but she realized as she stared at him that his chin and nose were his father's. Someday he might look like dear Edmund.

Isabel sighed. No one was about, and no doubt poor Carruthers still slept peacefully in her bed in the nursery. There was no help for it. Carefully she bent and gathered the warm little body into her arms — a little awkwardly for she wasn't used to this. He made not a sound as she carried him to her bed, but she was somewhat surprised at the solid weight of him. Gently she laid him on the bed and pulled the covers to his chin.

"Is he here?" Christopher's sleepy brown

eyes blinked up at her. His words were so slurred, she wasn't sure he was entirely awake.

"Who?" she whispered.

"The Ghost," he said, quite clearly now. "I dreamed he came and saved you, my lady."

She felt the corner of her mouth quirk up. "Saved me from what?"

He rolled into a little ball on his side, his eyes unblinking. "I dreamed you were crying in a tall tower all alone and the Ghost came and saved you."

"Ah," she said, her brows knit. What an odd dream for the boy to have. "It was only a dream, Christopher. I'm quite all right."

He nodded, a huge yawn splitting his face. "Then he did save you."

She blinked at this logic and Christopher began to softly snore.

For a moment she simply stared down at him, this child who would not go away, no matter how often she chased him. This child who demanded her maternal love, withered thing though it was. Her eyes suddenly swam with tears. She remembered Winter's repeated words: *If not I, then who?* She'd never be as saintly as he, but perhaps this one, small thing she could do.

She bent and kissed Christopher's forehead before climbing into bed herself.

Winter gazed down at Peach as she lay sleeping and wondered what would be best to do with the little Jewess. He didn't have much knowledge about the Jews in London — other than that they were technically illegal and thus a very secretive society. He could convert the girl, he supposed, and raise her as a Christian, but something inside of him balked at the notion of changing her so fundamentally. Of teaching her to lie all of her life.

At least she looked better than when she'd first come to the home. Her cheeks were filled out and were a healthy rose color, and she even seemed to have grown taller, if that were possible in such a short amount of time. Dodo lay against her, protectively cradled in one of Peach's arms. The little terrier eyed him warily, but she wasn't growling.

Winter switched his gaze to the other human occupant of the narrow bed. "Joseph."

Joseph Tinbox, who had been lying with one arm flung over his head and one leg hanging off the bed, opened his eyes groggily. "Wha—"

"What are you doing in Peach's bed?"

Winter asked mildly.

The boy sat up, his hair plastered to his skull in back and sticking straight out in front. "Peach had a nightmare."

Winter cocked an eyebrow skeptically. "A nightmare."

"Aye." The boy was wide awake and using his most earnest expression now. "I couldn't let her sleep alone after that."

"And you heard this nightmare from down the hall in the boys' dormitory?"

Joseph opened his mouth and then realized the problem: It was simply impossible to hear anything but a full-out scream from the dormitory at the opposite end of the hallway. He lowered his chin, peering at Winter from under his thicket of hair. "She's been havin' nightmares, she told me."

Winter sighed. The protective streak in the boy was a good one, but . . . "You've reached an age, Joseph, when it will no longer do to sleep in the same bed as a female, no matter how noble the reason."

He could see by Joseph's confused look that the boy had no idea of what he spoke. Still, it was the sad state of the world that people judged others not by the best that they could be but by the worst thought in their own hearts.

"Come, Joseph. Peach is old enough to sleep by herself," Winter said, holding out his hand. "She has Dodo to protect her, after all."

Joseph Tinbox gave him a look full of ancient childhood wisdom. "Dodo is a *dog*, sir. She can't answer back when Peach wants to talk about the things that happened to her."

"I'm sorry, you're quite correct," Winter said. He cocked his head. "Is Peach telling you all about what happened to her?"

Joseph nodded, his lips pressed tight together.

"I see." Winter glanced about the room, his brows knit. "Then perhaps a compromise is in order. What if you were to sleep in the cot next to Peach's bed? That way you could still hear her should she wish to talk, but you would both get a better night's sleep, I think."

Joseph thought the matter over as solemnly as a judge before nodding decisively. "That'll work, I 'spect."

He climbed into the cot and gave a great yawn.

Winter picked up his candle and turned to go. It would be daybreak soon enough. But Joseph forestalled him with a question.

"Sir?"

355

"Yes?"

"Where do you go at night?"

Winter paused and glanced over his shoulder. Joseph was watching him with perceptive eyes for one so young.

In that instant, Winter grew tired of lies. "I right wrongs."

He expected more questions — Joseph was usually full of them and his answer was too obscure — but the boy merely nodded. "Will you teach me how sometime?"

Winter's eyes widened. Teach him to . . . ? His mind instantly balked at the thought of putting Joseph in danger. But were he ever to ask for an apprentice to his Ghost, he knew instinctively that he could find no one with more courage than the lad.

He hesitated before speaking. "I'll think on the matter."

The boy blinked sleepily. "Thank you for letting me stay with Peach, sir."

Some sudden emotion swelled Winter's chest.

"Thank you for caring for her, Joseph," he whispered, then shut the door.

"Where are we going?" Christopher asked eagerly the next afternoon.

"To a place with lots of children," Isabel

replied. "You might find one or two to play with."

Christopher looked uncertain. "Will they like me?"

Isabel felt a pang. On impulse, she'd brought Christopher with her to visit the home. He'd been so happy this morning when he'd woken in her room and she hadn't scolded him. She thought he might enjoy the company of other children his age, but what did she know about children, after all? Perhaps this had been a terrible mistake. Christopher looked so apprehensive! He'd had very little experience with other children, she realized. Louise took him away to visit her once in a while, but she had no family and her friends had no children. Christopher had been rather isolated all of his short life.

She wasn't his mother, but Isabel felt guilty anyway. She should've noticed before now how lonely the little boy must be. And she realized suddenly that it was because of Winter that she was more aware. He'd opened something up deep inside her. Made her look at her life and world with new eyes. The thought made her uneasy. What they had was by necessity destined to be a short-lived thing. Someday — probably someday soon — she would have to walk away from

Winter. Yet the more time she spent with him, the more she was seduced by his grave, dark eyes. Those eyes saw her true self like no one had before.

Isabel shuddered. When she did leave Winter, it would be like pulling off a layer of skin.

"My lady?" Christopher's high voice brought her back to the present. She looked at him and smiled reassuringly.

"I don't know if the other children will like you," Isabel answered, "but I expect if you are kind to them, they won't find fault."

Christopher looked only marginally re-assured and Isabel gazed out the window with a silent sigh. No doubt Winter would think her a fool for bringing Christopher.

But when she saw Winter half an hour later, he had other matters on his mind. He stood on the home's steps, talking to Captain Trevillion, the dragoon officer.

Isabel picked up her skirts when she caught sight of the men and quickened her step toward the home.

"Good afternoon, gentlemen," she called as she neared.

Captain Trevillion swept off his tall cap and bowed from his horse, but Winter only glanced in her direction before his gaze landed on Christopher's small form beside her; then he turned back to the captain. "As I've said, I didn't catch sight of the Ghost last night, Captain."

Isabel's heart constricted. Dear Lord, was the dragoon captain suspicious?

"Yet you were out late, the children tell me," Trevillion said smoothly, worsening Isabel's fears. "Surely you must have at least heard something."

"Gunshots," Winter said mildly. "But I make it a habit to walk *away* from the sounds of violence, I assure you, Captain."

Captain Trevillion grunted. "The Ghost killed a gentleman last night, as I'm sure you've heard. I trust you'll alert me or my men if you hear anything about the matter?"

"You have my word," Winter said gravely.

The captain nodded. "Good." He turned to Isabel. "I'm sure you've heard the news as well, my lady. St. Giles is not a safe place to be walking around at the moment."

"Your concern warms my heart as always, Captain." Isabel smiled and gestured toward Harold, standing a respectful few paces behind her. "But I brought my footman with me."

"Is he armed?" the dragoon officer demanded.

"Always," Isabel assured him.

"Well, see to it that you're out of here by nightfall," Captain Trevillion ordered as if she were one of his soldiers. He turned the head of his big black horse. "And mind your promise, Mr. Makepeace."

Without waiting for their replies, he trotted away.

"Why was the soldier mad?" Christopher asked as he watched the retreating dragoon. He'd spent the entire exchange staring in awe at the big horse and its rider's impressive uniform.

"He's been working all night," Winter said gently, speaking directly to the boy. "I expect Captain Trevillion is tired. Have you come to visit, Christopher?"

"Yes, sir." The boy shyly leaned into Isabel's skirts. "My lady says there are children here to play with."

"And so there are." Winter gave Isabel a rare, wide smile that made her heart speed. "I'm glad that Lady Beckinhall thought to bring you. Have you come to teach me more manners, my lady?"

"Not today, though I fear our lessons are far from over." She pursed her lips. "No, after last night and Mr. Fraser-Burnsby's" — she glanced at Christopher — "demise, I think the contest between you and Lord d'Arque must be temporarily suspended.

Which is just as well, considering that you abandoned the ball without bothering to say your farewells to anyone."

"Your mission is indeed a difficult one," Winter murmured as he opened the front door, leading them inside.

"Humph." Isabel rolled her eyes, but she was in far too good a mood to argue etiquette this afternoon.

"I believe Cook has made some fresh buns this morning if you would like some," Winter instructed Harold.

"Yes, sir." The footman headed back to the kitchens.

Christopher gazed after him longingly.

"Perhaps we will have some buns as well in a bit," Winter murmured. "But first shall we see what the boys' class is doing?"

Christopher looked both apprehensive and excited at the mention of children. He said nothing but took the hand that Winter held out. Winter glanced at Isabel over the boy's head, his eyes warm.

They trooped up the stairs to the classroom level above the dormitories. As they neared, Isabel thought that the schoolrooms were unusually quiet, and when they entered, she could see why: The children were having their afternoon tea. Long tables had been set up, and each child had before him a steaming mug and a plate with a bun on it.

"Ah, I see we're just in time," Winter murmured.

Heads turned at his voice and the children chorused — after a prompt by Nell Jones — "Good afternoon, Mr. Makepeace."

"And a good afternoon to you as well, boys." Winter gestured to an empty seat on one of the long benches, his expression somehow amused even if he didn't smile. "Would you care to join us, Lady Beckinhall?"

She gave him a look promising retribution and his mouth relaxed into a smile.

He sat beside her and poured her a cup of the strong tea, adding milk and sugar without prompting before passing it to her. Christopher sat stiffly across from them, without drinking his tea, although he eyed the bun on his plate hungrily.

"Is that your mother?" One of the boys who looked about Christopher's age leaned over and whispered the question hoarsely.

Christopher darted a cautious look at Isabel. "No."

"D'you got a mother?" the boy asked.

"Yes," Christopher asked. "Don't you?"

"Nope," the boy said. "Don't none of us do. That's why we live here in the home."

362

"Oh." Christopher thought about that for a moment, then picked up the bun and took a bite. "I don't have a father."

The boy nodded sagely. "Neither do I. D'you want to see a mouse?"

Christopher looked interested. "Yes, please."

"Henry Putman," Winter said without looking up.

"Yes, sir?" The boy who'd been talking to Christopher looked over innocently.

"I do trust that the mouse is *outside* the home?"

Henry Putman wrinkled his brow.

Winter sighed. "Perhaps after tea you and Christopher can take it outside."

"Yes, sir." Henry Putman nodded vigorously and gulped his tea. "Joseph Chance can help us, too. He's the one who saved it from Soot."

A third little boy grinned over his bun.

Five minutes later, Isabel watched as Christopher trotted off with his newfound friends. The rest of the children trooped out as well. Apparently this was the designated hour for outside exercise. "You're so good with them."

"It's not that hard," he said. "One only has to treat them with respect and listen."

"Easy for you, perhaps," she said. "I

always seem to be worrying about what I've said to him — or what I *haven't* said."

He nodded. "I suspect that all mothers worry about how they raise their children."

She frowned. "I'm not his mother."

"Of course not," he murmured. "Yet you brought him here today. The last I saw you with Christopher, you were ordering him from the room. What changed?"

"I don't know," she said. "Perhaps some of your saintliness rubbed off on me."

He looked at her, one brow raised.

She sighed. "Or perhaps I got tired of hurting both of us by pushing him away."

He smiled, sudden and warm, and she wondered for a moment if he would ever laugh in front of her. "In any case, I'm very glad you brought him."

She shrugged uncomfortably, glancing about the classroom. Besides the long table and benches, there really wasn't anything else in the room. The marble floor was bare, and a lone bookshelf held a stack of slates and one book — from its size probably the Bible.

She looked back at him. "This room is very spartan. Surely there are funds now to decorate the home."

Winter raised his eyebrows as if surprised at the comment. "In what way would you

364

change things?"

"It's hardly up to me . . ." She trailed off and shook her head. "A carpet, for one. The floor will be very cold in winter. A few framed prints or even paintings for the children to look at. Curtains on the windows . . ." She trailed off again because he was smiling at her. "Why do you look at me like that?"

"I only admire the way you know how to make a building a home."

She snorted. "It's not that hard."

They were alone in the classroom now and he pulled her suddenly toward him, kissing her hard and fast. He raised his head again while she was still gasping. "Will you make my home a home, Isabel?"

She nodded, uncharacteristically mute, for he looked so satisfied. With dread she wondered if his words meant something more.

Isabel didn't know whether to expect him that night. Winter had made no sign — aside from that single searing kiss in the children's classroom — that he wanted to see her again.

Wanted to bed her again.

But she found herself in her library late that night after everyone else in the household had gone to sleep. She wandered around the shelves, trailing her fingers over leather and fabric spines, picking up a book now and again, only to set it down a moment later. Bah! She was as pathetic as any debutante yearning for a glimpse of a potential beau's carriage behind her mother's sitting room curtains.

When at last she heard the whispered slide of her library door opening, she couldn't even feign nonchalance. She whirled to see him and then her heart thrilled.

He was wearing the Ghost's disguise.

"Do you *want* to hang?" she scolded as she crossed to him. "Is it some impulse to martyr yourself for the inhabitants of St. Giles? Is it not enough that you give yourself night and day for them — now you must give your very life?"

"I have no wish for martyrdom," he said mildly as he watched her fling his hat and leather mask to the floor and untie his cloak.

"You have a very odd way of showing it." She scowled at the buttons on his tunic — it was that or weep. "If they catch you, they'll hang you as soon as possible, and there won't be a last-minute rescue as there was for Mickey O'Connor. There *isn't* anyone to rescue you."

"Isabel." He caught her trembling hands,

holding them firm even when she tried to pull away. "Hush. No one is going to capture me."

She *wouldn't* cry in front of him. "You're not invincible," she whispered. "I know you think you are, but you aren't. You're simply flesh and blood, as vulnerable as any other man."

"Don't take on so," he whispered, brushing his mouth over her neck.

"How can I not when you insist on risking your life like this?"

He picked her up and set her on the library table, standing between her spread legs. "I must find these kidnapped children. They need me, Isabel."

"Everyone in St. Giles needs you." She grasped his hair with both hands. "Yet if you needed them, they wouldn't care one whit. Why, they chased and beat you when you saved the pirate!"

"Should I help only those brave enough to help me?" he murmured as he bunched her skirts in his fists. "Perhaps only save those who pass some test of charity?"

"No, of course not." She gasped as he ran his broad palms over her thighs. She glared at him. "Even if such a test could be devised, you would completely ignore it. You rescue the deserving and the undeserving without regard. You're a blasted saint."

He huffed a single chuckle, and she noted with one part of her mind that it was the first time she'd heard the sound.

Then his hands were *there* and all thought left her mind.

He leaned close, watching her as his clever fingers found her point and gently stroked. "I'm sorry to worry you. I'd do anything to make you happy."

She opened her eyes wide and reached out to stroke his cheek. "Even quit being the Ghost of St. Giles?"

But he didn't answer — either because he didn't want to disappoint her or because her fingers working on the opening to his breeches distracted him.

He turned his face toward her just as she found the last of his buttons and slipped her hand inside. He was hard and hot, as she knew he would be, waiting for her impatiently. She grasped him as she accepted his tongue into her mouth, his fingers into her depths, and moaned. She knew she must be drenching him, but she couldn't help it. It had never been like this before — so urgent, so sparklingly real. All the colors of her world sprang into focus when she was around him. He made her quicken.

He made her come alive.

She was at the edge, but she didn't want to fall without him. She broke their kiss, gasping against his lips, "Come inside me."

He kissed her openmouthed, ferociously, sliding his fingers slowly from her sheath. His hips nudged her thighs farther apart as he brought himself closer to her center.

He pulled back just enough to look into her eyes. "Like this?"

She slid the head of his cock through her moisture, closing her eyes for a moment as she rubbed him against her peak. Then she looked him in the eye as she pushed him down, until he was just inside her entrance.

"Yes," she breathed. "Exactly like this."

Then he was shoving strongly inside her, widening her, stretching her muscles, making room for himself. She clutched his shoulders and wound her legs high over his hips, balancing on the edge of the table, entirely open and vulnerable to him.

He grasped her hip, withdrawing slowly, his eyes focused on the spot where his flesh was connected to hers. She felt the slide of his cock, the controlled strength of his retreat, and knew if he continued so gradually, she might very well lose her mind.

"Faster," she demanded, squeezing his shoulders. "Faster."

He shook his head. "Don't rush it."

And he reversed himself, inexorably plowing back into her, inch by inch. Slowly.

Too slowly.

"Winter," she pleaded, twisting against him, trying to find purchase, trying to hurry him.

But he suddenly lifted her, taking her right off the table.

She squealed, clutching at him, afraid to fall.

He stood with her wrapped about him like a limpet; then he inhaled slowly, his chest rising beneath her.

"Slowly," he whispered, and covered her mouth with his.

For a moment she forgot everything. His tongue was in her mouth, warm and strong, masculine and insistent, and his cock was pushed so far inside her that her feminine lips were spread wide. He had her. He was in control.

Then he began walking, still kissing her, and the motion was exquisitely seductive, a subtle nudging, a sweet, rhythmic rocking.

She moaned against his lips. "Winter."

"Yes," he murmured back. "Yes."

Then her back was against a wall and he'd braced his legs. Suddenly he was driving into her. Fast. Hard. Deep. Exactly right.

His teeth were bared, his lips pulled back, and his eyes glittered as he stared at her. *"Yes."*

She knew it was coming, feared she would lose all control. She caught his mouth, biting his lip, sobbing as she fell apart. He was so strong, so broad, so *right.* She'd never find another man like him as long as she lived. He was ruining her for any other, and the pleasure of it was beyond bearing.

She felt his muscles stiffen under her, felt him bear into her, thrusting the small of her back hard against the wall. He held himself there as his penis pulsed within her and his mouth softened under hers.

He was murmuring something, whispering, muttering, even as his body continued to spasm, and so great was her own ordeal that it took her several moments to realize what he said. And when she did, she pulled back, staring in horror.

He looked just the same, sure of himself, confident of his own ability. "I love you."

Chapter Fourteen

Finally, the Harlequin's True Love bowed
her head, folded her hands, and prayed
to the saints and angels and God himself
for the Hope she needed to save the
Harlequin from the ugly fate that
entrapped him. She prayed until the
moon rose that night; then, gathering
the Cord of Love, the Vial of Sorrow,
and her own Hope about her, she
rose and ventured out, her path set
for St. Giles . . .
— from *The Legend of the
Harlequin Ghost of St. Giles*

Winter knew at once that he'd made a tactical error. He scrambled mentally, trying to think. There was no use attempting to cover his mistake. *When you've exposed a weakness in battle, attack, don't retreat.*

It was too soon, he knew that, but there was no help for it now. He inhaled, catching his breath, and then looked her in the eye. "Will you marry me?"

Her eyes were already wide in shock, but her sweet mouth actually dropped open at his words. If the situation weren't so dire, he'd have laughed.

"Are you mad?"

As it was, he couldn't prevent his lips from twitching. "Some would no doubt think me so."

"I can't marry you!" He'd been expecting the blow, but it still hit him hard. Her face was so incredulous.

At least he no longer felt the desire to laugh. "Actually, you can. I am not promised to another; you are not promised to another. I have said I love you, and you have already given yourself to me."

They were still locked together, his erection not entirely subsided. She could hardly deny the point.

And yet she still did.

"I didn't *give* myself to you," she huffed, her face still flushed prettily from their lovemaking. "This was a moment of sport, nothing else."

She was a strong-willed woman, older and of a rank far above his. If he let her, she would ride roughshod over him. This, then, was where he needed to make a stand, cast a template for how they would get along in the future.

For he fully intended to be with her in the future — legally and sanctioned by the church in public, intimate and loving in private. He'd never bared his soul to another as he had to her. She saw his animal and had the temerity to pet it.

He loved her.

And he believed she loved him — even if she wouldn't acknowledge it yet. If he let her drive him away, they would never find this bond again. They'd be what they were before: two souls drifting, alone and isolated, apart eternally from the people around them.

He couldn't live like that again, and he wasn't about to let her return to that limbo.

So he leaned into her, using his greater strength and height to emphasize his words. Oh, and the rude flesh still embedded in hers. That he used as well.

He shoved his hips against her, reminding her of what they had just done, and said, "I had never bedded a woman before you. I made that plain. Did you think I let you seduce me lightly? No, I did not. *You* made a deal with me the moment you gave me entry into your body."

"I made no such deal!" Her eyes were

angry — and frightened — but he would not let her make him back down.

"Precious Isabel," he whispered. "You made a deal with your heart, your soul, and your body, and you sealed it with the wash of your climax on my cock."

She blinked, looking dazed. He'd never used such words before, especially not with her, but their bluntness was necessary.

"I . . . I can't marry you," she murmured almost to herself. There were tears in her eyes and she looked trapped. He mourned the anxiety this was causing her, but he would not let her go. "You're nothing but a poor schoolmaster. What makes you think I'd marry you?"

Her words were hurtful and he did not appreciate them, so his answer was crude and to the point. He tilted his pelvis into hers, sliding his reawakening erection against her slippery passage.

She gasped, her eyes locking with his, and he saw the moment when all her specious arguments fell away. When her hope of getting out of this easily died.

"I'm barren."

The words were stark, bitter. He heard them and then he heard nothing else for a little bit. He watched her sad face, pinched and somehow lonely as she told him.

"By the third miscarriage, I knew I'd never birth a live child," she was saying when his hearing came back to him. "Despite all the doctors that Edmund brought in. But it was the fourth miscarriage that was the worst. I bled for a very long time, and the doctors said I was lucky to live, but there was a price, they said. I was damaged beyond repair internally."

She said it calmly, but he knew she must've screamed and wailed at the news, for his Isabel was not a passive woman. She would've fought the verdict. Would've died trying to have another child. Thank God that was impossible.

Winter knew that soon, very soon, he would need to mourn the children he would never have. At the moment, though, he had but one goal.

"It doesn't matter," he said when she stopped to draw breath.

She looked at him almost scornfully. "Of course it matters. All men want children of their blood, and I cannot provide you with them. I can never have what other women have so easily. A baby — *children* — are lost to me."

"It is a loss, I agree," he said, gently withdrawing from her.

He let her legs touch the ground, but

when she would've fled from him, he simply picked her up in his arms and crossed to a settee, settling her in his lap like a little child. He couldn't count the number of times he had comforted weeping children in this position.

"Winter —" she began.

"Shhh." He put his fingers to her lips. "Hear me out. I cannot deny that I would've liked to have made babies with you. A little girl with your hair and eyes would've been the delight of my life. But it is *you* that I want primarily, not mythical children. I can survive the loss of something I've never had. I cannot survive losing *you*."

She was already shaking her head, disobeying his wish to be heard. "You're a young man, Winter Makepeace. You may think now that you don't care about your own children, but that will change. Why do you think I've never remarried? Someday you'll look at me and see a barren hag."

Something in her voice made him look closer at her. Her eyes were haunted, her face ashamed. "Did your husband look at you thus?"

"No. No, of course not." But she closed her eyes as if she couldn't bear some awful pain. "Edmund was always the gentleman."

"And yet he left you with his bastard to

raise. Salt to rub in the wound."

Her eyes flew open, desperate and wild. She shook her head even as she said, "I'll not be a millstone about your neck keeping you from having a real family. I couldn't bear for any man to look at me like that again, but especially not . . . not you."

That small stutter at the end of her speech made his heart swell. He knew then that it was only a matter of time and patience. Probably quite a lot of patience.

"I'll never look at you in any way but complete admiration." He stroked her hair soothingly. "You will never be a millstone about my neck. Rather you're the sunshine that brightens my day." He swallowed. "Don't you see? You brought me into the daylight. You've embraced parts of me that I was never able to let see light. Don't make me retreat again into the night."

She closed her eyes wearily. "It isn't enough. Don't do this to yourself — to *me.* Not even my money will make it seem worth marrying me in a couple of years."

He winced at her jibe. Her husband had scarred her deeply and she was mentally fleeing in panic. He'd not talk her into this right now. Gently he set her on the settee and got up, fastening his breeches. "It's evident that I'll not convince you tonight.

You're tired and I confess so am I. Let us leave this for the morrow."

Naturally she opened her mouth again, but he was expecting that and covered her sweet lips with his own mouth, kissing her until she softened.

Then he lifted his head. "And mind, precious Isabel, not to insult me too badly when we argue, hmm?"

He made sure to leave swiftly — before she could say more.

"My lady!"

Isabel opened her eyes to see Pinkney standing hesitantly by her bedside.

The maid proffered a folded scrap of paper. "My lady, this note came for you just now. The lad who brought it said he'd been paid a shilling extra to run it here. I think it must be important, don't you?"

The events of the night before rushed back into her mind before she could brace herself against them. Winter's proposal. Her own shocked decline. They'd enjoyed each other. Why did he want to change everything? Isabel just wanted to stick her head under the pillow.

She groaned. "What time is it?"

"Only one of the afternoon," Pinkney said apologetically. Of course. The lady's maid thought it the height of elegance to sleep in until midafternoon.

But Isabel was awake now.

She sat up in the bed. "Call for some coffee, will you? And let me see that note."

The note was folded and sealed, and Isabel broke the wax as Pinkney went to the bedroom door to order the coffee. She opened the message and read:

L. Penelope accompanies L. d'Arque to the home this afternoon. I think they mean to send Mr. Makepeace away.

— A.G.

Artemis Greaves. The lady's companion was risking her position. Isabel was already crumpling the note as she climbed from the bed.

He'd said he loved her. She couldn't think about that now. Not if she were to help Winter.

"My lady?" Pinkney looked startled when she turned and found her mistress already up and rummaging through her chest of drawers.

"Never mind the coffee," Isabel said distractedly as she threw the note into the fire. "Help me get dressed."

Ten minutes later — an extraordinary

record for her toilet, which nearly sent Pinkney into fits — Isabel was climbing into her carriage.

"If I'd only had five more minutes, you could've worn your new green military jacket," Pinkney moaned.

Isabel settled against the squabs, watching impatiently out the window. "But that's just it — I didn't have five minutes more. I only hope the time we did take didn't delay us too much."

The London streets seemed even more crowded than usual today. Twice her carriage was brought to a complete stop by animals in the roadway, and even when moving they hardly progressed at better than a walk.

It seemed to take agonizing hours to reach the Home for Unfortunate Infants and Foundling Children, but it couldn't have been more than half an hour.

Still, Viscount d'Arque's carriage was already in front of the home when they stopped.

"Wait here," Isabel instructed as she tumbled hastily from her carriage.

She ran up the front steps and tried the door. Locked. She lifted the knocker and let it fall, continuing with the racket until the door was abruptly pulled open. Mary Whitsun stared out, her face pale. From inside the home, Isabel could hear raised voices.

"Come quickly, my lady," Mary gasped.

Without another word, she turned and fled back inside.

Isabel picked up her skirts and hurried after. Dear God, what was Lord d'Arque shouting about? For she could hear that it was his voice that was raised now.

She and Mary Whitsun entered the sitting room just as Viscount d'Arque swung around from the fireplace.

"— know this murderer, Makepeace! You've already admitted as much. Give over his name, then, if you please, or I'll have you before a magistrate on charges of hiding a thief and murderer."

The scene was dramatic. Lord d'Arque looked as if he'd not slept a wink since the news of his friend's murder two nights before. His face was haggard, his eyes glittered maniacally, and there were actual stains on his coat and breeches. Beside him, the Earl of Kershaw and Mr. Seymour looked grim, while Lady Penelope seemed like she might burst from the excitement. Miss Greaves, standing behind her mistress, sent Isabel a guarded look.

In contrast to the tense little group, Winter stood by himself on one side of the room, still and watching. His face was closed so tightly that Isabel had no idea what he might be thinking. She wished in that moment that she could cross to him and stand beside him.

Impossible.

"I've already informed you," Winter said in a quietly dangerous voice, "that although I've seen the Ghost of St. Giles, I have no idea who the man actually is."

"Oh, don't prevaricate, Mr. Makepeace," Lady Penelope exclaimed.

He turned slowly to her. "Whyever would I do such a thing, my lady?"

"Whyever indeed," Mr. Seymour said softly. "Perhaps the Ghost is a . . . friend of yours? Or perhaps something closer? You've been absent twice now when the Ghost has appeared — at the opera and the other night at d'Arque's ball."

Pure horror coursed through Isabel's veins. If Winter was discovered, he could be hung for Roger Fraser-Burnsby's murder, innocent or not.

She started forward instinctively. "La, Mr. Seymour! What a silly accusation. Mr. Makepeace may have been late to the opera, but he escorted me into Lord d'Arque's ballroom as Lord d'Arque himself can attest. Are you accusing Mr. Makepeace of being able to fly from d'Arque's town house to St. Giles in seconds? Besides, many people have seen the Ghost. Would you accuse all of them of some deceit?"

Lord Kershaw bowed in her direction. "Quite correct, my lady. You yourself have had several tête-à-têtes with the Ghost, haven't you?"

"Are you accusing *me,* my lord?" Isabel smiled sweetly. "Perhaps you believe that I helped the Ghost kill poor Mr. Fraser-Burnsby on some lark?"

"Naturally not," Lord Kershaw said. "But what a happy coincidence that you should show up just in time to defend Mr. Makepeace, Lady Beckinhall."

She arched an eyebrow, carefully not looking at Miss Greaves. "Coincidence? Hardly. I had an appointment to tour the home today with Mr. Makepeace."

"We stray from the matter at hand, gentlemen," the viscount snapped. He'd never taken his eyes from Winter this entire time. "You can at least tell me where I might find the Ghost, Makepeace."

Winter shook his head. "I am as much in the dark as you, my lord. I know you do not wish to hear this, but I am not entirely certain that Mr. Fraser-Burnsby was killed by the Ghost in the first place."

Blood flooded Lord d'Arque's face, turning it an angry red, but it was Mr. Seymour who spoke. "You forget, Makepeace. There was a witness. Roger Fraser-Burnsby's footman described the murder in some detail."

"So I've heard," Winter murmured. "Strange that the Ghost didn't kill the footman as well so as not to leave such a meticulous witness."

"I haven't the time for this," Lord d'Arque said. "I'll find the Ghost of St. Giles with or without your help, Makepeace. Captain Trevillion tells me that his men nearly had the Ghost the night of the murder. It's only a matter of time before we catch him."

He started to go, but Lady Penelope forestalled him. "But what about your gift, my lord?"

Lord d'Arque stopped and turned, a strange, fierce smile on his face. "How could I have forgotten? I think it obvious from the last several days that I have won our little contest of gentlemanly manners, Makepeace. We can wait until Lady Hero and the Ladies Caire return to town to settle the matter, but it occurs to me that it might be easiest to present the ladies with a decision already made."

"I've told you I won't give up the home," Winter said flatly.

The viscount nodded judiciously. "I remember. But I wonder if you might be . . . persuaded . . . if I were to offer you an incentive."

Winter stiffened. "If you think money can sway me —"

Lord d'Arque waved a hand, cutting him off. "Nothing so crass. I have the best interests of the home — and its children — at the forefront of my mind always. I hope you do as well?"

Winter only narrowed his eyes.

"What do you mean?" Isabel asked sharply. She didn't like Lord d'Arque's oily platitudes. The viscount always worked for himself, which usually wasn't a problem, but with his grief over Mr. Fraser-Burnsby's murder driving him, d'Arque seemed entirely out of control. "What are you proposing, my lord?"

Lord d'Arque raised his eyebrows. "I only wish to bestow a naval commission on the eldest boy at the home, whomever that may be. I do think that you and Mr. Makepeace would approve of such a move?"

Isabel inhaled. A naval commission for a boy had to be bought and therefore usually went to the sons of gentry or nobility. To give one to an orphaned boy of no provenance was simply unheard of. What was

Lord d'Arque up to?

And then she realized: the eldest boy at the home was Joseph Tinbox.

A muscle in Winter's jaw flexed. "You're most generous, my lord."

The viscount inclined his head. "Thank you, I know. But of course there is a stipulation to such generosity. I can give the commission only if I am appointed the manager of the home. You would have to agree to step down gracefully. Right now."

Isabel was already stepping forward, shaking her head. "Now see here —"

But Winter spoke over her, his voice level. "Do you give your word of honor as a gentleman, my lord, that you will do this thing as soon as I leave?"

Lord d'Arque looked almost surprised. "I do."

"Very well. I agree."

"Winter," Isabel whispered, but he was already striding to the door, his features set.

She turned to Lord d'Arque, walked right up to him, and stood on tiptoe to hiss into his smug face, "I think I hate you right now."

Then she went after Winter.

Winter already had a soft bag out and was packing by the time Isabel found him five minutes later in a wretched little room at the top of the home's five flights of stairs.

She immediately yanked out the shirts he had placed into the bag. "What do you think you're doing?"

He paused, looking weary and patient and long-suffering, blast him. "I'm packing."

"Don't you dare act the martyr with me," she hissed angrily. "You're playing right into Lord d'Arque's hands."

"I know," he said. "It doesn't matter."

"Of course it matters!"

"I base my decision upon what I think best, not upon his reasons for making the offer."

"But you can't think it best for you to leave the home. For Joseph Tinbox to leave you and go to sea."

He turned back to the bag. "And yet I do."

She glanced desperately about the room, searching for something, anything, that would make him change his mind. The room was small and spartan, tucked under the eaves. It obviously had been meant for a servant, not for the manager of the home. The thought made her even more angry.

"Why?" she demanded. "Why must you always seek martyrdom? You dress as plainly as you can, you risk your life for those who would hunt you down and kill you if they could, and you even choose the most humble of the bedrooms in this home to sleep in."

He arched his eyebrows, surprised. "What's wrong with this bedroom?"

"It's a servant's bedroom and you know it," she snapped irritably. "And don't try to change the subject."

He knelt to reach under the bed. "I wouldn't dream of it."

She set her hands on her hips, aware that she was losing all traces of elegance in her agitation. "Lord d'Arque thinks you have something to do with the Ghost of St. Giles —"

"And he's right." Winter drew out his Ghost costume from under the bed.

"Are you mad?" she hissed as she hastily turned and locked the door.

"You keep asking me that," he murmured.

"With good reason!" She clenched her fists, rallying her argument. "He's only doing this out of revenge. He has no true interest in the home — it's a whim for him. How do you think he'd manage it?"

"Not well," Winter said as he folded his costume and tucked it into the bag. "But it's a moot subject: d'Arque has said himself that he'll hire a manager for the home."

"And do you truly think anyone could do as well as you?" she asked desperately.

He shot her an ironic look. "It's hard for me to answer that without sounding conceited, but no, I don't think anyone will do as well as I."

She threw out her hands. "There you are. You admit it yourself — you cannot leave the home."

He shook his head. "I admit only that my replacement will most likely not do as well as I. But the home won't suffer much overall, I think. Nell Jones has been with us nearly as long as I have. We have more servants now, a cook, and the Ladies' Syndicate to guide us. I believe the home will find a way to muddle through without me."

"The home might muddle through, but will you?" she asked softly.

He paused and slowly looked at her. "What do you mean?"

"It's everything to you, isn't it?" She gestured about the room. "You've said so yourself time after time. St. Giles, this home, the children in it. They're your life's work."

He nodded. "True. I'll have to find another life's work, I suppose."

Her heart swelled with grief. For him. For all he would not admit. "Where will you go, Winter?"

He shrugged. "I have resources. I'll find another place to live."

"And will you find another boy like Joseph Tinbox?"

"No," he said softly, regretfully, as he placed a few books in his bag and shut it. "No, Joseph Tinbox is quite unique."

"You love him, Winter," she said. "You can't let him go to sea."

He closed his eyes for a moment, and it was suddenly there in his face: all the grief, all the pain she'd expected before.

Then he opened them and his eyes were resolute. "It is because I love Joseph that I will let him go."

CHAPTER FIFTEEN

The Harlequin's True Love kept to
the shadows as she searched the
narrow lanes of St. Giles for the
Harlequin. Twice she fled
dangerous-looking men, and once
she had to hide in a doorway for long
minutes as a group of drunken louts
stumbled by. But no matter how hard
her heart beat in fear, she did not give
up her search for the Harlequin . . .
— from *The Legend of the
Harlequin Ghost of St. Giles*

Word travels fast in an orphanage. There
are plenty of ears, plenty of watchful little
eyes, gathering information and eager to
spread it.

All the boys were at lessons. The minute
Winter walked into the classroom half an
hour later and saw Joseph Tinbox, he could
tell that the boy had already heard.

"Joseph Tinbox, may I have a word with you?"

The other boys stared at Joseph as if watching a condemned prisoner. Joseph swallowed and rose from the bench he'd been sitting on. As the boy walked toward him, Winter noticed how tall he'd become. He could almost look Winter in the eye. Only a year ago he'd been less than shoulder height. Now he was nearly the height of a man.

Joseph stopped before him and said low so the other boys wouldn't hear, "Do I have to?"

The sound of his voice cracking on the last word nearly made Winter's heart split in two. "Yes, you must."

Joseph lowered his head and preceded Winter out of the classroom. Winter looked about the hallway for a moment, nonplussed, before leading Joseph to the sickroom. It was empty at present — Peach had felt well enough to join one of the girls' lessons.

He shut the door and looked at the lad. "You've heard, I take it?"

Joseph Tinbox nodded mutely. "Some toff wants to send me off to sea."

Winter sat on Peach's empty bed. "He wants to do much more than that, Joseph.

He's promised to buy you a commission in His Majesty's Royal Navy."

The grandeur of the name alone was enough to make Joseph's face break with awe — for a second, no longer. Then he resumed the stubborn expression he'd had upon entering the room. "I don't want to go."

Winter nodded. "Of course not. You've never been to sea, and you will be leaving everyone — and everything — you know. But I'm afraid that doesn't matter. You're going to have to be as brave as you've ever been, Joseph, because you simply can't pass up this opportunity."

Joseph's eyes darted to the bed Winter was sitting on. "Can't. Peach needs me."

For a second Winter wanted to close his eyes and admit defeat. Most of the children came to the home alone — bereft of both kin and friend. So it was doubly wonderful when they chose to make a friend. To become close to another child who was alone and lonely in the world. Joseph had, out of pure altruism, become Peach's protector . . . and friend. To tear apart such a bond was surely a sin.

But that didn't matter.

Winter leaned forward, his elbows on his knees. "Most of the boys who leave here become apprentices. You know that, don't you, Joseph?"

Joseph nodded warily.

"If they are lucky, after years of service, they might become a cobbler or a butcher or a weaver. All honest trades. All good enough lives."

Winter spread wide his hands. "But you, Joseph, *you* have the opportunity now to become more. You can become a gentleman. Once in the Royal Navy — as an *officer,* not a simple seaman — if you work hard, are brave, and act smart, you can rise far above any of the other boys here. Someday you might be captain of your own ship."

The boy's eyes widened before he bit his lip. "But the sea. What if I don't like the sea, sir?"

At that Winter smiled, for it was the one thing he was certain of. "You will. You'll learn how to sail a ship, listen to the stories of the older boys and men, and travel to wondrous lands far, far away from England. Joseph, it will be the most amazing adventure of your life."

For a moment Winter was sure he'd won the match. Had convinced Joseph that this decision was the best for the boy in the long run.

Then Joseph Tinbox's eyes landed on the

pillow, still indented from Peach's head. He stared for a moment, his eyes uncertain, and then he looked at Winter, resolute. "I'm sorry, sir. It sounds a treat, really it does, but I can't leave Peach by herself."

Winter swallowed. He felt so weary, so tired of fighting and fighting without cessation. Without even a little rest.

But that was maudlin self-pity.

"I'm sorry, too, Joseph Tinbox, for I fear you've mistaken the matter." He rose from the bed. "I'm not asking you to go. I'm ordering you."

Isabel sat down to a solitary dinner late that night in her private dining room. A fire crackled in the hearth behind her, there were fresh flowers in a small china vase on the round table, and Cook had made an excellent clear soup, but she seemed to have no appetite.

She'd been invited to a soiree, but with Winter leaving the home and Mr. Fraser-Burnsby having been murdered, she simply didn't feel like an evening out. Poor Lady Littleton would no doubt have a very sad showing tonight — if anyone came at all.

"Shall I bring in the fish, my lady?" Will the footman asked.

"Please," Isabel sighed absently.

She was still greatly disturbed both by Winter's proposal and his defection from the home. For that was what it was, no matter his reasons or how righteous he might think them. He'd given up the home for one child's future. That simply wasn't morally correct, no matter his arguments or how much Joseph Tinbox meant to him.

And then there was an even greater worry: Where *was* he? Pinkney had been excited to tell her earlier that the Ghost had been seen fleeing over the rooftops of St. Giles as Trevillion's dragoons gave chase. For all she knew, he might be lying gravely wounded somewhere — or worse, dead.

Isabel shoved her wineglass aside. She suddenly felt quite nauseous.

"My lady, you have a visitor," Butterman intoned with deep disapproval from the doorway. "He insisted that he see you, otherwise I would have turned him away. As it was —"

"That's fine," came a masculine voice from behind the butler.

Oh, thank God!

Winter stepped around the man. "Thank you, Mr. Butterman."

The butler stiffened. "Just Butterman, sir."

Winter nodded gravely. "I'll be sure to remember."

"Mr. Makepeace," Isabel said, "won't you join me for dinner?"

He turned to her, brows raised as if surprised — what else had he expected her to do, throw him out? — and said, "That's very kind of you, Lady Beckinhall."

Well. Weren't they terribly formal considering just last night he'd been thrusting into her wildly in her library?

"Please ask Mrs. Butterman to set another place," Isabel instructed the butler.

He left, somehow making his retreating back look shocked — as only a very good butler can.

The minute the door shut behind him, Isabel leaned across the polished mahogany of her dinner table and hissed, "Where have you been? There have been reports of the Ghost running about St. Giles all evening. I didn't know if you were risking your neck — *again* — or if the sightings were all false."

"Oh, some of them were real enough." He pulled out the chair opposite hers and sank into it. "I had a time of it, avoiding Trevillion and his men tonight."

Maddening man! He simply wouldn't give up — no matter how dangerous the streets of St. Giles were for him now. She didn't know whether to throw her cutlery at him or leap across the table and kiss him.

Fortunately, Mrs. Butterman bustled into the dining room at that moment with a maid in attendance. The silence between her and Winter seemed pregnant, but the housekeeper didn't appear to take any notice of the atmosphere.

Once Winter's wine was poured, Mrs. Butterman nodded to herself with satisfaction, asked if there would be anything else, and left the room. They were now alone, as Will the footman was still gone — presumably retrieving the fish course.

Isabel took the opportunity to ask, "Did you find the workshop that employs children?"

Winter shook his head, looking bitterly disappointed as he lifted his wineglass. "Only rumors. There're stories of children living in an attic somewhere, but my source — who I had to pay double to talk — was vague on the location. I tried one likely building but was driven away by the dragoons from another. I'll have to try again another night."

His going out night after night with the dragoons hot on his trail scared her to bits.

"I'm sorry," she said cautiously, "but can you at least wait a couple of nights before you go out again?"

He cast an impatient glance at her from

under his brows. "Every day I can't find them, those children are abused."

She shook her head and frowned down at her plate, wishing she could help in some way before another thought occurred. "And Joseph Tinbox? How did he take the news of his commission?"

"Not well." Winter sipped the wine, for a moment closing his eyes at the taste. Then he opened them and looked at her. "I had to tell him he has no choice but to take the offer. When I left, he was no longer speaking to me."

"Oh, Winter." She started to reach across the table to touch his hand when Will opened the door.

Will served the fish in silence, darting a nervous glance between Winter and her.

"That will be all," Isabel said firmly.

"Yes, my lady," the footman murmured as he backed out the door. No doubt all her servants were waiting in the corridor to hear Will's report.

Isabel sighed and looked at Winter.

He took another sip of the wine. "This is very good. Italian?"

"Yes, I just got it in." Her eyes narrowed. "You're the son of a *beer* brewer. How do you come to know about wine?"

Was that a hint of embarrassment in his

eyes? He shrugged. "I like wine."

"Just when I think I've come to know you, you reveal something entirely unexpected about yourself," she said.

"Ah." He set his wineglass down. "That's where you and I differ. I don't expect to ever know all of your secrets. I look forward, years from now, to making new discoveries each day."

"Winter . . ." Her heart near broke at the warmth in his brown eyes. She couldn't let him think that she might change her mind. "You know we have no future together."

He didn't reply, instead taking a bite of the fish, but his very silence shouted his stubbornness.

She sighed. "What will you do now?"

"I've thought that I might take up tutoring," he replied, "of a young boy."

Her brows knit. "Who do you know who has —"

He smiled as her eyes widened in comprehension.

"But Christopher is only five," she protested. "Far too young for a tutor."

"I've found that teaching children — especially boys — is best started as early as possible," he said, unperturbed. "I'll begin lessons with Christopher tomorrow."

"But . . . but . . ." She tried to think of an

excuse for him not to begin lessons with Christopher, but the fact was that Christopher would undoubtedly do well with some masculine discipline. Lord knew that he was nearly a feral child with only Carruthers trying to tame him.

"Good. I'm glad that's settled," Winter said as if she'd given her full and grateful consent. "I'll just take my things upstairs."

"Now see here —" she began before his last words sank in. She brought herself up short, blinking in confusion. "What?"

His smile had turned definitely wolfish as he pushed himself away from the table. "One of the benefits of being a private tutor instead of a schoolmaster: tutors live with the family. Now what room would you like to put me in?"

Three days later, Winter sat at a low table in Isabel's nursery. It was a room at the top of the house, but well appointed for all that. Tall windows gave in light and were properly barred at the bottom to forestall any accidents. An impressive set of tin soldiers marched along a bookcase and a rather battered stuffed lion lounged in the chair next to his pupil.

Winter pushed a plate of tiny cakes to the center of a table. "Now, then, Christopher.

Cook has kindly made fairy cakes for our tea. How many did she give us?"

The boy, sitting at the table opposite, leaned on his elbows to study the iced cakes. Each had a strawberry on top and they looked quite appealing.

"Twelve!" he said after a moment spent moving his lips as he counted.

"Quite correct," Winter said. "If we were to split the cakes between us, how many would we each have?"

Christopher's brow furrowed ferociously as he mulled over the question. Winter poured him a cup of milky tea with a spoonful of sugar as he waited.

"Six?" the boy finally asked.

"Indeed." Winter smiled his approval. "But six fairy cakes apiece would no doubt result in a tummy ache for you and the possibility of gout for me. Thus" — he nodded to Isabel as she entered the nursery — "we are very fortunate indeed that Lady Beckinhall has come to join us for our tea."

Isabel smiled. "Good afternoon, Mr. Makepeace. Christopher."

"We're doing maths, my lady!" Christopher bounced in his seat. "And Cook made fairy cakes for tea."

"Marvelous!" Isabel cast a sidelong smile at Winter as she sat. In the last few days, there had been a marked improvement in her comfort around Christopher. "What else have you discussed with Mr. Makepeace today?"

Winter took a hasty sip of tea, avoiding her eyes.

Christopher in contrast leaned forward conspiratorially. "The Battle of Hastings. Did you know that King Harold was killed by an arrow in his *eye?*"

"Really?" Isabel's voice sounded a bit weak. "And is that a proper subject for little boys, Mr. Makepeace?"

Winter cleared his throat. "I find when discussing history, the most, er, colorful moments are more apt to hold a boy's attention."

"Hmm." She poured herself a cup of tea, adding cream and sugar. "I had no idea that tutoring little boys was so, um, dramatic."

"It is a fascinating occupation," Winter said gravely. "For instance, Christopher and I are about to discuss division. Now, Christopher, we need to divide these fairy cakes equally among Lady Beckinhall, myself, and you. How many do you think we shall each get?"

Christopher wrinkled his nose in thought. "Five?"

"Ah. Shall we test your guess?"

Christopher nodded vigorously.

"Then please apportion out the fairy cakes equally."

Winter sipped his tea and watched as Christopher carefully placed a fairy cake on each of their plates in turn until all the cakes were gone from the serving plate.

"Good," Winter said. "Now —"

"Will we be able to eventually eat these cakes?" Isabel muttered, eyeing the cakes on her plate.

"Patience, Lady Beckinhall. Scholarship must not be rushed," he chided her. She shot him a look promising retribution. "Now, then, Christopher, can you count the cakes on your plate?"

Christopher counted. "Four."

"And there are three of us," Winter said. "So three times four is . . . ?"

Christopher's eyes darted between the plates before his entire little face lit up. "Twelve! Three times four is twelve, Mr. Makepeace!"

"Quite so, Christopher," he said with approval. "And now, Lady Beckinhall, we may eat our cakes."

"Huzzah!" cried Christopher as he attempted to stuff an entire fairy cake into his mouth.

Well. Table manners were a subject they

could discuss later.

He watched Isabel take a dainty bite of her cake, licking a crumb from the corner of her mouth, and felt his loins tighten. He'd hidden it well, he thought, but living in the same house as her, taking his meals with her — as she'd insisted — even simply breathing the same air was next to agony.

Winter grimly took a bite of cake and chewed. He'd vowed not to mention the subject of marriage again until she became used to the idea. Obviously he'd proposed much too soon for her tastes. Thus, he must play a waiting game, gradually letting her become accustomed to his presence in her life. And, he'd decided, it was best to abstain from sex during that time. A decision he was beginning to regret.

"Would you like some more tea?" She leaned over to pour herself another cup of tea, the movement affording him a wonderful view of her bosom. "Mr. Makepeace?"

He brought his gaze back up. She was blinking at him innocently. "Yes. Yes, of course."

This wait might very well kill him.

She smiled as she poured tea into his cup. "I hope you find your rooms comfortable?"

"Quite." He took a too-hasty sip of tea and scalded his tongue.

"The view is to your liking?"

He had a view of a brick wall. "Indeed."

She fluttered her eyelashes at him over the rim of her teacup. "And the bed. Is it soft and . . . yielding?"

He nearly choked on the bite of cake he'd just taken.

"Or do you prefer a firmer bed?" she asked sweetly. "One that refuses to yield too soon?"

"I think" — he narrowed his eyes at her — "whatever mattress I have on the bed you gave me is perfect. But tell me, my lady, what sort of mattress do you prefer? All soft goose down or one that's a bit . . . harder?"

It was very fast, but he saw it: Her gaze flashed down to the juncture of his thighs and then up again. If there hadn't been anything to see there before, there certainly was now.

"Oh, I like a nice stiff mattress," she purred. "Well warmed and ready for a long ride."

His nostrils flared involuntarily, for he swore he could scent her — soft and ready for him. If they were alone, if there was a bed nearby or even —

"Why do you ride your mattress, my lady?" Christopher asked indistinctly around a mouthful of cake. "I like to *sleep* in my bed."

"Um . . ." Isabel squinted as she tried to find an answer to the innocent inquiry.

"Lady Beckinhall sleeps in her bed as well, Christopher," Winter said without any emphasis at all. "Now remember not to speak with your mouth full and have some more tea."

The boy happily held out his cup.

Winter filled it, carefully not looking at Isabel. If only he could distract his appetites as easily as he did Christopher . . .

CHAPTER SIXTEEN

At long last the Harlequin's True Love
heard a shout and the sound of men in
combat. Instead of fleeing the violence,
she crept closer, peering around a corner.
There in a small square, she saw the
Harlequin fighting five men at once. The
men about him shouted and grunted with
the exertion of their labor, but the
Harlequin made not a sound himself as
he methodically cut his enemies down,
one by one . . .
— from *The Legend of the
Harlequin Ghost of St. Giles*

Isabel lay in bed that night, her silk coverlet
pulled to her chin, and wondered what she
was doing. She'd rejected Winter — told
him flatly that she could not marry him.
With any other man, the news might've
been met with relief: He could continue a
clandestine affair with her without the com-

mitment of matrimony. His choices then were either to continue as they were or to break the thing off.

Instead he'd managed to move into her household.

She wasn't naïve. The man was stubborn and proud. He hadn't given up his ridiculous notion of marrying her. Perhaps he really did love her.

She closed her eyes in the darkness, her heart squeezing painfully in fear at the thought. She hadn't let herself think it before now. It was simply too terrible to contemplate. She wasn't like him, a person capable of deep caring. She'd shied away from strong emotions of any sort practically all her life. In her heart Isabel knew: She simply wasn't worthy of his love. Someday he'd find that out, and when he did —

There was no sound, but she felt a movement, a shifting of the air in her room, the warmth of another presence.

Isabel opened her eyes. He was there, at the foot of her bed, a single candle in his hand, dressed only in shirtsleeves, waistcoat, and breeches.

"Forgive me," he whispered as he set the candle down. "I could not stay away."

She lifted herself on her elbows, her pulse beginning to speed as she watched him unbutton his waistcoat.

"It's an oddity, actually," he said, almost as if he were musing to himself. "My self-control is rather strong as a rule. I've managed to keep the secret of the Ghost for nine years, from both friends and family. I don't lose my temper often. I've sustained wounds and never by action or word let anyone know, even if it meant cleaning and sewing up a wound myself."

He shrugged out of his waistcoat. "I think, objectively, that we can agree that my control is better than the average man's. I was, after all, celibate until I met you, and nearly content with that state of affairs."

He folded his waistcoat and placed it on a chair. "But then I *did* meet you and everything flew out the window, including, it seems, all of my rules of behavior, which, I think, is entirely your fault."

That outrageous remark prompted Isabel into speech for the first time since he'd entered her bedroom. "*My* fault?"

He nodded, as somber as a judge. "Indeed. Let us look at the facts. You joined the Ladies' Syndicate for the Benefit of the Home for Unfortunate Infants and Foundling Children and immediately began a campaign of taunting me."

She sat fully up, fascinated both by this

line of thought and the fact that he was now removing his shirt. Really, his chest might be her favorite thing in the entire world.

Not that she was about to tell him that. "Taunting?"

"Taunting." He folded the shirt as well, the muscles in his arms rippling in a quite distracting manner. "The little quips, the sly looks letting me know you'd once again thought yourself quite clever as you shot a dart at me, the low, provocative bodices —"

Isabel involuntarily glanced down at her bosom. "My bodices aren't provocative!" Well, not *all* the time, certainly.

He glanced at her sternly. "Provocative." He flicked open the buttons of his fall, and she nearly forgot what they were talking about. "And that doesn't even take into account the later double entendres, the lessons in flirtation, and the dancing lessons in which you took every opportunity to touch my buttocks."

"I never, ever" — *hardly ever* — "touched your buttocks. On purpose." She opened her eyes as wide as she could and cast a look of shock and innocence at him that would've melted a Spanish Inquisition priest's heart.

He lowered his brows into a thunderous glance and stripped off both his breeches and his smalls, revealing an erection that stood nearly vertical and stretched to his navel.

"You," he said softly, menacingly, as he advanced to the bed, "are a wanton seducer of innocent young men, too unworldly to escape from your wiles, even supposing they wanted to."

He was up on the bed, looming over her so suddenly, his heat beating against her, that she squeaked.

He braced himself on one arm and ran his other hand down from her throat, between her breasts, over her belly, to her mound, where he spread his fingers wide in possession. For a moment he simply stared down at his hand covering her femininity.

Then his gaze rose to hers and she saw that all teasing had left his eyes. They had gone so dark they were almost black. "How could I help falling under your seduction? How could I help succumbing to your lures? Is it any wonder at all that I'm here tonight?"

She swallowed, for she'd never seen him in this mood. She realized now that his earlier joking had hidden the fact that he almost seemed to resent her and her "lures." "What do you want?"

His eyelids drooped as he examined her

mouth. "Oh, you know very well what I want."

He didn't wait for answer or permission. He simply took her mouth, opening his own wide over hers as if he could swallow her.

As if he could make her his.

He licked and nipped at her lips, never letting her draw him in more deeply. Controlling and guiding their lovemaking. She could feel his naked chest under her palms, the strong, excited beat of his heart. His heat and tension were all around her, yet she could not get him to lie upon her. To seduce his tongue into her mouth.

She whimpered under his teasing onslaught and she thought she heard him chuckle.

That made her yank her head back and dig her fingernails into his chest muscles.

"No," he said firmly as if to a child. "I am the one in charge tonight, my lady. I am the one who holds the reins."

He rose over her, athletic and quick, and grasped her hips to flip her over.

"Oof!" She struggled to get her hands under her, but now he had chosen to lay his entire length over her, pressing her into the mattress. "Winter, let me up."

"No," he murmured in her ear. His hot breath stirred the hair on the side of her head as he gently brushed back the locks. He stroked her hair as if he had all the time in the world.

As if his thick cock weren't pressing firmly into her bottom.

She wore only a thin silk chemise to bed, the fabric as delicate as tissue, and no barrier to the feel of his body on hers. In fact, it seemed to heighten the sensation, allowing him to slide against her with exquisite friction with every movement.

"I adore your hair. Do you know that?" he whispered. "I used to dream about it in my lonely monk's bed, long mahogany locks twining themselves about my limbs in my sleep. I'd wake aroused and aching and cursing you."

He tilted his hips into her bottom, his cock sliding sweetly against her, as if to emphasize his words.

She felt her center go hot and liquid, yet she licked her lips and challenged him. "I don't believe you. I've never heard you swear, even when you were in great pain."

"I consider it a sin to take the Lord's name in vain," he said as he smoothed aside her hair, baring her neck. "Yet you drive me to sin."

His mouth was on her skin, at the tender place where her neck met her shoulder. He licked her there, as if he would taste her essence, as if he was experimenting. Then suddenly he bit, his teeth sharp and hard, and she gasped.

"Do I hurt you?" he asked against her skin.

"No," she said shakily, for no matter his aggression, he didn't. He was always gentle with her, always aware of his greater size and strength.

"You hurt me," he said conversationally. "Daily. Hourly. Second by second."

"I'm sorry." She tried to turn, tried to take his face in her hands and tell him that she didn't mean to, truly. She only did what she thought best for them both.

But somewhere along the way, he'd finally lost his infinite patience.

"No." He bit her again, like a stallion chastising a mare. "We do it my way."

He ran his hands down over her sides, sliding over the silk, until he found the hem of her chemise. Then he drew it up, slowly, inch by inch, teasing her with the feel of each bit of her skin being exposed to the night air.

For a moment his hips lifted from hers as he palmed her bottom, his hand hard and hot. His thumb found the crease of her cheeks and he ran it down, lightly, almost tickling, sending all her senses on alert. He paused where her bottom met her thighs and then swiftly thrust his fingers between her legs.

"You're wet," he said, and although his words were light, nearly conversational, he couldn't disguise the deepening of his voice.

Her arousal aroused him. The animal taking over the human body. Except animals felt no love. No regret or sorrow.

She wouldn't think about that right now. His fingers were teasing her from behind, making her lift her hips in supplication. She felt wanton as he inserted a finger slowly into her sheath. The fit was snug from behind, and she thought of how tight his cock would be from this angle.

She bit her lip, closing her eyes, feeling as his finger slid in and out of her, her passage as slick as the silk of her chemise. For a moment his hand abandoned her.

"I like this scent," he said, his voice whispering against her ear. He placed his hand on the pillow near her face and she smelled it as well: her wetness. Her arousal. "Your scent. Exotic, secret, purely primal. My cock wants it. I lose my mind when I smell you."

She moaned. She was growing wetter with his words. Why didn't he simply turn her over and take her? She wanted him as well.

But his hand trailed down again, leisurely almost, moving to the side of her hip. "Lift for me."

She obeyed and he slipped his hand under her, finding her from below. He spread his fingers, thrusting through her folds.

"Wet, so wet," he muttered.

He urged her thighs apart with his knees settling between them so that she felt his cock, insistent and hard, at her entrance. She wasn't sure he could even manage it from this angle. She was nearly flat on her belly. But he pushed and she felt him breach her, the big round head parting her folds relentlessly, the stretch of her muscles so sweet.

He paused as if considering and then thrust again, pushing inside, making a place for himself within her warmth.

She gripped the pillow by her face, wanting to rise up on her knees and push back. To hurry this along to its inevitable conclusion.

But he was too strong, too stubborn. He gave her no leeway. He flexed again and another thick inch slid inside her.

She thought she heard him groan, but it was drowned out by her whimper of need. He opened his mouth against the back of her neck and suddenly thrust hard, seating himself fully.

She nearly came around him.

Carefully, delicately, he found her clitoris with his fingertips and simply held his forefinger on her. He didn't have to do anything more — her own weight and his on top of hers pressed her down against his finger. She tried to circle her hips, to move against that one finger, but she was impaled from behind, held immovable but by his wish.

"Now," he whispered, and withdrew his cock an incremental amount. So tiny, less than an inch, surely. So small it should hardly matter at all.

But when he thrust back inside her, quick and hard and nearly brutal, the movement sent her hips grinding against his hand, trapped between her and the mattress. Sent her gasping for breath as the sensation spurred all her nerve endings to a nearly painful pleasure.

"I love you," he whispered as he thrust again. And again. Each movement controlled. Each devastating in its effect. "I love you."

She lost all concept of time. She lost her place and surroundings. She couldn't remember who he was — who *she* was. She lost her mind.

Because the pleasure/edge of pain was so sweet, so infinitely divine, nothing mattered but that it continue. She'd been seduced, enthralled, drugged by his lovemaking. At this moment it was all that mattered in the world to her.

And he didn't stop. He was panting now, his breath sawing roughly in and out of his lungs as he thrust in and out of her, his movements becoming jerky.

"Come, damn you," he growled in her ear. "Drown my cock in your liquid."

And the earthy demand was too much. She convulsed, trapped between his fingers and his cock, utterly in his power as he continued his unending thrusting, beyond hope and dreams and human regard.

She was a being of feeling and nothing but, shimmering pleasure sparking through her veins, making her heart beat, making the soles of her feet tingle. She was everything and nothing and it was all because of him. He was drawing out her orgasm, making it last, and it seemed he would never stop pumping into her.

But he was only mortal after all. She felt it when it overwhelmed him, too, this wondrous sensation. He jerked against her, his finger pressed hard against her as his cock slammed all the way into her passage, and he simply held himself there, twitching, as his seed flooded her.

He muffled a shout against her shoulder.

And then she drifted, liquid and soft, nearly insensible from bliss. He was heavy on her back, slumped against her, his breath hot on her ear, but she didn't care. It was almost comfortable, and a mad idea rushed into her brain to ask him to stay the night. What matter if the maids found him in the morning? It was her house, after all, and she a widow. Surely —

He rose off her in one lithe movement, and her body immediately became chill without his covering heat. Wordlessly, he pulled on his breeches, scooped up his clothes, and picked up the candle.

And left her room.

Winter slid through the night like the Ghost he was. It was long past midnight now, and the streets of St. Giles were grim and black, but he hadn't been able to sleep after leaving Isabel. He'd thought that he'd try again to find the rumored children living in an attic. He'd followed such rumors before — again and again — only to be disappointed, but that hardly mattered. Tonight he needed physical activity. Tonight he needed to forget.

His beast had escaped tonight. He'd broken his vow to stay away from Isabel simply because he'd found it impossible to continue to do so. And when he'd come to her, he'd made love to her like an animal made mad by lust. She'd been wet, though, beautifully, wonderfully wet, so perhaps she hadn't been as appalled as he by the primitiveness of his possession of her. She hadn't been scared and that was good, for the darkness within himself certainly scared him. It was as if she'd unlocked a cage that once opened could never again be shut. The beast was out now, free and untamed, and it *adored* her. Her snapping wit, the vulnerable place inside her, even the hurt that her barrenness had caused her. And especially the look that came into her blue, blue eyes when he touched her at her center. Oh, the beast liked that especially.

He growled under his breath as he leaped between buildings. The space was too great, the jump too dangerous, yet he landed on the other side easily.

Perhaps love unfulfilled had made him a demigod.

Blasphemous thought. He stood on the roof, the moon casting her light against his back and the angled rooftop door in front of him. He shook his head, trying to clear it of emotion entirely before he drew both his swords and kicked in the door.

It swung inward on broken hinges, crashing against an unseen wall. The room revealed was without light. Several dark forms began to rise, clumsy with sleep and confusion. Winter's eyes were already accustomed to the dark. He had the advantage of surprise and higher ground.

Always attack from above if you are able.

The ghostly voice of his mentor whispered in his ear even as Winter leaped to the room below. He landed on the largest form — a man with huge shoulders, reeking of sweat. The man had gotten only as far as his knees, but Winter's weight knocked him face-first to the ground. He wasn't moving, so Winter swung to the next man, slapping him on the side of the head.

BANG! A gun went off, the flash blinding everyone in the darkness.

Winter closed his eyes and continued fighting. Years ago, Sir Stanley had made him practice his sword craft with a bag over his head for just this reason. He felt a body stumble against his, and Winter elbowed the man high in the belly. There was a thump as the man fell and then he heard the scurry of fleeing feet.

Winter opened his eyes.

The man he'd just knocked down was struggling at his feet. A half-dozen strange machines in the shape of overlarge chairs sat against the walls of the low attic room. Otherwise the room was empty besides the body of the first man, still insensible from Winter landing on him.

Disappointment slashed through Winter, making his grip rougher than usual when he hauled the man to his feet.

"Where are they?" he asked, because there wasn't anything else to do. "Where are the children?"

To his astonishment, his victim waved to the far end of the room. "There."

Winter's eyes narrowed in suspicion. Either the man was trying to get rid of him or it was a trap, but in any case he had to investigate.

He took the man by the coat collar and dragged him to the far end of the room. As Winter got closer, he could see that there was a small door in the wall. Hope began to bloom in his chest and he fought it back savagely. He'd found hidey-holes before. They'd all been empty or occupied by adults.

There was a stout wooden bar across the

door and Winter lifted it before cautiously opening the door. It was even darker than the outer room, a hellish little pit without light or hope. The air fairly reeked of despair. At first he thought the ghastly little room empty. Then a small shape moved. And another. And another.

A little girl's face emerged from the pit, thin and starving. "Please," was all she could say.

He'd found them. He'd finally found them.

"You have a visitor, my lady."

Megs looked up vaguely from the open book on her lap the next morning. She couldn't remember how long she'd been sitting here in the library with the book as disguise, but there was an empty cup of tea by her elbow, so it evidently had been quite some time.

"I'm not receiving visitors," she said dully.

"Oh, surely that doesn't apply to me." Lady Beckinhall sauntered into the library behind the butler, nodding a dismissal at the man.

He looked relieved as he left the room.

"I've come to take you out," Lady Beckinhall announced, peering at a huge Bible on a stand.

"I've got a headache."

"All the better, then," Lady Beckinhall said briskly. "Fresh air will do your head good."

"Usually doctors prescribe bed rest for a headache," Megs pointed out.

"They prescribe bed rest for *everything*," Lady Beckinhall said somewhat obscurely. She turned from the Bible, her expression softening. "Please? It's been almost a sennight since Mr. Makepeace left the home. I estimate Lady Penelope has about run it into the ground by now. I thought we should at least go see."

"Mr. Makepeace left?" For a moment Megs felt a stirring of interest.

"Yes. Two days after —" Lady Beckinhall winced and stopped, looking at Megs helplessly.

Two days after Roger died.

Megs looked back at the book in her lap, the words blurring. "I can't. I'm sorry."

She felt Lady Beckinhall coming nearer. "Why? Why can't you leave?"

"I just can't."

"What is it?" Lady Beckinhall laid a cool hand against her forehead. "Are you really ill? Have you seen a physician?"

"No!" Megs moved her head aside. "It isn't that."

"Then what?"

The words were out of her mouth before she could catch them. "I'm with child."

She opened her eyes, glancing up, and caught a look upon Lady Beckinhall's face that she'd never seen on anyone before. She literally went gray, her eyes wide with horror.

Oh, lovely. Apparently she'd shocked the unshockable Lady Beckinhall. "I'm sorry," Megs muttered inanely. "I don't know what I was thinking to tell you. Forget I ever —"

"You were thinking that you needed help." The look was gone from Lady Beckinhall's face as swiftly as it had appeared, color beginning to seep back into her cheeks. "And fortunately, you've told the right person."

CHAPTER SEVENTEEN

When the Harlequin slew the last man,
the Harlequin's True Love ran toward him,
but as she did so, he turned and sprinted
away, as fleet as a stag. For many hours,
the True Love pursued the Harlequin,
never losing sight of him, until he came
to bay against a dead end. Quick as a
wink, the True Love darted forward and
threw the cord braided from her own
hair over his upper body, drawing it
tight so that his arms were trapped
against his sides.
In this way, she bound him with
her love . . .
— from *The Legend of the
Harlequin Ghost of St. Giles*

Isabel entered her pretty little dining room
and paused. She and Lady Margaret had
never made their trip to the orphanage.
Instead, she'd returned home, written and

posted a letter on Lady Margaret's behalf, and now was ready for luncheon. But Winter was sitting at the rosewood table, a single cup of tea before him. That was odd. Winter usually ate a scandalously early breakfast and then left for the nursery or for a study she'd let him use. Yet he was still here hours after lessons with Christopher should have started.

"What is it?" she asked without preamble.

His gaze didn't rise from his teacup. "I found them."

She darted a quick glance at the footman standing in the corner pretending not to listen. "Tell Cook there'll be two for luncheon." She waited until the footman had left before asking Winter, "Found who?"

"The children." His voice was dead.

She frowned. "But that's good news, surely?"

His gaze finally rose to hers, and she saw that his eyes were red-rimmed and sunken. She revised her earlier thought: It wasn't that he'd gotten up late this morning. He hadn't gone to bed at all.

She pulled out a chair and eased into it. "Tell me."

He spread his hands before him and looked at his palms as if trying to understand his past or future. "They were in an

429

attic of a house divided and then divided again into a warren of rooms. Fifteen girls all crammed into a room with no windows, no ventilation, and a ceiling that was no more than my shoulder's height at its tallest. Not a one smiled in happiness or even relief when I opened their barred door and rescued them. I think they had given up hope."

She closed her eyes, mourning those children hidden away and used. Mourning Winter's pain. "But you did find them. They'll learn to smile again."

"Will they?" he asked, and she opened her eyes to see him shaking his head. "I don't know."

"Where are they now?"

"I brought them to the home. Knocked on the door and stood in the shadows until the door was opened and they were let in, safe and sound. They didn't move, didn't try to flee while they waited."

The footman returned followed by two of his compatriots bearing platters of cold meats, cheeses, bread, and fruit.

"Just set it here," Isabel said, waving to the table. "We'll serve ourselves."

She waited until they'd trooped out of the dining room again before filling Winter's plate with a selection of everything on the table. "Here, eat this."

He stared down at the food as if it were something he'd never seen before. "There were adults in the outer room when I first got there, but most ran away. I did restrain one man, but he seems odd in the head. He couldn't tell me who was behind the workshop. Who the aristocrat was who made money off the backs of little children. Perhaps he never saw d'Arque."

She was pouring him a fresh cup of tea, but she paused in the act. "Lord d'Arque?"

"Yes." He ran his hand impatiently over his hair. "I told you: I found that scrap of paper with his seal in the hand of a child I rescued from these people."

She arched an eyebrow and said gently, "You told me that you'd found the scrap of paper in a little boy's hand in St. Giles. You never said the little boy was connected with the workshop people you were looking for."

"Didn't I?" He frowned, looking terribly weary. "Well, he was. People in St. Giles call them the 'lassie snatchers,' for apparently they like girls for their work. Little girls have smaller fingers and are more nimble for fine work."

She knit her brows. "But I can't see Viscount d'Arque being involved in this."

Winter gave her a jaundiced look. "I

recognized d'Arque's coachman as one of the lassie snatchers."

That made her pause for a second. "Did you talk to the coachman?"

"Yes." Winter grimaced. "He said it wasn't d'Arque."

"Well, then —"

"And then the coachman ran away before I could get anything else from him. For all I know, he was simply covering for his master."

"Or perhaps he was speaking the truth," Isabel said. "I know you don't like the viscount, and I admit he can be quite annoying, but that doesn't make him criminal. That doesn't make him the sort of person who would let a little girl be hurt for money."

He shook his head. "I think you're biased."

She remembered the look on his face when Lord d'Arque had flirted with her at the Duchess of Arlington's ball. "I think you may be biased as well."

He shrugged moodily, not speaking.

She took the opportunity to serve herself some cheese and fruit. "Why don't you show Lord d'Arque the scrap of paper? Ask him who he wrote it to?"

He gave her an ironic look but remained silent.

She poured herself a cup of tea, adding a dollop of milk and a spoonful of sugar before sipping. "What were they making in this workshop anyway? You never said."

"Stockings." He sounded bitter. "Can you imagine? They work these children to death to make lace stockings with fancy embroidered clocks on the ankles in the French style for silly ladies."

Isabel's chest felt tight with sudden dread. She set down her teacup. "Have you seen the stockings?"

"Not until last night," he replied. "They left a box of finished clocks behind to be sewn on the lace stockings later."

They were alone in the breakfast room. Isabel got up and rounded the table to Winter's side. He looked at her quizzically until she placed her foot on the chair next to his and lifted her skirts.

"Did the clocks look like this?" she asked quietly.

He'd frozen, staring at the dainty pink, gold, and blue embroidery on her ankle. It was oversewn onto a stocking that was white lace from the sole of her foot to over her knee. Delicate, enormously expensive lace, sold for a fraction of what it would cost elsewhere. She'd been a fool.

His eyes rose to hers. "Where did you get those?"

She let her skirts fall and lowered her foot to the floor. "My lady's maid, Pinkney, got them. I'm not sure where, but I know she was thrilled by the price."

His mouth tightened grimly. "Could you call her here, please?"

"Of course," she said, keeping her tone calm as she crossed to the door and gave the order to the footman outside.

Winter was terribly angry, she could see. *Silly ladies.* Did he think she was one of those silly ladies he'd spoken of? The ones who never cared who made their stockings as long as the style was the latest? Well, she *was* one of those ladies, wasn't she?

She sank into her chair, waiting for Pinkney.

He didn't say anything else, instead staring at the table between his hands, a line incised between his brows.

The door opened to the breakfast room and Pinkney came in. "You wanted to see me, my lady?"

"Yes." Isabel folded her hands in her lap. "I want to know about the lace stockings you have been buying for me."

Pinkney's pretty forehead wrinkled. "Stockings, my lady?"

"Where did you get them?" Winter asked, his voice dark.

Pinkney's blue eyes opened wide, a mixture of confusion and fear in them. Winter looked quite daunting at the moment. "I . . . I . . . that is, there's a little shop on Baker Street, my lady. The shopkeeper has the lace stockings in back. One has to know to ask for them."

"And how did you know?" Isabel asked.

Pinkney shrugged helplessly. "One hears rumors of such things, my lady. Where to find the latest kid gloves, what cobbler makes the finest heeled slippers, and who has lace stockings made in the best French fashion at half the price. It's my job, my lady."

Pinkney looked at them with an odd sort of dignity, for she was quite right — it *was* her job and she did it well.

"Thank you, Pinkney, that will be all," Isabel said quietly.

The lady's maid curtsied. "Yes, my lady." She turned to leave the room.

"Wait." Isabel swiftly lifted her skirts again and rolled down both stockings, removing them. She held out the limp bits of silk lace to the lady's maid. "Burn these along with the others, please."

Pinkney's mouth had dropped open when

Isabel lifted her skirt in front of Winter. Now she snapped it shut. "Of course, my lady."

She took the stockings and fled.

"Why did you dismiss her?" Winter asked abruptly. "She might have known more if we'd questioned her."

"I doubt it." Isabel shook her head. "She's a superb lady's maid, but I think all the minutiae of her position — the things she just enumerated — take up every available bit of her mind." Isabel shrugged apologetically. "She's not that interested in anything outside of fashion."

Winter shoved back from the table. "Then I shall go and visit this shop on Baker Street. Perhaps the shopkeeper can give me more information."

"But what about Christopher?" Isabel asked. "Don't you have lessons for him today?"

Winter turned and glanced at her from the door. "Indeed I do, but his mother, it seems, had other plans. I was told that she took him away on some errand very early this morning."

"What —" Isabel began, but he was already gone.

That was odd. Louise visited Christopher only once a month — if that — and usually only for an afternoon. She rarely woke before noon, let alone rose from bed.

Sighing, Isabel ate her luncheon. Should she have vetted all the clothes that Pinkney brought to her? Made sure they were made in legitimate workshops? Or should she simply give up fancy lace stockings, heeled slippers made of gold cloth, gowns that took months to embroider?

She could dress like a female monk, ban all color from her life . . . and go quietly mad within the week. She *liked* extravagant gowns, pretty underthings, clocked stockings, and all the other fripperies that Winter no doubt frowned terribly upon. She could no more stop wearing them than a peacock could divest himself of his feathers.

Well, then this was yet another reason that they couldn't marry. Even if Winter truly did love her, he couldn't help but be disgusted by her delight in clothing and jewels. It was yet another nail in the coffin of their affair. They simply were not matched in any way.

Isabel wrinkled her nose and mashed what remained of the cheese under her fork tines. She should be glad to find one more reason to give him of why they should not, could not, *would* not marry, and yet all she felt was a dismal roiling in her tummy. Her brain was convinced, but her heart rebelled.

The door opened and Isabel turned, glad of a diversion from her gloomy musings.

Louise swept in, her cheeks pink, her eyes sparkling, her golden hair highlighted by a pink ribbon rosette, and — if Isabel weren't mistaken — she wore a new dress. "Oh, Isabel, the most marvelous thing has happened! I've found a protector and he's given me a *house*. I can take Christopher to live with me by the end of the week."

Isabel's mouth opened, but no words emerged. Louise continued to chatter about her new protector, and the house she would soon have, but it was as if her voice were muffled.

Isabel had accepted the responsibility of Christopher only reluctantly and because really there hadn't been anyone else to look after him. He'd been a burden, an innocent reminder of Edmund's infidelity and her own barrenness. She should be glad that Louise had finally found a way to take care of him herself. A child needed his mother, and Louise, no matter how flawed, was Christopher's mother.

And if she felt some small disappointment in Christopher's leaving, that was only to be expected. She'd grown . . . fond of the boy.

"I'll come fetch him tomorrow, shall I?"

Louise said.

Isabel blinked. "Yes. Yes, of course. That will be quite all right."

And it would, wouldn't it?

Late that night, Winter pushed open the door to his room in Isabel's house, weary both in mind and spirit. The sight within brought all his senses to the alert, however: Isabel lay in his bed, and from what he could see, she wasn't wearing anything.

He closed the door behind him. The room she'd given him was much nicer than his former room at the home. On the same floor as her own bedroom, it was, he suspected, a guest room rather than one usually assigned to a servant. The bed was large and comfortable, and there was just enough furniture to make the room pleasant: a chair to sit by the fire, a chest of drawers and a dresser with a basin and pitcher for washing. She'd made sure, he was certain, to give him a room that he'd find homey without being ostentatious.

"What are you doing here?" he asked.

Her eyelashes drooped and a smile played about the corners of her lush mouth. "Why, Mr. Makepeace, I know our lessons were short, but I do think I covered enough for you to be able to understand why I might be here."

Her tone was so brittle that he immediately was worried. "What has happened?"

She pouted. "Must there be something wrong for me to be here?"

"In these circumstances, yes." He crossed to the bed, looking down at her. "Tell me, Isabel."

She turned her face aside, saying nothing, but her sweet lips trembled.

He could not bear the sight. He climbed into the bed fully clothed and gathered her warm little form against himself, smoothing back her glorious hair. "Isabel."

Her breath caught raggedly. "Do you remember when you first came here and you met Christopher?"

"Yes," he murmured into her hair, wondering where this was leading.

"I was quite cold to him," she said.

"Isabel," he protested.

She swiped at her face. "No, I was. He's but a little boy and it wasn't his fault, but he reminded me of everything I don't have — everything I can never have — and I just couldn't stand the sight of him. He made me feel too much. Back then I wished desperately that Louise would simply take him away. Find another home for him to live in." She caught her breath. "You're going to laugh, but my wish has been granted."

He closed his eyes in sorrow. She'd just begun to open her heart to the boy. Just begun to let herself feel some joy in their relationship. To have Christopher taken away now was a terrible blow.

"I'm sorry," he said. "Where does she plan to go with him?"

She twisted her fingers in the front of his coat. "She's found herself a protector — a rich importer of goods. That's where she was this morning: She'd taken Christopher to outfit the both of them in new clothes at this man's expense. He dotes on her, Louise says, and has leased her a fine town house."

He frowned, staring over her head. "That does not sound like it would be the best place for the boy to live and grow up."

She stilled. "I thought the same, but I fear my affection for him is clouding my judgment. I want Christopher to be happy. Surely he would be happiest with his mother?"

Her voice was both hopeful and fearful as she asked him the tentative question.

He sighed. "I don't know if he would or not. All I know is that he seems quite happy here. *You* seem quite happy to have him in your house with you."

441

"Yes, but what I feel and think isn't the point," she said earnestly. "I should think only of Christopher and his interests. I need to do the right thing."

He laid his head against hers, breathing in her scent, content simply to hold her. "Sometimes doing the right thing is no sacrifice."

Isabel lay against Winter's wool coat, the coverlet pulled to her shoulders, listening to his breath under her ear.

"There's more." His voice rumbled against her cheek. "More than Christopher, isn't there?"

She burrowed into his warmth. She didn't want to face it, didn't want to think about it. Couldn't he simply make love to her and make her forget?

But he stroked her hair gently instead. No one had ever done that before, and she thought now that she might forever miss his hands in her hair when he left.

"Tell me," he said.

She squeezed her eyes shut like a little girl, as if not seeing him would make the telling easier. "I saw a . . . friend today, a dear friend, and she confided to me that she is expecting a child."

His hand stilled against her hair before

442

resuming. "I'm sorry." His voice was a deep whisper. "I know that must've been hard for you to hear."

"It shouldn't be," she insisted, balling her fingers in the lapel of his coat and tugging. "I should be able to hear joyous news and celebrate with a friend. I shouldn't be so small, so concerned only with my own problems. I should be a better person."

His chest moved beneath her cheek as he shrugged. "So should we all."

"You don't need to," she whispered. "You're perfect the way you are."

"I'm far from perfect," he murmured. "I thought you would know that by now."

No, the more she knew him, the more perfect he became: selfless, strong, kind, caring . . . the list went on and on. In contrast, she felt small and mean and undeserving of love.

"You don't know the worst," she said.

"Then tell me."

She inhaled to steady herself for her confession. "My friend is not married. The child she carries is out of wedlock. Naturally she's distraught. She hardly knows what to do. In her despair, she wept as she told me her plight, and all I could think was . . ."

It was too terrible; she couldn't say the words.

But he knew them anyway. "You wished the babe was yours."

"Why?" She jerked back from his embrace but still clutched his lapels. "*Why?* Why must she carry a child who will destroy her life while I . . . while I cannot —" She couldn't go on. Her throat was clogged with all the tears she'd held back for years.

He wrapped his arms around her and for a moment she resisted, pulling back. Her fears, her little jealousy, her weeping, were all so horrid. So ugly. He must hate her or at the very least feel pity for her, and pity was the last thing she wanted from him.

It wasn't fair that he of all men should be the one to see beneath her protective façade.

But in the end she did relent, because he was Winter and she'd realized in the last several days that she could never resist him for long. Somehow he'd become more than a lover, more than a friend. What he was to her she couldn't put into words, but she was very much afraid that it was permanent and forever, as if he'd embedded himself into her very flesh.

Pray he never found out.

She turned her face up and kissed him like an untried girl, her lips soft and closed, her face wet with tears. Her eyes were closed as she kissed him and she could feel when his arms stiffened.

He pulled away. "Isabel, we shouldn't, not with you feeling this way."

He *did* pity her — she could tell by the look on his face. He was going to set her aside, leave her because he could no longer face her.

She flung back the covers and lunged at him, all but knocking him to the bed and climbing atop him.

"Don't, Isabel," he said, but his voice had already deepened, roughened, and she knew she'd have him soon. She could feel the fabric of his breeches and coat against her naked skin.

She caught his face between her palms and kissed him again, her mouth open and needy — for she did need him, more than he'd ever know. He groaned under her mouth, angling his head for better access to her tongue. He tasted of wine and man and need. He tasted of everything she'd never thought she'd wanted but somehow had sought all along.

He tasted of Winter.

"Isabel," he whispered, his fingers trailing along her cheeks. "Isabel, no."

"Why not?" she murmured, nipping his lips, stroking his jaw. "I need you now. I need to forget."

His eyes were sad. "Perhaps you do, but not this way. I'll not be used as a male whore, and you, my darling Isabel, are better than this."

Her head reared back involuntarily. She felt as if he'd hit her.

"How do you know?" she asked viciously, scrambling away from him. "Perhaps I see you as no more than a male whore. Maybe I'm not any better than this."

He was up and over her so fast she didn't even have time to gasp. He wound his arms around her, pinning her arms to her sides, holding her fast, and when she looked up at him, into his face, she expected to see anger.

Instead she saw compassion.

It was too much. She inhaled, the breath searing her chest, breaking open her heart, spilling all the rage and fear and disappointment out into the open. She cried, great, heaving sobs, blinded by her own tears, her mouth open in a silent wail.

He gathered her closer, his face against hers, and rocked her in his arms as if she were a newborn babe.

But his gentleness only gave fuel to the fire of her despair. She twisted, hitting his shoulders with her balled fists, convulsing in her grief. He only held her tighter, murmuring soothing sounds as she sobbed for the marriage that hadn't lived up to her dreams, the miscarriages, and the children she would never have. The grief came boiling out of her, hot and ugly, too long suppressed, too long denied.

She sobbed until her hair was matted with sweat, until her eyes were swollen, until her weeping quieted and she could hear what Winter said as he rocked her.

"So brave," he murmured into her hair, stroking it. "So beautiful and brave."

"I'm not beautiful," she rasped. "You shouldn't see me like this."

She must look like a hag, and the horror of her gauche tantrum and her naked vulnerability made her hide her face in his shoulder.

But he placed a gentle palm under her chin and turned her face back to him. "I'm privileged to see you like this," he said, his eyes fierce. "Wear your social mask at your balls and parties and when you visit your friends out there, but when we are alone, just the two of us in here, promise me this: that you'll show me only your real face, no matter how ugly you might think it. That's our true intimacy, not sex, but the ability to be ourselves when we are together."

She stared at him, stunned, and laid her palm against his cheek, rough with the day's stubble. "How can you be so wise?"

He shook his head. "Not me. You were the one who started this. You were the one who showed me the way."

He gave her too much credit, but she was too tired to argue the point.

He rolled to his back and settled her against him. "Sleep."

She closed her eyes and obeyed, but as she drifted off, the realization came to her:

She loved this man, now and forever.

CHAPTER EIGHTEEN

The Harlequin was bound by love, but he still stared from sightless white eyes. The Harlequin's True Love carefully unstopped her glass vial of tears and, standing on tiptoes, tilted the vial over his eyes. At the first drop on his eye, the Harlequin roared, thrashing his head back and forth, but the True Love persevered, washing both his eyes with her tears of sorrow. When the vial was empty, she stepped back and saw that his eyes were once more brown and seeing . . .
— from *The Legend of the Harlequin Ghost of St. Giles*

Winter woke before the dawn the next morning. Isabel lay beside him, breathing deeply in sleep, smelling of soft, warm woman. He thought of what he'd told her the night before: *Sometimes doing the right thing is no sacrifice.* Perhaps it was past time that he took his own words to heart. If he was to marry Isabel, he must give up being the Ghost of St. Giles. All along, the idea had been brewing at the back of his mind: He could not have Isabel and be the Ghost, too. It was the reason, after all, that he'd remained celibate so many years: The Ghost was an all-consuming job. A married man, on the other hand, must make his family his first priority, and he'd do nothing less for Isabel.

But before his Ghost disappeared for the last time, he needed to finish the hunt for the lassie snatchers and the "toff" behind them. He needed to confront d'Arque and either discover he was the toff or eliminate him from the search.

And there was one more thing he must do.

Quietly he rose, dressed, and placed a few things in his bag. He looked at Isabel. She slept deeply, one hand curled under her chin like a small child. He had the urge to kiss her before he left, but in the end suppressed it — he didn't want to wake her.

Outside, London was only just beginning to wake. A sleepy maid knelt on the step next door to Isabel's house, polishing the door, not even looking up as he strolled by. A milkmaid called out saucily to him as he passed and he nodded in return.

By the time Winter made it to St. Giles, the sun was up fully, but the sky was so overcast it looked like evening. He pulled his long cloak about himself, glad he'd decided to wear it today. If he wasn't mistaken, there would be rain before noon.

The home was up, of course, the single kitchen window bright. He knocked softly at the back door.

Mistress Medina opened the door, her normally neat cap askew. She raised her eyebrows at the sight of him. " 'Ave you come back to the 'ome, then, Mr. Make-peace?"

"I'm sorry, no," Winter replied. "I gave my word to leave and so I have. But I wonder if I might speak with Joseph Tinbox out here." He gestured to the alley.

Mistress Medina's lips pursed. "Don't seem right, it don't, you not being able to come inside the 'ome. And Lord knows we need you."

She ducked back inside before he could comment.

There was a series of thuds inside, followed by an angry shout.

Winter cocked an eyebrow at the door. It sounded as if active warfare were going on inside.

A minute later, Joseph Tinbox came outside. His hair was down instead of tied back properly and his waistcoat had a stain on it that looked older than breakfast.

The boy stared at his feet, his mouth turned down at the corners. "Whatcha want?"

"I've come to say good-bye to you, Joseph," Winter said gently. "You're to report to your ship tomorrow, aren't you?"

Joseph nodded, mute.

Winter looked away from his sullen face, beset with sudden qualms. Perhaps this wasn't the right thing for Joseph. Perhaps the boy would hate him for the rest of his life, blaming Winter for sending him to sea and the hard life of a sailor.

But he wasn't going to be just a sailor. He would be an officer. The position opened up the possibilities of a career, of good money if not wealth, of a home someday in the country. This commission would change Joseph's entire life in a way that nothing else could: it gave him the freedom of a gentleman.

Winter looked back at the boy. "I trust that you'll write, Joseph. If not me, then Peach and Nell and all the other children at the home."

The boy's lip trembled, but he muttered,

"Yes, sir."

"To that end, I have something for you," Winter said. He set down his soft bag and drew out a wooden box.

Curiosity had always been one of Joseph's defining characteristics. He leaned forward now, peering at the box. "What is it, sir?"

Winter unlatched the box, opening the flat lid. Inside was a small glass jar of ink, papers, various newly sharpened pens, and even a tiny penknife. "It's a traveling writing box. My father used to take it with him when he went to the country to buy hops. See? Everything is fitted neatly so they shan't move or be spoiled if the box is shaken."

Winter relatched the box and stood, holding out the box to Joseph. "I'd like you to have it."

Joseph's eyes widened to saucer size and he opened his mouth, but nothing emerged. It seemed that Winter had succeeded in rendering the boy speechless. Joseph took the box and stood a moment simply staring at it.

He ran the fingertips of his right hand delicately across the worn surface of the top and looked up at Winter. "Thank you, sir."

Winter nodded. For a moment he was speechless as his throat worked. When his voice emerged, it was gruff. "Joseph, would you like to shake hands?"

The boy's lower lip trembled. "Yes, sir." He held out his hand.

Winter took it and then he did something he'd never done to any of the home's children. He bent, awkwardly, and drew the boy into a hug, writing desk and all. Joseph's free arm came about his neck and squeezed fiercely. Winter bent his head and smelled jam and boy sweat. *This is what it is like to feel with all one's soul.*

Winter stepped back, blinking. "Take care, Joseph."

The boy's eyes were sparkling. "I will, sir." He ran into the home, but an instant later poked his head outside the door again. "And I'll write you, sir. I promise."

He was gone then and Winter stared at the door, his throat thick, wondering when next he'd see Joseph Tinbox again. Would the boy thank him for sending him to sea? Or curse him?

Winter tilted back his head, feeling the first ice-cold drops of rain spatter against his face. Either way, he'd make the same decision again.

"I thought I'd had your word to leave the home, Makepeace." Viscount d'Arque's voice came from behind him.

"You do, my lord." Winter turned slowly, gesturing to the closed kitchen door. "You'll notice that I'm on the *outside* of the home."

D'Arque stood with his friends the Earl of Kershaw and Mr. Seymour in the alley behind him.

The viscount grunted suspiciously. "Well, see that you stay away. I can always renege on this bargain."

"No, you can't," Winter said pleasantly. "You gave your word as a gentleman. Renege and I'll make sure the news that you broke your word is in every breakfast room by noon the next day."

D'Arque looked startled by the sudden steel in Winter's voice. Good. The man needed to learn that he couldn't play with lives.

Mr. Seymour cleared his throat. "If you're not here to visit the home, Mr. Makepeace, then why are you here?"

"I believe I could ask the same of you," Winter said. "I do notice both you and Lord Kershaw hanging about the place quite a lot."

Lord Kershaw stiffened, clearly offended by Winter's familiar tone, but Mr. Seymour merely smiled sheepishly. "You'll have to forgive us gentlemen of leisure, Mr. Makepeace. An orphanage is quite fascinating in its own way. 'Sides, we heard that the Ghost of St. Giles delivered a pack of feral children here the night before last. Kershaw and I thought we'd see what it was about."

"Ah, then your mission is not so very different from my own," Winter replied. "I'm interested in finding out who was holding these children. To that end, I thought I'd search again the place where the Ghost found them."

"Indeed?" Mr. Seymour looked eager. "You know where they were found by the Ghost?"

Winter nodded, watching the man. Only Seymour seemed interested in the illegal workshop. Kershaw was yawning and d'Arque merely stared into space as if thinking of something else.

"Then with your permission I would like to accompany you and investigate the site as well," Mr. Seymour said.

Winter frowned. "I had thought to go alone . . ."

"But two pairs of eyes are better than one, don't you think?" Mr. Seymour asked.

"True." Winter glanced at the other two gentlemen. "Would anyone else like to participate in our investigations?"

Looking bored and impatient, d'Arque, shook his head. Lord Kershaw raised his eyebrows haughtily. "I think not."

Winter nodded and turned to Mr. Seymour. "Then shall we proceed?"

"No," Isabel said with all the authority she could muster, which as it happened, was quite a lot. It was early — much too early for fashionable calls — but Louise had arrived just after Isabel had risen.

Louise's pretty eyes opened wide. "But I'm Christopher's mother. He should be with me."

"Yes, that's what I thought at first as well," Isabel murmured as she poured tea. She'd invited Louise into her sitting room to discuss Christopher. "But then I considered the matter and realized that wasn't quite true."

Louise blinked. "You can't mean I'm not his mother."

"In a way I do, actually." Isabel held out the teacup and the other woman took it absently. "You see, Christopher has lived with me ever since he was a baby. I provided for him, saw that he was clothed and fed and had a competent nanny, and lately I've enjoyed his company as well. You, on the other hand, see him once a month, if that, and have never thought to inquire about his welfare."

"I . . . I've been busy." Louise's mouth looked mutinous.

"Of course you have," Isabel soothed. This next bit was going to be tricky. "But that's just it, don't you see? You have a busy social life with so many things to do. Do you really want a little boy around, getting in your way?"

Louise's brows drew together.

"And I" — Isabel waved her hand, indicating her town house — "have this great empty house. It just makes sense that I keep Christopher and raise him. And besides, I've come to love him."

Louise's brow cleared. "Well, since you put it like that . . ."

"Oh, I do," Isabel murmured. "Have some more tea."

"Thank you." Louise stared down at her cup, looking very young. "I can visit him still, can't I?"

Isabel smiled, relieved and so happy she felt like twirling about the room. Instead she said, "I'm sure Christopher would like that."

Fifteen minutes later, Isabel watched as Butterman shut the door behind Louise.

She turned to the butler. "Has my carriage been called?"

"Yes, my lady."

"Good. Please inform Pinkney that I wish to go out."

She paced restlessly until the lady's maid appeared and then hurriedly entered her carriage. The ride to St. Giles was uneventful, which made her even more impatient when at last they arrived.

Isabel stepped down from her carriage outside the home and found herself looking around eagerly for Winter. Silly! Just because he wasn't at her house — had gone out without a word to her, in fact — didn't mean he'd left her. Of course, his bag was gone, too, but one ought not to panic over that. He'd left behind his clothes — what there were of them — and surely such a frugal man wouldn't just abandon wearable clothes.

Would he?

She took a deep breath, steadying herself before she mounted the steps to the home. Harold followed at a discreet distance behind her. She'd thought they'd reached a new accord last night, but perhaps she was wrong. Perhaps, despite his protestations, she'd driven him away with her theatrics. Wretched thought!

Well, she could at least inspect the home while she was here. Lady Hero, Amelia, and the younger Lady Caire were all still away;

Lady Phoebe was a girl and could hardly act alone. That left her to see if Lady Penelope was dressing all the boys in primrose coats or making the children march in circles or any other idea that flew into her scattered brain.

Isabel knocked on the front door.

Usually it was opened at once, but there was a very long wait this morning. Isabel tapped her toe, glanced at the sky to see if it was about to rain, and started when something crashed inside.

She raised her eyebrows at the still-shut door.

Which suddenly opened. One of the smaller girls — oddly still in her night rail — stood there with her thumb in her mouth, staring at Isabel mutely.

Isabel cleared her throat. "Where is everyone, darling?"

The child pointed down the hall behind her.

Well. Isabel raised her skirts and prepared to enter.

"Shall I stay out here, my lady?" Harold asked anxiously.

Isabel looked at him and then back into the home from which an odd screeching sound was coming. "I think you'd better come in with me. You, too, Pinkney."

The lady's maid had been loitering near the bottom of the steps but now climbed them reluctantly.

The hallway looked normal enough — if one discounted the long smear of something green at child height. Isabel peered closer. The smear looked suspiciously like pea soup. The sitting room was empty — except for a broken bowl on the floor — and the kitchen seemed normal enough save for the angry muttering of Mistress Medina. Something thundered across the ceiling overhead, and Isabel picked up her skirts and hurried up the stairs.

She was nearly to the top when Soot came tearing past, closely followed by Dodo, trailing a long red ribbon tied around her neck. They went roaring down the stairs, and then Isabel heard the scrabbling of dog and kitty claws on the marble floor below before a scream and a crash from the kitchen.

Oh, dear.

She ran the rest of the way up the stairs and to the first classroom, skidding to a stop in the doorway and ducking only just in time as a small missile went whizzing past her head.

Sadly, Harold wasn't so quick.

"Ow!" Harold picked up something from the floor. "They're flinging walnuts, the little buggers!"

Pinkney clapped both hands over her mouth to muffle a giggle.

"Oh, I'm so sorry, Harold," Isabel said faintly, for she was busy staring in horror at the classroom. Who knew that such well-mannered, sweet children could do . . . well, *this.*

To one side, a pitched battle was going on between some of the younger boys, apparently without any rules at all, for they were using slingshots, pillows, and what looked like the remains of their breakfast porridge. On the other side of the room, relative quiet reigned as the babies who could just walk intently painted the wall with more porridge and what looked like jam. In the middle, a bunch of girls had made a maze of tables and benches and were busy hopping from one to the other, screeching at the top of their lungs.

And in the midst of all this, Lady Penelope stood, her face a mask of stunned confusion. "Children," she pleaded. "Children, *please.*"

As Isabel watched, a glob of porridge hit Lady Penelope's lovely hair and stuck, sliding a bit over her left ear.

Naturally, Isabel started forward, ready to confiscate slingshots, yank girls down from tables, and wash a passel of babies. She opened her mouth, about to give a stern command . . . and then she thought about what she was doing. If she saved Lady Penelope now, helped her run the home and discipline the children, then there would never be a need to call Winter back to the home.

"Oh, Lady Beckinhall!" Lady Penelope had caught sight of her. She held out dainty white hands pitifully. "Surely you know what to do with children? I sent Artemis down to fetch Lord d'Arque or Nell or the cook or one of the maids or *anyone,* but she hasn't returned. You don't think they've captured her, do you? Tied her up and stuffed her under a bed?"

Lady Penelope essayed a laugh, but it came out more a frightened titter.

Isabel looked at her gravely. "I'm sure I have no experience with children, my lady, but in any case I wouldn't be able to help. Mr. Makepeace has only ever been the one who could control these children. Didn't you know? They come from *St. Giles.*"

"But . . . but . . ." Lady Penelope raised her hands to her head and unfortunately found the porridge stuck there. She let out a scream that for the moment made all the children pause.

Isabel backed from the room. "Oh, dear. I expect I should go find Miss Greaves, oughtn't I?"

She whirled and was halfway to the stairs before she heard the wail from Lady Penelope. *"Waaaiiit!"*

Isabel climbed back down the stairs much more sedately than she'd come up, Harold and Pinkney trailing along silently. She tried the sitting room again first, and then went back to the kitchens.

Miss Greaves sat at the kitchen table with the cook, a pot of tea between them. Miss Greaves leaped to her feet at the sight of Isabel. "Oh, my lady. I was just . . . just . . ."

"Having tea, it looks like," Isabel said soothingly. "I wouldn't mind a cup myself. Harold, can you find Lord d'Arque for me and request he come speak to me?"

The footman nodded and trotted from the kitchen.

"Now, then." Isabel sat and poured herself a cup of tea before glancing up at the cook and Miss Greaves. "How long has it been like this?"

Miss Greaves heaved a sigh.

The cook grimaced. "Almost as soon as Mr. Makepeace left. It's been a right riot 'round 'ere. The little monsters don't pay a whit of attention to anyone. Got Lord d'Arque quite smartly on the back of the 'ead with a walnut, one of 'em did."

Mistress Medina sounded almost pleased.

"Lady Penelope did try," Miss Greaves said earnestly. "She brought hothouse cherries for the children the second day, but —"

"Pits," Mistress Medina said succinctly. "Not to mention cherry juice stains right proper. Any 'alf-wit knows *that*."

"I think she would've handed the home back after that," Miss Greaves murmured, "if it were not for Lord d'Arque's insistence that they keep it. He hasn't even bothered to hire a manager."

"But why?" Isabel asked.

"Because," Lord d'Arque said from the doorway, "it irritates Makepeace for me to be here. That's why. Besides I'm right in the middle of the Ghost's haunting grounds here. If he shows, I'll be the first to hear about it."

Miss Greaves squeaked at his entrance and hurriedly made her excuses. Mistress Medina rose from the kitchen table, her very slowness an insult.

Fortunately, Lord d'Arque was in no state to notice. He leaned against the doorway, almost a parody of insouciance, obviously the worse for drink. "Do you still hate me?"

"Oh, yes," Isabel said sincerely. No matter

what his reasons — if there were any — he'd hurt Winter very badly. Her loyalties were quite confirmed. "But I've come with a question for you anyway."

Lord d'Arque pushed off from the door-jamb and walked overly carefully toward her. "Given him up? Come for a real lover?"

She wrinkled her nose. "I've never known you to be crude before."

He sank rather abruptly into the chair opposite her. "Sorry."

She studied him. Something was obviously tearing at his soul. Perhaps Winter was right. *This* d'Arque might very well do something shady and immoral. "I want to ask you about your coachman."

"My coachman?" The viscount blinked as if that were the last thing he expected. "Don't tell me he's in trouble — I only hired him the other day."

It was Isabel's turn to look puzzled. "I thought you'd had him for months."

Lord d'Arque rolled his eyes. "No, that was my old man. He disappeared while we were attending the opera. Damned inconvenient. I had to get one of the footmen to drive me home, and the man had never handled the reins as far as I could tell."

Isabel frowned, thinking. Had someone killed the coachman to keep him from tell-

466

ing Winter anything? If so, that hardly exonerated Lord d'Arque. She pulled the scrap of paper with his seal from her pocket. "Is this yours?"

He leaned down to peer at the paper, his brows drawing together. "It's my seal, certainly, and this is my handwriting." He turned the letter over, staring at the misspelled words there. "Looks like someone reused the paper for a note." He shrugged and straightened. "Where did you get it?"

"It was found in St. Giles," she said. "And I would very much like to know what it was doing there."

"How should I know?"

She pursed her lips impatiently. "It's your letter."

"Do you remember everyone you write to?"

"Actually, yes," she said. "Because the people I write to are usually personal friends."

He stared at her a moment. "Let me see that."

She handed the scrap of paper over.

He peered at it, turning it over. "Well, it says October . . ." He looked up at her suddenly. "Why do you want to know whom I wrote to anyway?"

"Because," she said with a hard smile.

"Why do you wish to conceal whom you wrote it to?"

"I don't." He shrugged again and let the paper fall to the table. "I write my grandmother when she's out of town — but she was in London during October. I might've written this to a paramour or . . ." He frowned, thinking.

"Who?" she whispered.

"I wrote a note on a matter of business to Seymour in October."

Her heart skipped a beat. "What business?"

He shook his head. "It was a delicate matter. I gave my word not to reveal it."

"Adam."

He smiled suddenly with some of his normal attractiveness. "I do like the way you say my given name."

"I haven't the time for this," she said sternly.

He sighed. "Oh, all right. Seymour had a moneymaking scheme he wanted me to invest in. I declined in a letter."

"Why did you decline?"

"I've found that moneymaking schemes are a good way to lose *all* one's blunt." He smiled, dissipated and handsome. "And despite my devil-may-care exterior, I have the heart of a conservative miser."

"Hmm." Isabel thought for a bit. Was Mr. Seymour's moneymaking scheme somehow connected to the lace stocking workshop? Or was the whole thing a false trail? "What was Seymour's scheme?"

"I don't know."

"What?"

The viscount shrugged elegantly. "We never got as far as specifics. I declined at once."

She grimaced. "Very well, I'll ask the man himself. I'll visit Mr. Seymour at his home." Isabel rose, gesturing to Harold, but Lord d'Arque was shaking his head again.

"He's not there. We met Makepeace when we came here. He and Makepeace set off together for the place where the Ghost had rescued all those girls the other night."

Alarm caused Isabel's hands to tremble, but she made herself ask calmly, "Did anyone go with them?"

"No, they went alone. Why?" The viscount was staring at her curiously.

"It's probably nothing." Isabel tried to think. She looked at him. "How did you come to hire your former coachman anyway?"

"What very odd questions you're asking this morning," Lord d'Arque murmured. He threw up his hands at a fierce glance from her. "All right! Seymour recommended him, in fact."

Oh, God! Mr. Seymour must be the aristocrat behind the workshops, and Winter had gone off with him alone. Why else would Mr. Seymour do that except that he'd realized that Winter was the Ghost and wished to kill him? How could she get to Winter in time to warn him?

She balled her hands into impotent fists. "I don't even know where they've gone. I don't know where the workshop is."

"Well, that's settled easily enough," the viscount drawled. "I do."

Her mouth dropped open. "*You* do?"

He smiled, looking almost boyish. "Makepeace told us where the place was before he left with Seymour."

Winter paused beside a tall house, looking up. Four stories plus the attic. This was the building that he'd found the children in the night before last.

He lowered his gaze to his companion. "This is the place."

"You're sure?" Seymour looked doubtfully at the building. "It looks like all the others around here."

"I'm sure," Winter said. "Would you like to go first?"

470

"Oh, no," Seymour said. He smiled and gestured. "After you, Mr. Makepeace."

Winter nodded and entered the building. It had been divided up into multiple small rooms, each for let, some sublet again, and some with beds rented yet again within the rooms. A typical St. Giles house. Luckily the stairs were here at the front of the house and they wouldn't have to travel the warren to find them.

Winter started up the stairs. "I was surprised to see you and Lord Kershaw in St. Giles today."

"Really?" Seymour's voice echoed off the bare walls eerily.

"Mmm." Winter turned a corner. "Why were you here?"

"We came to help d'Arque look for Fraser-Burnsby's murderer," Seymour said. "The Ghost of St. Giles. You still know nothing about him?"

His voice was suddenly very close.

Winter paused and turned, unsurprised to find Seymour on a tread just below him. "You move very quietly, Mr. Seymour."

The other man was no longer smiling. "So do you. I noticed on the walk here that you're quite at home in St. Giles."

Winter smiled thinly. "I have lived here for nine years. And, no, I don't know anything about the Ghost."

"You're sure?"

"Very."

Winter started up the stairs again, aware that the other man followed him closely. The house was old and made odd noises — creaks and groans. This time of day it was mostly deserted. The inhabitants were out, scrabbling for what money they could earn or steal so they could afford to sleep tonight in this wretched place.

If they were attacked, probably no one would hear. And if anyone did, they were very unlikely to do anything about it. People minded their own business in St. Giles out of desperate necessity. They might as well be trekking through some African desert.

"I was surprised you knew about the children the Ghost brought to the home," Seymour said. They were nearing the top floor now.

Ah, at last. "Were you?"

"You seemed to know almost before any-one else outside the home. Almost as soon as the Ghost himself."

"I have my sources," Winter said easily. The climb was making him warm and he folded back the edge of his cloak.

"Your sources must be nearly as good as the Ghost's."

"Perhaps." Winter paused outside a small door. "The workshop is in here. Would you like to go in first?"

"Please, Mr. Makepeace," Mr. Seymour said.

Winter looked at him a moment and then opened the door. The outer attic room was even smaller in daylight. The wood from the broken roof door lay on the floor in jagged pieces among a layer of dust. Oddly, the machines were all gone.

Behind him the door to the attic room closed.

Winter felt the jolt of warning rush through him.

A moment too late.

When he turned, Seymour already had his sword drawn. "I think you'd better kneel before me, Mr. Makepeace. Or do you prefer to be called the Ghost of St. Giles?"

CHAPTER NINETEEN

Now the Harlequin could see, but he still
stood mute and unmoving before his True
Love. So once more she stood on tiptoe,
this time kissing him on the cheek before
whispering, "Remember how we once lay
together, love?
Remember how we became lovers and
hoped for a future?
That future is alive and here."
And taking his hand, she laid it upon
her gently swelling belly, where a
new life grew. Thus she made him
touch Hope . . .
— from *The Legend of the
Harlequin Ghost of St. Giles*

She'd pushed him away from her again and
again, but she never thought he'd go far.
He'd always be in her life, always be in this
world, living his own life, perhaps marrying,
managing his home, *happy,* damn it.

Winter Makepeace wasn't supposed to die. Isabel simply couldn't conceive of it. He was too athletic, too young, too *vital*. He wasn't like other men. He challenged her. He saw all her faults — and they were myriad — and he said he loved her anyway. If she lived a thousand lifetimes, she'd never find another man like him, and she didn't want to.

She loved Winter Makepeace and no other.

The thought was dizzying. Isabel actually stumbled in the dank, awful St. Giles alley.

"Are you all right, my lady?" Harold said as he caught her arm.

"Yes, yes," she panted. "We must *hurry.*"

The way to the address that Viscount d'Arque had given her was too narrow for her carriage. Besides, one moved faster on foot in St. Giles — the alleys and lanes twisted too much for a carriage and horses. So she'd run all the way. They'd left d'Arque behind, for the man had been far more the worse for drink than he'd at first appeared. Harold jogged along beside her, though she'd ordered him to go ahead. He'd stoutly refused, saying St. Giles was too dangerous for a lady alone.

Which was right, but that wouldn't save Winter if Charles Seymour were even now plunging a dagger into his back.

A tall house loomed up ahead.

"That's it," Isabel gasped. "Hurry!"

Harold yanked open the door and they started climbing a nightmarish length of stairs. Around and around they went, never ending it seemed, and the entire time Isabel climbed, she listened for a shot. The cry of a wounded man. Voices raised in anger.

And heard nothing.

At last they made the final turn and came out on the attic level. Straight ahead was a mean little door, and Isabel rushed it even as Harold flung out an arm to catch her back.

The door burst open and Isabel's momentum sent her crashing into the room — and into the back of a man.

Strong arms wrapped around her and for a split second everything was calm.

Then a voice spoke above her. "Ah, Makepeace, I believe your inamorata has joined us."

Winter felt the sweat slide down the small of his back. He'd suspected the moment that Seymour volunteered to accompany him to the workshop that Seymour was the "toff." Seymour had been the only one of the three aristocrats who had been inter-

476

ested in Winter's knowledge of the workshop location — knowledge he could only have if he was the Ghost of St. Giles. When Winter had seen the other man's sword, triumphant victory had swept through him at the confirmation of his hunch, but in the next instant Isabel had come barging in.

Seymour now held Isabel tightly against his chest, his arm across her throat. Winter had felt the excitement in a fight, he'd felt the thrill of danger, and the pain of a hit.

But he'd never felt fear.

Seymour flicked a glance at Harold the footman, who was hesitating by the door uncertainly. "Throw down your pistol, please, or I'll kill your mistress."

Harold dropped the pistol he carried.

Seymour smiled at Winter. "Now. The Ghost of St. Giles is known for having two swords with him at all times. True, you're not dressed as the Ghost at the moment, but, please, humor me. Open your cloak, Ghost."

Winter opened his cloak and held the edges apart, looking into Isabel's wide, blue eyes. She was terrified. That alone signed Seymour's fate. "It's very kind of you to come save me again, my lady, although I would've thought Harold would know better."

Behind her, Harold shrugged by the door.

She licked her lips. "I love you. No matter what happens, I love you, Winter. If —"

"Enough." Seymour yanked hard on her neck, cutting her off. "I seem to see a hilt peeking from your cloak lining. Place both your swords on the ground — slowly — and slide them across the room."

Winter's chest was full of the splendor of Isabel's love, but he couldn't linger over that now. He did as Seymour said.

"Now kneel."

Winter shook his head gently. "No. If I kneel, you'll kill me and then kill Lady Beckinhall. I really don't see any incentive to do so."

For a moment, Seymour looked nonplussed and Winter used his distraction to drift closer.

"I'll . . . I'll kill her," Seymour sputtered.

Winter shook his head. "You kill her and I'll kill you, swords or no swords. There'll be nothing holding me back. Really, it's a matter of logic."

"If it's a matter of logic," Seymour said with dripping sarcasm, "then what do you suggest I do?"

Winter tilted his head. "Fight me man-to-man."

"No!" Isabel strained against the arm

around her throat. "You're not armed, Winter! Don't be a fool."

Seymour grinned. "Very well."

He shoved Isabel aside in a sudden movement that sent her to the floor and leaped at Winter, his sword aimed at his heart.

Isabel landed painfully on her hands and knees. *Winter!* She sobbed as she rolled to see if he'd been killed with Mr. Seymour's first sword thrust. To see if he was dying right now, his life's blood spurting from him.

But Winter had his cloak wrapped about one arm, using it to defend himself as he maneuvered toward his swords. As she watched, Mr. Seymour thrust and thrust again, the point of his sword landing in the wadded cloak each time.

But the price of such defense was evident: A dark, wet stain was spreading over the cloak wrapped about Winter's arm. Dear God, if he was crippled, this would be all over before he reached his own swords.

Isabel looked frantically about and saw Harold's pistol. It lay against the wall behind Mr. Seymour. She began creeping toward it.

At that moment, Winter lunged for his swords, his right arm outstretched. Mr. Seymour followed, stabbing vindictively.

Winter rolled aside, his long sword in his right hand, just as Seymour's sword point pierced the wooden floorboards where he'd just lain. Winter jumped gracefully to his feet and lunged at Mr. Seymour.

Isabel reached the pistol and grasped it in both hands, lifting the heavy thing and pointing it toward the fighters. But Mr. Seymour and Winter were now in a straight line comparative to her. If she shot and missed, she risked the danger of hitting Winter and killing him. She caught Harold's eye and he started forward, but she waved him back. Anything he tried would bring him closer to the fighters — and into her own line of fire.

She held the pistol level and aimed at Mr. Seymour, waiting for her moment.

Seymour parried a lightning thrust from Winter. "You were supposed to be unarmed. This isn't fair."

"Oh, you aristocrats," Winter hissed, stomping forward in attack, "you make your own rules that must be followed by all but are only in your own favor."

Mr. Seymour sneered, batting aside Winter's long sword. "It's the natural order of things that the mighty will rule over the meek. If you don't like it, then plead your case before God."

And he struck, as quick and vicious as an

adder, ripping a long tear in Winter's waistcoat. Isabel moaned, low and terrified.
Winter's waistcoat immediately began to
darken, and as he moved, blood spattered
to the floor from both his left arm and his
side. Dear God, he was losing so much
blood! He would weaken if this didn't end
soon. But the men were still too close
together for her to shoot.

"You're good," Winter panted, skipping
back from another thrust. "But then you
aristocrats often are — what more do you
have to do than to endlessly practice your
sword craft?"

"You may learn the art of the sword," Seymour sneered, "but it's like a parrot talking:
he only mimics what he doesn't truly understand."

He lunged and Winter caught the attack
with his own sword, the blades shrieking as
they slid against each other, each man bearing against the other with his full weight
and strength. Winter's blood smeared the
floor and his rear boot slid in it, forcing him
to stumble to the side to avoid the tip of
Mr. Seymour's blade.

Mr. Seymour grinned. "Thin stuff, your
commoner's blood. I shall paint the walls
with it when I'm done with you."

Winter raised his eyebrows at the theatrical threat. "You make your money off the backs of little girls. Don't think that I'll let you win here."

"Perhaps you won't have that choice," Mr. Seymour grunted. He darted to Winter's opposite side.

Finally! Isabel pulled the trigger. The gun exploded with a deafening *BOOM!* The recoil laid her flat. She struggled to rise and for a moment simply stared in horror.

Winter and Seymour were locked together, so close they might be embracing. Dear God, had she shot them both?

Then Mr. Seymour slid bonelessly from the embrace and Winter looked up.

"Oh, Winter!" Isabel didn't know how she got there, but suddenly she was in Winter's arms, kissing him awkwardly, tears slipping down her cheeks. She'd almost lost him. If she hadn't fired when she had, he would've —

She glanced down at Mr. Seymour and frowned. "But where is the gunshot wound?"

Harold cleared his throat. "You missed, my lady." He pointed to a large hole blown into the plaster of the wall.

"I missed?" She looked up in time to see Winter scowling at her footman.

Instantly he smiled down at her. "But it

was very close. I'm sure that had you had time to aim, you would've got him through the heart."

"Humph." He was humoring her outrageously, but under the present circumstances, she could hardly protest. "Then how did he die?"

Winter lifted his sword. It was smeared with blood. His own face was white. "I let the beast out."

"Oh." She reached to touch him; he was too calm, too reserved. She could almost see him retreating back into himself.

"Jesus!" Lord d'Arque's voice came from the door. "What happened here?"

He was staring about the room in horror. Isabel froze. If he chose to bring Winter up on murder charges, she would have a very hard time defending Winter. He was a commoner who had just killed an aristocrat.

"Your friend Seymour attacked Lady Beckinhall," Winter said before she could speak, his voice hard.

Viscount d'Arque blanched. "Attacked? Dear God, my lady, I hope you are all right?"

"Yes." Isabel touched her throat delicately, wincing at the bruised skin there, relieved that he was properly appalled at Mr. Seymour's actions. "Thanks to Mr. Makepeace

483

and my footman. They both risked their lives to save me."

Lord d'Arque stared down at Mr. Seymour's body. "When you said Makepeace was in peril from Seymour, I thought your imagination had run away from you."

"Yet you kept following me anyway?" Isabel asked softly.

"Seymour was acting very strange after the girls were found here," Lord d'Arque said slowly. "Whenever I mentioned questioning the girls, he made sure to deflect my attention. And then he had become obsessed with Makepeace. Kept saying he was the Ghost of St. Giles and had killed Roger."

"I was under the impression you thought that yourself," Winter murmured.

Lord d'Arque glanced at him. "Maybe for a bit, but it's simply too outlandish — that a schoolmaster should be a masked madman. And why would you have killed Roger anyway?"

"I wouldn't have," Winter said soberly. "I don't know who killed your friend, my lord. I wish I did."

Lord d'Arque nodded, looking away for a moment. "I suppose Seymour was behind this dreadful business with the enslaved girls? That was his moneymaking scheme?"

"Yes," Isabel said. "He meant to kill us so

his secret wouldn't come out."

"Awful." The viscount passed a hand over his forehead. "To make money that way — by the labor of little girls and in such a wretched place." He looked around the cramped little room, then back at them. "I cannot find any pity in my heart for Seymour. He more than deserved his fate, but his wife is a rather nice woman, you know. The scandal when this is revealed will kill her."

"Then don't let it," Winter said. He smiled grimly. "We can say that the Ghost has claimed another victim."

Lord d'Arque nodded. "Leave it to me."

CHAPTER TWENTY

For a moment, the Harlequin Ghost of St.
Giles stood still, staring at his True Love,
his palm upon her belly where their child
grew. The True Love held her breath, for
this was her only chance. If he did not
recognize her, did not return to the day
and to the living, she had no other means
of waking him from the spell. So she
waited, watching him, as the sun began
to dawn on St. Giles . . .

— from *The Legend of the
Harlequin Ghost of St. Giles*

One week later . . .

"I have a letter for you, Peach." Winter held
out the paper with the carefully printed address toward the little girl.

Peach, who had been sitting with Dodo
on her bed, practicing her spinning, looked
up. She took the paper reverently, turned it
over in her hands, and gave it back. "Please,

sir, what does it say?"

Winter had received reports from all the teachers at the home since his return as the manager and wasn't surprised at her request. Apparently Peach had never been taught to read.

A matter he'd soon see remedied. But for now Winter sat next to the little girl on her bed. She'd been assigned a bed and a small trunk for her possessions in the big girls' dormitory, for after questioning, Peach had confessed her age to be eight years old.

"You see your name here?" Winter pointed to the address.

"P-E-A-C-H," Peach carefully named each letter.

"Very good." Winter smiled at the girl and opened the letter. He tilted it so she could see and ran his finger under the writing as he read:

Dear Peach,

I'm writing you this here Letter before my Ship leaves London. She's called the Terrier and she's Brilliant! When we come back to London, I'll take you to see Her. I'm to sleep in a kind of Swinging Bed. The older lads say as it might take a while to get used to.

Anyway, I hope you and Dodo are

Well. Mind you listen to Miss Jones and Mistress Medina and the rest, and if Mr. Makepeace should come back, you Listen to him, too. He's . . .

Winter had to stop and clear his throat at this point.

Peach looked at him curiously. "What does he say?"

Winter blinked a little and continued:

He's the Best Man in the World.

Your Friend,
Joseph Tinbox

Winter gave the letter to Peach. The little girl stared at the handwriting for a moment before sighing and folding it carefully.

"I wager you'll be able to read that yourself by the first snowfall," Winter said softly.

"Really?" Peach brightened for a moment, then looked doubtful. "Winter is a long ways away."

"It'll be here sooner than you think." Winter stood but then impulsively squatted in front of the little girl, taking her hands in his. "I'll be writing a letter to Joseph soon. Would you like to include a note of your own?"

"But I can't write."

"I can help you."

Peach peered shyly at him. "Yes, I'd like that."

"There you are," Temperance called from the doorway.

"Sister" — Winter rose, went to her, and pulled her into a hug — "you've returned."

"Winter!" She pulled back, looking at him oddly. "What was that for?"

"I'm glad to see you." He shrugged.

"But" — she glanced at the room full of children, all of them staring curiously, and pulled him into the hall — "you never hug. And did I see you holding that little girl's hands?"

He blinked. "Yes?"

Temperance laid the back of her hand on his forehead. "Are you feeling all right?"

"Of course." He batted her hand away and smiled down at his sister. "How was the house party?"

"Dreadful!"

"Really?"

"Well, no," she sighed. "Some of the ladies were actually quite nice and there were ruins nearby to explore, which I enjoyed."

"So the experience was not as bad as you thought it might be."

"Are you going to tell me you told me so?" she asked suspiciously.

"Not at all." He stared at her a moment, wondering.

"What is it?" She nervously touched her nose. "Have I got a spot?"

"No, but something's different," he said.

"Oh!" Her cheeks, which seemed rounder somehow, turned rosy. "You're not supposed to know yet."

"Know what?"

"I'm expecting an Event come winter," she said primly.

"Really?" For a moment he felt a tiny pang, somewhere near his heart: Isabel would never experience this particular joy. And then a grin spread across his face. "How marvelous!"

"Thank you." She bit her lip but couldn't hold back her own smile any longer. "Oh, I'm so excited, Winter. You have no idea!"

"And Caire?"

She blew out an exasperated breath. "He's so nervous you'd think *he* was the one to carry the babe. But that's part of the reason I came here. I have a favor to ask of you."

He raised an eyebrow.

She clasped her hands in front of her. "I wonder if I could take Mary Whitsun away? To come live with me. Caire wants someone to help me if I should feel unwell, and after the baby comes, we'll need a nursemaid.

She'd be perfect, and besides, I've missed her terribly since I left the home. Please?"

"Of course," Winter replied, delighted. "I think Mary Whitsun would quite like that."

"Oh, wonderful!" Temperance beamed up at him. "I suppose with that settled, I ought to get back."

He blinked. "Get back where?"

"To the Ladies' Syndicate for the Benefit of the Home for Unfortunate Infants and Foundling Children," Temperance said with a touch of asperity. "Didn't you know we were holding a meeting in the sitting room downstairs?"

"Now?"

He felt the surge of energy through his veins. If there was a meeting of the Ladies' Syndicate, then Isabel would be here. He hadn't seen her in a sennight — not since he'd killed Seymour. During that time, he'd been busy with reclaiming the home and helping the traumatized little girls who had been used in the workshop, but that hadn't been the main reason he'd stayed away from Isabel.

His darkness had come to the fore that day. He'd killed a man — something he'd never done before. Taking a life wasn't something to be done lightly. He'd prayed over the matter, considered if he should let

Isabel go for her own good. But there was another side to his darkness; he'd always known that. When he'd let it free, he'd also set free the ability to hug Temperance. To take a little girl's hands in his own to comfort her. He knew now that he would never be the manager his father was: distant, reserved, but kind. Instead he would care too much, worry too much, grieve too much when a child was lost. And when a child succeeded? When one thrived or was rescued? Then he would probably be overjoyed.

He couldn't change that about himself, even if he wanted to. That was simply the kind of manager he was destined to be, and he thought he could now live peaceably with that fact.

But there was one person — one lovely, stubborn, wicked lady — whom he couldn't live without, and apparently she was sitting downstairs at this very moment.

A week had been entirely too long.

"Excuse me," he murmured to his sister.

"Where are you going?" Temperance called after him.

"To find my destiny," he replied.

"*What* were you thinking?" Isabel watched with amusement as Amelia Caire raised a patrician eyebrow sternly at Lady Penelope.

492

Amelia had just got back into town last night, apparently because of a letter Lady Margaret had written weeks ago.

"I'm sure I had the best interests of the children at heart." Lady Penelope opened her pansy-purple eyes wide in appeal. "And Artemis said it was a good idea."

Miss Greaves, who had just taken a sip of her tea, choked.

"I understand that Mr. Makepeace confiscated three and thirty slingshots," Lady Hero said thoughtfully. "I'm not sure I've seen that many slingshots in all my life."

"We've had to have all the classrooms repainted as well," Amelia said. "*And* four beds have had to be replaced."

"Cook found another cherry pit this morning," Lady Phoebe piped up brightly. "In the flour in the kitchen."

All of the ladies looked down at the scones on their plates. Lady Hero carefully set her plate aside, looking a tad green about the edges.

"Well, I thought it was an experiment worth trying," Lady Penelope said stoutly. "If I'd not brought in Lord d'Arque, we'd never have learned not to give the children hothouse cherries as a special present."

She looked about the room as if having scored an important point.

Amelia sighed and Isabel felt for her. No matter how harebrained Lady Penelope was, she still held the heaviest purse of any of the ladies. They would simply have to learn to put up with her.

"I think we shall have to make a law that Mr. Makepeace be the one *and only* manager of the Home for Unfortunate Infants and Foundling Children," Amelia said. "All those in favor, please raise your hand."

Several hands shot up. Lady Penelope raised hers to shoulder-height, which, in Isabel's opinion, still counted. Lady Margaret, however, simply stared at her lap — as she'd been doing since the meeting had begun.

"Megs?" Lady Hero whispered gently.

"What?" Lady Margaret looked up. "Oh, yes." And she raised her hand as well, making the vote unanimous.

Isabel had the feeling that Lady Margaret had no idea on what she'd just voted.

Amelia nodded, satisfied, and began pouring a second cup of tea for all the ladies.

Isabel took the opportunity to lean toward Lady Hero, sitting next to her. "I'm so pleased you came to town, my lady."

Lady Hero smiled. "We were ready to return from the country."

"Then your husband accompanied you?" Isabel murmured.

"Oh, indeed. He has most urgent business in London." Lady Hero glanced at Lady Margaret.

Isabel nodded, glad that things were being seen to. "I hope he proves successful."

Lady Hero smiled rather sadly. "Lord Griffin is used to success — even in matters that seem to have no happy outcome."

Which was, Isabel supposed, the most that could be hoped for.

The sitting room door opened.

Isabel turned to look and caught her breath. Winter stood there, his face quite stern. She'd been planning on cornering him after the meeting. He'd spent the last week avoiding her and she was quite tired of it.

But it appeared he'd changed his course.

His bow was short and he never glanced at any lady but herself. "Might I have a word with you?"

She gulped. "I . . . I'm sure when the meeting is —"

"Now, Isabel."

Oh, dear. She felt the blush heat her cheeks as she hurriedly got up before he could say anything else damning. As it was, the other ladies were suspiciously quiet.

She went out into the hall. "What is it?"

He simply looked at her and she saw

everything she meant to him on his face.

Her heart clutched. *Now?* He wanted to do this *now?*

Last-minute panic seized her. "I'll never have children," she hissed as quietly as she could, because it must be a free time, for the children were all flocking down the stairs. "I'm too old, too rich, too much above you in station, too —"

He silenced her by the simple expedient of kissing her. There, in the home's hallway, in front of the entire Ladies' Syndicate and what must be most of the children, soon to be *all* of the children, for whoever wasn't there to witness the embrace was being urgently called by their brethren . . .

And she didn't care. She wrapped her arms about him and kissed him back, fiercely, joyfully, this man she loved with all of her flawed being.

He pulled away, only far enough to whisper with smiling lips, "You've well and truly compromised me this time, Lady Beckinhall. I think you ought to save my poor reputation and marry me."

She looked into his warm, strong, loving eyes and voiced her remaining doubt. "You'll never have children if you marry me."

And he did the strangest thing. Winter

496

Makepeace, the man who never laughed, threw his head back and *shouted* with laughter.

He looked down at her and grinned, sweeping his arm toward the stairway, now crowded with children of every shape and size. "Oh, my precious Isabel, *these* are my children — the children of my heart, the children of my life's work. I'm the father to dozens of children and plan to be the father to hundreds of children in the future. Come. Say yes, be my wife, and help me raise my brood."

"Yes," she whispered, and when some of the children leaned forward, unable to hear, she shouted the word: *"Yes!"*

Winter grinned and kissed her on the mouth, fierce and quick, and then turned to the waiting children of the home. "Children, it is my great honor to tell you that Lady Beckinhall has consented to marry me."

For a moment there was awed silence and then a great roar went up: "HUZZAH!"

Winter laughed again and picked Isabel up by the waist, swinging her around, high above his head.

"HUZZAH!" the children cheered, half-maddened by delight.

"Nell!" Winter shouted to the maidservant standing among the children. "I think this calls for scones for everyone at tea."

That prompted the biggest cheer of all and then a mad scramble as the children raced to find seats for tea. Nell beamed as she brought up the rear, and even Mistress Medina dabbed at her eyes with her apron as she hurried back to the kitchen.

"My dear, I hope you haven't ruined a perfectly good orphanage manager," Amelia said drily from the sitting room doorway. Her expression softened. "But I wish you all the happiness possible."

"Thank you." Isabel's eyes grew misty and she received a congratulatory kiss from each of the ladies, even Lady Penelope, who looked quite bewildered.

"Let me escort you to your carriage," Winter murmured in Isabel's ear.

She nodded quickly, for she wanted a few more minutes alone with him. But as they neared the door, quick footsteps came behind them.

They turned to see Mistress Medina, holding out a small key on a ribbon to Winter. She winked. "I almost forgot in the last week's flurry. Thought you might want the key back, sir. Wouldn't want all those slingshots to get loose again."

Outside, dusk was just beginning to descend.

Isabel waited until the home's door closed behind them. "What was that all about?"

Winter actually looked a little guilty. "Well, when I left the home on d'Arque's orders, I gave this key to Mistress Medina."

She looked at the innocent little key, realization dawning. "And it . . ."

"Unlocks the cabinet where I keep all the slingshots I've confiscated from the boys." He nodded and beamed. "I actually have quite a collection. I've been acquiring them for nine years, you see . . ."

She giggled at the thought of Mistress Medina arming all the little boys in the home. Poor Lady Penelope! She'd never stood a chance.

Winter tugged her cape closer about her neck. "Are you happy?"

"Ecstatic." She smiled up at him. She felt so free suddenly, as if a great weight had been lifted from her shoulders. "Let's have a short engagement. I want to move into the home as soon as I finish decorating it."

"Decorating?" His eyebrows arched in amusement.

"Decorating," she said firmly. "It's much too austere for children. I want to bring Mr. and Mrs. Butterman, and Will and Harold the footmen, and of course Pinkney, though she's liable to expire from shock from living

499

at an orphanage, and of course I'll have to bring Christopher and Carruthers."

He stopped suddenly, facing her. "Christopher didn't leave with his mother?"

They'd not spoken since that night when everything had been so rushed.

"No." She looked up at him, so grateful for what he'd brought into her life. "I took your advice and told Louise that I wanted Christopher to live with me. As it turns out, she was quite relieved — it seems that a small boy isn't very conducive toward romance."

The corners of his mouth twitched. "It depends on the type of romance, I think."

Then he was kissing her again, his mouth so warm and full of life that she entirely forgot where she was and kissed him back enthusiastically.

"I do love you," she whispered as she pulled away. "Now and forever. I realized it when I thought you might die at Seymour's hand."

"There was never any chance of that," he murmured. "Not when I had you to live for."

"But . . ." She trailed off, her eyes widening as she glanced over his shoulder.

Winter turned to look.

A man stood not half a dozen steps away,

dressed in harlequin's motley, black jack-boots, and a long-nosed mask. As she gaped at him, he nodded and tipped his black, floppy hat before leaping to a low-hanging balcony and thence to the roof where he disappeared.

Isabel looked up at Winter. "What . . . ? How . . . ? *Who* . . . ?"

He smiled and leaned down to kiss her on the nose before whispering, "I told you I was the Ghost of St. Giles, but I never said there weren't others as well."

As the sky lightened in the east, the Harlequin Ghost of St. Giles shivered. When the dawn's first rays touched his face, he shuddered. And when at last the sky was blue and the sun yellow overhead, he wept.

"Forgive me, my True Love," he gasped as he sank to his knees. "Forgive me, for I was in a place of darkness, neither in this world nor the next, and I forgot who I was and what you meant to me."

"I forgive you," the True Love said, and kissed his lips. "For you are the light of my world. I love you more than life itself."

"And I love you as well," the Harlequin said. He laid his palm upon his True Love's belly and looked at her.

"Let us leave this place and marry so that we can bring our Hope into the world together."

And so they did. The Harlequin and his

True Love left St. Giles, married, and
lived happily ever after . . .
But beware, my dears! For 'tis said that
even in his happy new life, the Harlequin
sometimes grows restless on a moonlit
night. There are those who say he returns
to haunt the streets of St. Giles, wearing
his tattered Harlequin's motley and
wielding two sharp swords.
And when he does, murderers and
thieves, those who would harm the
innocent, and those whose evil deeds are
done by dark tremble at the mention of
the Ghost of St. Giles!
— from *The Legend of the
Harlequin Ghost of St. Giles*

Godric St. John jumped silently down into
his town house garden and then crouched,
motionless, and waited for a full minute.
The precaution was most likely unneces-
sary. Since Clara's death — and a long time
before she'd passed away — no one had
cared about his comings and goings.

Still. It was good to keep in practice.

When nothing and no one moved, Godric
slowly rose to his feet. He slid from shadow
to shadow, making for the door at the back
of his house that led into his library. Tonight
had been mostly wasted. He'd chased a thief

and then lost him in a warren of back alleys, scared off a possible footpad from a pieman returning home for the night — the pieman hadn't even known his peril — and seen Winter Makepeace kiss Lady Beckinhall in the middle of Maiden Lane. That almost certainly meant a marriage — however oddly matched the couple — and Winter's retirement from their . . . hobby.

Godric grunted as he opened his library door. One fewer Ghost meant —

"Good evening, Mr. St. John." The voice came from the shadows obscuring the old leather armchair near the fireplace.

Godric swung in that direction, crouching low, his swords already out and up.

The vague shape in the corner tutted. "Now, now, Mr. St. John, there's no need for violence, I assure you."

"Who are you?" Godric whispered.

The man leaned forward into the faint light cast by the embers in the fireplace. "My name is Griffin Reading." Godric could see now that he had an elbow propped on the arm of the chair and something dangled from one finger.

Godric paced forward and the shape resolved itself into a mask: long-nosed, leather, black. Exactly, in fact, like the one he wore upon his face. Exactly like the spare mask that *should* be hidden in his bedroom.

But evidently wasn't. Godric looked at Lord Griffin.

Who smiled without humor. "I have a proposition for you."